KICKING TOMORROW

KICKING TOMORROW

FOR ROBERTA

a novel by
DANIEL RICHLER

with Peace —

Daniel Richler

AUG. **M&S** *2002*

Canadian Cataloguing in Publication Data
Richler, Daniel
  Kicking tomorrow

ISBN 0-7710-7469-7

I. Title.

PS8585.I33K52 1991   C813'.54   C91-093644-7
PR9199.3.R34K52 1991

Printed and bound in Canada

McClelland & Stewart Inc.
The Canadian Publishers
481 University Ave.
Toronto, Ontario M5G 2E9

Acknowledgements
Many thanks to Jack McClelland for his tough editorial advice and
his fierce support. Also to Ellen Seligman, Jennifer Glossop, and
Linda Williams for whipping this thing into shape; to Hélène Holden
for the rah-rahs so many years ago; to Janet Turnbull for her hearty
laughter; and to the Ontario Arts Council for keeping me in paper
and typewriter ribbons.

For my mother, Florence

DO YOU LIKE THIS GARDEN
THAT IS YOURS?
SEE TO IT THAT YOUR CHILDREN DO NOT DESTROY IT!

– Malcolm Lowry, *Under the Volcano*

1

ROBBIE BOOKBINDER FIGURED THAT BATTLING OPPRES-
sion, routine, mediocrity, and parents had given his eyes
a gunslinger's squint; they appeared to him to have been
fried in the sandy skillet of some Mexican gulch – thou-
sand-yard eyes, *El Topo* eyes, pale blue panes on an arid
sky. But when he took his spread-legged square-jawed bell-
bottomed stance in the doorway of the living room to
confront his old man, he caught a reflection of himself in
the mirror by the light switch and realized, sadly, that this
magnificent stare was largely a figment of his own imagination. Not remotely like a Man With No Name. Not even
close. Bummer. For he suddenly saw that in moments of
conflict he had a pathetic kind of canine attention about
him – the heavy bangs of mongrel-brown hair, the flat
nose on the same plane as his forehead, his face as well-
fed as a pedigreed pup – a dumb mutt pausing on the
verge of comprehension, panting hard, wondering,
Where's the stick?

He barrelled on angrily anyhow, with all the taut collected energy of a little boy lolloping down a hill unable to
stop; he stood in the door of the living room – which
smelled of whisky and farts, like a saloon – fists on hips,
and shot his question.

"Dad, what the fuck – pardon me – do you *do*? Exactly."

Dad lay flopped on the couch, a bottle of Canadian Club on the carpet between him and the TV, the husk of an orange peel high up on his swollen beebody abdomen. He groaned his patented Groan of Ages, turning over, in Robbie's slit-eyed view, like some spiced beast on a spit. Meanwhile *Lapointe's at the blue line!* It's so late in the season the ice is soft and steaming, but still *he winds up for the shot, he shoots, he* – no! *Off the goalpost!*

"Look, aum, Robbie. Now's not the – OK? Your timing is – I'm so tired I can barely – why don't you come and, aum – "

"Chris*sake*, Dad – "

"All right, all – " He leaned up on one elbow. "Look, there's nine, ahh, what do you – numbers, okay. And a zero for good measure. I jumble them up." Then turned over into the hot pillows, and went back to sleep.

Arf arf, so funny Robbie forgot to laugh. Stamping down the stairs to the dungeon now, the walls there thick with posters pinned up one over the other – shredded skins of colour peeling like the lining of an acid stomach, as Dad once so wittily pointed out – plus a Canadian flag hanging from the ceiling, red marijuana leaf where the maple leaf should be. Robbie crouched down on his haunches, knees on either side of his ears, fingers sprung taut on the carpet before him. He looked up to burn a hole through the ceiling, heating the couch springs to roast Dad's prone arse, and singing under his breath, *All parents must die, all parents must die.*

This little pop ditty with major chart potential he'd made up himself, and it was the blistering bone-crushing opener as he pictured himself towering over Montreal on gigantic amplified billboards, driving adults mad with grief. This wasn't music, this was *war*, and he churned hot saliva around in his throat to make it: he kicked holes in the walls of the den as the vicious viscous stuff spat out from the

10

neon jaws of jean stores, head shops, brasseries, and pinball parlours all along Ste-Catherine Street. He punctured the asbestos ceiling tiles with his broomhandle, yelling into the bristles, buzzing the sound systems of the Ritz Carlton hotel and the Place Ville-Marie shopping centre, making mincemeat of their PA systems. Kicking beanbag chairs across the floor he gave authority figures an instant headache wherever they were: down at Station 10, on the Métro, at Jarry Park as Tim Foli stepped up to the plate, in funeral homes even – as Dad had once said, this stuff was loud enough to wake the dead. At Saint Joseph's Oratory the heavy vibrations of his amplified guts caused the crutches and braces discarded by the faithful to fall clattering across the flagstones, sending echoes around the great dome. In a snowstorm of polystyrene pellets his supersonic voice jammed cop cruisers, cabs, and airport towers, blitzed through banks to make the money jump in the trays, and disturbed the electrical currents of dental offices to grind the patients' teeth unpleasantly. Ladies and gentlemen: the horrible HELL'S YELLS!

At breakfast next day, rising at the crack of noon, he found Miriam's and Barnabus's cereal bowls on the kitchen table, the oatmeal dregs hardened to cement, the spoons stuck fast, plus a memo Dad had left:

Re: your group. How about "Halitosis."

Robbie read it over his Sugar Krunchies, an upward-curving line of milk forming between his lips in spite of himself. He could just see the old clown putting on his livid display of *Night of the Living Dead* gums, arf arf, going for an orange from the fruit bowl. *Braiins*, thought Robbie, *All parents must die*.

Slumping downstairs again. Through the mould-skinned mud-splattered window at the level of the garden's rhododendron bushes, a fine summer's day glimmered greenly. Out there in the city the Olympics were setting up, hot on the heels of the Stanley Cup, and pageantry was in the air. But Robbie lurked. He'd already lurked there all winter – after his high school burned down and sweet Ivy was taken to hospital – wearing his attitude like so much rusting spiked armour; having drunk from the bitter cup of experience he was lording it these days, like Yertle the Turtle, over all he could see. He'd spent the lingering bleak thaw-months of winter mulling over the terrible things he'd witnessed, absently rubbing his prickling guilty skin, dropping Quaaludes in his beer. Xmas his parents had bought him a fifties-style Coke machine, which he'd since meticulously repainted to read, in the trademark wavy lettering, *Cocaine*, and stocked to dispense a pharmaceutical variety of drugs. There was a bitter pungency – the reek of hash oil – and a label that read,

REFRESH YOURSELF! ONLY 5 CENTS!

Refreshed, he'd brooded at the dungeon's frosted, then dribbling windows, and listened to his hair grow, down to his shoulders by May, as long and tangled, as invested with puissance and vertu, as the manes of the exiled Merovingian kings of the Dark Ages. He stared into the smeary sun, cheerless as a plain aspirin dissolving, and planned on not ever being nice to anyone again.

Nine numbers and a zero. So it was corporate something. Or legal something. Or – *government* something? Or all three. Same difference; he worked for the Man. Unlike Robbie, who worked for no one. Like the Hell's Angels (the knights of new, slewing and smoting in search of their Grail – the bottomless amphetamine-still), he was a one-percenter, riding outside of the law. He was free, he could do what he wanted with his days.

For instance, just on a whim, if he wanted, today he could pay a visit to Dad's office – to bug the ass of the old geez more than anything, score a free lunch maybe, try to talk about the school fire, unburden himself a little, provoke some concern, even seek advice re: Ivy, or at the very least, if his timing was – aum – , get a lucrative kiss-off for the afternoon.

That morning a brief torrential rainstorm had flushed the mugginess of the city into the St. Lawrence River, leaving cars and buildings gleaming and the mountain benevolently green. Now he strode down Westmount's steep streets barefoot, side-stepping the worms that wriggled on the sidewalks, rinsed up from the lawns. He descended into the city and, look, the good vibes were all around – like, check out this smiling guy with a headband and loon pants, handing out leaflets from a Navajo satchel.

WHO ARE THE REBELS?
Today's long-haired Youth . . . or You the Parents?
WHO WERE THE REBELS?
The Carpenter of Nazareth and his odd bunch of
long-haired, bearded, robed, and bare-footed,
System-defying disciples? . . . Or their sanctimonious,
hypocritical, God-defying persecutors?

"Have a nice day," the smiling Child of God said.
"Right on," Robbie said, saluting with his fist.
Downtown the sidewalks heated up fast – he had to pull a sun-softened blob of bubblegum from between his toes, leaning for balance against the mammoth sculpture on the plaza outside the Canadian Imperial Bank of Commerce. A brass plaque on the sculpture read, Henry Moore – *Woman in Three Pieces*. The gum clung like a sweet leech, a cat's cradle of gooey gossamer strands between his fingers.
He signed in and received directions at the lobby security desk, but still he got lost and wandered around, his feet flip-flopping on the cool floors. He rode the elevators up and

down for a quarter of an hour. He read the directories, but Dad wasn't listed by name, and the exact office eluded his memory. Something to do with race horses, hadn't he once said? Robbie asked a woman in a suit. She suggested Human *Resources*, but when he located it the secretaries looked at him funny. He felt totally out of place. It was like meat storage in there, it was so efficiently air-conditioned, and he was dressed for summer: *Cannabis Sativa* T-shirt, cut-off jean shorts, that was it. He asked a couple of men toting briefcases. They exchanged glances like he was a freak. Making him feel unreasonably self-conscious about his toenails. He made a face at them, steely and pointed as a tactical nuclear missile; what did they expect, the city was a filthy place to live, *K*? They each made several chins at once and threw their hands up. No one knew a Monsieur Bookbinder. Not in this department, anyway. Nor in the next. Nor the next. He opened one door – onto a stuffy half-lit hallway, as it turned out, and a concrete stairwell. Bummer. The door clacked behind him resoundingly. He tried to go back, but it had locked shut from the other side. *Major* bummer. Down the hall he found a series of locked doors, some clanging iron stairs, a smaller airless corridor, twenty more flights of stairs, and finally a reinforced door that regurgitated him onto the sun-bleached sidewalk. He glared up at the skyscraper and pointed at his temple with his index finger to blow his brains out.

Stamping away, he went by the Smiling Idiot Child of God again, passing out his leaflets.

"The truth will set you free! Kohoutek is coming! God is sexy! Can you help with a donation? You look like you're in need of Salvation!"

"Oh, *fuck* off."

Away then to the Middle Earth Record Store, the one with a notice in the window that read:

WE SELL NEEDLES

which allowed him at least one small chuckle today. And emerged with a stash five minutes later: two psilocybin buttons, noble Princesses of the Waters, costing him five Bank of Banana dollars apiece. He bought a can of Brador in a brown bag from a dépanneur, chewed and washed one button down . . .

. . . aimlessly meandering now, checking out the head shops and record stores, parking himself on a bench to monitor the sidewalks overflowing with American tourists; pretty soon he feels a degree of 4-D *StonerVision*! The passersby moving with the pixilated rhythm of models in a Japanese monster movie, and the colours of the set of the world like wet enamel paint. His nose poised over the lip of his beer can, sniffing up the malt aroma along with the cruddy odour of the paper bag, he does his best to resemble someone whose very shadow falls across the sidewalk like a threat: in a menacing variation on the theme of throwing breadcrumbs to pigeons, he tosses grit beneath tourists' feet. Robbie squinting grimly at these dumb squares: *The Fat, the Ugly, and the Stupid.* He shoots them dry-gulch glares. Next to these lard-legged lumpy-assed cowboys, Montrealers look to him ultra-European, sleek, mellow, and fine . . .

. . . in forty-five minutes the air is close and thick, the Earth's icecaps have melted and the city's a vast warm fishbowl; the sky is heaving like water's surface seen from a minnow's POV, the skyscrapers are dissolving like sand in the sea, clocks are dribbling from their ornate stone housings, people are happy cartoon sea-monkeys with crowns and sceptres. Robbie is swollen, water-logged, seasick, and his face is numb. He's flat on his back on the still-damp apron of grass in front of the Church of St. Anthony. Directly above him, in mid-air it seems, is a giant Mickey Mouse hand made of orange plastic, as big as a float in an Easter parade, fixed to a pole. He's not too surprised, he's seen a number of these hands before, all over town, pointing like Flying Fickle Fingers of Fate, drawing people's attention to pieces of open-air art, parts of an exploded exhibition timed for the Olympic extravaganza. This one's pointing down at Robbie. *Boy in Three Pieces.* He props himself up on an elbow, looks around. Realizes now he's lying in the middle of a circle of rocks, a mini-Stonehenge, the shadows cast long in the late-afternoon sun. He glugs down half his beer, eyes closed, loving the way his eyelids flame a brilliant orange, extinguishing to reveal a sliding envelope of blood vessels bright as rivulets of lava, cooling as this ancient place sinks hissing to the sea bed. And again he's thinking about sweet Ivy, Ivy, Ivy; he wishes he wouldn't but he can't help himself, her wrists wriggly-slick like two hot eels as he tries to pull her from the burning school attic for the hundredth time . . .

Sitting up an hour later, he's coming down a little, and look now, tottering along in his direction: Rosie. Balanced precariously on a pair of purple Candies, desperately short-sighted, scrunched-up paperback in one hand, pencil in the other busily underlining, Rosie periodically looks up at the world with her repertoire of perplexed expressions, stepping off sidewalks with the abandon of a person stepping off a cliff, recognizing objects only at the last minute – apologizing to a car – all the while having, it looks like, some intense dialogue with the spirits of her fuzzy universe; *listen to this, sky; listen, flowers; listen, lovely old building.* Robbie lies back on the grass hoping she'll go by.

She doesn't.

"Bob, hey wow! How ya DOIN? I can't believe my eyes, you're just the PERSON! I was just thinking; why do men have to spit in the street? I mean *what*, do they have more *saliva* than women?"

She plops down on the grass, her temples streaming with perspiration. Robbie examines her closely, still seeing the world in flashes through a mushrooming fish-eye lens: in the beautiful metal sunset – copper and sodium flashes, nickel and cadmium sparks – the pores of her cheek are big as pockmarks, and each one contains a drop of radioactive rainbow water . . .

She crosses her legs like scissors, reverses them, and again, and tucks a hand snugly between her thighs. Only to unfold herself as if she's been found out doing something wrong.

"Wow," she says when she sees his eyeballs shuttle. "First time I see you in MONTHS and you're *already* making me self-*con*scious. You should know I DO that, *Bob*, because of my DADDY. I've always embarrassed him sitting this way. But I *like* to when I'm feeling forlorn. I want to have a baby." She tilts her chin up proudly, sweeps her hair behind her ears, pulls it out again, wraps it around her fingers and sucks the end of a tress. Clacks her gum, squints at the street, and pushes her other hand between her thighs. Stops. "I know I *know*, don't LOOK at me like that – I'm just a chamber of horrors, aren't I? In my own abusement park."

Robbie sticks his index finger to his temple and cocks his thumb back to blow his brains all over the Church of St. Anthony's lawn.

"You never called," she says, resting her head on his shoulder. "And now I can see that you hate me. I'm not *blind*, you know."

Rosie's fleshy and pink as the gum she loves to blow. And she smells of the stuff, which she chews with a vengeance. Robbie catches an image of the time she once bit her lip too hard in anger, the gum appearing between teeth streaked with blood like ruddy marble. Now she's obviously fresh from an afternoon shift at L'Enfer Strip;

17

she resembles an ancient Egyptian vampire – black lip-stick, black leather mini-skirt, slashed black tank-top (nip-ples as large as raw bee-stings, he sees so close, and the stitches of her bra strap spun from crackling plutonium), pale white flesh showing through slashed black tights, jet black hair spiked upwards with sugar and water – just like, she says, these so-called *punks* are starting to do in England.

"Hey, Rosie," Robbie says lazily. "Check this. See the Queen on the dollar bill? And on the back, the Prairies divided in two by the infinite road?" (The paper money's opening up to him like a Cinerama screen. He doesn't know about her, but he can even hear the wind combing the wheat . . .)

Rosie squints. "Uh huh."

"Watch as I roll it."

"Oh, I don't do that stuff, thank you. My metabolism's *way* too speedy. I know cos I'm reading about the eerie case histories of feral children. Also, anorexia nervosa, amenorrhea, coelacanths, the Gaia hypothesis, and Veli-kovsky's startling predictions which have actually chal-lenged contemporary science. What do you think?"

"Pay attention, Rosie, please. Look into it, like a tele-scope."

"Yeah, OK, so?"

"See the Queen standing by the road now with her thumb out?"

"No."

"Farm out! She must've hitched a ride."

Rosie frowns, snatches the bill to examine it closer. Robbie rolls his eyes in disbelief. Then he drifts off, reflecting grimly on the fact that not a single American has side-stepped that menacing shadow of his all afternoon. The shadow has lengthened, he's feeling smaller. He shrugs and woozily thinks, I seem tame to Yanks because they're so jaded. Well, who wants to be like them. I'm glad

I'm a decent fucken upstanding Canuck. Then he timbers back onto the grass and blacks out.

It was dusk when he was shaken awake. Two men were standing above him: a priest and a cop. He knew the cop.

"Glorious sunset that was. A real Michelangelo," said Officer Gaunt, ever affable, smiling behind his scrawny shrub of a beard, his red eyes watery like he'd been laughing till he cried. Even when his beloved German shepherd had keeled over (Robbie's first unsavoury thought on awakening) after some asshole had mixed Drano into his dog food, Gaunt persisted with his relentless bonhomie. And now he was making an extra-nice face for Robbie's benefit and holding open the rear door of his car like a chauffeur.

"Where're we going," Robbie called out from the back. "Dog pound? Pick out a new mutt?"

His tongue curled up like a snail. Up front, just the sound of the two-way and the cruiser's engine straining up Côte-des-Neiges' steep incline towards Beaver Lake. He stared at Gaunt's red neck, splotchy where the regulation cut was freshly clipped. The short hairs on the nape of Robbie's own neck creeping, like someone was petting him the wrong way.

"Hey, sorry 'bout your woof," he said, leaning forward all contrite with his nose divided in four by the grill. "Wonder what asshole would of done a fucken thing like that."

They had come around to the north side of the mountain, taking the long way home for sure, overlooking the Nôtre-Dame-des-Neiges cemetery now. The smog was a purple haze above the gravestones. Gaunt pulled the cruiser over. A couple of cars drove past. Robbie slunk down in his seat.

Gaunt rested his arm on the top of the front seat and

turned, speaking over his shoulder. "Why do you deliberately make life tough on yourself?" His trademark tones of exasperation. "With all your privilege, lad."

"Hey, hey – you a cop, or a parent?"

Gaunt scratched his beard and sighed. "So tell me, since we've not yet had the pleasure of a heart-to-heart. I've been asked to ask you – how'd you manage to – you know – do what you did?"

The base of Robbie's spine slick beneath his T-shirt now. "*I* dunno. What?"

"Jesus crawl back on the cross for comfort. Just *tell* me, please."

"Oh. Rescue my girlfriend you mean? Too much, am I getting an award?"

"No, not in a manner of speaking. Though that was a very heroic thing you did there."

"Have you heard from her?"

"No, but her father says, and I quote, if you so much as dream of her he'll recommend you get a horsewhipping."

"Yeah, so. I could care less. He already made a pitch for that, fuck. Luckily my Dad sent him a memo which said that horsewhipping is against family policy."

"You and Ivy ever spend time in the attic?"

"The . . . *school* attic? Uhh, let me think. Uhh, no."

"Never?"

"Never."

"Not even once?"

"Never, I said."

"You're sure."

"I'm sure."

"Sure you're sure?"

"Fuck, I was in class the whole time, ask anybody . . . can I go now?"

Gaunt turned the ignition, pulled the cruiser back onto the road. "Okey doke," he said, and sighed.

In five minutes they were in front of the Bookbinders'

home. Robbie could see, with some relief, that no cars were in the driveway and the lights in the house were off.

"Fuck off now, do," Gaunt said, smiling in the dash light like a satanic butler. "There are people, you know, myself included, who worship the ground that's coming to you."

Later that night, while Dad snored and Cournoyer scored to clinch the Habs a reprieve in overtime, Robbie was upstairs snooping. Ears primed like a bat's, he pulled out forbidden drawers and tried on a few dainty ensembles. Not as much fun as it sounds; Mom so mistrusted him that the antique armoire was almost certainly booby-trapped – drawers left open and shut with only *apparent* randomness, bras and stockings flung in with only *apparent* abandon. It made him knot his cheeks and gnash his teeth and lose his boner to be forced to remember so many sneaky details, to put everything back exactly where it was in the first place. And did sweaty fingers leave visible stains on satin panties? Would his big feet leave an impression in silk stockings? Would his animal toenails make them run? And would Mendoza, the family dog who is now panting and slobbering at the bedroom door, somehow stool on him?

He rifled through Dad's desk (*him too* – envelopes, pens, and keys arranged in incredibly devious asymmetries) and plundered the pockets of a pair of big elephant-brown baggy-ass pants that lay in a trampled mound at the foot of the bed, thinking all the while that at the end of this energetic day you could hardly accuse him of a lack of *curiosity*, not knowing what his old man did. Exactly. It was plainly that: the Generation Gap being what it was in the mid 1970s, communication at home was as rare, as slim, as *bogarted* (in his expert estimation), as a joint rolled with prime Hawaiian hay. The end. All parents must die.

2

FOLLOWING MORNING, AFTER HIS SHOWER, HE STOOD IN front of the mirror and swabbed a patch clear. His hair was kite string tangled in a tree. His body plump-white and muscleless as a larva. And pizza-face, gross himself out. He leaned close, nose to the glass, nose to nose, chin to chin. And weird, eh, how elsewhere the universe was spiralling vastly, crackling with energy, and elsewhere the planet was busting apart with political crises and unnameable emotional traumas, and here his world had shrunk down, like a dwarf star collapsing in on itself, to his concern for this one little disgusting pimple. And so suicide was out of the question this week, for sure. Die young but leave a beautiful corpse, remember that.

He squeezed himself into his bell-bottoms, squirmed around, doing knee bends, tiptoeing, till his cock and balls were reunited to one side like a squishy packet of Gummi Bears. Pulled on a paisley headband, a belt buckled with a Harley-Davidson eagle, plus his authentic Canadian regiment D-Day combat jacket with the red curtain fringes sewn on the cuffs and the Ban-the-Bomb patch on the back. He selected a T-shirt that bore an image of Keef Richards of the Strolling Bones, a photo taken just minutes before he'd died of a mysterious brain haemorrhage. (Or so it was rumoured; Robbie'd heard it otherwise said that the singer had injected himself with a horsecock-needleful of crystal meth, diluting it with water drawn up from a toilet bowl, and that he'd been careless – for apparently, Spit Swagger, the group's drummer, had just thrown up in the same toilet, and Keef had neglected to flush it before dipping the syringe in. Robbie had yet to verify the truth of either story.) The image had been printed on a film of sticky plastic and ironed on at the Prairie Buffalo T-Shirt Emporium and Head Shoppe, in the Alexis Nihon Plaza. After three washes the cheap shit was already breaking up, but Robbie preferred it like that; the chips reminded him of the way oil paintings and frescoes crack apart after a century or two, and they invested Keef's portrait with the decadence and intrigue associated with historical decline. Keef's imperially bored expression registered no surprise at his own head exploding: the Twentieth Century Schizoid Man had kept his cool to the end. And there was a caption:

KEEF LIVES

over which Robbie had scrawled, in fat black Magic Marker,

SUCKS

"Oh. You look extremely GROOVY," Rosie told him when she showed to pick him up. (Apparently, they'd made a plan – out on the lawn of the Church of St. Anthony – though he was fucked if he could remember what for, exactly.) He shot her back a nasty stare. He knew it wasn't in her nature to be sarcastic, but just to be sure.

Down in the dungeon they shared a beer. "I like this place," she said, looking around. "It's a living *womb*." She curled a strand of hair around her index finger, thought-

23

fully. "I can never trust men, I've decided." Tucking the hair behind one ear.

"Yeah," Robbie replied, good-naturedly, for he knew she couldn't be thinking of him; he, Robbie the Gallant, exempt from the company of Men Women Don't Trust.

"Like for instance, you should have *called* me. We had a good time in the winter, *I* thought. What if I hadn't never bumped into you yesterday?" Slipping a hand between her thighs, looking at the ceiling. "Boys smell like fast food, I think, which is too bad. . . . " Squinting at the marijuana leaf flag. "Anyway I've decided I'll give myself a gin abortion if I have to. But I have to say I would still want the baby. In *principle*." And opening them unself-consciously wide.

"Chrissake," Robbie said. "What happened?"

"Oh, mellow out, Bob." Clamping them shut. "Give me my space will you? Nothing happened. I'm just saying *if*. I mean, every time I'm alone with my boss he's all over me. And, ouch, he's so ROUGH. Here I am – delicate little Rose. Five-foot-six, forlorn, circulation cut off by pantyhose invented by men."

"Rosie, uh. Maybe the way you – maybe you, sort of, lead him on."

"Oh yeah, typical – *see no evil* . . . " she snapped, clacking her gum angrily at him now. "You and he and my Daddy would get along like *houses* on fire. I don't LEAD the guy on. He doesn't *need* to be led on." Then she crossed her legs with what Robbie took as an expression of finality. And uncrossed them again.

It was June 24th, she reminded him – St. Jean-Baptiste, Quebec's Fête Nationale. So they took a Boulevard bus to Côte-des-Neiges and walked from there, high up to Beaver Lake, where Mount Royal's southern plateau looked over

24

the city and – on days when the wind blew the haze away – all the way to the St. Lawrence River.

Robbie, who liked to sit right in front of the amplifiers, was stunned with disappointment to see how many people had got there before him. He staked out a little territory, as much as Rosie's beach blanket would cover, somewhere in the centre of the anthill of humanity that bristled with flags and waving arms, and soon they were both lying beneath a big sky getting a buzz off a bottle of fizzing warm apple cider.

All over the mountain, while the music played, children tugged on kites and families perspired around barbecues; French-Canadian hippies handed out political pamphlets and flags with fleurs-de-lis on them, mimes in whiteface did their utterly compelling act of standing still or being stuck inside glass boxes – the only whiff of violence (apart from the fact that the music was so loud fish were floating up dead on the surface of the lake) was a story that circulated in the crowd about an incident involving the Montreal chapter of the Satan's Choice and their arch rivals the Dead Man's Hands, over a cocaine deal. Another story had it that several of the bikers had gang-banged a teenage girl in the bushes, on the east side of the mountain under the giant electric crucifix. But there was so much peace and love and music and political fervour in the air that no one was about to get het up over a little thing like that.

Robbie lay on his back watching smoke curl lazily upwards, listening to the music performed on a stage half a mile away, and thinking about how the word humanity has the word ant in it. The earth was a vast dish tipping, revolving vertiginously in a luminous universe, the centrifuge pulling him around like a great, lethargic fairground ride. He could barely see the stage at all, but there was so much sweet metal music spilling out from the banks of speakers, like a drawerful of cutlery crashing to the floor, that his skull was numb, and there was still enough noise left over to smack against the rows of houses at the edges of the park and bounce right back again.

He tried to estimate how many people were there. It was certainly the biggest crowd he'd ever been in. Maybe even bigger than Woodstock!

"A partir d'ici et pour un an!" the immensely popular Yvon Deschamps dictated into the microphone, his arms outstretched.

"A PARTIR D'ICI ET POUR UN AN!" the crowd responded as one massive, joyous voice from all over Mount Royal.

"J'vais pas parler l'Anglais!"

"J'VAIS PAS PARLER L'ANGLAIS!"

"Dey're not gonna speak Hinglish because dey don't know *ow* to speak Hinglish," Robbie chuckled to himself, splitting a match down the middle to make a flimsy roach-clip.

Rosie squinted around and whistled low. "You know what, Bob? There's a *renaissance* going on here. The best and heaviest music in North America, the best and heaviest BOOKS, the best ART, the heaviest POLITICS. It's crazy, but right now there's a genuine *revolution* happening, and no one in the outside world even knows about it."

"The best and heaviest dope," Robbie murmured.

Politics was not his strong point, but as far as he dug it, Quebec separatism went like this: the *pea-soups* had had it up to here with being bossed around by the *Anglos*, who had all the money and the culture and the smarts. It was Dad who called them pea-soups, because that was their national dish, but to Robbie's generation they were *pepsis* – that's because, and Robbie was sure he had read this in a scientific magazine, the average Québécois drinks eighteen gallons of pop a year; that's tops in Canada and second only to certain southern U.S. states. Anyway, now the pepsis wanted a spot guaranteed on the hit parade, and in their own language; they'd tried bombings and kidnappings before, but today a whole lot of pepsis felt the only way to be was out of Canada altogether.

That was it, in a nutshell. Robbie meanwhile is preoccupied with working enough spittle up in his dried-out mouth to moisten the end of an enormous spliff before the glowing tip falls off and burns Rosie's back. And Rosie meanwhile has pulled a copy of *The Compleat Illustrated Handbook on the Psychic Sciences* from her beachbag.

She rolls over, shows him. "Palmistry, astrology, dice-divination, cartomancy, moleosophy, dream interpretation, telepathy *and* ESP, graphology, yoga, and omens."

"Moleosophy?"

"The study of moles and their meaning. I have one on the aureole of my left nipple. Look, see?" Robbie looks. "It means I'm an active, energetic person. Want to meditate?"

He shrugs. Can't hurt. Rosie whispers to him his confidential personal mantra, cupping her hand to his ear – *forrum* – and shows him the lotus position. . . .

He has trouble concentrating. Not just because he's stoned, and not because he's at a rock concert; it's just that the benefit of repeating a Sanskrit word over and over in his head and picturing nothing but a white screen, utter nothingness, for twenty minutes, frankly eludes him. Dad would probably laugh that it shouldn't be such an impossible task for Robbie of all people, but he'd never appreciate the real problem: Robbie's Sanskrit word sounds too much like the *Montreal* Forum, and Yvan Cournoyer and the Canadiens keep skating in to push a puck around and score on the power play. In his mind Robbie calls an end to the period and brings on the Zamboni to clear the ice of tuques and ice-cream wrappers and frozen spit, in slow ovals, and fill his mind again with utter white. But it's futile. He opens his eyes a fraction and peeps over at Rosie. She's sitting with an upright back and her fingers poised, her eyes wide open, vicariously enjoying his perfect transcendence. . . .

"Good try!" she says. "Now gimme your palm. Boy, I'm reading *everything* these days. Tea leaves, toenails, bus transfers, toast. Fate leaves fingerprints all *over* the place."

Everything except intelligent books, thinks Robbie the Big Reader, rolling his eyes. He knows Rosie wants his palm only to make physical contact with him, and her extreme eagerness makes him retreat farther. Though in the end his curiosity wins out.

"Ivy?" Rosie says. "Lemme see. Hmm. No, I don't think so. I don't see her in your future at all."

He pulls away, wipes the damp on his jeans.

Rosie shrugs, then crosses her arms to pull off her tank-top; points her toes in the air, and slips off her tights. Then she stretches out on her belly beside him in a minuscule black bikini, closes her eyes, and demands he oil her all over.

"I'm so short-sighted I can't see the stage anyway," she says. "You can give me the play-by-play while I listen."

How cheap and greasy mascara looks in the bright sun, he thinks. He examines her body, sees how her curves are traced with swirling trails of hair – not dyed black like the hair on her head, but gold as a bumblebee – on her cheeks, on her arms, down her back too. Her shoulder blades like wings. Her wasp waist. The startling rise of her rump and the tantalizing shadow where her bikini-bottom spans the valley; her golden down disappearing there like a pollinated path.

He looks up to see a couple of guys, hairy as buffalo, ogling her too. He gives them a defiant look, like: Bug off, this is MY queen bee. Pours a palmful of baby oil on her back, and works it in. Rosie reaching back with one arm and deftly unhooking her bra. But after Robbie sees them turn away, he thumbs her flesh without enthusiasm again.

He's really saving himself for Ivy. Just because Rosie and he made out last winter in an episode he'd rather not dwell on right now thank you very much, doesn't mean he's *committing* himself, exactly.

Soon he's aware of her standing up. He hears her voice, up in the clouds, saying she's going in search of a Johnny-on-the-Spot. He watches her buzz off as he remains cross-legged on the beach towel, his fizzing warm bottle between his thighs, all pumped up as happy and buoyant as a multicoloured hot-air balloon.

Now his perception has become microscopic. With the hot bubbles of alcohol burping up the back of his nose and tickling his nostrils, and the sun gripping onto his shoulders for a blazing piggyback, his focus is all on the skin of his hands and feet. The land map of veins and freckles is pocked and reddened from the grit embedded there; swatches of grass are mashed into his ankles, fallen asleep from hours of sitting, and the tiny criss-crossings of his skin are like landing strips on a pinkish plain. The grit like scattered boulders. The blue veins like monster worms. And up above, his eyelids feel huge, lowering as slow and heavy as canvas awnings over the entire world. He swallows to pop the underwater pressure in his ears. More bomblets of cider explode in his nose like tiny depth-charges. Bathysphere of booze. He's going down, safe and sound and abso-tively posi-lutely answerable to no one . . .

. . . when he eventually came down, Rosie still hadn't returned. That was the first thought he had given her in an hour. Or two. Well, the crowd was humongous, she was bound to get lost for a while. After ten more minutes, however, he grew anxious. Maybe she didn't like him any more; maybe she had taken off. With someone else. He twisted around and craned his neck to find her, but the crowd was too immense.

Then he caught sight of her, and she was wandering off

29

in the wrong direction. He thought of yelling, but there was no point – the music was way too loud, and he'd be risking his life to call out in English in *dis* crowd – so he just stood and waved, like a castaway on a desert island. She drifted off aimlessly, like a boat with a luffed sail. He fired a shot into his temple and rolled his eyes. Now pepsis were shouting at him to sit down; the buffalo guys threatened to tie his shoelaces together if he didn't.

Rosie was a bobbing pinpoint on a sea of bodies, tacking back, more or less. Veering off again. Now only ten or twenty paces away. She wore a worried expression, not much else. He shrugged and sat down. She was so close, surely he didn't have to call out. She stepped right by.

The buffalo guys wolf-whistled. One of them, an oily polka-dot bandanna bunching up his stringy hair, stroked her hand and cooed, "Taberouette, t'es ben cute, toi. Viens faire un tour par ici."

Rosie looked down at him angrily, whipping her hand away, and said, "Fuck off, you stupid boy. I can't understand a thing you're saying, but I know I don't like it. I'm trying to find my *friend*."

"Ayy baby," he said, "come ere an sit in my lap. Qu'est-ce qu'y a, j'fais pas ton affaire?"

The other one had a row of fleurs-de-lis tattooed across his shoulders. He grabbed her ankle. Rosie shrieked. "Ayy baby," the animal said. "Chu pas assez grand pour toi? Viens donc ici an sit on my *face*."

Before Robbie could decide what to do, she had wrenched herself free and, kicking the guy squarely in the chest, toppled over backwards and landed with a plonk on her own towel.

"Bob!" she said with a wobbly voice, and Robbie saw in the bright sun how flecks of mascara were suspended in her tears. "Why didn't you shout where you *were*? I was *scared*. I couldn't *find* you."

"Hey," he said, irritated. He held it against her that she should allow herself to be seen crying. Ivy never would. She wouldn't allow you to have such a picture of her, like a drooling animal, in your memory. "Don't cry, K? People're looking. Really, Rosie, why don't you just wear glasses. Or contacts, if you're so vain?"

She looked at him wildly. Her lip was trembling. She rolled her gum into a hard little ball and pinned it between her front teeth. "Bob, I think I hate you. I'm being hassled by a couple of goons and you're embarrassed cause I'm *crying*? Fuck off, you stupid jerk."

"Uh, gee, Rosie." He put his hand on her knee. "I'm sorry. You mix me up, that's all."

She brushed it away. "Yeah, isn't that typical. *I'm* being threatened with rape, and you want to talk about *your* personal crisis. Well, take off if you can only think about yourself, OK?"

She turned her head in the direction of the stage. Robbie watched her with nervous interest. She was batting her soggy eyelashes and chewing her mouth. He knew she wasn't enjoying the concert; that more than anything she wanted to talk. And sure enough: "I mix you up, do I, you poor confused thing? Here's what you should know about me, then: I don't wear glasses so I don't have to *see* all the goons who want to hassle me. It's OK if I only have to hear them, well, it's *partly* OK, but if I look them in the face I'm DOOMED. That's all they want, and I won't give them the pleasure."

"What about working at your club, then?" Robbie said, superciliously. He'd been wanting to get around to this for a long time. "All men do there is stare, and you give them lots of pleasure."

"But standing real close and staring the customers down is, well, it's *different* – it's like, when they look into their drink as if they've found something floating around in it,

31

they're just like little boys. And anyhow, the bouncers *protect* me in there. Out in the REAL world I don't *want* to see too clearly."

"But, Rosie, maybe if you didn't, uh, dress the way you do, you wouldn't attract so much, you know, attention."

Rosie punched him in the arm and gave him a resentful glare. "You sound like a politician," she said, her voice clogged. "What should I wear? Rusty spiky armour? Why should I change the way I *dress*? Sexy is fun, although the way most men behave, you'd think it was a THREAT. Why *should* I change the way I dress. Men should change their *minds*, instead, like, turn 'em in and get a new, improved model." She blew her nose on her towel. "I'm all forlorn now, Bob. I want to leave."

Robbie felt shitty. Truly he did. He held her arm, like a male nurse, guiding her through the crowd. On the bus he stared hard at anyone who might be curious as to why her eyes were wet. The bus passed through Westmount, only one stop to the park now. He prepared to stand up, taking her hand.

"Oh no, not me," Rosie said. "I'm going all the way home. *Alone please*."

Robbie pulled a glum face, real hangdog, like the sun and the dope had warmed and softened it to Silly Putty. He slumped his head down between his shoulder blades. He held onto her hand sorrowfully, gave it an ingratiating squeeze. At last she looked at him.

"Bob!" Squinting in disbelief, shifting her weight away to get a better look. "You look so sad. Have I really upset you? Wow. Now, that – is – DYNAMITE!"

In the middle of Westmount Park was a brightly painted booth equipped with a sound system, known in the neighbourhood as the Kiosk. There was a concrete clearing around it, with blistered wooden benches, provided by the municipality to keep all the trouble in one place. Across the park, past the swings and past the library on Sherbrooke Street, you could always hear the supreme heaviosity of guitar riffs, whumping out over the trees.

It was mostly Anglo-Quebeckers who gathered there, Westmount High students, famous in the city for the achievement of being perpetually stoned. (Years ago Robbie's parents had refused to send him there for fear of Bad Influences, but look now, he thought, at least this school is still standing.) These cats liked to just hang out, revving their bikes, perching on the backs of the benches like patched-up parrots, smelling of patchouli and savage B.O. They smoked joints and grooved, sunlight flashing off the little mirrors embroidered into their Indian-cotton frog shirts. And the main thing was that to maintain your cool, you had to act unfriendly. You had to sit there looking like a Strolling Bones album cover, just being a lizard with a sewed-up mouth, sitting in twilight, in the crack between worlds, Castaneda-wise, not releasing a drop of emotion. Now Robbie wondered why he'd come. He looked around him with a sinking heart. He'd been so *up* until he saw these long faces, these indolent bystanders, these pseudo-hippies gone prematurely to seed, still waiting, he observed sourly, for another generation's revolution, still playing someone else's old romantic records. *The Lugs. The Head. The Yores.* He knew better. The CIA had defused the sixties by bombarding the hippie community with downer drugs and chemical mindfucks. If you doubt it, just look around. Like, six blocks over and a short hike up the hill Canada's coming apart, it's having a revolution all of its own, *and none of these turkeys even knows about it*. To Robbie, the sixties was a dirty word; he'd found out what a scam it all was – just before the fire razed his school down to several rows of seared gym lockers, he'd caught a glimpse of how it all worked – he'd been backstage. Ivy had shown him.

Brat was here, wearing a Vietnam combat jacket with the sleeves pinned up to reveal his thalidomide hands – fins really, crab claws without a shell – which he was now using to pass on a roach, with surprising dexterity, the strange economical speed of dwarfs. He was cool as all get out; he acknowledged Robbie and Rosie's arrival by blinking slower than normal.

Louie Louie called out heartily. "*Ayy*, allo, white man! Taberslaque! You can see your religion in dose pant!" Big hulking Louie Louie in army surplus shit-kickers and a brown bomber jacket as buffed and battered and caked in dirt as the hide of the old bull itself. Extending a meaty fist. Yes, Louie Louie was a pepsi, the son of the janitor at Westmount High, and once assistant janitor himself, who'd been embraced by the Westmount clique by virtue of the high-quality weed he dealt; he used to store the stuff in toilet rolls, high up on a stockroom shelf where his bent old man could not reach, and open shop in the cans at lunch hour. That was before Officer Gaunt made a good-will appearance, on tour with his lecture entitled, *Pot or Not?* and brought in his dog for an inspection of the premises. The way Louie Louie talked about it now, is papa was taken de hearly retirement, hosti.

Joggers and mothers passing by with prams looked askance at the tribe, and Robbie felt pleased to be thought of as party to trouble. Louie Louie was such a gronker, closer to seven feet than to six, his hair short as a GI's, his eyebrows shaved off, eyes as dull as gunpowder, neck as thick and dirty as a tire; he now worked in a poultry factory at the eastern end of the city, where it was his job to chop the little beaks off newly hatched chicks to prevent them from pecking one another to death in the overcrowded cages where they were fattened for slaughter.

"I'm *also* reading *The Bible and Flying Saucers*," Rosie announced, pulling yet another ragged paperback from her beach bag. She held it up for Brat to see, pointing to the photographs as if teaching a baby. "It's like, when you read Psalm 104:3, *He makes the clouds his chariot*, what do think that *really* means, guys?"

Robbie passed buttons of mesc around, popping one right into Brat's mouth.

"No, really," Rosie said, accepting one with her tongue stuck out and then placing Robbie's hands on her shoulders and making his fingers massage the muscles there. "What does it mean?"

"It means you shouldn't believe everything you read," said Robbie, who was reading nothing at the time. And his hands had turned to wood.

Time passed and people sat. It was incredible how the Anglo cats there could sit and sit and sit, saying zilch in *either* of Canada's official languages, not least Robbie himself, with his KEEF SUCKS T-shirt proclaiming the sum total of his commitment to the maintenance of intelligent life on our fair planet.

Half an hour later he was feeling brutally nauseous, which was a welcome change in tempo, at least. By then Rosie had turned away to read the palm of some furry freak in a crushed-velvet shirt. Robbie observed them with a seasoned stoner's intellectual disdain. These people, with their ankhs and vibes and karma and signs. This bullshit, this time-wasting, this inertia, this empty decade. The only authentic thing they'd inherited from the sixties, he thought, was a terminal case of superstitious mindwarp. The vanity, he thought, to imagine you're part of some cosmic plan, that you can find a personal reference to yourself in any cheap paperback index of the zodiac. And still in his mind he was stuck on Ivy, Ivy again, who was addicted to reality (so she used to say), and the last he saw of her in the hot smoke: her glistening wrists, slipping from his grasp . . .

He went off to throw up in the bushes, returning, immensely relieved, to wash the mesc's soapy taste down with beer . . .

. . . he hears himself say something, to no one in particular,

pigs, fuck,

in two voices, one for each ear, out of sync like an effect on a heavy record; the one euphoric, made light with giddy foolish amusement – the source of which he can't determine at all – the other flat and foul as death's own burp. He's frightened by the intensity, the sudden shift, and his skin crawls.

And in fact has anyone, may I ask, seen or heard about Ivy?

Yow! Eek! These are Brat's first words. *The devil's own daughter.*

Two hours now Robbie's pelvic bones have ground against the bench, and at last the lamplit world begins to bloom. The stained-glass park slips and slides all around them, peeling away like the acetate cells of an animated cartoon. The multicoloured leaves appear gloved in a malleable varnish, and each one has a distinct musical personality. The trees now chiming. Sucking up tones from the Earth's core and dispersing them into the star-filled air. The chocolate-brown earth humming. And the four of them on their backs watching this verdant orchestra in its bonging bowl of midnight blue milk, speaking only in bursts.

School's fucked, he hears himself say. *Heh. I mean look at me. If this is the best they can do.*

A crescent moon flits by like a swallow, white as talc, leaving seventy-five powdery tattoos of itself across the stomach of the sky.

Uff, the gronker goes. *Uff uff.*

Robbie watches a crystal-mint leaf detach itself from a twig and tinkle down. And an epiphany, playing itself out like the tumbling flakes in a kaleidoscope: we're all rushing down the cosmic flow. Consciousness is just an illusion. We only *think* we're thinking. Thoughts are only circuits flashing, we're really juicy robots programmed into this microchip galaxy. Man, I hope I remember this later. Turning his neck and through his jellied windowpanes he sees Brat on his back with a foot propped on a knee and his head on a swollen root, still and solid, enamelled like a garden gnome with his arms chipped off.

Bob, Rosie says. *I see love colours when I ball. You?*

Robbie turns to her. He likes Rosie's ski-jump nose, her plummy lips, but she's too, he has to say it to himself at the end of the day, too *clingy*. She doesn't hold a candle to Ivy, who showed so little affection that when she *did* touch you, you knew she probably meant it. Frankly, he's turned off by the way Rosie likes to hug all the time in public places, pressing her nose behind his ear and making his neck wet with her breath; demanding epic-length backrubs and smelling as she does of frangipani and Bubble Yum. When she clambers onto him like she has now, squeezing his waist with her thighs, he thinks with distaste of what he's read in *Bosom Buddies* magazine about girls enjoying horses between their legs due to a phenomenon known as *equus eroticus*. He's embarrassed for her; he figures a person should communicate their sexual style subtly, not announce it like some three-ring circus. He makes like a lizard with a sewed-up mouth. . . .

At midnight they move on, sluggish, smuggling a bottle of St. Antoine Abbé apple cider into the Westmount Roxy, the air musky with passion flower and hashish, and get blotto watching *Woodstock*. (It's Robbie's nineteenth time. Ivy used to work here, and in the good old days he always got in for free.) Rosie sucks his fingers and makes them sticky. He's vaguely aware of this. She lays her head on his shoulder, lifts it, lays it down again, lifts it, lays it down;

weird, he imagines he has a large feathered wing, just one, restless, ruffling, twitching heavy on his shoulder. He concentrates hard on the movie, wishing after all that he'd been a part of that whole groovy business, that whole exuberant crowd. A crowd with a purpose, doing its own original thing. And he might have been part of something today, but for Rosie's emotions. He rocks out, although by three a.m. he finds himself melancholy once more, unexpectedly so, given that he knows every frame in the film by heart. Ridiculously sad in fact, weeping – as he discovers when his lips taste salt – to see that field of garbage during Hendrix, for it looks exactly like what he feels has been bequeathed to him as a seventies guy. He feels so ambivalent, he hardly knows himself. People were part of something back then, or so it was reported. All he senses he's a part of is some Great Hangover; he's grabbed at the end of the sixties and, like a lizard's tail, it has come off in his hands.

3

THE COTTAGE SEASON IS REVVED UP, MIRIAM AND BAR-nabus are out of school for the summer, and Mom's back. Where has she been? A certain continent. Truth is, Rob-bie's stoned again, and wasn't really paying attention that closely when she plopped her luggage down, and got it all confused when she described the documentary she'd been making about, about – spices . . . species? . . . faeces? Same difference; whatever it was, knowing Mom's show, it was probably bad news for nature.

Anyhow, now it's rush rush rush to get out of this hot smelly town, and the Bookbinders nod to the other West-mount families packing up their cars in their driveways sprinkled with apple blossom. A routine Robbie despises, and he makes no bones about it. Dad has to tell him, "Sorry, Robbie, but in this fam – I, this house is out of – look, we're locking up for the summer. That is non-negotiable. I don't want you having some, some – "

"Some whut? Some whut?"

"Some *harsh* party," Barnabus says. "I heard him tell Mom."

"*Hushed* party is what he said, STUPID," Miriam says. "*As is your wont*, Rob."

"Won't *whut?*" Robbie demands. Fists on hips, red-eared

and steaming, he shoots the Rubinsteins a withering stare clear across the street, tosses his hair off his shoulders, rests the knuckles of one fist on the hood of the car, instantly yanking them off the burning metal.

"Look," he spits. "You can tell Dad I'm wasting my teens away slaving over a hot lawnmower. It's the wilderness out there, not a croquet lawn. It's futile, I'll tell you that much for free – keeping that place the way Mom and Dad like it is like digging a hole in the ocean."

"Dad says you're too angry about nothing and that we need quality-intensive time together," Miriam says snittily, going back to her *Owl* magazine.

"Hard family labour, he means."

"And Mom says next time we'll buy the Alexis Nihon Plaza so you can hang out in the mall."

Grumbling, he stuffs a sack full of groceries (he's been *forced* to do this) under the hatchback and squeezes in the back seat with his brother and sister. Mendoza the boxer jumps in too, slobbering on his lap. Robbie slams the door extremely hard. It's suffocatingly hot as they wait for Dad to switch on the air-conditioning. The car has the familiar stink of sticky coffee at the bottoms of Mom's *Hello World!* TV-show mugs, the reminder of last week's french onion soup that slopped over during the dirt-road stretch of the trip, and the repulsive memory of Barnabus's abruptly reviewed lunch, all three courses.

"Oh. Now. Chrissake. *SBD.* Who's the dirty pig?"

"He who smelt it dealt it," Miriam says.

"He who denied it supplied it," Barnabus says.

Robbie rolls down his window and hangs himself out. A breeze cools the damp creases in the crooks of his arms. *Puh PUH duh duh PUH*, he taps out a demon rhythm, gingerly, on the shell of the car. *Puh PUH duh duh DUH. All families must die . . .*

. . . at last they've driven off. And Robbie's won a victory: he's waved goodbye and is strolling back down the garden path now like he's the owner of this big old house. Turns up the stereo to rock the foundations and sings along at the top of his lungs, churning his throat up hot and raw, all alone in the place that from the neighbours' point of view must have just become a jumping jukebox.

The doorbell rings. It's Ivy, fresh from the hospital. Her skin is tender and white, as her petroleum jelly-soaked bandages have only recently been removed. They feast on pizza and agree the clams on it look like little denuded vaginas. They drink freely from Dad's liquor cabinet and in the living room play Ivy's favourite game, the one in which they take on mystery characters and meet for the first time, again and again. On this woozy evening she's a writer of erotic literature living in Paris at the time of Debussy and Cocteau and Gide, although Robbie wouldn't know what that means if you spelled it out for him. She's sitting on the tapestried couch, squinting against the setting sun, the smoke from her cigarette hanging in the light like a nest of crafty thoughts. He's pinned to the carpet like a hairy butterfly, twitching, hands fluttering, fishing for flakes of cork on the surface of his wine. Reluctantly he settles on Keef Richards of the Strolling Bones, but then, with shame, realizes he can't think of a thing to say in order to become *Keef Richards, to pull on the heavy mantle of his glory, to adopt the supreme voice of a generation.*

Robbie loves Ivy, but how he's starting to hate her, too. She just sits there with the cool of the Sphinx, her legs drawn up and her knees tucked under her chin, her skirt tantalizingly slipped off her thighs. She's sizing him up through her otter-brown eyes, head cocked insouciantly, as if she were unaware he can see her labia squeezing out in the shape of a plum pit, wrapped in the tissue of her panties like fruit on display. When she knows perfectly well . . .

... he sighed and shifted in his seat, for the car, vibrating steadily on the highway, was causing the thickly-stitched seams of his far-out sprayed-on bell-bottoms to pinch his scrotum.

They drove two hours from Montreal through the Eastern Townships to Kilborn Centre, the car's shadow rippling and tumbling over the drab flat fields, the Madame Patates, the gas stations, and the farmhouses advertising worms. Now, in Robbie's humble opinion, regardless of what the Quebec Tourism brochures said, Kilborn Centre was an oily little armpit boasting a row of burger joints and tacky souvenir stores on Main Street, and a fish canning factory on a lakeshore crawling with foam. Motorbikes clustered together in the mangy central park next to a Baron Bulgingburger's franchise. Bikers hung out drinking beer and listening to music – the old ladies with PROPRIÉTÉ DE HELL'S ANGELS on their T-shirts, the brothers with their stitched-on colours and studded leather vests and stupendous beerguts and psycho mountain-man beards. They peed, too, against the war memorial plastered with bird droppings, a bra dangling aloft from the soldier's upstretched hand. Dad said, "Jesus, look at those smelly, aum ... " and remarked that the statue had no right to be there because, during Conscription, the French Canadians had disgraced themselves by fleeing the towns and hiding out in the bush.

"Chickenshit pea-soups," Barnabus said, and Mom turned to give Dad an almighty look. Just like on TV! Grilling some industrial-strength polluter. Robbie sank low in his seat.

The Bookbinders had to drive through Kilborn Centre to reach the heart of the Townships. Lush, rolling, contented, the last rural bastion of Quebec's well-to-do Anglophones, the Townships were drawn together by great Lake Kilborn, whose southernmost tip touched Vermont, U.S.A., where fancy restaurants served seafood specialties on

42

boardwalks with a view. The cottage was on the lake, situated near a Benedictine monastery that once produced Stilton and apple cider. Mom commented that their Stilton had never been aged properly, and the cider had always been unpalatable, and the architecture of the monastery itself was impossibly gaudy, but that as long as the monks had owned all that land, at least the bay had been quiet. Not like now.

"Play with me, Rob," Barnabus pleaded. "Like you used to. In the old days when you were nice."

"Oh, shut up, Barn," Robbie snapped. "It's not my fault if Mom's ruining the atmosphere."

When Mom just commented on things off-handedly like that, you always knew there was more to follow. Mom's casual comments were, in Robbie's view, tips of icebergs, fins of sharks. And sure enough, as Barnabus sulked and Mendoza panted with his great chops wobbling, she got her shit in a knot. If you were a regular viewer of *Hello World!*, you'd know why already, for only last week, standing on the family's own shoreline, she'd detailed the failure of the monks' operation: if their Stilton hadn't been quite so rubbery, she reported, the cider so unpalatably sweet, etc. etc., they might never have had to sell their land; now the EPX Chemicals Corporation spelled way worse trouble for the Townships. Spell that P-O-L-L-U-T-I-O-N.

Robbie stared at the horizon. Start with monastery, end up with provincial politics and a whole lot of gobbledegook like chlorophenols foliage erosion inhibited nitrogen fixation by symbiotic bacteria heavy metals in the soil fecula on the beach acid loadings all over Quebec and thanks to elevated levels of mercury in the sediments, worsening breakdown in the foodchain. You couldn't match the degree of Mom's rage, you could never catch up. So, if you were Robbie, you just shrugged your shoulders and brooded like an old factory under clouds of toxic thoughts, and waited for Dad to *really* get her dander up by telling her further studies were – that acid rain and, aum – may be *preventing* – that nature does, nature kills more species than hu – that the monks were just as bad as EPX, pumping their raw sewage into the lake, and so on.

"Yes," Barnabus said. "*Poo*lution."

And after that the inevitable brittle silence. Mom should know better, Robbie thought. This is the way it always ends – not with a bang but a simmer. Mom *thought* too much; she never allowed things to simply be what they seemed – they were always propelled by devious invisible mechanisms, rife with Machiavellian schemes, tragically booby-trapped. In her forensic view, it never just rained – someone was seeding the clouds. There was never just a thaw – it was nuclear experiments in the Soviet Union. Birds never just flew south – it was NASA screwing around with magnetic north. Robbie was never just out late – he was doing drugs, abusing nature like everyone else these days.

"It's S.P.E.C.T.R.E.," he said. "The evil empire. They're behind it all. We're all gonna die. Anarchy and destruction is their goal."

"Oh, *is* it, really?" Mom said, retrieving her sense of humour at last. "Well, that's OK, then. I thought it was something serious."

"Poo is their goal," Barnabus said.

When the Bookbinders bought their place, it had been a weed-rich wilderness, all rocks and spiky fern and maple trees. Hunters must once have lived or roomed in the cottage, for when Robbie had first been sent out to battle the tall grass, spent cartridges were snapped up clanging into the teeth of his mower. If he'd of known what was in Mom's mind as far as landscaping plans, eh, he would of applied for a transfer to some other family, in an inner-city ghetto maybe. Knee-deep in bracken, eyes streaming, sneezing like a demon, he'd knotted a *Cannabis Sativa* T-shirt around his face for protection against the clouds of aphids, airborne pollens, spores disgorged from the mouths of dock and pokeweed, silky dandelion pappus, and vintage Canadian thistledown, frisking in his wake like malevolent nose-nymphs.

When the Bookbinders moved in, there had been a patch of runner beans in a corner, and that was about it – a rusty two-handled saw, some old taps on the maples blocked with hard sap. But Mom had said, "I want a proper garden," so she marked off a bramble-choked area as big as a hockey rink with a temporary electric fence, borrowed some pigs from the neighbouring farmer, threw pignuts in there, and the undergrowth was gone in a month. But that was not all.

"Symmetry," she said. "We need to set the axis of the garden to avoid monotony, and our new French windows want a clear view onto the lake."

If a thing was six inches out, they had to dig it up and move it over. If a beloved plant wouldn't take well to moving, everything else had to move. And weed-killer was an environmental no-no; it was hand-weeding all the way.

"Did serfs of old suffer like this while scything the hay?" Robbie demanded. "How come evilution hasn't taken care of allergies? You should put in your show how pollution's making our noses *de*volve."

"We need a tranquil space," Mom had said absently. She stood by a heap of prunings with her hands on her hips, squinted around, and spat a mosquito from her lips. "The drama of a hidden hedgenook, Robbie. Think, the mystery."

One year she went crazy for golden privet, the next for muted colours and variegated leaves. One year, she despised little herb gardens, the next she was growing cinnamon, allspice, pepper, castor beans, sago, and guava. By this time there was a cobbled forecourt, little statues –

45

stone angels, stone pigs – and a summerhouse with climbing roses, clematis, and honeysuckle, and the garden had become the set for *Hello World!* You'd think the show could have afforded a gardener by then but *no*, the only thing the network was trimming were costs.

How he despises the country! While Dad lies prone indoors, watching the Olympics, Robbie lounges in a deck chair overlooking the lake – *The Sneezable Kingdom* – beside a mounting pile of soggy Kleenex. His eyes sting, he has streaming catarrh, his throat's inflamed, the roof of his mouth itches like mad, his teeth throb. He watches a bumblebee so plump with pollen it has to drag itself across the hot stones to the shadow of his legs for relief. The great white legs of Robbie, Cruel Lord of the Bees. Mendoza there too, sweating saliva from his tongue, *plip, plip*.

Out on the glassy water a Laser's sail luffs in the wind. Down the hill Mom's bent over a clay urn encouraging chives to grow, her bottom raised to show off the label on her jeans to all of nature, mosquito netting wrapped over a broad-brimmed straw hat and tied with string around her neck. Humming to herself in a samba rhythm, "I'm Sgt. Pepper's Lonely Heart's Club Band, yes I'm – "

Robbie honks again with the sound of a trumpet being cleared of spittle, and she looks up – like a cow interrupted at her grazing, he observes unkindly – the mosquito net casting a soft shadow across her cheeks and nose.

"There are solutions, you know," she calls up, and begins to list homeopathic cures for hay fever sufferers, like *Arsenicum album* and *Pulsatilla*, but Robbie knows all about that thank you very much; he's already been through her catalogue of wild poisonous plants to identify the psychedelics indigenous to the Townships: out in the fields and forests around Kilborn, foraging with Mendoza, he learned about *Lycium halmifolium* the Matrimony Vine,

Morning Glory, Jimsonweed, Angel's Trumpet, and a variety of magic mushrooms with juicy names like *A. phalloides* and *G. esculaenta*, although the only thing he dared try was something called Black Henbane. The dog was smarter; he turned his nose up at that, too. Not only is it foul-smelling, but also seriously toxic, as the quantity you need to ingest for recreational purposes is dangerously close to the quantity that soon had Robbie lying under the eaves of the boathouse with no saliva at all in his mouth, trying to retch onto the sandy ground. Finally he did upchuck, right into Kilborn Bay, neatly beside some stiff trout that had washed up on the beach. Then a motorboat zoomed by dragging three dazzling babes on water-skis, and their wake slopped the puke back onto his bare feet.

He passed part of draggy, swollen June planting marijuana seedlings among Mom's vibernums, observing to himself that here at least was one plant to which he was not allergic. The rest of June he spent leaving taps around the house running, wearing odd socks and, one evening, forgetting to gather up a sheaf of love letters he had written to Ivy, spilled beer on, and laid out to dry on the kitchen table; the letters were drenched in a bilious mixture of hops, rage, devotion, and lust, each blotted word like a miniature Rorschach test for all the family to see. And when he came down to breakfast the next day – lunch, really – they all looked at him funny.

Thus June crawled, and July, and Robbie mourned Ivy all the while. Lingering in bed, lurking in the bath, sprawled on the lawn, he thought about that metaphor they use in those lavender-coloured booklets you suddenly find lying around the house when your sister is entering her Difficult Phase: that vaginas are like flowers. He had seen a similar thing in a book of pastel paintings by Georgia O'Keeffe, a favourite of Mom's which had been lying around the house a lot longer. Ivy's *labia minora* were large and ruffled, as Robbie remembered them, and made him think of speeded-up films of lavish dewy flora blossoming in the space of seconds: her sex flowering beautifully into womanhood, Nature preparing her pistil for the penetration of his proud stamen.

He skulked around the house, soft and swollen as a stewed fig, sneaking looks at the thirty-five varieties of bras and nylon nighties in the weekend supplements. He thought of those devices Victorian parents once forced adolescent sons to wear – a spiked penis collar with a bell – alerting everyone to their unnatural stirrings. It made him crazy to be so muzzled up. He wanted to strip down all free and naked, to leap and frolic in open fields, his penis wagging as happy as a puppydog's tail; he saw himself hurtling through the air like a sperm whale, leaving a trail of milk and honey on the fields below.

Which is more or less all he did through July, and all through August, too. By the end of the month, however, he'd succeeded only in magnifying his savage libido, boiling himself in his own juices, like a bug floating in a glass of brandy left out in the sun. So he tried something new. What he did he did surreptitiously – he wouldn't give anyone the satisfaction of knowing he was doing anything *creative* with his time – from his bedroom cupboard he pulled out his easel and oils, blew the dust off his palette, loaded up with a two-four of Molson and a cassette machine, and marched out with Mendoza to Maple Point to paint.

He chose a promontory that commanded the long stretch of lake past Owl's Head to the south, the pine-bristled Hogsback ridge rising up a mile closer, and nearer still, only there a year now, the EPX chemical factory. He stripped to the waist and took off his shoes and socks. Brown pine needles had made a thick soft mat on the ground, and a number of maples, leached of colour, had tumbled down the slope before him to soak and peel on the lakeshore. This spot had always been thickly camou-flaged, just perfect for smoking reefer at a crouch; now the fallen trees permitted him to spread the easel's legs several feet back from the ridge, plus his painting gear, his two-four, a blanket, the cassette player, and still designate a spot for Mendoza to slobber on.

Weird thing was, from here the factory looked beautiful: nestled in the green valley of the Hogsback, its cluster of chalk-white chimneys, pipes, catwalks, gantries, and towers of scaffolding looked as pristine and alien as the Apollo moon unit in the Sea of Tranquillity. Whatever noise Mom said the factory made was drowned out by wind and wave. A delicate ribbon of white smoke rose from a central chimney, weaving languidly through the pines, tickling the back of the Hog. Robbie thought of the Group of Seven, years before S.P.E.C.T.R.E. seized power, trekking out across the Canadian Shield, writing their poetry amongst the crystal streams, struggling to express the massive, un-spoiled, unspeakable beauty in words. How would Robbie, in his turn, do something original for himself and *paint* this land today? How do you paint invisible poolution, chlorophenols foliage erosion inhibited nitrogen fixation by symbiotic bacteria heavy metals in the soil fecula on the beach acid loadings all over Quebec and thanks to ele-vated levels of mercury in the sediments, worsening break-down in the foodchain? He stood half-naked with a hot, carrot-fat reefer fuming between his lips, toking back smoke as thick as Plasticine, and like Keef Richards bent over his guitar, bore down on the bitter pleasure of depict-ing the apocalypse.

Thing was, landscapes had never been his bag. He'd always preferred to get horny over nudes of the late nineteenth century. Statistics show that 99 per cent of teenagers conceal *Bosom Buddies* magazines in a drawer, but Robbie felt as much of that stewed-fig feeling coming on when he pored over nudes by Rubens and Bouguereau, sneaking them out of the parents' library, stuffing the enormous volumes under his T-shirt as he tiptoed upstairs. Sure, these nudes were fatter than your average centrefold, but they never did anything frightening, like throw you a full frontal or pull apart the cheeks of their behinds for you to see all the bits you didn't need to see. Art experts droned on and on about bogus concepts like affronts to popular morality, and superb mastery of the use of perspective, and allegorized portraits, and manifestos of sacred and profane love, but they never came out and said what they obviously meant. It was obvious enough to *him* what the painters had in mind with all that elaborate drapery snaking between the ancient models' thighs, and all the surfaces of their bodies smooth and sugary, free of bum pimples and track marks. (Although Robbie never looked at girlie magazines, well, hardly ever, whenever he did he'd always check out their arms to see if they were junkies, which he figured would explain what drove them to exhibiting themselves so crudely.)

The world in raging *StonerVision!* now, projected on a curved screen, like this were a scene in some lakeshore drive-in movie. A Hendrix tape unravelling Nature's very DNA, as his knife-edged thrashing guitar-licks shred the air. *Third Stone from the Sun*. Robbie's nose is thick with the sweet pungency of oil and linseed. He's vigorously mixing earth into his paint, grass and bracken crushed between his damp palms, smutched with phthalo and burnt umber. Pure titanium white for the factory. When a bead of sweat soaks his eyebrows, he dabs at his forehead for some of that too. Mendoza's panting. Robbie lunges with his paint-brush for the plipping tongue. Unwise. The dog snaps at him, barks, and takes off into the woods.

50

Ivy had a body a lot like one of Rubens' nudes: oblong and waxy pale. With wide feet. And a belly that swelled out like a Bouguereau. And breasts as pale and delicate as bubbles of milk that looked like they'd be cool in your palms. Ivy, who hated her body, and deliberately burned her arms with cigarettes when she got too drunk.

Suddenly across the water there's what looks like a crowd gathering. Some kind of kerfuffle. Vehicles, a dozen people maybe, right in front of EPX. Robbie's squinting, it's hard for him to tell from here – in this heat the surface of the lake buzzes and blinds. He clicks the tape off with his toe, standing stock-still to get a better listen, but now his ears are trampled under wind. He shrugs and toes the tape on again.

In some of those old paintings, usually the ones featuring harems or hell or catastrophes befalling all of mankind, you could eyeball a dozen nudes at one time, the whole batch of them languishing in states of undress, some of them bound and helpless, some being ravished by Romans or devoured by monsters. You'd never find that in a magazine like *Bosom Buddies*. Robbie wonders if, while the paint was still wet and sexy on the canvas, the painters ever got it on with their models. He also wonders what it must have been like to see some of these paintings in a shop window in the days before magazines; if, in the privacy of their homes, people ever tugged off in front of them.

He bends down to pick up a dead bee, sticks it rudely into a blob of cadmium yellow. Thinks about something Mom has said – that honey bees are particularly sensitive to air pollution, and that when they suffer so does the pollination of plants, seed production, and the fundamental regrowth of vegetation. Right, and everything gives you cancer.

Oh, here's Mendoza back at last, and what's he got in his jaws. A rat? Robbie's moving in air as heavy as the linseed oil, *cumulo nimbus* weighing heavy on his shoulders. He bends down. *Here, boy. Show me.* Chrissake! A chipmunk. Without any hair.

He sits down to clear his brain. Becomes aware of his sunburnt cheeks, stretched over the bone. On the opposite shore the crowd has clustered tightly together. Round a particular tree, it looks like. A sound cuts across the water: a chainsaw. Then the crack and crunchy tumble of the tree, booing, chanting, and finally a police siren, swallowed up by the wind. Meanwhile, Mendoza's licking the ground ferociously. Robbie whacks him. Dumb dog. Mendoza throws up.

In time, coming down, he rubbed off the pine needles that had pressed into his skin, and took his first square look at his Great Work of Art.

Then, grimly, he took the canvas and smeared it, face down, across the ground.

4

LABOUR DAY WEEKEND, AND HE WAS SO HORNY THAT EVEN replays of Nadia Comaneci, performing perfect tens in her white-and-red striped gymnastics outfit, looked to him as concupiscent, as vulval, as Hans Bellmer's ball-jointed pornographic doll. (A coffee-table book – a post-Freudian museological survey of erotic art that took in voodoo fetishes, African clitoridectomies, and the misogyny of Picasso – was the best he could sneak up to his bedroom that night in the absence of a copy of *Bosom Buddies*.)

So the next day, the last Saturday of August, he split. He would have told someone, but at lunch time, when he came downstairs, no one was around to tell. So he just took off.

He never felt more a part of his nothing generation than when he was alone; alone in a concert crowd, alone at the family dinner table, and especially alone with a beer on a hill by the highway. He walked with his thumb out, standing under overpasses spray-painted with seagulls, symbols of the international hitchhikers' fraternity: a white one indicated a first-class spot, blue meant OK, red meant you could wait for a ride till the cows came home.

The cows were, in fact, preparing to come home when

he finally scored a ride, as far as Châteauguay, three-quarters of the way. Tramping across the Champlain bridge, his feet aching and his socks crusted with dirt where his sneakers had broken open, he rejoiced to see Montreal's skyline fencing the mountain, the brown air like bruised sky above it and, as he approached, the great cubes of glass breaking up the myriad reflections of new and old architectures like the images in the eye of a bluebottle fly.

The city was still blindingly bright, packed with people, and hot as an oven. It was as if humidity had an arse and had squatted down right over Peel and Ste-Catherine. Cars flashed in the glare. The tar on the roads was soft. Office buildings exhaled their dry, dead breath onto the side-walks through rumbling grills. He walked with his hair loose and his shirt flapping open, combing the people-streams hoplessly, foolishly, for Ivy, his heart lurching like that of a dumb lost beast whenever someone with her gait, her hair, her pale complexion bobbed up in the crowds.

His tongue scooping psychedelic camel-dungy mush-room-slime from his teeth, now he's on vulcanized feet, numbly bumping into people as they loom up stretched or squeezed, like versions of himself in a fun-house mirror. Catches blips of conversation in his sponge ears, bubbles of gummy telekinesis like the speech balloons that float around in cartoons. *HEY!* YOUNG MAN! YOU LOOK LIKE YOU'RE IN NEED OF *SALVATION!* Laughs at a sun- and meths-crazed rummy who's stopped traffic, kneeling down in the middle of the street to worship a bus. Robbie's bent on despising him until the pigs come along to infringe upon the stinky old guy's liberties, at which point he asserts a sudden kinship by standing next to the cruiser; Robbie the civil watchdog, eyes as big as saucers, monitoring police brutalities.

He buys a can of beer and stops in Dominion Square to play chess with old Joe Smolij, the rubby with the brambled

beard and the SMASH CRASH GAMBIT sweatshirt, as blackened with street-grime and oil as the undercarriage of a
diesel truck, who keeps up a running commentary above
the din of traffic throughout games he never loses. "Make
a moof make a moof," Joe says, stamping a pawn onto his
corrugated checkerboard and punching the stop-clock.
"Time is money. Money is freedom. Oh oh oh no no –
never expose your king, boy without a brain. Some patriot,
some colonial, ha! You looss, but don't feel bad. Nobody
think fast in this heat."

"Wow." Robbie stares at his paralyzed pieces, barely out
of the gate, his beer can still cool between his thighs. Fool's
mate. Joe's lungs are obviously custom-finished to process
carbon monoxide to his brain. "Fuck."

Joe looks hard at Robbie, scratches a sunburnt potato of
a nose. "I don't make no boozy moofs. I don't get angry so
quick."

Robbie's taken aback by the answer. He's not angry
with Joe. He *thought* he was enjoying himself. He forks out
his dollar, smiling to prove it, says goodbye and strides on,
loving the tickle of sweat at the back of his neck, running
his fingers up his slick spine, rolling past soft rubber
skyscrapers under a flexible sky. From University Avenue,
where the highway deposits drivers downtown, he trucks
westward to Atwater, where Canada's first McDonald's is
pumping out its patented sweet greasy-meaty smell. And
here, too, is the Forum, home of the Habs. Home of the
Habs, yes, but more significantly, where the Bones played
in the 120 degree heat for an hour and twenty-three
magnificent minutes back in the summer of '72: for blocks
in all directions, the sashed and macraméd windows of
apartments had been propped open with loudspeakers
heralding the group's arrival, the marquee featuring their
name the way a church posts a Sunday sermon. Within,
the stage was a dragon writhing in a bath of blood, Spit
Swagger's testicles dangling like a sack of tennis balls

down one leg of his white, sequinned jumpsuit. The show was two hours late; rumour had it Keef had fainted backstage. *From drugs, I imagine*, Mom said. *Yeah*, Robbie said, saluting with clenched fist, *from drugs*. And when he got home, he discovered his sweat had dyed his thighs and penis a jeany blue. All this, by the way, was when Robbie was the Bones' biggest fan, bar only Ivy. Now, of course, he hates Keef's guts and for some very good reasons, reasons he brooded over most of the winter and is sick to death of now and does not want to discuss, thank you very much. He lopes on up Atwater past the great rock temple like a yellow-eyed wolf, into the heart of Westmount, to the park.

But the park is quiet. The Kiosk's still locked up for the summer. Bummer. He shoots himself in the temple, *blam*, then takes Plan B, which is buy a screwdriver from Pascal's, go to the house, crawl unseen beneath the bushes, force the little dungeon window open, and once inside have the place to himself. His bohemian love-pad. He'll lead his friends in by the back door, past the sign Dad has posted that reads,

ALL YE WHO ENTER HERE ABANDON DOPE

straight down the back stairs to party till they puke.

The window splinters from its casing with a loud crack. He kneels in the sweet humid earth and waits, his heart pounding loud in his ears. A strand of spider web clings to his lips. Rhododendron leaves reach under his shirt and clamp onto his damp back. He pulls the window back and slides head-first into the basement, bringing in with him a cascade of earth that fills his nose and mouth and scatters across the carpet.

The dungeon's cool darkness smells of mildew, stale beer, and African-musk incense. The moisture has warped his record jackets; mould is growing on the patches of carpet where friends puked the last time they'd partied there.

Upstairs, the fridge reverberates on. Then switches off automatically, leaving the house in stillness again. Robbie with a heavy head stands in the hallway at the foot of the stairs, cleaning earth out from his nostrils with his thumbs.

"Hello-o," he calls up. "Is anybody ho-ome?"

The old house swallows up the words. Settles on its foundations. Robbie becomes aware of its electrical nervous system, of its groaning arterial piping, like the sound Dad makes heaving himself onto the couch after a hefty meal. *Felled by food*, he hears Miriam say.

In the living room, the television screen has accumulated dust. The rubber plants too. Three-month-old newspapers lie on the floor announcing political events that were of unbelievably small interest to him even then. He plinks on the piano, high notes only. Outdoors the cicadas send out their really weird buzz, like loudly amplified electric cables.

He stands before one of the windows to the west, the stain in the glass fiercely illuminated by the setting sun – after Rossetti, a noblewoman in a flounced alizarin dress and the caption,

Gather Ye Rosebuds

He walks into the kitchen, and suddenly the hallway telephone rings. He reaches instinctively for the receiver. Then thinks better of it.

On the kitchen counter by the fridge lie the leftovers of the family's last hectic meal, a Pyrex dish filled with oily water, a skin of tiny bubbles clinging to its sides, and the outline of a baked eggplant in the bottom like a fossil from the Palaeozoic era. Above the stove a blackboard reads, in Mom's handwriting,

insoluble aluminum phosphate
– indigestible to trees –

Robbie picks up a piece of chalk and writes,

S.P.E.C.T.R.E. was here

On another wall, the kindergarten classics: Robbie's own prize-winning watercolour abstracts, wonky houses and blobby animals. Chunkily signed. The runny, muddy paint and warped paper with curling corners, stuck there with crinkly scotch tape. Plus Miriam's world-famous portrait of a man fresh out of the shower, a circus attraction to be sure, with a cock to do a horse proud dangling there in red crayon. And marked at the bottom, DADDY BEFOR AND AFTR. And all around him diagrams indicating articles of clothing to be worn. SHERT. RED SOX. PANTIES.

Only girls wear panties, Robbie hears Barnabus say.

Yeah, well, I wish we could take the stupid thing down now, Miriam snaps in his ear. *I did it years ago and I'm thirteen now if you don't mind. I find it really disgusting.*

The sun has set now, and plunged the house into throbbing darkness. He opens the fridge cautiously. A sliver of cold light cuts across the kitchen tiles. In the fridge, some concentrated tomato paste. He squeezes the tube and licks the end. Two Jerusalem artichokes. A jar of wheat germ. Some fine imported horseradish. Lard in wax paper. Blackstrap molasses. Yoghurt culture. He closes the door and mutters, "Fuck." Then louder, "Food food everywhere and not a bite to eat."

Cops patrol Westmount regularly during cottage season, or so Dad has warned, so Robbie dares not switch on a light. He didn't think of this when first entertaining his Bacchanalian fantasies for the weekend. Bummer. Sitting on the floor in the dark, he makes a furtive phone call, counting the holes in the dial with his fingers. His voice sounds flat in his ears.

"Hi, can I speak to Ivy."

"No. I'm sorry. She is gone away." Ivy's Grendel mother.

"Who is calling, if you please?"

He hangs up. Immediately the phone rings again.

"CHRISSAKE," he shouts. "No one TRUSTS me around here."

He makes two more furtive calls, to Brat, to Louie, allowing four rings only, but no one answers. He sits down on the chair and listens to the last of the evening traffic. The silence closing in like pillows on his ears. He makes for the dungeon, holding on to walls. Lurks down there like Gollum in the damp, nostrils curling up at the mildew. Funny, how all winter long he lurked in this upset-stomach, steeped in bitter contentment, taking acid pleasures from his solitude, and now look: sunstruck and defeated, he lays down on a gutted beanbag chair and falls fitfully asleep, hugging the crunchy pillow and pretending Ivy is lying there beside him, breathing gently with her hand curled against her throat.

Next morning he turned the living-room stereo up to full, yelling ALL PARENTS MUST DIE! He opened a tin of maple syrup and poured a bowl of stale Sugar Krunchie crumbs. Into that he mixed water and a generous drop of cherry leb hash oil. He read the blurbs on the box. There were FREE! plastic endangered species, offered both in French and English. How educational, he thought. Our bilingual culture. . . .

He loses track of time. He must have been there munching the same soggy mouthful for at least twenty minutes now, for suddenly the record is going *scrrtcch scrrtcch*. He gets up to change it, then returns to his Krunchies 'n' Hash. Stares at the watercolour gallery. SHERT. PANTIES. RED SOX. Dirty sox, he thinks, smelling his own fiendish feet with his magnified sense of smell. He drags himself up the stairs. Sits on the landing, takes off his socks and leaves them on the hallway carpet. Kneels in the bathtub, staring at the water rushing from the faucet, the level rising fast. He imagines himself a mercenary knight in rusting spiky armour, trying to forge a brook on his way to Agincourt, the water past his knees. If his horse falls, he wonders, will he be able to unhitch his heavy skin in time, or will he drown with his helmet on?

Scrrtcch scrrtcch. Chrissake. He hates the house so quiet. Only the sound of this roaring brook, and the record like crickets chirruping. He stamps down the stairs, leaving spludgy footsteps in the carpet behind him. In the den, intending merely to turn the record over, he's distracted by his own reflection in the TV screen – as if in a foe's dull breastplate. He unbuckles his Harley-Davidson belt and shakes it at the box, one of the first on the market with remote-control, which bursts into life. An evangelist is doing his hilarious sin and repentance number. Robbie jangles his belt again. And lo, if it isn't *Hello World!*

He's just in time for the regular *Environment in Vogue* bit. This week there's a sequence, edited to jaunty music, of women in the street balancing themselves with briefcases or shopping bags as they lift their heels to inspect fresh runs in their stockings; women in Washington and New Orleans are complaining about damage to their nylons, apparently in greatest numbers after wet and windy days, and this is now being linked to the high saturation of sulphuric acid in those cities' atmospheres! Amazing, but true! After the commercial, Mom comes on, and there's some kind of kerfuffle. The camera pulls out to show she is hugging a tree. In fact, she's *chained* to the tree. The camera's bobbing violently, jostled by a crowd. It's still so close up it's hard to tell how many people are there, but glimpses of white scaffolding in the background tell Robbie exactly where she is before she announces it. He sinks to the soggy carpet to watch.

"Planet Earth is 4,600 million years old!" Mom has to shout over the roar of a chainsaw. "To get a clearer picture, imagine Earth is a forty-six-year-old person! We know nothing about her childhood, the details of her youth are sketchy, but we can deduce that she began to blossom at forty-two!" The camera lurches wildly. For a moment, there's sky and a great spread of branches and leaves. The chainsaw bites into wood. It sounds like screaming now – the camera tilts down, and Mom's talking a mile a minute. Robbie stares, picking cereal from his teeth. "Dinosaurs appeared a year ago when Earth was forty-five. Mammals grazed on her front lawn eight months ago. Man-like apes dropped around for cocktails the middle of last week! Last weekend everyone stayed indoors for the Ice Age!" Mom's voice is shrill and distorted now; people are booing, and the tree begins to crack. As it falls she's pulled up and over with it, her hair in her mouth, sawdust covering her clothes, her skin, and the black foam rubber of her microphone. Three pigs are pulling her feet first from under the chain. As they haul her off to a waiting cruiser she just about shrieks, "Modern man's been in the neighbourhood for four hours! An hour ago he discovered agriculture! The industrial revolution began one minute ago! In those sixty seconds of biological time we have made a toxic garbage dump of – " The door of the cop car slams shut. The microphone cable goes taut as the cruiser moves off, then limp, but she rolls down the window and hollers, "Have yourselves a fine Labour Day weekend! See you next week same time same channel! I'm Abigail Bookbinder for *Hello World!*"

Robbie shakes his belt again. The screen crackles with static and falls silent. Poor reporting, he thinks, she never mentioned *noise* pollution, like she always does to me. So what is that, anyway, the third time she's been arrested? Second time in front of EPX, at least. She oughta get a real job.

He slips his belt through the loops on his jeans, shaking his head. Decides to return to the Townships, help bail

Mom out maybe. On the way, he might even look up Rosie at the club where she works, bring her to the cottage for the weekend. Farm out concept! He exits the house barefoot. Leaving the front door wide open behind him and the bathtub taps on full.

5

WEIRD HOW, JUST BECAUSE OF ONE LITTLE OVERSIGHT, your entire life can be ruined. Robbie pondered this, later that same day, as he sat beside Rosie on the bus to the Townships. Short of joining the army, what was he going to do now? He sat paralyzed with guilt, ignoring Rosie's exclamations.

"*Look!* A *Madame Patate* stand. How LOVELY! Look, a brown *brook*!"

His forehead was blistered with cool sweat; he was trying to convince himself that it wasn't *his* fault the house in town had been suffering from dry rot. Why else would the piano have fallen through the floor so easily? One little inch of water wasn't so heavy, surely. . . .

Halfway to Rosie's club, he'd realized he needed his shoes; barefoot downtown is one thing – different strokes for different folks, OK – but in the country it's impractical; if he was going to give Rosie a tour of the weed-, leech-, and insect-infested countryside, he needed his sneakers. So he'd returned to the house.

Major bummer.

The green deep-pile carpet in the living room looked like the Sargasso, with a seaweed-slick continental shelf at the door of the study plunging ten thousand leagues to the depths of the basement den. The house was a dripping lagoon, *plip, plip,* smelling nastily damp. He had slapped up the wet stairs to turn off the bathtub taps, and sat down on the rim and wept. Bummer of the century! Now he pictured his records floating in the flooded dungeon like vinyl lily-pads, the pellets from the beanbag chairs clustering like white algae; his sketches, too, including some nude studies of Ivy, saturated, blotting, dissolving. And now with the thrum of the Voyageur bus in his ears he was wondering, should he blame it on burglars? Or not tell at all.

When he and Rosie appeared on the terrace, Grandma Bethel put her hand to her mouth, the lenses of her horn-rimmed glasses magnifying the astonishment in her eyes. Close up for the kiss, her cheek was as soft as the pad in a lady's compact.

"I can't believe he's so *tall*. And look!" Robbie obliged her, bowing his head so she could reach and rummage. "You can't tell these days if they're boys or girls. Oy, what a kid!"

"Hey," Robbie said, seeing Barnabus in a white shirt, and Miriam in a dress. "Why so spiffy? What's the occasion?"

"Seder!" Barnabus said. "We almost didn't have it, 'cause Dad said he was going to leave Mom in prison for the weekend to teach her a lesson."

"He was joking, stupid," Miriam said.

"Seder in September," Grandma Bethel said. "God forgive me."

"It's all my fault," Mom said. "I was just too busy in the spring. That's when I was arrested for the first time, remember – well, the first time this year. It was a bitch. The network president told me our ratings were slipping. So I said to him, how do you make dioxin in gulls' eggs *entertaining*? Anyway, Mother, you know we do this for the kids. It's better late than never."

"Oh, don't worry about me," Grandma Bethel said, "I understand perfectly. Do what you think is best for the children. You said it, I'm behind the times. Who am I to want everyone to be as old-fashioned as me?"

Robbie dressed up. Awkward in his suit and tie, trying to pump the nervous guilty bubbles of air from his heart, he opened the fridge for a beer. He cracked one open and sat back to watch everybody working in the kitchen. In the dining room Dad pored over a brand new Haggadah, stiff scotch in hand, moving his lips as he read.

"This is not the draft I'm – " he said. " '*Non-Sexist, Yet Traditional*,' hmm. Where do the eggs, aum, shouldn't we crack them open first to see if they're boys or girls?"

"Don't be gross," Miriam said. "You dip them in the horseradish."

"No, darling," Mom said. "The eggs are dipped in the salt water when we tell the story of the Exodus."

"Oh my," Grandma Bethel said, one eye uneasily on Rosie, who looked like a death-watch beetle. "I know you don't need my help, but we're not meant to eat any eggs at all. There should be just one, roasted, in the middle of the table. You look at it, as a symbol only."

Robbie, in his simmering gloom, thought, Don't lose your shorts over it. The only good thing about tradition is that it's in the past; the way old people talk about heritage you'd think they did a good job on the world before handing it down. We should just start again, a little nukular war wouldn't hurt nobody in the long run. But just to be nice, to participate in family life a little – as Mom has demanded not infrequently – he asked, "A symbol of what?"

"That's a very intelligent question!" Mom said.

"Yes! It's a symbol of rebirth," Grandma Bethel said, delighted, "and of the burnt offering that was made every day of the feast during the existence of the Temple in Jerusalem."

"Far out," Robbie said flatly. "Thanks a bundle."

"Can I wear a hat this year, Daddy?" Miriam called out.

"Why not," Grandma Bethel sighed. "It's a non-sexist Seder. I'm sure God, praised be She, won't mind a bit."

Robbie poured a fresh beer into his mug. Still buoyed up by the acknowledged excellence of his question, he was planning a second. How the family would miss him when he was gone, and wish him back like the prodigal son.

"Grandma," he said with the applied earnestness of a student of the Talmud, thumb poised thoughtfully on the cleft of his chin, twirling a strand of hair between his fingers. "I've always wondered, and since I don't speak Hebrew, what exactly 'coleslaw' means."

"I'm sorry," Grandma Bethel said, looking at him with her huge eyes. "I don't understand your joke."

Everyone turned to look at Robbie. The ice clinked in Dad's drink. "What makes you think it's – ?"

"Yiddish, then," Robbie said, cross now. The old familiar goatishness growing on him now as palpably as horns and a beard.

"No . . . "

"Well, it's always in kosher delis, right? All I thought was maybe it had a religious meaning or . . . . "

Grandma Bethel's eyebrows arched like Hallowe'en cats above the rims of her glasses. "Oy *yoy*," she said. "No, no, my darling."

Suddenly, Miriam slapped her palms on the table top, and howled with laughter. She stood up and and danced round the room with glee, wrestling Mendoza to the floor, woofing in his ear, "Hey, Mendoozle, what do *you* think coleslaw means in Yiddish? Robbie wants to know. And how about *pastrami!* That's an ancient Hebrew word, if I'm not mistaken. And *carnatzel* and *rye bread* and *dill pickle* hahahahahahahaha!" Falling on her back now, hugging Mendoza's head as the beast scrabbled with his claws on the tiled floor. "And *apple cobbler* hahahahaha!"

Mom said, "OK, OK, Miriam. Don't be cruel."

"But he likes it when I wrestle."

"No, darling, don't be cruel to Robbie."

Robbie bit his lip to hold back the tears of humiliation.

"This clam chowder is the *best*," Rosie said brightly. "My Daddy owns a diner where they make clam chowder, too. From FROZEN! Although I have to say it makes me queasy queasy queasy. I believe in *mermaids*, that's why. I have a very old soul. Did Bob tell you I also have two webbed toes on each foot? If I slit them and then had a baby, I wonder, would she, too? I'm *so* happy I'm chowing here tonight, I often feel all forlorn. Pass the salt PLEASE and THANK YOU."

Everyone stopped to stare at her. Robbie, taking some small consolation that there was one person at the table more foolish than he, leaped up to gather the soup bowls, laid the cutlery for the next course, plonked fresh ice cubes into the water jug, topped up Dad's glass, and helped Mom go baste the lamb.

"You're so charming together," Mom whispered to him. "It's lovely the way you just let her be herself. My father was virtually illiterate too, but my mother always made him feel ashamed."

And Miriam said, "She's one scrambled egg, coming up."

"*Barukh ata aum Adonai Elohaynu* aum – " Dad managed. "*Melekh ha'olam borei p'ri ha'adamah*." Then everyone read aloud in unison,

"Blessed are You, Eternal One, Provider for the Universe, Who Brings forth fruits from the Earth."

"All right. You may drink the first cup of wine on the – aum – agenda."

"Hey, being Jewish is *great!*" Rosie said.

67

"By the way, Robbie," Mom said. "I can't tell you how handsome you look in a tie. Will you pass the celery around now?"

"K," Robbie replied, "but only if you tell me what celery means in Hebrew," and everybody laughed with relief.

"Actually, darling," Grandma Bethel said, "that's another good question. The *karpas* is a symbol of springtime and the miracle of nature's renewal. The salt water you dip it in represents the salty tears shed by the Israelites when they were in bondage."

"Yeah well, I can relate to that at least," Robbie said, and everybody laughed again.

"*Barukh ata Adonai, Elohaynu Melekh ha'olam shehek-heyanu . . .* "

Robbie going under now, thinking, *Bondage.* Picturing the oppressed Israelites building the pyramids for Pharoah, making bricks in the baking sun, sweating in those grotesque leather masks with zips across the mouth. And thinking, Whoa, where do some thoughts come from? Though he knows: he's seen ads in *Bosom Buddies* magazine.

"I have a question now," Barnabus said. "Why aren't girls circlecized?"

"Oh, brother," Miriam said, and Grandma Bethel put her hand to her cheek.

"I have a better strategy for you, Barnabus – " Dad said. "Page eighteen, The youngest person at the table, OK?"

"But why aren't girls circlecized?"

"It's very simple," Mom said. "Girls don't have penises."

"Oh, I see. Thanks," Barnabus said. And frowned. "What's that got to do with it?"

"Excuse me," Rosie said, "I believe in the Middle East they *do* circumcize teenage girls. Their clitorises! Picture the mutilation! Men'll do *anything* to put women down. . . . "

"What's a clitoris?" Barnabus said, and now Grandma Bethel put her face in both hands.

Robbie still seeing that image hovering above the table. He tried to erase it by quickly closing his eyes and shaking his head. The image wavered. That's all it is, he tells himself, a wavering image, a desert mirage. I'm not responsible. Someone else conjured it up. It's the devil out there in the dunes, uncirclecized, naked, and cruelly sunburnt; he's grinding hot sand between his palms and callused shaft and he's in a rage because it's getting under his fireskin. When he spills his sulphuric semen in the desert's belly, lo: Satan's babies are scorpions. *Robbie Robbie stop*. But the harder he tries to shake the picture, the harder it clings to his eyeballs.

When he came to, Miriam was giving him a scornful look.

'I think someone should take this book back," Rosie said. "The pages are backwards."

"Page thirteen," Dad said, and Robbie could see he was concealing a grin behind his Haggadah. "Robbie, please."

"K," he replied sullenly. "*The wicked child inquires in a mocking spirit: What mean YE by this service?* Hey, wait a sec. How come I get this one every year? I notice it's not wicked 'son' any more, so why not give it to Miriam?" No one looked up from their books. "K, OK. *Saying YE and not WE, he/she excludes himself from the household of Israel. Therefore thou shouldst turn on him/her and say: 'It is because of that which God did for ME when I came forth out of Egypt.'*"

"Now, children," Dad said. "According to the Haggadah, *maror* means bitter herbs. We eat it as, as – as a year-end review, to recall how the Egyptians edged our ancestors out of a lot of valuable property."

"I love horse relish," Barnabus said. "I want lots."

"*Radish*, dumbhead," Miriam said. "And you're not supposed to like it. You're supposed to think sad thoughts about your forefathers."

"Not to mention your fore*skins* I should think," Rosie said.

"Who are they?" Barnabus said.

Who indeed, Robbie thought. Let's face it, Jews are losers. He was thinking of the Hasidim up around St. Urbain Street, boys of his own age all in black with fur hats, even in summer, and sidecurls like some dreary parody of party streamers. They weren't taking part in the world. Not like Robbie was. When they grew up they'd make their wives shave their heads, and wouldn't touch them when they were on their periods. What would they think of Ivy, the time she showed Robbie her biggest secret, well, one of them, anyway: how she daubed menstrual blood on her lips with her finger for lipstick.

"OK, Barnabus," Dad said. "Before we eat, go and open the screen door. That's to invite Elijah the Prophet in for a drink of wine. See, here we place his executive cup. Later you'll get up again to close it, and when you come back you can check the level to see if he – aum – skimmed his percentage."

"If Elijah was really real and was a ghost," Barnabus said, "he could pass *through* the mosquito screen."

"Oy," Grandma Bethel said, pinching his cheek hard, "you kids are so *smart*."

Dinner was served, and the talk turned to politics, which wasn't Robbie's thing, exactly. He'd tried to keep up by flipping through magazines, opening them just wide enough to see the colour and type riffle by, but never wide enough to read them. And listening to the parents talk was the same; as if the conversation were being riffled too. "PLO," Dad was saying, "recognize aum right Israel exist conflict ideological political Jerusalem last year aum."

"Solving problems," Mom interrupted, "Middle East political settlement Gaza ideological conciliation diaspora Arabs Jews war Holy Land."

"I think Ghadaffi's lost some weight," Rosie said. "He's looking great these days, for a mad tyrant."

"Abby," Dad said, "when the Knesset – "

"Darling, don't talk to me of the *Knesset!*"

"No, darling, let me finish. When the Gush Emunim – "

"Wait!" Rosie said. "Let's ask Bob what *he* thinks!"

Robbie, who had, until this conversation, been under the impression that the Gaza Strip was a place where girls in the Middle East like Rosie worked, held his knife and fork upright, grease sliding down onto his thumb.

"Ha!" Mom snorted, "I'll give you *Bob's* political analysis of the last five years: February '72, SALT signed – the Alpha Jerks play the Montreal Forum. November '74, Nixon re-elected – the Big Racket wows 'em at the Concert Bowl – "

"Actually . . . " Robbie said as mildly as possible (the flooded house still weighing heaviest on his mind), "it was the Paisley Noses at the Concert Bowl."

"June '75, the Watergate hearings underway – Pink Phlegm zonks 'em at Place des Nations . . . "

"Aum, kids, did you – I read that Ringo was the real brains behind the Beatles."

Robbie's ears burned red. Did she have to needle him so hard? Plus it wasn't fair using her professional TV technique on him like that. He felt small, the same way the victims on *Hello World!* appeared: looked down upon by the camera and miniaturized, while the shots of her lent her imperial authority. He put a gun to his head and fired.

"I think Bob has a wait-and-see policy," Rosie said. "I admire that."

"Yeah," Robbie said. "Zackly."

"My eye," Mom said. "But all right. If you want. Robbie tell me, what is this *Knesset* we were referring to?"

Thinking hard about this one. And regretting having drunk so greedily. His forehead was wet. He burrowed into the meat, carving aside the fat. And ventured, "It's a, um, potato dumpling, right?"

"That," Dad said softly, "is a *knish* you're, aum – "

71

Robbie's lips gnarled up all sad and ugly, and everybody looked at their plates and made like nothing remotely funny or ridiculous had been said at all.

"Anyway children," Mom continued, coolly changing the channel, and Robbie went under again. "What you must understand is that Passover is not just about olden times. When it talks about the trials of our forefathers we should also take it to mean the ones in the twentieth century. I'm talking, of course, about the Holocaust."

Robbie Bookbinder, ten years old, standing on the back of an old armchair in the living room in town (an old armchair that he more recently found just about floating down the front path), *his head close to the ceiling. Reaching up to tip down a fat book with a yellow star on its binding, and wondering if his fingers will leave prints in the dust. The late afternoon light is closing in around him, buzzing like flies. Against angry grey skies, the naked women with broad black smudges of pubic hair standing in the mud. And this is the first time he saw that women have pubic hair. The ditches of blood-blackened bodies, the smoking chimneys, the grinning soldiers posing for pictures. Robbie turning the pages faster and faster, in bunches now. And Mom suddenly striding into the living room. "Robbie, you startled me standing way up there." Guilty Robbie slamming the book shut. "Oh, come on, what is it, we have nothing to hide on these shelves. Show me." Robbie confused now, and saying, "But Daddy said I shouldn't." Mom says, "That's only because it will make you so very sad."*

Miriam was quizzing round the table. "And you, Barnabus?"

"I believe in the gospel according to Jesus Christ," he said, knees on his chair and reaching for more horse relish.

"I believe in millions of gods all at once," Rosie said.

"Aum, we're still . . . commissioning studies."

"Mommy?"

Mom pulled another face Robbie had seen on TV, and

it usually meant trouble too, but all she said was, "I don't think it's a good time to talk about it."

"What better time than Seder?" Miriam demanded.

Mom sipped her wine and dabbed her lips with her napkin. She leaned forward with both elbows on the table. "Well," she began, "with all due respect to your grand-mother – "

"Not me, surely," Grandma Bethel said.

"With all due respect, I can't put faith in a god who's constantly allowing innocent people to be murdered. In the camps babies were boiled in the fat of their parents while their brothers and sisters looked on. A god like that must be indifferent or wicked. I'll have nothing to do with him."

Robbie poked at the squidgy lamb with his fork. Impressive, he was thinking, she should hand out pamphlets, but Mom turned on him. "Don't you like it, darling? Or is your mind on the Paisley Noses?"

"No, no," he said. "It's yum." He stabbed a piece of, of – a celebrated violinist, a Viennese intellectual, a much-loved aunt – right into his mouth, chewing with his lip curled up.

"I'm sorry, Bethel," Mom said.

"No, don't you worry about me," Grandma Bethel said.

"What about you, Grandma?" Miriam said. "What do you think about God?"

"I don't know. That was a hard act to follow."

"I think Grandma doesn't want to, aum," Dad said quietly.

"Why not? Everybody else – "

"Grandma lost some people in the war who were very close to her," he explained with his hand on Miriam's arm.

"No, no," Grandma Bethel said. "Grandma doesn't mind, dear. You want to know do I believe in God? Of course."

"But Mommy just said . . . "

"Mommy can say what she feels."

"But what about your friends? I mean, the ones who died."

"Not just my friends, my darling. My mother. And father. And my brother, too."

"But aren't you mad at God?"

"I have some questions I'm planning to ask Him. That's for sure."

"I think you're being sexist, saying *Him*," Rosie said.

Finally Robbie burst out, "There is no God, don't kid yourselves. And if there was one that'd killed *my* Mom and Dad, I'd shoot first and ask questions later."

"Oh, Robbie," Mom said. "That's very sweet, but God didn't kill Grandma's mother and father."

"Seriously, I'd tell him to go fuck himself."

"Robbie, please – "

"There you – you're getting – take it down a notch, please."

He was close to tears again. Same for everyone else this time, but he was too involved in his grand élan to notice. He was thrilled. An issue he finally cares about and, unbelievably, they want to shut him up.

"I can't tell Him such a thing, dear," Grandma Bethel said, her eyes big and moist as fishbowls.

"Why not, for Chrissake?"

"It's certainly not for Christ's sake!"

"But why not?"

"Because, that's all."

"Because what?"

"Because . . . He's . . . " Grandma Bethel said, her voice trembling. "Because He's . . . all I've got . . . " Now she was weeping, fumbling in her enormous lap for a corner of her napkin, "left."

"Mother, Mother," Mom implored her, "that's not true. You have us. You know that."

74

"Bethel – " Dad said, helplessly.

Robbie was as embarrassed as everybody else, but he was secretly pleased he had provoked such a reaction. It would start her thinking about life. Stop wasting time, get real. Of course there's no God, not one who'll answer your prayers, that's plain as the nose on your face. He made a wiggly mouth, mimicking her this time, and exchanging a smirk with Rosie. But Rosie was staring tragically at her plate. Only Dad saw him.

"Robbie," he said, "do you want to get out of here?"

"Uh, no thank you. I was only . . . "

"No, I mean, just get OUT! This meeting is adjourned. Go away, buzz off. We don't want you here any more."

"But – I – what about the songs after the meal? We have to find the hidden *matzoh*, and – "

"We'll manage without you, thanks. Just go away, scram. It's clear this is meaningless to you. Just, just, get OUT."

"K, fuck, K. Bye, then." He pushed his chair back and stood up, knees shaking. The family and Rosie turned their heads all together to follow his flight. He tore at his tie and ripped off the buttons of his nice white shirt to reveal KEEF SUCKS, grabbed the executive cup and chug-a-lugged the Prophet's wine. Then he lit out into the night, giving the porch door an almighty slam, to sulk down on the water with the dock spiders.

The next morning, from his bed, he could hear the phone ringing off the hook. As if things weren't bad enough. All activity was clearly futile now. Adolescence had been one great rip-off in the first place – not even a full decade, just seven measly teen years – but civilization as Robbie knew it was definitely over. What could he do but kill himself? Throw himself down a chimney at EPX. Stick his finger in an electric socket to make a human amplifier. Out on the lake motorboats farted, and water-skiers shrieked. The beech trees scrabbled at his window to come out and play. He lay there imagining the sound of Hell's Yells – all scraping feedback, the sound of exhaust. This dying planet gets the electric guitar for its funeral, a steely annoyance, an army of men with black ice for armour, shouting violent disharmonies. A vengeful sound, a music to rape and pillage by. A sound for burning down schools.

That's when Dad knocked on the door and said through it, "Robbie, are you there? I think it's time for a, aum – "

Robbie hoped for a moment that he had come to announce a raise in his allowance, his *salary*. Though he didn't really expect it. As Dad waited at the door like that, politely, like a nervous servant, Robbie pictured him as the scrawny, pimple-ridden teenager he had once been, fleeing Russia – or was it Poland his parents came from? Or Germany? Or was it his *grand*parents who did the fleeing? Robbie had never got the story down, exactly. On a black freighter anyway, or so he imagined, mastur – aum – bating furtively when he could, somewhere in the belly of the rusting hold, and then growing up to ascribe the same furtiveness to all future generations of teenagers. When it was not Robbie's thing at all.

Then Dad barged in, just like that. He sat down at the foot of Robbie's bed, right on the hillock where Robbie had shuffled off his pyjama bottoms under the blanket, and said, "Listen – aum – " He gazed out of the window, unable, as per usual, to look Robbie in the eye. Robbie figured he regretted his harsh words from the night before. "The police phoned from town. I'm sorry to – they found a pair of – "

Stinky sox, Robbie thought, grimly, remembering them now, left there on the top of the stairs like a couple of turds.

" – and, aum, 'S.P.E.C.T.R.E. was here' on the blackboard in your handwriting, I'm afraid."

"Yeah, well I don't see why you hafta blame *me*, exactly."

"Look, I think, we think, Mom and I, that you've – how can I – ? Basically, you've overstayed your welcome. All right? We'd like to give you a month to find a job, if you don't mind. And a place of your own. We're quite angry with you, I'm sorry to say."

Robbie shrugged. "So anyway," he said, weakly trying to change the subject, "how's poor Grandma?"

"It's not that we don't – Mommy and I just think that you should – aum, I'm not good at this – it's a question of being proactive, not reactive. One day you'll thank – you'll see this as a, the incentive you needed to make your, your mission statement. Right now you have to prioritize. Analyze. School's clearly not your, aum, bag – "

"Hey. It's not that it's not my bag, as you so sarcastically put it – "

"No, I never – I only meant, since you didn't mention university all summer, we assumed you weren't interested."

"I *am* interested. It's just that there's no way I'll even be *accepted*, so what's the point of trying. Look – after the school . . . well, you know, burned down, OK, the principal told us he understood we were too traumatized to do our final exams. Fuck – pardon me – *I* wasn't traumatized. I was *counting* on a final exam. So suddenly they're judging us on our term performance. What a drag. Plus we got an aptitude test – you wouldn't remember – in French, of course. Double drag. How can they judge what's good for me if I'm not allowed to talk about myself in my own freakin' language? According to the test my IQ's around 78. A retard. Now at this point in time I know I'm not exactly a Nobel prize-winning physicist, but come on. Seventy-eight! The Bureau of Educational Research, Université de Chibougamau. What do they know about young people like me in Chibougamau?"

"They have young people in Chibougamau, I'm sure of

that," Dad said. "But I don't – aum – sorry, what *were* your results?"

"That I'm ideally suited to be an undertaker, fuck. And second, a tie between librarian and army officer. Rock star isn't even on the list. I guess they don't have those in Chibougamau."

"Well, ahh," said Dad.

"I know what you're thinking. That I'm a complete fuckup."

"No, that's – "

"Your son, the burger flipper."

"Well. As a matter of fact, Baron Bulgingburger is nothing to be ash – "

Robbie glared hard at his toes. "The Baron is *not* where it's at," he mumbled. "I'll tell you that much for free."

"Excuse me?" Dad said. "Where *what* is – aum – *at?*"

Robbie rolled his eyes and scrolled his lower lip downwards to reveal his teeth, tightly packed like sardines in a can.

"Look, aum, since you and I . . . why don't you take a tip from someone you admire instead, like, well, Rosie. She has a good sense of her limitations. Give yourself a realistic mandate, too. Ask yourself, What are my basic skills? What's my performance potential? Channel your rage. One day you'll thank us. Life is what you make it, you know. Oh, and Grandma says goodbye. She took the early bus to town." He squeezed Robbie's collarbone. Weird, that was the first time they'd touched since the spanking days, except those occasions when Robbie's fingertips had brushed his big palm collecting allowance.

Robbie sat, stunned that retribution had struck with such unequivocal suddenness; he would have preferred to tease out the torture of the guilty secret all weekend. And the idea that he would one day thank his parents for such foul treatment didn't make him feel any better at all.

When Dad left the room, he sat up in his bed, with his guts in a knot and his throat as tight as a collar and tie. The Generation Gap, he reflected, is a brook bordered with poison envy that old people have polluted by dumping their own crappy resentment into it. But for all his rage he was ashamed that he hadn't beaten his parents to the punch, and been the first to think of leaving home.

See, Robbie hated Keef Richards' guts, but at least the guy had done things his own way, leaving *his* old man in his dust. For the Strolling Bones wrote songs not just about the crimes of totalitarian regimes around the world, but of parents too: as the story goes, Mr. Richards, Sr., had spent his life's savings so his son could attend a fancy private school that would give him a chance to rise up through Britain's hobbling class system. But all the school had done was force him to wear a nancy little uniform, and instilled in him bourgeois attitudes that almost cut him off completely from his real brotherhood (which, he said, was the disenfranchised of England, the salt of the earth, and not a gallery of pseuds and citied intellectuals). He had deliberately failed his exams, causing his father to despair, and returned to the ranks of the honest working class, which these days, he said with stinging irony, meant you didn't work at all. In an argument that's become part of the Bones' mythology, Keef put the issue of paternal devotion this way: "Da, if the only way to save me from dying was to eat a bucket of snot, would you?"

"Aww, son," Mr. Richards had replied, "don't go being a blithering idiot."

"No, really, Da," Keef had insisted. "Would you do it or no?"

Now Keef's father was broke and wouldn't speak to him, but Keef didn't care because his patricidal hit songs had made him a fucking fortune, and his old man was so deluded by middle-class aspirations that he was as good as dead, anyway. He was a rootless fool, Keef said, quoting somebody Robbie didn't know, divorced from the full-bodied blood of the land. *All Parents Must Die*.

Mom was in her study downstairs, sheltered from the midday sun, curled up in the bay window, poised on needlepoint cushions, her ankles crossed like Copenhagen's *Little Mermaid*. She was sifting through heaps of newspapers, clipping articles for *Hello World!* Always weeding, Robbie thought.

"*Blues*papers," he said, leaning against the doorjamb. "What's the point? The Generation Gap. S.P.E.C.T.R.E."

Mom kept reading.

Ah ha, the ignore routine. No one in this house shouts when they get mad. Confrontation's a thing for families without table manners. The Bookbinders just stew. He knotted his cheeks to parry and looked around, casual as someone waiting for a bus. Herds of plants were bunched on shelves, trailing onto the parquet floor. They stirred, alert to his presence. He thought of stepping forward. The floor was a maze of bunched papers, stapled notes, luxurious Italian stationery in crimson and cream, blotters and pads with suede covers and gold-thread tassles, articles clipped and sorted and stuffed into envelopes according to some secret system of hers.

Without a word still, she reached down, pulled a copy of *Rolling Stone* from the heap at her feet, and held it out between her thumb and index finger, at arm's length, like a dead something. She never even looked up. He took it with resignation and dragged his feet into the garden, leafing through it idly, wondering what was the point of starting anything, since she had already clipped a third of it out. It was just like life in the seventies, as far as he was concerned: edited out and handed down. He felt like rolling it up and tossing it back through the window. He felt like throwing it in the lake. He felt like toking up and throwing himself in the lake. Yes, come to think of it, he really did feel like committing suicide, throwing himself in front of Rosie's slalom-ski, as she blindly sliced the waves. "Life is what you make it," was one of Dad's favourite bromides, but Robbie had sussed one thing out for sure: life ain't all it's cracked up to be. And another problem was, he had in fact tried suicide once, but it hadn't exactly agreed with him. He hadn't had the basic skills required.

That's what he told Ivy once. Which, come to think of it, was where all the trouble began.

6

IT REALLY WAS ALL IVY'S FAULT.

They had met only nine months before, at Collège Blanchemains, in Outremont, a dirty whale of a building dating back to Confederation, with intestinal corridors and iron teeth around the windows. Robbie's parents sent him there to master French; without French under his belt, Dad had warned, the world of business in this province, not to mention politics, would be closed to him when he got older. *Business?* thought Robbie. *Politics?* He was horrified. *Older?*

He didn't meet Ivy Mills until December, but he already knew her name because he had stalked her all semester, often standing behind her on buses, peeking over her shoulder at the books in the crook of her arm. His nose had brushed the back of her hair. She smelled of something warm and sweet, weighed down with the mulched odour of rotting fruit. The classes were sexually segregated, if you can believe that in this day and age, but there was a co-ed cafeteria, and when he finally had the courage to set his tray down across from her, he smelled her breath and knew for sure.

"You drinking?"

Was she startled by his urbane opener? He couldn't

gauge her reaction. Fact is, his body was fighting down such a nervous riot that if she had sprouted horns and a black tongue, he couldn't have gauged that, either. What she did was merely draw her cup close to her chest with one hand, holding her place on the page with the other, and say, "What's it to you?"

His bowels went all soft, his stomach filled with air. His appetite evaporated up his throat. The clanking and clattering of the cafeteria with its cutlery and strings of silver Xmas tinsel whirled around his head, and the small distance between Ivy and him fell away like a yawning gorge. He managed, "You reading?"

". . . Uh huh."

"*Who* are you reading, may I ask."

"George Sand," she said. "Says on the cover, doesn't it."

"He good?"

Ivy sighed and rolled her eyes. "God. She's incredible."

She carved up her hamburger, one-handedly, with no more apparent interest in it than in him. She ate in large mouthfuls, eyes on her plate, fork loaded and waiting for her to swallow. The buttons down the centre of her navy cardigan were mismatched, he saw, the cuffs turned inward, and there were little round holes in the front. Moths? he wondered. Reefer? Through the holes he could see her skin. *Therefore, Watson, she is not wearing a bra.* He glanced at her bosom, searching furtively for a tell-tale shadow, there where she held her cup still. He looked for the slightest tumble of wool, the shallowest valley. . . .

Suddenly, she was speaking to him, looking straight at him for the first time. "You want a map? You'll need one."

"No, I – uh."

He asked where she lived. She told him, murmuring disinterestedly, *just Montreal.* He asked if she liked music. *Maybe.* He asked what she thought of the school. *Sucks.* So, what *was* she drinking? *Brandy.* Then she went back to her book.

He was in love. Her impossibly wide mouth, filled with crooked teeth, how beautiful. And she hadn't told him to fuck off or anything. Even if her attitude was (as it seemed to be), No one else in this hole speaks English so you'll have to do, that was good enough for him.

"Since you're a reader," Robbie ventured, unfolding a piece of paper from his pocket, "perhaps you'll appreciate the finer points of this." He slipped the page across the table.

GRAMMATICAL USAGE OF THE WORD F---

As an adjunctive: the f---ing cat.
As a suburbanite clause: Watch out for the cat, f---.
As an odddverb: I f---ing ran over the cat.
As a nown: What the f---, it was just a cat.

And so on. Arf arf, hilarious, no? Ivy scrunched her hair. He'd used the school Gestetner, got giddy sniffing the papers as they rolled off, and then distributed them right before class, inviting entries for a French companion volume.

"I got back two measly submissions," he told her, "both from this dork named Gaston Goupil. *Chu f---e*, which means I'm wasted, and *f---ser*. That means, for your information, to skip. School."

"He is a dork," Ivy said darkly. She wasn't laughing too hard at the grammarian, either. "If I were you I'd steer clear."

"You know Gaston?"

"We-ell."

She offered him a sip. He took the cup and watched her over the rim, licking to savour her saliva. She pushed a plastic barette tighter into her hair above her left ear. Her hair was coarse and untidily chopped, and she scrunched it constantly. It had no particular colour, either, as if she had tried and botched several different jobs at once: a patch of chestnut there on one side, with a streak of sandiness, a tawny clump on the other, like a ferret or a polecat. And this impression he had of her being akin to a fox, or a marmot, or something in a field, was heightened by her brown eyes and broad cheeks, and by her nose; it was like a muzzle, a lively nose that seemed to leap forward as if it had an opinion of its own. How he wanted to reach over and stroke it!

"I'm Robbie Bookbinder," he said, finally.

"I know," Ivy said. "Abigail Bookbinder's your mother, from that show *Hello World!* My family watches all the time. She was in the news – didn't she get arrested protesting a dam project in James Bay?"

"Yeah, well, she's always. . . . Me, I'm in Hell's Yells."

"What's that?" she grinned, showing a mouthful of crooked little teeth. Covering it quickly with her hand. "A gargle? Or a gargoyle?"

Then she got up, leaving her tray – and Robbie – behind. He watched her go, hoping she'd turn around to acknowledge him, but she walked right out of the caf without stopping.

He chased after her, at a discreet distance. In the corridor he watched her pull a great Afghan coat from her locker. He slipped on his own army-green parka with the RAF target on the back. Then she strode out of the school, crossed Avenue Van Horne, and disappeared into the dépanneur there. He leaned against a tree, and waited. When she came out, he waved, tentatively, but she was engrossed in rolling a cigarette, and didn't seem to see him. He followed her down the street, trying to catch whiffs of the very smoke that had whirled inside her lungs. He followed her through Outremont, down Park Avenue, past the pool halls and souvlaki joints, south towards Mount Royal. And when, finally, she turned around and looked at him, she had rolled a cigarette for him, too, and was lighting it with hers, end to end.

It was the first time he had ever *fucksed* school. They

88

walked, far from the chalky overheated classrooms, two flecks against the snow-covered mountain. Their fingers and toes frozen stiff, they kept strolling all afternoon, fuelled by the liquor Ivy poured from a silver flask. They walked until they came back down to the Main, where Schwartz's delicatessen exhaled spicy steam through the grill above its door, and piles of pickles and carnatzel and hunks of hot smoked-meat sent condensation dribbling down the windows. Up the street, rolls of carpeting and bolts of cut-price cloth grew hoarfrost where they stood on the sidewalk. The pages of secondhand paperbacks on outdoor stalls were brittle with cold, and cracked when they flipped through them. Up and down the streets an elderly generation of immigrant Greeks, Italians, and Jews negotiated with halting steps the blisters of black ice on the pavement.

With prodding, Ivy talked about her family. *Have one, in a way*. Brothers and sisters? *Some*. Her Dad? *A barber*.

"A barber?" Robbie repeated, chilled to the bone.

"Not a hairdresser, note. Hairdressers are for faggots."

"They're not for everyone, agreed."

"A barber with a strop and razor, keeping up tradition. He's for royal rule, too. Hangs a picture of the Queen. The revolving pole outside's a Union Jack. Your father?"

"Um, well – "

Ivy looked amused. Her breath, hot and alcoholic, hung in the air between them. "You don't have to be embarrassed. I don't care what he does. Why, is your family poor, like mine? I would have thought your mother makes a bundle!"

"Well, ah – " Robbie said.

"Or maybe you're rich, but subscribe to the idea that it's cool to be poor and have a bad attitude."

"Well, no, I – "

"I do, and I'm not ashamed of it. It's 'necessity's sharp pinch' that got me where I am – my excuse for a father certainly couldn't afford to send me to Blanchemains. As far as I'm concerned, getting on a special educational program like I did – because I'm *smart* – mostly means I can be as bad as I like."

"Right," Robbie said. "Exactly."

"Hey look!" She gripped his arm. "That woman in the fur coat. She's a whore."

"How do you know? Wow. Do you know that person?"

"God, no. What do you think she's doing, waiting for a parade?"

They walked and walked until the sky and the snow beneath it turned purple and the street lights flickered on. Robbie couldn't think of a thing to say. Ivy had clammed up, too. They walked. He was feeling grim. They obviously had nothing in common after all.

"Time to go," she said at last. And embraced him violently. Their noses bonked, but he barely felt a thing. He heard his frozen parka crunch, and smelled warm beeswax and brandy escape from her Afghan coat. She opened that wide mouth, so full of crooked teeth the thought struck him that she must have an appetite for things he'd never even heard of yet. He closed his eyes and allowed himself to be devoured. It was hot and wet in there, and his entire being was engulfed in the kiss. His soul slithered down a dark-red, ribbed tunnel, and when they lost their balance together on the ice, he was surprised to find it was rush hour all around them. She finally released him. He watched her climb onto a bus. Then he turned and raced all the way home, knees buckling and the breath in his throat rasping so cold it barely made steam.

Ivy worked most evenings behind the candy counter at the old Roxy Cinema. That alone would have been enough reason to go out with her, for Robbie got to see *Woodstock* seven times in two weeks, all for free. But over lunch one day she told him the cinema had acquired an uncut 35mm copy of *She Stoops to Conquer*. "And I don't mean Oliver Goldsmith," she whispered, with a confidential smirk.

"No, of course not," Robbie replied, pushing his lower lip up and nodding his head like he knew *exactly* what she was talking about.

Back in the forties, the Roxy had been the home of the Empire Burlesque Follies of Montreal – he'd heard stories of his grandfather going there to see Les Girls de Montmartre for only twenty cents. Now, an electric marquee was bolted over friezes of the theatre's original Egyptian motif, that once depicted Osiris and Horus and Thoth ogling bare-breasted, feather-topped dancers; the city atmosphere had smudged and disfigured them, but Robbie preferred them that way; history seemed to lurk there.

He lined up to say hi at the candy counter, his heart turning over like an egg in boiling water. Ivy was up to her chest in carob bars and packages of Trail Mix. Her breath was heavy and sweet. "Oh, *hello*," she said. "Don't you look groovy." Surreptitiously, she showed him a brown-bagged bottle she had stowed under the counter beside an Ayn Rand novel. She smiled with her mouth all full of teeth like a stuffed pocket, and Robbie was in heaven.

It was hot in the cinema, and the crowd was as quiet as if they were watching a thriller. The music was jaunty, like an ad for a holiday resort, but it was a great leaning tower of Penis that was projected on the screen. Robbie had never seen anything like it. And who was it up there also, but the one and only Kiki Van Garterbelt, star centrefold of *Bosom Buddies* magazine. He searched for a seat in the dark, but was forced to perch on a step by the fire escape, feeling conspicuous in the red glow of the EXIT sign above him. Kiki had the giant penis in her mouth, and the silence in the cinema was deafening. When the penis ejaculated there was a cheer from the audience; the same spontaneous cheer Canadian airline passengers let out when the pilot has managed a tricky landing, after which everyone laughs, realizing they weren't the only ones afraid. And, right after that, there was a shout from the back of the room, and the image faded and the screen went white. The house lights were switched on and everybody turned their heads around to look.

"Raid!" someone shouted. "Les boeufs!"

Chrissake! Robbie fought to gather his jacket and flee, but there was a stampede in his direction and people were trampling over him to get to the fire escape. Someone stuck a shoe in his groovy oversized flares and tumbled forward, landing with a knee on his chest. Robbie was in a forest of legs and shoes and laughing, pushing people. His head-band was yanked off. Then he was dragged aside by one arm and it was her saying, "*Here, this way,*" and after a scramble the two of them were hidden behind the cinema screen, peering between the curtains with their breath held fast. The police had blocked the doors. They were checking ID and taking names. Ivy took him by the hand and led him deeper backstage. She seemed to know it well, deftly manoeuvring through the dark obstacle course of cables and sandbags, rusting spotlights, splintered flats, and mounds of dank, mothy material.

He hadn't imagined there would still be so many re-mains of the old burlesque house. Behind the screen and in the wings, plaster sphinx heads and thrones of pha-roahs that had once dominated the walls high above the auditorium lay on the floor like the finds at an archaeolog-ical dig; they had been shorn off the walls to accommodate the automatic pulley system for the new movie curtains, and were now a damp and crumbled ruin, the damask and lapis lazuli paint flaking.

"What did you think of *She Stoops To Conquer?*" Ivy said.

"It was – OK," Robbie said. "Compared to all the other – but – it seemed to me it . . . it showed you everything except, except . . . love. If you know what I mean." He wasn't sure just how honest or dishonest he was being;

what he said was true, but he really wanted to show Ivy what a sensitive guy he was, and his disingenuousness was as clear as the impression his headband had left across his forehead.

"God, yes," she said. "Of course. What did you expect?"

Still higher, off the precarious ramps and wrought-iron galleries, were the dressing rooms. Each narrow cell had a countertop filthy with greasepaint and dust, and a mirror bordered with sooty lightbulbs. On the floor in one room was a brown paper bag, darkened at the bottom by some viscous liquid. They peeked: the bag had been filled with haemorrhaging bait. A family of dead mice clustered there, bloated with their own blood.

He blew dust off an old Empire Follies program, its cover corrugated with moisture, filled with photographs of sultry artistes posing topless in their sequinned muu-muus, hands poised like girls on game shows, bare thigh thrust forward. Jacquie Diamantine, Regine Argent. They wore luminescent lipstick and clotted eyelashes. The Three Manzoli, beaming acrobats with Brylcreem flying, and the internationally known Lance Falwell, a blond Adonis, the program claimed, with the voice of an angel.

"Look at the ostrich feathers and the rhinestones," Ivy said. She was standing close, to see, and her arm was firmly pressed against his. Turning a page, their hands touched.

"This one, piled high like a wedding cake. Looks like a Dr. Seuss," he said.

"And the breasts on that one," Ivy whispered. "Have you ever seen anything like?"

"Well," Robbie said, thinking hard about what he really felt and determined not to end up lying again for no good reason. "They're pretty nice, I guess. But just cause they're big like that, uh, – "

Bingo. Ivy took his hand and pressed it to her chest.

The next day they *fucksed* school altogether and lurked in the Bookbinders' empty house. They got drunk, and fondled – whenever Ivy initiated it; the first time Robbie laid a wooden arm across her waist, she jolted away and said, "One track-minder, one night-stander." The next she was a wildcat, biting his lips, yanking at his ears, mashing his testicles, forcing his hands to squash her breasts. When his fingers brushed her pubic hair, sprung tight as a mattress within her unsnapped Osh Kosh B'Gosh's, she recoiled. "You just want to get into my pants," she said. He couldn't make head or tail of her.

Ivy smoked and read aloud to him. She carried several books in her satchel, and they were thumbworn, broken-spined, booze-crinkled, and densely underlined volumes with the pages raggedly cut. "Baudelaire, he's incredible. Listen: *It is essential to be drunk all the time. That is all: there's no other problem. If you don't want to feel the appalling weight of Time which breaks your shoulders and bends you to the ground, get drunk, and drunk again. What with? Wine, poetry, or being good, please yourself. But get drunk.*"

Robbie's lap warmed under Ivy's weight, his head resting on her back, the afternoon waning, filling up the drunk old house with a grey, gruelly light. The rush-hour traffic at a whishing pitch on the slushy streets outside. He took a hit off of her cigarette, and the nicotine made him nauseous. "That's only because," he told her when she looked at him funny, "while weed is organic and natural, eh, the chemicals in tobacco always throw me for a loop."

She wriggled free of his embrace. He watched her walk over to the bookshelf. And the way her body moved inside her dungarees, like she was sweetly, naturally, doing the twist! What was it like, he wondered, awestruck, to never have to worry about the way you look, to just be beautiful. How does she fall asleep with herself at night? If he were her, he figured he'd be up caressing himself till dawn.

"This place is a treasure trove," she said. "At my house the parents say there shouldn't be books, we'd only wreck them." She ran her fingers along a row of books like she was searching for a secret button to push, and stopped at *Nadja*, just one title of hundreds there that Robbie had always found easier to dismiss as boring, than pull out and try. "André Breton," she said. "This book's incredible. Your parents have good taste. The architect of Surrealism. In one bit they're driving in the country, he's at the wheel and she covers his eyes. Whew! The motto is, *Beauty will be convulsive, or not at all.* Isn't that incredible?"

"Uh, sure," Robbie said, pushing his lips out to help him figure it. "You bet."

After that they necked and rolled about on the floor, and just as they were getting hot and heavy, Ivy said she wanted another drink. They swigged mouthfuls of raw anise straight from a bottle in the parents' liquor cabinet, and when their gums were numb, Robbie went to the kitchen to top it up again with water.

"Don't be an idiot, Ivy said, "That'll make it go yellow."

Down in the den he showed off his sketches – first the nudes copied from the classics, then his own surreal bestiary, a bunch of stuff he feared was way too crude to show; a mean-spirited collection all right, unkindly conceived, rudely rendered, about as appealing as spit on the street.

"It's just stuff, for fun only," he said, his cheeks blooming hot. "I did them years ago."

Ivy smoked, and examined them for a long time. There were scrums of figures, bullock-headed, all muddy blots of ink and furious scribbles, the lines scratched deep into the surface of the paper; there were smeary, thrashing blurs with gills, and shark's fins slicing through the backs of jackets; there were other figures laid down blobbily, smudged and scuffed, some rubbed with ash from Dad's cigarettes, some with spittle and snot to wrinkle the paper, some bled on, some torn up and messily glued back together; there was a likeness of himself as a sperm whale flipping, another with a storm of charcoal for a facial expression, another with his head dripping, exhausted, from a toothpaste tube, and several others repeatedly sketched and rubbed out and sketched over again to give an uncertain, woozy, dazed effect. Ivy gingerly turned the pages by the corners, careful not to smudge them, and whistled appreciatively.

"God," she said. "You must know more about art than me."

"It's not my best, of course," Robbie said.

They played a game, taking turns to lick each other's tongues and kiss the crooks of their arms, and Robbie's face was wet and cool from Ivy's saliva. He insinuated his palm against the startling flatness of her loins. When she pulled his jeans off, he felt buoyantly naked, his bottom foolish – the bottom that had only ever been presented in public before for a spanking. His penis felt pumped up with air. When she pulled off her Osh Kosh B'Goshes he was surprised by her skinniness, by the bones in her knees, the tendons in her thighs, and the traces of hair there. With their shirts still on, they hugged and pressed their hipbones together. He smelled the tart exclamation of her vagina, and when he pressed the tip of his penis against her, he was astonished at how resistant a mat of hair he was being asked to penetrate. He had always imagined, when he had dared to imagine it in such detail at all, that this would be a soft and accommodating entrance, but it turned out to be a surprisingly resilient, compact anatomy of flesh and bone and pubic hair. After years of gazing at peach-fuzzed photographs, all gauze and satin and cinnamon colours, it was all surprisingly, well, *physical*. His ears filled with the din of breath and

96

skin. Then the front door slammed upstairs. It was Mom home from her vacation at Three Mile Island.

After that, he figured they were seeing each other. If you could call it that. She was such a strange stray cat – she never called, she wouldn't give him her phone number or let him walk her home, she never waited for him outside school, she rarely spoke her mind, and she had no friends to keep him informed of her latest mood swing.

When they did meet – in the caf, at the bus stop, at Pendeli's Pizza near the school – it was by accident. She'd look up from books by writers like Jean Rhys or Colette or someone equally obscure to Robbie, and pull a reluctant, wide smile across her face and then look down again, always to finish her sentence before saying hello. He'd have to stand there with his heart thumping, and the distinct impression he was interrupting not just her reading, but her whole life. Still, she always ended up taking his hand and holding onto it outdoors, until he thought he'd lose the circulation in his fingers.

At night, after she hadn't phoned, he'd lie in bed like an eel in a hot pie of sheets, and astral travel over the city to her bedroom. It wasn't to peep; just to be beside her when she awoke. He'd lie on his back and weave together a flying carpet with gossamer fibres spun from sleepydust. He'd waft over snow-topped chimneys and late-night streets, and materialize in her bed like a body's warm sleeping odours. He'd just lie there beside her, full of the purest intentions, picturing her body without emphasis on the sexual parts, like a Barbie. Maybe they'd press their hips and thighs together, and maybe he'd caress her nippleless breasts, but never more.

Because French-Canadians were in a belligerent, secessionist mood at the time, the back of Robbie's head was made the frequent target of snowballs packed with grit. But, a month before he met Ivy, he had made peace with some of the more apolitical guys in the school, by virtue of his good nose where killer-weed was concerned. This he had established by fluently razzing Gaston Goupil for trying to fob off some bum hay on the boys.

The clouds overhead like quick dark knives scraping snow from the icy sky this Monday afternoon; six of them gathered in an alley, making a huddled flapping circle, and passing a sample joint around, pulling their fingers out of their mitts only long enough to pinch the diminishing roach, press it against their chapped lips, and fumble it on. The burning smoke, the rasping naked throat. They waited, stamping their feet. After a few minutes everyone shook their heads and peered suspiciously at Gaston from behind their curtains of hair. "Ayoi," Robbie said. "C'est le big bullshit, ça. C'est le Colombien ben cheap, pas le super stuff. Rien que les seeds et twigs. Fuck moi. Quel rip-off, hosti." He demanded a second joint. And then another, just to be sure . . .

. . . after the fourth the stone's coming on at last. Robbie's body feels like a frosted fungus, the air thickening around him and moving sluggishly, and it becomes suddenly inexplicably hilarious to him that in Québécois the word for being stoned is *gelée*, which means frozen. He's also chuckling at the fact that he picks up more of the language out here than he does in class, although he knows it's not the sort of education his parents think they're paying so dearly for. The older furry freaks are checking him out, uncomprehending, and Gaston's looking fierce, but when Robbie looks up to see their scraggly hair and baffled expressions he thinks of *One Million Years B.C.*, and laughs even harder. These fucken doorknobs. Well, it's not long before they're all laughing for no good reason and returning to class, and Robbie feels he has pacified the tribe and no more will they try to push his tongue against a frozen drainpipe for being a *maudit bloke*, which means damn English-speaking Canadian, or a *sale juif*, which means dirty Jew. At the very least, if anyone whips a gritball at him in this condition, he won't feel a thing before he thaws out.

"Remember I suggested once that you steer clear of Gaston Goupil – " Ivy asked him the next morning. Robbie had staked out Pendeli's Pizza way before school began and intercepted her when she came in for a coffee and a smoke. " – now I'm telling you."

"Why? He's just a low-life. A scam artist."

She leaned forward. "God. Do I have to explain everything?"

He leaned forward, too, to kiss her nose. How sweet of her to be concerned for his safety. Her face bore a thick skin of white pancake, the crude boundary visible under her chin up to her ears, and Robbie imagined her undressed, like a cabaret performer with a luminous head. And how he loved her voice, so soft, like a sweet-smelling ghost, never rising above a whisper! She sat back abruptly, tugged at the sleeves of her cardigan, pulling them over her wrists.

"Look," she said. "If I have to explain, then you don't deserve to know. Maybe we shouldn't be together. I wish I was somewhere else."

"But – "

They sat in silence. She opened a book, pressing it flat on the table to read, absent-mindedly rolling cigarettes between nicotine-stained fingers. When the butts became too small to hold, she squeezed the pinches of remaining tobacco back into a plastic pouch. Then she poured a capful of brandy into her coffee cup, and one into Robbie's. He watched the operation, admiring her fingers, thinking how lovely they were, a little plump, a little yellow, but lovely still, with the cuticles bitten to the quick, with little red blotches, little pinpricks, in the soft flesh between her thumbs and index fingers, but all the more tender for that.

Finally she looked up and sighed heavily. "OK, so. Look over there. Who do you think that is, by the playground fence? By the exit."

Robbie lowered his head to peer under the ALL-DRESSED SPECIAL painted meatily on the inside of the window. He stuck out his lower lip and tapped it with exaggerated thoughtfulness.

"Well, well, speak of the devil. I can tell 'cause his hands are hanging lower than his knees."

Ivy rolled her eyes impatiently. She yanked at her hair. "Yes, but can't you see who he's *with*?"

A school bus pulled up beside the schoolyard and disgorged a zooful of primary schoolers, all in puffy snowsuits like Michelin men, yelping and tripping and making each other eat yellow snow, followed by one straggler whose coat had been turned backwards like a straitjacket, and bound with the idiot strings on his mitts. Gaston and his companion turned their backs and walked away, slowly, with their heads close together. Gaston, Robbie could see, was wearing his prerequisite pepsi outfit – platform boots with big round toecaps, flares flapping above his ankles, plaid shirt, red-and-black lumberjacket – but the other guy was more menacing; he wore oily jeans, a belt made from bullet shells with a bunch of keys as fat as a fist dangling from it, and a leather jacket with a sleeveless jean vest on top.

Just before they turned the corner, the menacing guy's heap of greasy hair was whipped upwards by a gust of frozen wind. It took off like a caveful of bats, and Robbie caught a quick but unmistakable glimpse of the design on the back of his jacket: a hand of bullet-holed playing cards, pairs of black aces and eights with a skull-faced joker in-between, and in Gothic lettering the words

DEAD MAN'S HAND.

"Chrissake," Robbie said. "Do you *know* those guys?"

"God. If I have to explain – "

"No, *really*." He was fascinated, drawn to the violence of bikers with the same nervous intoxication, the same thickening of the blood that *Bosom Buddies* magazine aroused in him; whenever that stuff reared up, stretching the surface of safe and decent routines like a sudden boil or an unexpected erection, he couldn't help himself. "Really," he repeated. "I mean, the Dead Man's Hands is the gang that killed a Hell's Angel a while back, right? They stabbed him thirty-seven times, and shot him twice in the head, and injected his veins with battery acid. And then, like, he crawled to a hospital and *lived* and eventually ratted on everybody 'cause even he was scared shitless. He's a police-protected witness now, right, with a luxury jail cell and a twenty-five-dollar weekly allowance just for cigarettes. All the Dead Man's Hands have F.D.W. tattoos on their penises which stretch into *Fuck De World*, right? Oh, and they wear aces and eights because that's the poker hand Wild Bill Hickok had when he was shot in the back. That it?"

"I don't know," Ivy said. "But I guess you have all the facts. . . ."

101

7

ON THE BUS BACK TO TOWN FROM KILBORN BAY, ROSIE commiserated with him. "Hopefully things will work out for you as they did for me, Bob. After I got caught accidentally on purpose sawing the heels off of my daddy's girlfriend's fancy shoes, I thought we'd *never* talk again. Isn't it hilarious how you 'n me are such *losers*! Maybe you could stay at my place."

"Yeah. Hilarious," Robbie said despondently. Besides some leftover matzoh and *maror* he'd wolfed from the fridge before fleeing the cottage (to remind him of the sadness of the Jews in exile), he'd barely eaten all day.

"Or I have friends at the club who could put you up. Same ones who helped me when *I* was kicked out."

"What? Like that guy in that cult? In Paspebiac? The one that's waiting for the end of the world? Don't be idiotic."

"Pierre 'Moses' Thibeault you mean. Stop being funny. It wasn't a cult."

"It's called *The First Doomsday Cult*."

"Well, it's not a cult *per se*. Although I did get bored waiting for the end of the world with them. Did I ever tell you they sat on the floor and played Monopoly for sex? For *days*. After a while I had the distinct impression he was *cheating*. Hey, I tell you what. To cheer you up, after my shift this aft, I'll buy you a ticket for the Strolling Bones."

Robbie had never had the slightest intention of going to see the Bones. He'd taken Rosie to the country specifically to avoid them. That's what he was ruefully thinking to himself as he waited for her in the Alexis Nihon Plaza that evening. Frankly he hated the Bones with all his might; he despised Keef Richards' guts, and he didn't give a damn about their Absolutely Very Final That's All Folks! Tour of Triumphant Return. He used to be their world's biggest fan, bar only Ivy, but he had grown up a lot since those days. If Keef had an assassination complex just because a crazed fan had once hid in his hotel bathtub and bit at one of his testicles as he stepped in to take a shower, nearly severing it, Robbie could *really* give him good reason now. That's what he told Rosie when she joined him. "It's like Dad always said, the guy looks like a Neanderthal and he can't play for beans."

"Oh, you're just saying that 'cause of what happened with you and him and Little Miss Sunshine," Rosie said, and linked her arm with his. She swept the hair back from his face and kissed him on the end of his nose, called him her seeing-eye dog, and left him with a smudge of black-and-blue lipstick there.

The plaza was packed. The noise level had soared to obliterate the Muzak. The air was charged. On a regular day a kid could get cautioned by a pig just for loitering here, but an hour or two before a concert, forget it. Kids ruled, OK? They perched in rows on the staircases so that shoppers loaded down with bags had to step over them; they took up all the stools around the Pogo and Orange Julep counters so you had nowhere to sit if you had been on your feet all day; they scoured the aisles of the supermarkets and department stores like locusts, making the cashiers and floor managers wild with suspicion; they crammed into the automatic photo-booths, piling six laps high, so there was no point in even waiting for your turn; they leaned and slouched and loitered as much as they pleased along the balustrades, like crows on telephone wires, like ragged jackdaws with an eye for shiny things, until it was time.

Robbie and Rosie had met on Sub-Level 2, by the Prairie Buffalo T-Shirt Emporium and Head Shoppe. They checked out the posters and the pins and the bandannas and the toker accessories in the window. They were just standing there at the window, not being a menace to society or nothing, when Officer Gaunt loomed up smiling, with another, bigger pig behind him, dressed in plainclothes. As conspicuous as Norbert the Nark.

"Hey, quit hassling me, man," Robbie said in a hushed, urgent voice. "You're making people paranoid."

It was true. People were speaking out of the corners of their mouths and watching beadily. Robbie knew exactly how they felt; he had often seen kids get hauled off in a half-nelson, wearing the only expression you can in the face of such obvious social injustice: stunned disbelief that it's happened to you and not someone else equally guilty. Robbie knew they were watching now with a mixture of raw dislike for the pigs and amused condescension for him for being so dumb as to get caught.

Gaunt crooked a finger at Rosie. "Would you mind terribly if we just had a private word," he said, ushering her away by the elbow. She tugged her arm out of his grasp, and stood there blinking ten paces off, out of earshot.

Gaunt returned, crossed his eyes at Robbie and grinned. "My mother always said they'd stick if I persisted in doing that," he said, "but sometimes I think it's the only way to see eye to eye with little pricks like you."

"Wassat supposed to mean."

"It means you lied to me when we last had our little chat."

104

"Oh?"

"Mother of Jesus," Gaunt sighed, and then winked sala-
ciously. "Lead-pencil drawings on piled-up sheets of paper
do leave lovely clear evidence after a fire. We reconstituted
some of the carbon remains. I have to say, you're quite the
artist."

"Gee, thanks," Robbie said, genuinely proud, but regretting that he had been so proud to actually sign them.

"So you did spend time in the attic. And you must know
how the fire got started."

"Fucked'f I do."

"Were you or were you not there?"

"No, man, I told you – I was definitely in class when the
alarm went." Robbie leaning with one hand against the
window of the Head Shoppe. The sales clerk looked pointedly at him through the glass, and when Robbie peeled his
vermin fingers off, there was a row of oily fingerprints left
behind, like a nervous run of eighth notes on a stave.

"You see," Gaunt said, "it's quite strange, really. After the
fire the key was still in the attic lock, welded fast."

Robbie pulled a face, as if to think. "So?"

"So, you're a flip little bastard. You don't care at all, do
you?"

Robbie had to think about that one. Care about what?
He hesitated, looked above him. Up there at the balcony
rail was a gang of Bones fans, replete with studded wristbands and top hats, feathers and coloured hair. They were
leaning and watching and waiting like glittering vultures
now, and Robbie wondered if any of them would have the
courage to drop a pearl of spit, or, like the naked cherubs
of Renaissance ceilings, pee a golden shower. He pulled
a tight smile, trying to be nonchalant for their benefit: *yep,
no sweat, just rappin' with the fuzz.* Finally he said, "Why
should I? Wasn't my insurance policy."

"A person *died* in that fire."

"Right, I knew that."

"Oh you did, did you? How did you know?"

"Someone told me, I forget exactly."

"Well, doesn't it make your skin crawl to think of it? A – person – dying – in – a – fire."

"No. I mean, yes! Pends on the person, I guess. I mean who it was that bit the biscuit. You see it on TV all the time, which these days numbs young people's emotions. You can't afford to get upset every time it happens. For your metal health. But you're right, it is terrible in principle."

Staring match. Robbie's Man With No Name eyes vs. Gaunt's watery red ones.

"Metal health," Gaunt repeated. "Oh – by the way, may I introduce Detective Sergeant Husker."

"Listen," Husker said to Robbie confidentially, like they'd known one another for years. "We have a little investigation going on here, and we need your help. OK, my friend?" Up close, he had the bleeding complexion of steamed beef. Abattoir breath. Thick stringy vocal cords. Robbie nodded, and his Adam's apple grated. "Now. Did you know the dead boy's blood was full of heroin? When I say boy, I mean about your age. So again, for me, what were you doing up in that room?"

"*Art.* Whaddo you want me to say, that we did smack? *Fuckaff* – sorry. Sorry 'bout that, sir. I mean, I don't chip, I'm clean. Look at my arms. No tracks, man. Chrissake, whaddo I have to say?"

"So you deal."

His breath was really appalling. Robbie stepped back and said, "You kidding? Where's my brand new Cadillac, then? I wouldn't be hanging out with all these low-lifes if I was dealing *horse*. I'd be a celebrated dealer to the stars. And don't say I'm a pusher, neither, 'cause I ain't. Get away, why donchou."

"All right, all right," Husker said. "Go enjoy your concert, and stay the *fuck* out of trouble."

"We are on your side, you know," Gaunt said. "There was

106

once a time when all I wanted to see was a policeman on his backside, too. You're quite the artist. You should put your talent to work one of these days, make a decent living."

"Yeah," Robbie said. "I'm gonna forge money."

The other in-place to be before a summer concert was outside Atwater Park, right across from the Forum; the brimming streets, the pigs swinging their sticks like beefy promenading ladies with parasols, and the seasoned potheads smirking behind their backs. The smells of incense and reefer, of patchouli and dirty denim, of fresh-mown grass and puke. The furtive dope deals and pepsis saying under their breath as they passed you by, *Ash, hacid, mesc*. Crowds were massing around the main doors, under the elevators shaped like crossed hockey sticks. Rosie clung to his arm.

"I *hate* it when pigs harass a young person for no good reason. What did they want from you?" She giggled. "Did they think you're a *druggie*? Pigs are so dumb going by appearances. *I'm* the one holding, but they don't hassle me cos I look so *sweet* and *innocent*!" Then she bit his earlobe and murmured hotly, "I get so aroused before a big show, Bob, I get premature elation."

"Yeah, well, I'm sorry if I never made it clear," he snapped, shrugging her off, "but I'm not going."

Ticketless fans hung around outside in the blistering heat, trying to outwait the scalpers who were fanning themselves with handfuls of unsold whites and blues. Robbie thumbed the ticket Rosie had slipped in his pocket. He mingled, sized up one likely innocent knob with short schoolboy hair and mumbled, "Greatest rock 'n' roll band ever. Absolutely Very Final That's All Folks! Tour of Triumphant Return. Ever, truly. Last chance to see a legend. Fifteenth row, hundred clams."

"Rip-off, man. Guy over there's got fifth for eighty."

107

Robbie took twenty.

Rosie looked at him, all forlorn. "Hey. I *bought* you that ticket."

Robbie shrugged back at her sharply. "I never asked you to. You know I hate these guys with a passion. I'd kill Keef fucken Richards with my bare hands if I had the chance."

"Aren't you going a little overboard?" Rosie said with an indulgent smile, trying to take his hand. "Your anger's way out of line. And you're *scary* when you get like this. Please, Bob – *talk* to me."

"If I have to explain, then you don't deserve to know," Robbie mumbled, unconvincingly.

"*What* did you say?! If you *what*? Now, where have I heard *that* turn of phrase before?"

Robbie turned abruptly and lost himself in the crowd. He felt cheap and desperate, leaving Rosie like that, but he couldn't help himself. For if he could find it in himself to turn back now, what would his anger have been worth in the first place?

He was the only one going this way, wriggling up the thick stream of bodies to spawn his rage. He wove around back to the Forum's stage door, and lurked by the Bones' fleet of equipment trucks. Back in '72 some wigged-out pepsi bozo had placed a bomb beneath one of them and blown it up. That had been political, that act, though Robbie couldn't say why exactly. But he could think of other reasons to do it again, now. He read the sign in the window of the roadie tour bus where the destination is usually slotted:

GASHMOBILE

He spat at the windscreen. His spittle flew low, into the dead insect-fur on the radiator grill. Then a long black limo, so long it had a double set of wheels at the back, slid around the corner, silent as a shark in black water, and paused in the driveway, shitting a white cloud of exhaust behind it, while the aluminum stage door rolled clattering open. Robbie ran over and hammered his fist on the car roof. It bonged like an Indian drum. He pressed his nose to the window, but it was opaque. A security guard shouted and chased him away.

The sun had set a virulent blackened red, as if its rays had sliced the sky and soaked the cotton clouds with blood. He launched himself off for the comfort of the Roxy, stopping at a dépanneur for a six-pack along the way. What was playing tonight, he wondered. Farm out: *Woodstock*.

He slouched in the back row and got systematically ripped. Besides him, only five people were watching. By the time the scene with all the melancholy sixties garbage came on, he had peed three times and passed out on the sticky, gum-pimpled floor. The usher, shutting the place down for the night, didn't see him there and left him alone in the darkness.

His stomach ached, and his gums still bore the tang of raw onions from the *maror* that morning. The saliva in his mouth was so thick and viscous he could run it between his teeth like sour Jello. He shivered vigorously in the dank air. Hey, he thought blobbily, this wouldn't be such a bad place to live. And tumbled into a bitter foaming sleep, as if someone had stuck a straw in his brain and blown hard through it . . .

. . . he's with the family, waiting for a flight to leave from Dorval airport. Quebec is seceding to become the fifty-first state of the U.S. Indignant, rather than becoming Franco-Americans, the Bookbinders are moving to Ontario.

A siren goes off that sounds a lot like an industrial vacuum cleaner. There's an announcement over the PA that Ghadaffi has lost some weight, but not enough; now he's feeling forlorn and declaring war on everybody. The air is thick with grief. Robbie feels so profoundly sad it's like a stone is lodged in his throat. He's sitting on the floor beside the luggage and Mom's ruffling his hair. Everyone in the departure lounge knows it's the end of the world, and they're very quiet. But Dad's trying to pretend things aren't all that bad. He's yammering with all the forced gaiety of a hostess at a dreadful cocktail party.

"So, Robbie!" he says. "Ahh, do tell us about Hell's Yells' plans for their incredible World Domination Tour!"

8

THE MORNING AFTER IVY HAD POINTED OUT THE DEAD
Man's Hand, and been so deadly serious about Gaston
Goupil, he ignored his Sugar Krunchies and headed out
early for Pendeli's. There he sat, finger-painting the formica tabletop with grease, his stomach clenched sick from
the acid coffee poured there. Ivy didn't show until the last
minute. She was red-cheeked and breathless, her white
pancake visibly splotched onto her earlobes. By that time,
in spite of himself, Robbie had whipped himself into a
sweat picturing Gaston and her in bed making dirty love,
this way, that way, this way again; he tortured himself as
they smoked hand-rolled cigarettes, drank brandy for
breakfast, and arrived late to school together. Yes, because
come to think of it, she was almost always late. Her eyes
were always puffy, too, like any serious toker. Obviously
she and Gaston were a secret number. Why else would she
refuse to explain a thing?

"If I have to explain," she said when she saw his long
face, "then you don't deserve to know. The sneaky mother
counted the tampons in my box in the bathroom. We had
the fight of the century."

"Really? So – "

"So she should know better. Ever since I was anorexic

111

my periods haven't come regularly. I get maybe eight a year, tops. You'd think she'd be relieved for me, but *no*, she had to say something. I bet she's told all of her seven good Catholic sisters on the phone about it, too." Ivy licked a rolling paper so angrily that Robbie feared she might cut her tongue.

"Uh, well, how long's it been? It."

"Three months, I guess. Big deal."

"Well then," Robbie said, tentatively. "There's no chance of you being pregnant by me, ha ha. Is there."

"Well, no-o. I mean there was only that once, at your house, and you didn't even go inside. God, this is embarrassing. Look, it's such a tiny hole. I sit in the bath and soap doesn't go up, it's against gravity."

"Well, did you maybe sleep with somebody else?" Robbie asked. Casually as possible.

Ivy gave him a fox-in-the-grass look. "What's the difference," she said. "Maybe I've slept with lots of guys. Maybe not."

"Well, have you?" Despite himself, he had let an accusatory tone into his voice. His stomach dropped.

"I'm not going to give you the satisfaction of an answer," Ivy hissed. "If I have to tell you . . . "

Outside the school, as the bell rang, he stuck his neck forward to kiss her, tentatively and not a little guiltily. She grabbed him like she was saving herself from falling off a roof. She unzipped his parka while they necked, opening her dufflecoat and pressing her body to his. She clutched his hands and guided them under her shirt and urgently thrust her knee between his legs. Robbie, grabbing a breath, looked over her shoulder and saw they had attracted quite a crowd. Kids were smirking, several wiping their noses on frosty mittens. And now Ivy was biting Robbie's neck.

"Hey," he said. "Don't be crazy."

Abruptly she withdrew. "What's wrong with crazy," she

snapped, and shot him an almighty expression. Then she pushed him off and slipped away over a snowbank to the girls' way in.

He chased after her, calling out, "Sorry! Sorry!"

"OK," she said. "You want to *fuckse* with me? I'm in the art room after lunch."

Robbie's teacher this morning is Monsieur Nul, who throws things at the slightest provocation, whose fly is permanently, maybe deliberately, undone, and who daily exhorts the kids to excel at their studies before the Chinese and the Jews take over the world. There's a test re: hypotenuselesses and angles of complete irrelevance, but Robbie's stoned again, having toked up in the can on some fine Afghani smash, and is busy being FUCK the outlaw biker with his skull ring and oil-caked jeans, singing, under his breath, *"Getcher motor ruh-nin, headout onna highway . . ."* He's slouched way down in his seat, with his blue Beatle boots propped against the back of the chair in front of him, his arms slung high up over the desk top like he's straddling a cool chopped hog fuelled and vibrating with sheer anticipation – a Harley-Davidson '59 DuoGlide with mile-high custom handlebars and a low-rider seat over a flaming gas tank – tearing a strip down the tarmac. . . .

FUCK pulls over to prop the bike up on a hill overlooking a playground by the side of the highway. Up at a window, an imprisoned schoolboy is watching him: poor Robbie Bookbinder wishing he, too, were out here enjoying the smells of the roasted earth and the bike's ticking hot engine. FUCK crooks one finger at a sullen-looking girl with a face like a fieldmouse who's refusing to join in an organized game of volleyball. *What a bitchin' split, ain't she one hot mama.* He swings her into his bucket seat and squeals off down the road. Robbie, meanwhile, has some trouble putting his gentler ache into words. He looks on

113

longingly and considers how edible the surfaces of her must be. Sweet and bitter berries. He passes a hand over his chest and cups an imaginary breast. Closing his eyelids, slow and contented as a lion on a sunbaked rock, and wishing, wishing he could for once be possessed of the comfort he imagines sexiness gives a girl. And when he opens them again, there's M. Nul smiling behind his beard. And the whole class is looking too, among them the impeccably neat Nono, sporting a nifty pair of mustard double-knit slacks and a case of acne like an all-dressed pizza; Pharte, with four eyes and a spine so straight you'd think his bowels were rock hard from end to end – who plays, it is rumoured, le soccer all alone with his mother after school; and Boniface, as skinny as a praying mantis, poised above his test paper like he's saying grace before gobbling the baby answers alive. Robbie shoots glares all around, like, what *is* this? I honestly cannot relate! What have *you* geeks got that makes you so damn superior?

At lunch he went to the neighbourhood dépanneur run by *les p'tits juifs*, which means the little Jews; they were very little, indeed, the old man and his wife – when they reached their hands over the counter for money, their tattooed wrists slipped out from their sleeves, and that made all the pepsis smirk.

There are winter days in Montreal so cold you can crack the air over your knee. Robbie frequently split at lunch hour, insulating himself as he did now, by chug-a-lugging three or four stubbies of Champlain porter as he circled the block, duh-dumming heavy nose guitar solos under his visible breath, knapsack clinking in rhythm with his step. When this time the bell finally rang, he was affectionately writing Ivy's name across a snowbank in hot, steaming pee.

The art room was six storeys up, in the old building's attic. He pushed through the clot of students, raced up the

114

twisting stairwell, and hid in an upstairs can. Well, what was the point of sitting at his desk, now? His fingers were so numb he could barely fish out his little hardened weenie (Ivy's name being so short he'd returned with a still chilled and swollen bladder), let alone hold a pen in class. He snuck up two more flights to the uppermost landing. From so high the clatter of the classrooms sounded remote. His rock 'n' roll heels were loud on the creaking wooden floor, and left coins of slush behind him. He crouched, listening to doors close, one by one. He felt like a lurking young ghost, a poltergeist from some earlier century's educational system; the victim of one brutal thrashing too many, doomed to wail over an eternally stinging bottom.

The attic door was locked. He knocked and waited. Ivy opened it a crack.

"Come into my parlour," she whispered.

"Too much," Robbie whispered back.

"I'm wasting my time in English class, so they let me. Like I said, being smart is an incredible excuse to be bad."

"Far *out*. I'm gonna tell 'em as far as English, eh, tests and that equal a ditto waste for me, too."

She locked the door. "Come see."

She had spread a large sheet of cloth over a table and, copying from a book, was well into an intricate design; an interlacing of tendrils and bunches of fruit and flowers – mango, pomegranate, banana, hibiscus – populated by a variety of beasts.

"It's batik," she said. "Lookit. In Indonesia they use metal printing blocks, but if you're a purist, like me, you use this."

She held up a wooden-handled tool with a small copper vessel at the end, pointed like the nib of a busted fountain pen. The vessel was hinged with a simple copper tab and filled with molten wax. Ivy demonstrated, pulling back the tab with her thumb and drawing the vessel carefully across

115

a length of half-finished cloth; she left a shimmering snail's trail of wax that dulled as it sank in and dried. "Then you dunk it in the dye. Colour by colour. The dark colours, like indigo, they go on last. Finally you boil off the wax. Up comes the pattern, like magic."

"Like an Easter egg," Robbie said. "Far-out smell. First thing I noticed about you."

Ivy frowned at her design. "Beeswax and paraffin, from Sumatra. It's imported specially. There's a company. . . . Look how when you crack the wax like this the dye seeps in and makes a marbly effect. This is *supit urang*, which is pincers of the lobster. See. Here's a peacock. Here's a phoenix – "

"You should add a TV set, and some hockey sticks. That would make it a truly Canadian work of art."

" – and a *kala* mask. It's supposed to look like a lion." She stopped to glare at him. "You're right, I'm useless. I bet you could do a better job."

He hooked his chin over her shoulder. "No," he said. "It's really well done."

"God," she said, shrugging him off. "I hate when people watch me. So *quit*. Lookit, there's paper and pencils in the drawers over there. Why don't you do something for yourself?"

"K, I'll draw you."

"*I'll* kill *you* if you try."

He laid out several sheets and sharpened a pencil. While she worked he sat poised, looking her over, following the curves of her, weighing the air around her.

"God, I hate you," she said.

He tried the leaping line of her nose, but his hand was tense. He erased, tried again. *Wrong, fuck.* Erased again. The pencil squirmed between his wet fingers.

A while later he gave up, crumpled the paper. Despondently looked through the window. The afternoon was getting on. Two jets made white slices across the sky like skates on dull grey ice. Ivy had a small gas campstove lit, above its blue flame a pot filled with simmering beeswax. He wandered over. He made to dip his forefinger in, but she stopped him.

"Don't touch, you idiot. You'll go and burn yourself and knock the thing over. Here. Let me show you something else."

First she opened the window. Then she speared a little ball of hash on the end of a brooch pin she had pulled from her cardigan. Slowly she heated it at the flame, and, when it was soft enough, transferred it to the bowl of a little silver pipe she pulled from her Afghan coat. Then she held the pipe over the flame, and as the drug sizzled and burnt, she sucked up great lungfuls of its acrid smoke. The room was plunged into ash-grey air, and Robbie felt zonked enough just standing next to her. This stuff was way heavier than hash – as soon as he had a real toke he felt sleepy and sick.

"Man," he said, sitting down on the floor. "Are you ever full of surprises."

"*Life will be convulsive*, don't you remember? *Or not at all.*"

"I think so. Yeah, right. I get it now."

She plops a sheaf of drawing paper on his lap, and rolls some pencils clicking across the floor. Robbie looks at them stupidly. His arms are filled with lead. Then she undresses. Just like that. And sits demurely on a chair, arms folded, legs braided. This is her torso: as light and flat as a packet of Sugar Krunchies; slight, squared-off shoulders, a flat chest, and a boxy pelvis. He picks up a pencil. It's like balsa wood, yet it also weighs a ton. He concentrates as hard as he can, but his sketches are still shrunken and scratchy and tense, headless and footless like an ancient Roman ruin. Then, in a murky grab at inspiration, he adds a flourish from the headless neck, a quite unrelated arabesque. *Fun.* He draws some whirly

117

clouds, some paisley hills. *Yahoo!* Pretty soon he's doodling out of control, and signing it extravagantly before he's even done.

I know what you're thinking, Ivy says, or seems to have said. She's looking shyly over her bare shoulder. *I have a body like Gumby.*

Yeah, maybe, he says, abruptly straightening his back. *But no way I can concentrate on drawing now. This heavy stuff, or what.*

What do you mean, maybe. Fucker. It's opium.

Whoa. Figures.

She pulls him up by his hand, not a little roughly. *C'mon,* he distantly hears her say. Still nude, she leads him to the top of the stairs. It's dark here, a corridor with doors to two or three other, smaller rooms: a bathroom, a locked storage space, and a cubbyhole nearly as bare as Ivy at the end. He's sleepwalking now. The tiny cell contains a single stained glass window, a chipped porcelain chamberpot, a kneeling stool, a brass bedframe without a mattress, and a white shadow where a crucifix once hung on the wall. *They think it's locked up,* Ivy's saying, *Curious . . . tried the door . . . olden days . . . old Grande Dame Blanchemains . . . incredible . . .*

He sniffs the cool musty air. Looks out through the window. Feels like they're checking out an apartment. She stands with her hand on the brass bedpost, her luminous head above her naked shoulders, pale as a ghost. He laughs uncertainly and says, or hears himself say, or what did he say? He can't remember.

Together they watch the first-graders plop about on the ice rink below. They stand hip to hip in silence, hearing the distant shouts, the traffic on the slushy streets. Robbie rubs his forefingers and thumbs together, and the tips are numb. A gust of wind, and a veil of snow is pulled across the window from the outside, the gutter its curtain rail. He clears his throat. The dust up here is making his sinuses ooze. Like Siamese twins he and Ivy stand, the conjoined hip not like bone, but glowing coal. He wants to laugh, he wants to cry. What was that, did she pull her hip away, or was she just falling off balance, the way you will when you're trying to hold so perfectly still? Will they get married, or are they already breaking up forever? Distantly, a ruler cracks on a desktop and a class erupts in laughter. *School's out forever.* Ivy blows her bangs off her forehead. Then turns and stamps back into the art room. Robbie's bowels are turned right upside-down now. His guts sink slowly like chilled tripe in a jar. After a while she returns fully clothed, Afghan coat and all. She holds out his khaki parka. And the next thing he knows she's dragging him down the dark stairs like a dummy.

"What a mess. You look like you're in need of a haircut."

When Robbie first met Ivy's father, it was not under the best of circumstances, mainly because Robbie was stoned again and had the roaring munchies. He sits on the carpet, noisily wolfing Cheese Puffs from the big glass bowl on the living-room coffee table, while Mr. Mills paces and quizzes him about his father's occupation.

"Well, my mother, she does a TV show." Cheese Puff crumbs cling to his hair. He tries to brush them out, but his fingertips are a gooey orange and only make a worse mess. Mr. Mills meanwhile twiddles his thumbs like he's winding up some vicious mechanism in his fists. Robbie pegs the guy for a malevolent teddy bear, with the straw emerging from his head where the little round ears were yanked too much as a baby bear, the stitches coming out of his tight little smile.

"Like all children, I see you like junk food."

Robbie nods. Cheese Puff earthquake in his ears. Mrs. Mills meanwhile is sitting at the kitchen table in the adjoining room of this tiny apartment, chopping vegetables.

"Compare at New York, Montreal is a safe city," she's saying. Robbie puts his hand to his chest, mouthing, *me?*, but she seems to be talking to herself. "Those tourist I saw, they ad nylon windbreaker from Allemagne là, with the best rainproofing. Alors les Allemands, what can you do, they are like that, an they ave cultural centres. That fellow e move so fast, e was a football player, I know, you don't ave to tell me, I'm more intuit then you think."

"Did you know," Mr. Mills says, just pleasantly chatting, "that French Canadians drink the most pop in Canada? And did you know that sugar and caffeine have a negative long-term effect on learning in children, so it's scientifically proven that pepsis are the most stupid people from sea to shining sea?"

Robbie wonders if this really is a test. Pulls a weak, ambiguous smile. And now the Cheese Puffs are all gone. He's eaten the entire bowl. Ivy's brother darts his head into the room to look, and then the sister does the same, head and shoulders only, like a Punch and Judy puppet show. At last Ivy appears, dressed for the school dance. She pulls a long face and drags him up by the hand.

"Wow," Robbie says in the corridor. "Do people still *think* that way?"

"What do you expect? The father's all for royal rule over the Dominion. He collects proven facts about pepsis. You're an idiot to come here. I never asked you."

The stone was wearing off now. He wiped the sweat from his forehead. *Terrific timing, stupid.* He padded gingerly after her as she led him through the dim apartment; the Mills lived in a cramped box in St. Henri, a scoop of gravel south of the Canadian-Pacific tracks. Besides its smell of batik, the first thing he noticed was that there were rim marks all over the furniture; some fresh and sticky, some a faint outline, some buffed but still visible in pale circles where previous layers of lemon wax had been clouded over.

He felt privileged to be there; he was hushed and appreciative, absorbing all the precious details of the Place Ivy Lived In, like it was a church or museum. There was where she bathed, there was where she curled up to read, there was where she studied, there was where she slept. He saw the place criss-crossed with trails of her gentle energy, luminous as a snail's.

Her bedroom was a jackdaw's nest, a warren of lustrous stuff: a tuba with a dull skin of tarnish stood on its mouth in the corner; a futon lay in another, buried under batik cushions; a swollen-bosomed chest of drawers sat in a third, her underwear everywhere so that Robbie didn't know where to look. Books, magazines, and sheafs of paper spilled off bowing shelves. On a desk was a mannequin's head with a veil and an ostrich feather, a tin of aniseed balls, a shoeboxful of cassettes, a Ouija board, and a boxed record set: the classic Strolling Bones' live album, the famous rare R.I.P. Keef Richards limited-edition, containing the vial of Keef's actual blood. He picked it up reverently as a CP train rumbled by Ivy's window.

There were four guys in the Bones: Spit Swagger, Bile, Jerusalem Slim and, of course, Keef. They had been through thick and thin since the sixties, suffering the death of only one of their founding members, whose name no one could recall. They had rats-nest hair down to their shoulders, and wore elaborate outfits like the decadents of the nineteenth century – wigs, ruffs, calf stockings, a plague of beauty spots – layered over with post-nuclear accessories like can openers, Saigon mirror sunglasses, burnt and bullet-shattered guitars, and leather jackets bristling with half-inch shells like the armour on a small herd of metallic stegosauruses. They were in Tangiers in this photo, Keef sipping mint tea and smoking a sebsi from a calabash pipe on the balcony of the Toubkal Café, and the others were striking bored and arrogant poses for the camera. Their skin was pockmarked, their legs were like stalks, and their sprayed-on satin pants threatened to come apart at the seams. They wore bored expressions with smudges for eyes; they looked as if they were all about to nod out, and probably would, as soon as the photo session was over.

"This is a valuable collector's item." Robbie said in awe. "You must be a real fan."

"I'm not a fan. I worship him. Look, he signed it for me."

"You *know* him? Isn't Keef dead? My Dad says one day they'll dig him up and think he's evolution's missing link. When we were kids, Dad took us to see *One Million Years B.C.*, and he said, Hey look, Keef Richards finally found a job. Laff riot, eh, my Dad?"

"Oh, he's not dead," Ivy said breathlessly. "That haemorrhage thing was just an experiment to push the limit of his existence. Now he says he knows there's nothing after life, and that *God* spelled backwards is *doG*."

Robbie wasn't so sure of that, exactly. One story he'd heard was that Keef was in such bad shape he used to blow blood through the holes in his harmonica, and things really bottomed out the day they were taping an appearance on the Sonny and Cher show; all that was required was a little lip-synching, but Keef wasn't into moving his lips that day – they'd called a break, and then he'd almost died in the studio can, attempting to move his rock-hard bowels. Robbie hadn't heard *doG* mentioned at all.

They sat down on the bed cross-legged, knees touching. Ivy spilled a bunch of old photographs from an envelope, some of them faded grey-and-white, square, with a date stamped on the serrated border. She flipped through them quickly, tossing them down without comment. Baby Ivy in diapers. Ivy cuddling her sister. And in the more recent ones, Robbie noted sourly, Ivy with a lot of male friends, with greasy denim jackets and bunches of keys as big as fists dangling from their belts. In one picture, two of them were holding her horizontally above their heads.

"Oh, who's that there?" he said, real casual, and his question rang in his ears. An infected question, he knew. But still he needed to hear the answer. She lit a cigarette first.

"My oldest brother. Who did you think?"

"I wasn't sure, I – "

"Typical. You're jealous, right?"

"No, not exactly, I – "

"Well, while you're being jealous of the people in my past, you could get jealous of all the boys I *haven't* met yet. There's going to be pictures of them sooner or later. My brother's in jail. This one's of me when I was anorexic."

"Wow. Like a concentration-camp victim."

"That's why I'm so fat now."

"You're not fat now."

"In the hospital they dragged me out of bed and took off my shift. The doctor and the nurse held me up by my armpits and stood me in front of a mirror. I could see all my bones, all hung up in a bag of skin. I didn't recognize myself at all. This is me in Grade 7. That's when I first did acid. And this is me and my tuba teacher."

"He's hugging you. Were you friends?"

"And this is me when I ran away to Paris."

"Do you ever look polluted!"

"All I did was drink anise. Want to hear my writing?"

Robbie listened and Ivy read. She punctuated her sentences with puffs on her cigarettes, pausing when a train rumbled by, absently brushing flakes of tobacco from her pillow. And in the impossible deliciousness of the moment, Robbie wished he were a flake of tobacco on that pillow!

"i drink myself sober tasting the tears before they are revealed
how can we love a child so lost within a heart hardened to stone
i hate to be held close and feel warmth yet so many have walked

123

*in and penetrated me touched my soul leaving me to bleed i put
on a face and paint my lips with my own blood and go somewhere
crowded to feel lonely together God Bless the miserable Bleeding
Hearts of Artists les artistes qui cherchent l'angoisse they're all
you need to brighten a lousy day you don't dream it you have to
be it i have kissed farewell to my dreams and gone out to play on
the tracks with the naive idiot hopefuls of the world."*

She looked up with flushed cheeks. Scrunched her hair
up, gathering it off her forehead. Rolled a fresh cigarette,
while the old one still smouldered between her lips. "What
do you think?" she whispered. "Is it incredible?"

"Um, well," Robbie said carefully. "Yes. *Really* incredible. But it's like, hard to tell, such a short bit. I dunno what
to, exactly. Aumm. Shouldn't we go to the dance now?"

It was a dance, but they didn't dance. Ivy brooded in a
corner, Robbie fretted that his evaluation had not been
generous enough. He offered to buy her a Cott's Cola for
a mix; they'd been nipping from a bottle of white alcohol
– the generic kind with the moose label that you could get
at the Société d'Alcool – and raw, it caused him to shudder
like a washing machine on the rinse cycle. He went off
across the crowded gym.

When he returned she was gone. He looked around,
searching the strobe-lit crowd on the dance floor. Under
the basketball hoop on the other side of the gym he made
out Gaston Goupil's friends, lined up against the wall like
they'd been hung there to dry. And two of them at least
had dressed formally for the dance: they were wearing
black sleeveless jean jackets with aces and eights – Dead
Man's Hands' colours – all over them. King Dork himself
wasn't there, Robbie noticed, drinking his fizzy teen drink
and watching the couples slowdance to "Je T'Aime . . . Moi
Non Plus" as tentatively, feet as uncertain, as old people.

Eventually Ivy reappeared, looking dishevelled, her hair raked upwards like wet fur.

"What happened, what *happened*?" he said.

"Ask me no questions. . . . " she spat.

After the dance, one sullen hour later, they held hands at the bus stop, still saying nothing. The cold air stuck Robbie's nostrils together. Ivy's snout was running, pumping out steam. They had to wait a long time for the Westmount bus; all the other kids were going the other way, and soon Van Horne was desolate and silent – only laughter somewhere in the neighbourhood, clattering over the hardened streets. Robbie stamped his feet to bring back the circulation. Ivy bent over double with her Afghan coat hanging open, frozen to the bus stop like an Arctic fox in a trap. Now that laughter came unexpectedly around a corner, coming hard with the clink of heavy keychains and the crunch of hobnailed boots on ice: Gaston et Co., beers in hand, smiling way too congenially. Robbie put a pistol to his head and fired.

"Awé donc, mon hosti chienne de bloke."

"Let's go," Ivy said quickly. She pulled Robbie's arm and tried to walk away, but the pepsis sandwiched them, slapping their backs like good old friends, and hauled them into the alley behind the school. As they faced off under a lamp post, Robbie thought of the way the *Montreal Star* would interpret this situation; they'd call it a *political* confrontation, one in which the angry French Canadians, who have been exploited by the maudit anglais for centuries, are finally bucking the yoke and turning on their oppressors. This conflict may *appear* to be about some bum weed or a girl, but it is really a microcosm of the healthy secessionist struggle.

"Hé, mon p'tit gar. Fa frette dewowr, hein?"

"Hey, man," Robbie said, super-diplomatic at this street corner summit meeting, and putting on his quackingest joual accent. "Ça va tu ben, Gaston? Ain't it past your bedtime, guy?"

Gaston looked at his friends, and jerked a thumb in Robbie's direction. "Qu'i v'en manger une bonne." Then he hugged Ivy hard. In return she shoved his nose with the base of her mittened palm. "Ayoi!" he said, holding his nose. "Maudite marde."

That made his friends guffaw. Robbie laughed too. He was thinking, Well, that's that, and not looking out when a fist knocked his face sideways. Actually, he saw the fist before it hit, just for a second. He thought about how to stop it: he could duck, or he could put his free arm up to protect himself, or he could hack his assailant's arm sideways, just like in those kung fu flics where Bruce Lee goes *chop chop* in slow-mo. Or he could get smacked in the face, which is what he did. His front teeth stung and his nose throbbed – a stabbing pain that made him aware of just how thinly the flesh is laid over the skull, of how the head's a lump of bone. He put his hand to his mouth to check for blood, but he was wearing mitts just like Ivy, and all he got was a mouthful of bland wool. Distantly, he heard her hiss, "God, just fuck *off* va te faire foutre OK?"

Someone gripped Robbie by the back of the neck. He was bent over and squeezed tight, his head against a studded belt. A bunch of keys hanging from the belt scraped against the bridge of his nose as he was hustled forward in a swirl of clothing and buffeting bodies and hissing from Ivy and a couple more *ayoi*'s. They marched him further down the alley into the shadows. He tried to wrench free, but he couldn't make the slightest move, appalled at his own weakness. He was bent so low he feared he'd fall on his face. The heaps of snow and ice that zoomed by below him were a dark Alpine landscape as seen from a small, pitching aircraft. He saw the glistening of trickled ice on an iron drainpipe ahead of him. *Chrissake*. He clamped his mouth shut, tucked his chin to his chest. He was yanked back up by his long hair. Gaston held his jaw, pushed his face against the icy pipe and said hotly in his ear, "Lèche ça, mon chum." Robbie could turn his head only a fraction. He rolled his eyes to find Ivy. His head was swivelled back and the nostrils of his bruising nose were squeezed together. When he opened his mouth to breathe, his head was shoved forward again. His teeth banged against the metal and his tongue, his tongue stuck fast.

All in a flurry, then: Ivy screaming, Gaston and his pals going *Har har mon hosti*, the close wail of a siren, Gaston shouting *Les boeufs!* and taking off across the ice. A policeman with cigar breath and a badged Cossack hat, strings hanging down from the ear muffs, closely examining Robbie's predicament. Robbie feeling more shame than pain, Ivy on his other side saying I told you about those guys you should listen to me next time OK. I better go to Pendeli's for some hot water. Robbie going *elllh* and swivelling his eyeballs like a poor dumb beast. He's trying to gently peel his tongue from the pipe, but when he does there's a sensation of deeply embedded needles. And in this winter night air his eyes are very blurry and warm with tears, which at least may melt this terrible ice.

That weekend she took him to her brother Olly's place (the one *not* in jail, he guessed) on a brand-new development plot in Côte St.-Luc. It was still under construction, all trailers and gouged frozen earth, plywood skeletons and exposed insulation, unshingled walls wrapped with candy-stripe sheathing, each house resembling a child's sketch of the perfect home, and you counted the fifth salted driveway on the crescent to identify Olly's. As they got off the bus, Robbie brooded that Ivy hadn't even asked how he felt.

"I know what you're thinking," she said, when at last she noticed his long face, "but why should I waste words? You're obviously happy enough to see me. And you've been talking non-stop for the last half-hour, so your tongue's obviously in working order. What else do you need from me?"

He shrugged and asked her what her brother did.

"Stuff."

"What kind of stuff, exactly?"

" – "

"K, OK, I know. Ask you no questions you'll tell me no lies."

He'd never live in a suburban nightmare like this, not in a million years. When he got famous he'd buy a Tudor country estate like Keef's. He'd read about it in Mom's *House and Garden*: Addams Family style, with spiky trellises on the roof and a spidery weathervane, creepy tangled vegetation flourishing on the grounds, a real garden of delights: Venus flytraps, poison ivy, grotesque warty mushrooms, mammoth hollyhocks, mad Van Gogh sunflowers, and ferns as impenetrable as bales of barbed wire. If Robbie had a garden – not the trimmed rectangle the size of a bridge table that passed for a yard around here – he'd plant all those things too, plus install a moat with an alligator to take care of mailmen, and kids who'd thrown their frisbees wild.

"Oh, hey, don't point that thing at guests!" Olly's wife Karen said. "Cissy, I said put that gun *down*." The two-year-old stood at the front door clutching a dull black pistol in her sticky fists. Robbie pulled a game smile, looked at her fat little legs, the ketchup and the crumbs on her face, the rubber diaper as swollen as a dinghy.

"You're thinkin these kids have unusual hobbies, eh," Karen said, smiling back apologetically. "Collectin Nazi memorabilia an nat?"

"No, no," Robbie said, taking a chair, real casual, at the kitchen table. "Different strokes, right?"

There were two other children, one still an infant in a towering highchair, the other a five-year-old grabbing only at things Cissy had already picked up. And, oh look, Robbie's Mom was on the television on the counter, turned up loud. She was doing a sunny story on disappearing vacation spots and the erosion of archaeological treasures by air pollution. Now there was a tug-of-war over the Luger. Karen bent down to separate the babies, and Robbie got a faceful of cellulite – the loose trunks of her thighs, squeezed into an old pair of denim cut-offs, favourites from a slimmer time – crossed with red striations where the seams had bitten in.

"Bendin down like this," she said, "always makes me think about how the worst part of a prostitute's job eh, apart from standin in the freezin rain, is bendin down to look in cars. They must have terrible bad backs, specially since they gotta stand fer hours on them stupid heels."

"That's not the *worst* part," Robbie said, but the words came out more tersely than he had intended; he'd figured on starting a cordial conversation, but he now realized what a sour mood Ivy had put him in with her infuriating silences and evasions. And, *Chrissake*, what kind of psycho family was this? His whole body had stiffened with moral rectitude. "I mean, what about the job itself?"

"Aw, who is this guy, Ivy honey?" Karen said, patting Cissy's diaper and wrinkling her nose.

. . . and did you know, Mom was saying, your hair dyes are tested on the eyes of rabbits? And how about the expression 'mad as a hatter' – hatters used to soften fur with mercury to make felt linings, but now it's been documented that mercury poisoning will result in shrunken brain cells . . .

"Way I see it," Robbie pronounced, taking a righteous

slurp of beer, "if they're not happy they should take a job at the Baron." Mom was in front of the Great Pyramid of Giza now, and now Big Ben, and said *G'bye World!* Karen switched the TV off, and exchanged a glance with Ivy.

"OK, you guys, I'm just gonna change this little monster. Why doncha play pool if you want?" She laughed and looked dead at Robbie. "We got a real table, down in the den. Betcha get tired of just playing *pocket* pool, eh, Mr. Big Balls?"

Downstairs Ivy put on a Bones record and racked up, while Robbie snooped, his cheeks still burning. On a desk with a typewriter, *The History of Firearms*. He flipped through it idly. The typewriter, he noticed, sat on a place-mat whose rubber bristles made up a Harley-Davidson logo. There were some cheap pool trophies on a shelf, and a heavier-duty one fashioned from a camshaft and mounted on a block of wood with a plaque.

"Oh. Your brother ride a bike?"

"If you say so," Ivy said. "Your break."

He inspected a photograph propped against the trophy. There was Karen, and a bunch of guys with heavy beards and filthy jean jackets and keychains and tattoos. Chris-sake, Robbie thought. The real McCoy.

He broke, sewered the cue ball. Soon after that, as Ivy hunkered down to pocket her fourth ball in a row, he looked around some more, just to prove how losing didn't faze him a bit. On one wall hung two Indonesian shadow puppets – two demons, it looked like – on another a Day-Glo poster of a groovy couple fucking against a cosmic backdrop, and on a third a Strolling Bones mirror featuring Keef Richards naked and nailed to a cross backwards, his spine pushing out the flesh like a row of spikes. Into the mirror's frame was tucked a strip of photos from an automatic photo booth, and there was Spit Swagger grinning darkly and Karen crammed in on his lap, shirtless, braless by the third snap, and laughing by the fourth.

"Wow," Robbie said. "Does Karen *know* Spit?"

" – "

A few feet away from the mirror was a coatstand. Hanging from it was a black shirt. A patch representing a hand of cards had been sewn on the shoulder. Robbie held the sleeve up to get a better look. Ivy put some wicked English on the cue ball. Five cards sprayed with bullet holes: pair of aces, pair of eights, and one joker skull. "Chrissake," he said aloud. "Olly's a Dead Man's Hand, isn't he?"

"*Chrissake*," Ivy mimicked. "No, not at all. If you must know, he's the president."

"Wow," Robbie said, gingerly feeling the sore tip of his tongue.

From behind the desk Ivy pulled out a heavy sheaf of papers, fatter than a phone book, bound in a blue file.

"Transcripts, lookit," she whispered proudly. "This is every phone call made to and from this house for the last two years. Exhibit 'A'. The RCMP says that after the Mafia and the Angels and the Outlaws, they're the most powerful organized-crime group in the province. They know who Olly is, they've been trying to nail him forever, but he's so incredibly clever nothing sticks. A couple of guys got some time, but not Olly. He's respectable. He's rich too: rule of the club is that his salary always matches what the prime minister makes."

"But, like, I know all about bikers, right," Robbie said.

"That must be nice for you," Ivy said, stiffening.

"Yeah," Robbie said. "Does he have a Filthy Few patch?"

"What, that says he's killed for the club? Don't be an idiot. The only thing like that he ever boasted about was the time the neighbour's cat kept him up meowing all night. He told me he lured the cat in with a kipper, smashed its brains out with a hammer, put it in the deep freeze overnight, and put it back on the doorstep, paws up, with the neighbour's morning paper in its mouth. Isn't that incredible?"

Olly Mills arrived home. Robbie had expected him to be at the vanguard of a roaring metal horde, all spit and greasy hair and Nazi helmets, spewing salt and ice behind them, but looking up through the casement window he could see the wheels of a nice mustard Chevrolet pull up the driveway without so much as a squeal. Olly was taller and leaner than Robbie, his hair was shorter too, and he barely had a beer gut at all. He looked like a dentist, home from Sunday golf.

They sat around the kitchen table, the babies splashing on the floor in an inflatable Scoobie Doo wading pool. Olly was quiet and gracious and Ivy was more alert than Robbie had ever seen her. She asked questions, told him awful stories about school, fetched him beers, gave him a shoulder rub, and explained anything he wanted to know. Robbie sat there like a hairy gargoyle, despising her utterly, and trying to work up the courage to ask Olly if he knew Gaston Goupil and if, by any small chance, he could ask him to lay the fuck off. Olly picked Cissy up and dandled her on his knee, and Robbie thought of all the newspaper stories he had read about how bikers are the scum of the earth, gun runners, extortionists, hired killers, drug dealers, robbers, porn dealers, loan sharks, professional rapists, and lords of the white slave-trade, all in a day's work. And here he was in the kitchen of Mr. and Mrs. Burb. What outrages had Robbie read about, and registered with a mixture of revulsion and awe? There was that story about a biker's old lady in St. Jovite who wouldn't participate in a gang bang, so her old man nailed her to a pine tree – she didn't scream or even protest, and only went to hospital because the infections in her palms made it impossible to give hand jobs to customers. Then hadn't three Aces and Eights been fished out of Lake Kilborn just last summer? Cops said it was a gang war because the bloated bodies had been wrapped in sleeping bags and anchored with chains and cinder blocks, which was the Hell's Angels' trademark.

An hour later, Robbie was shaking the hand of the president of the Dead Man's Hands goodbye.

Ivy kissed her brother and said, "I left the batik for you in the living room. See you."

As they slid around the icy crescent, Robbie was exploding with questions he knew Ivy would never answer. He tried one anyway. "Neat. Olly do batik too?"

" – "

They rode the bus home in silence.

9

LIKE DAD HAD WANTED HIM TO DO SO BAD AT THAT BUM-
mer of a Seder, Robbie buzzed off. He got out. He got *way*
out – two damp nights on the Coke-skinned floor of the
Roxy, and two more chilly ones sitting propped up inside
the Westmount Kiosk, with the wind buffeting the wooden
walls. Finally Rosie found him in Dominion Square, ar-
guing noisily over a game of chess with Joe Smolij, and
took him home for a hot bath – even old Joe, who smelled
like a bowl of mouldy polewka, had flared his thistly
nostrils when Robbie first put his dollar down. True to her
word, meanwhile, she'd spoken to a friend who, luckily,
had moved out of her apartment that Labour Day weekend, and needed a new tenant to sublet immediately.

"Sorry I didn't get a better price for that Bones ticket,"
Robbie said, by way of thanking her.

"S'OK, Bob," she replied, kissing him. "I know what it's
like sometimes, not to see the woods for the trees."

"Mn-hm," he said doubtfully, hoping that by this sylvan
metaphor she did not mean the better aspects of herself.
He thought of a Chinese fortune cookie he'd once read:
woman's heart like hotel – room for everyone, and *that* was more
like Rosie; her heart was as big as the Holiday Inn at

Niagara Falls – way too big for him, too indiscriminately accommodating, with DOUBLE ROOMS AT CUT-RATE PRICES! – not his style at all. In fact he felt kind of sorry for her. K, it was nice that she was helping him out, just this once, but she'd have to realize that since he was on his own now it would be *unhealthy* for him to lean on his friends too much; put more plainly, she'd just have to stop glomming onto him.

That had been a week ago. Now this cool September morning in the neutral light of dawn, the walls of his mouth numb with bourbon, the stuff of his brain swollen up, he had the experience of swimming over rooftops. Having drunk himself sober and stayed up long enough to overcome fatigue, he was staring out the bedroom window of his new apartment on Berdnikoff Avenue, through its membrane of pale dirt, thinking. Feeling. In jags. The only colour out on the street was a crackling neon billboard displaying the latest in Eccelucci's famous line of sensuous lingerie. The street was deserted here, under the eastern bluffs of the mountain. Clouds scudded over his new neighbourhood with its spiked iron fences and dusty doilied windowsills and dark apartments. On the sidewalk, a tricycle lay abandoned on its side, its frame wet with morning dew, a piece of bedraggled string trailing from its handlebars. Like a newborn baby bike.

Robbie had the second floor of four, accessed by a winding staircase with curlicued iron railings. Similar staircases braced similar buildings all down the street, some twisted and some straight, each one with a skin of cracking green paint as thick as bark. Across the road he could see the windows of other apartment hollows, each with a blue fluttering TV heart, and through the floor Mom was giving the third degree to some industrialist about miscarriages and stillbirths. The mist had shrouded downtown, leaving only the broken teeth of the city. The rain-streaked concrete bunkers they call apartment buildings squatted cinder-grey at intervals, as if this was all that was left after the apocalypse: Montreal reduced to a stone garden, eerily quiet, its population evaporated, people's phantom shadows printed on the walls and sidewalks, cars welded to the roads.

Rosie was crashed on his mattress, Brat on the floor wearing sunglasses with a crumpled cigarette behind one ear. Louie Louie had already crawled off to the poultry factory, holding his head and complaining of a shrunken skull. What a night. Robbie could only remember it in one big bundle: the jammed toilet at Arthur's Hideaway stinking of urine. Mirror's gone, smashed long ago, nothing but a shiny steel plate on the wall now. Him peering in. His anamorphous reflection, the real him: *his metal soul*. People are shoving in line for a turn at the urinals, scribbling, leaning over, comparing notes. The concrete graffitied walls. GO HOME LES MAUDITS BLOKES. He's suffering from a bashful bladder – the pepsi goon squad's threatening to squash his incredible shrinking penis against the cold and slimy porcelain, and all he wants is a private, unpolitical pee, thank you very much. Standing there thinking of waterfalls. Complicated mathematical equations. Anything. Hopeless, he's terrible at math. It's hypotenuseless. Faking a shiver, turns around aching and ashamed. Happily spies a vacant cubicle just then. Inside he leans with one foot braced back against the lockless door. Balanced on the other foot aiming as best he can. Wad of bloody tissue swells in the bowl. His own piss sounds like rain on a cardboard box. Pops a Quaalude and starts to count his money from an envelope. Amazing: one thousand clams. His kicker for this new life, tax free, all in cash. Plus a note, in Mom's handwriting: Lots of luck, darling. Don't spend it all in one place. When she handed him the envelope and Dad shook his hand, he'd wanted to say, No thanks, I'll manage. But he didn't, so here it is. A flushing from the Ladies on the other side of the wall draws the water in his toilet down a little, and now the tissue looks like a jellyfish with its network of pulsing transparent arteries. He tries to stuff back all the bills, but a fiver slips out and twirls into the toilet. Fuck it, proclaims Robbie the Rich spitting royal spit, kicking the flush handle with his sneaker. Rolls back up the stairs bandy-legged, like a squid in warm water. This is the life, wallowing in the buzz of guitars like skiffs skipping on choppy whiteheads, fish with aluminum wings, seagulls with jet engines, electric veils of seaspray on the breeze. At the bar a jagged redhead sits alone, stirring her drink with a long fingernail. Robbie leans up against that amazing bleeping new video game called *Pong* – you bounce a little square blip (the tennis ball) off a little rectangular blip (the racquet), and welcome to the twentieth century! Pulls out his envelope. Robbie the Mighty, laden with booty, having pillaged, ready now to play *Pong*. The redhead's hair is lacquered into antennae, her tile-red leather gear layered like armour. A boiled but living lobster. He imagines her naked, skinny and pale, ochre freckles all over her flesh. Exoskeletal ribs and rust-coloured pubic hair, sharp as razor blades. Heels on her feet that would slide out of her boots like the flesh in a crustacean's claws. Their eyes meet now. Her expression: complete and utter disdain. Robbie shrugs and returns to his friends at a battered round table. Buys everyone a brew, winning many pledges of allegiance. The big buzz at the court is re: their old men. Brat's is stinking rich, he owns Lovely Enterprises. Louie Louie, tabernouche, is papa as retire an watch de hockey an de game show all de days. E tink Louie's a failure, but, calice, e'll be surprise. Rosie's Daddy wishes he could have his daughter back, the one with the long blonde hair who used to read *Cosmo*, not this vampire queen, this utter stranger who comes home only to feed and fight. *Just shows to go ya*, she says, *home is where the hurt is*. Lovely Enterprises meanwhile distribute plastic squeezers for toothpaste tubes and sno-globe paper-weights and portraits of clowns on velvet. Hey, someone's got to do it. Lovely Tunes for the perfect office environment. Lovely sentimental memory cards and posters. Lovely bargain-basement makeup. Lovely kiddie party loot bags, whoopie cushions, X-ray Spex, and square egg-makers. Soon the human race will expire, the cities will erode and rust down, leaving only Lovely Enterprises' non-biodegradable empire. Alien archaeologists will sift through mountains of the Lovely plastic shit and have one bizarre time reconstructing this society, fuck. Ferocious chainsaw music thunders over the PA, sending strong alternating currents underground – the figures on the dance floor are tattered rats leaping about in an electrified cage. Robbie goes to the pool table, the felt blotched with booze and blood. A clutch of biker mamas, *bitchin splits*, are shooting a game. He lays a sawbuck on the table, grabbing a tipless cue like a lance. No one picks up the gauntlet. They play in a grim, defiant silence, stabbing at the cue ball with authority, cigarette smoke crawling up their cheeks, eyelids convulsing in squints, thorny-rose bumblebee death's head chained-flesh tattoos slipping out from under their clothes as they bend over. Ignoring him completely. No matter: later, how much later he can't remember, they're all leaning against the scratched and greasy aluminum counter of the Baron Bulgingburger at St-Laurent and Ste-Catherine. At his grand invitation. The lobster lady too, a dozen other people he doesn't know. The oily hair. The animal hunger. Dogs and burgs spitting on the grill. His bladder full of hot beer. Cops and rockers in line for coffees. There's a rubby with a split head and dried, ketchup-caked hair lined up beside a stunning transvestite in a Louise Brooks coiffe and a lamé tube dress, and the whole banquet's on Robbie. Chin on fists, now, watching with disdain the guy in the mustard- and relish-coloured Baron outfit as the poor bastard struggles with the order. Drop of sweat falling slow-mo from the guy's forehead onto a sizzling burger and Robbie thinks, *Not if it was the last job on Earth.* Louie goes, *Un penis, all-dress hOK, avec cum, blood, coodies, de works.* Rosie snapping *If that little wiener reminds you of your dick I hope you have a lot of technique to make up for it.* Laughing, spluttering spittle onto the counter, Robbie goes, *Turdburger pour moi, two order of spark plug.* Brat howling, drumming flippers on the counter. Louie Louie doubled over, headbanging and screaming. *Chose là, ah ouais, un JAVEX. Deux PENIS, un RINGWORM all-DRESS UFF UFF UFF.* And the guy in the Baron Bulgingburger outfit announces nonchalantly into the microphone: *trois penis deux turd all-dress deux spark plug deux javex un ringworm.* Weird fucken night. Later still, at Robbie's new place, everyone drinks his beer smashing bottles against the radiator playing records at crusher volumes. All except the Bones' *Greatest Shits*, which gets tossed about his new apartment like a frisbee. And then nailed to a wall. What else. Clumps of hair, smell of glue. Rosie's face laughing close up, silver bubblegum tumbling about on her tongue like a pinball. She's cut Robbie's hair and dyed it purple and glued it up like porcupine quills. A *punk*upine. Shaves his eyebrows too, at a sinister aquiline angle, an eagle's wings plunging. Then bites him on the neck. He likes her, and could spend more time with her, if only she could make some serious adjustments to her personality. Because her idea of what makes a person interesting is all wrong: *Remember, Bob, when we met, you were with Ivy and I was completely nude!* Now the room's thick with people and smoke, hot and sulphurous as a matchbox crammed with fresh-burnt matches, and Robbie, knowing he's being an asshole, stuffs a twenty dollar bill into her bra and drifts away across an ocean of nervous ecstasy, buoyed up by the idea that this is *his* place, all this noise is

139

bouncing off *his* walls and making *his* ceiling tremble. Then realizing it's almost midnight and he's not been tucked in yet. Chest heaving *whoa!* over a wave of worry: without *his* mother will he ever manage to take care of himself? A cigarette butt he's swallowed with his beer is floating like a raft on an incredible journey through his digestive system. The subterranean garden of guts. The squeezing fleshy tunnels. The acid baths. Placing the frostie like a cold snub-nosed pistol to his forehead he crawls to put a record on. On his knees before the stereo set he has an ecstatic vision of himself with Hell's Yells, swinging his arms in an arena somewhere in the American Midwest, lights searing, stage like a raft on pitching water, guitars howling, and his own heart amplified like a big bass drum. The crowd throws up a bristling undersea garden of hands in murky poppling water, He Him Himself in the eye of this musical hurricane dressed like a killer ballerina, like a blood-stained peacock, like Poseidon on angel dust. But thinking, Mom and Dad would not be impressed. *Oh, but this is silly, darling.* Little Robbie like a raw deboned chicken suddenly, emasculated and wishing he could do it like Keef – mindlessly, meaninglessly, with total abandon. *Convulsive or not at all* – plunging through a massive pane of glass in outer space, plunging through it with knees tucked into the chest, head-first with the glass splinters slicing past the ears like shooting stars and heels like exhaust pipes. The image fast as a blink. Silly, really, but leaving no time for respectability or conscience or pigs or disappointed parents or anything. If Hell's Yells aren't abandoned they won't be worth shit. *What're you going to sing about then?* Rosie asks. *How about the environment, like your Mom. Acid snow. Sizzling springtime, and robins dropping out of the sky.* Robbie barks, *I don't give a FUCK about the environment*, and feels his hardened hair pointing like horns up above. He lives downtown now; there *is* no environment downtown. Vibrating like a rattlesnake he's finally shuffled off his tender family skin. He doesn't need anyone any more. Sucking on the nozzle of a glass water-pipe, gagging on the acrid yellow smoke. Holding it down with a wet snap of his nasal passage. Exhaling and passing the bong to Louie Louie. And now Brat has thrown up in the toilet. A spectacular topographical map of his delinquent evening that sits like a loose soufflé on the seat which in his haste – his arms are too short – he has neglected to lift. Against the tiled floor, a grin crawls across his white face like a wet centipede. *Technicolour yawn, man.* Robbie meanwhile is trying to concentrate, please: Hell's Yells will be terminally dinful, he announces, toxic waste for city ears, a wall of shattered sound, white noise, urban congestion, a soundtrack of trashcans and traffic. Rosie says, *It's easier to describe ugliness than beauty. All this silly rage! And you can't even play an instrument!* Seething, Robbie tells her that's irrelevant, all the beauty in the world has already been described, and technique is passé – you need only kick the instruments screaming around the stage. *By the way, Rosie, did you upchuck too?* For Rosie smells of vomit. *No, Bob, I cleaned up Brat's barf for him. If you object, I can try and put it all back where I found it.* She turns her back for him to rub since as she says he has no other instruments to play. Robbie standing on the brink. A bridge of nerve endings sagging between him and her. Maybe he does love – no, he's only confusing it with gratitude. The roof of the world is descending now, its old air heavy as wax in his ears. *Oh, for heaven's sake*, she says, taking his hands and placing them on her shoulders. *You don't have to look like I've sentenced you to* death. *I'm not really in love with you, don't be frightened. I'm in* like, *that's all.* Robbie staring at the back of her head, his fingers have no muscles at all. Which is when he has his inspiration. Makes his stomach spin to think of it, but he's grinning too. Here he goes. It's all or nothing: he must go for broke, he sees. Spend every penny his parents gave him. How else will he ever be sure to do his own thing?

So, as the sun swam up the skim-milk sky, disturbing a pale film of curdled clouds, Robbie sat at the window of his new apartment with his remaining money laid out on the sill. Amazing: only twenty bones left. How fast a thousand went! Cruelly hungover, he watched the air pop with tiny sparks, synaptic explosions, and had a staring match with the luscious Eccelucci model on the billboard outside; when the model posed for the picture, she had looked straight at the camera so that now, wherever you were, she seemed to be fixing you with her gaze and defying you not to want to undress her. Robbie pictured the nerd at the Baron downtown wiping the counter for the last time.

Midnight madness, that's what it had been – Robbie leaving everyone in his dust, cabbing it down alone to Old Montreal, to St-Antoine where the pawn shops are. Scurvy Music's FULL MOON MIDNIGHT MADNESS SALE! *WE MUST BE CRAZY!* and he'd splurged his entire wad on some battered old shit – though a thousand bones didn't go far at all. That was OK with Scurvy; he said he liked Robbie so much he'd give him a discounted instalment purchase plan and throw in free delivery. The plan had a lot of pages stapled together: interest rates, forfeits, repossession clauses, payment schedules. Robbie figured, s'cool, Hell's Yells will make triple this in half the time.

And so, later that afternoon, when Rosie opened her eyes, he was lying face up beside her with his sneakers and parka on, and he'd kicked slush on the bedsheets. She popped her gum back in her mouth and, squinting, felt her way to the bathroom to put her makeup on before he awoke. But he was only pretending to sleep, suppressing chuckles, just relishing her reaction. For, out in the hallway, and in all six remaining rooms of the apartment, there were amps, amps everywhere; big, black, bolted, silent with their cables coiled up, stacked and marshalled like sinister Jack-in-the-Boxes, enough noise-pollution equipment to bring the building down like Jericho. Should anyone be so wicked enough as to switch it all on.

10

EVENINGS, DURING HER BREAKS FROM THE ROXY CANDY counter, Ivy began to phone Robbie. Too much! Major advance in the relationship. Problem was, while he wanted to believe it meant she loved him, he could never be sure, exactly, because phoning him up was all she did; she wouldn't actually speak. Robbie would sit at his end, waiting and wondering, trying to picture her. He'd sit and listen to her lips burst softly as she smoked cigarettes. Was she reading a book with the phone cradled on her shoulder? Was she drinking from the brown paper bag under the candy counter? Was he expected to talk? Or maybe this was all some cruel joke, for every now and then he'd hear someone approach her and elicit the sort of lively response she never had for Robbie. Then, with him feeling empty and sad and blaming himself for not being able to galvanize her like other people could, she'd say, abruptly, "Have to go. Kiss," and Miriam would look up from a comic book at the kitchen table and say, "Boy, you didn't make a sound for ten minutes. Whoever that is, she must be one big blabbermouth."

Worrying only about Gaston at first, Robbie now found himself jealous of everyone Ivy knew; since she refused to tell him of the guys in her past, he figured he had reason to be jealous. And because she told him nothing of her past, he had to assume that she was hiding things from him in the present as well: he was jealous of Gaston and Olly, and he was especially jealous of the guys in her dreams – Keef, for example – and since he had come that far, he allowed himself to be jealous of the guys in her future, too.

He didn't enjoy being jealous, but she forced him; she delighted in telling him about the people she wished she was with, people who really knew how to live. The infamous Nicola Lingus, for example, who took a bottle of gin to bed with her every night, and was raped as a child and slept in her bra so her breasts wouldn't sag; who lived off the royalties of that incredible hit song Keef gave to her for her birthday, and survived an odyssey of heroin addiction only to die choking on a pastrami sandwich. Ivy said she wished her life was half as full.

Although Ivy identified with all the vulnerables, kooks, and suicides of the world, she never yearned to dig up Robbie's secrets. In a way, Robbie was glad of that, because when he tried to think of things to impress her, or things to make up, nothing came. The more she told stories of people she admired, the more he felt bland, humourless, uninventive, and without potential. How, for instance, could he ever compete with Spark Combo? There was a guy who knew no limits: an acolyte of Anton Szandor LaVey, he only wore clothes purchased from the estate of Aleister Crowley, played poker only if the stakes were a night with his opponents' daughters or sons, carried condoms in Byron's snuffbox, and died a tragically slow death, strangled by cancer of the throat.

"I never really understood," Robbie said, squeezing out a generous attitude, "what exactly Spark Combo did with his life."

"Nothing, of course," Ivy said. "That's what's so incredible. He was the world's only living castrato, but he refused to record. He'd sing only at dinner parties. I wish I was there. Wouldn't you love to live like that? Just be king of all you can see and be drunk all the time?"

Lying in the dungeon, with Ivy in his arms and a bottle of Mateus on his chest, he had to agree with that much, at least. He gazed at her flesh up close, likening the innocu-lation scar on her shoulder to a flaw in a Greek vase, something done deliberately, in deference to the Gods, to spoil an otherwise perfect thing, and considered how her skin had the resiliency of sliced apple flesh exposed to the air for a day.

"Here, this scar," she said, "this is where the mother stabbed me with a fork when I was just a bitty baby. And this row of bruises is pretty recent, the father's left-handed see. You've got to be cruel to be kind, he told me, quoting Shakespeare, then walloped me on the head with a com-pendium of the Bard's plays I'd borrowed from the library. Oh, and these, these are track marks I guess."

While Miriam and Barnabus watched TV upstairs, Rob-bie and Ivy did the babysitting with their shirts off, sticky backs in a vinyl beanbag chair. The crunching of the polystyrene pellets, the swish of their skin, the snapping of an elbow. Him slyly stealing looks at her nipples that stood up as high as pencil erasers, and asking himself what his favourite parts of the female body were. He knew Louie Louie would say, "De tits." And Baimy would say, "The cunt, of course," but for him it was the drift of dark baby down at the nape of her neck, the crooks of her arms, the dual dimples in the small of her back. He gazed at her body lazily, and as his eyes drifted from their moorings, the image of her subdivided and dissolved before him, and it looked like her ethereal body was lifting off her material one.

"Do you sometimes feel like you're the only person in the world?" she asked him. Well, him, in a way. "How do you know you exist at all? What does it *feel* like to think? At

146

AA they tell you to look to a Force, to help you contact reality again. Reality? I'm addicted to it, but I'm trying to kick tomorrow all the time. I mean, where's the borderline? Where are the doors of perception? What is decadence? What is depravity? Sometimes I feel like barbed wire is being dragged through my veins."

Robbie thinking, – , but squeezing her shoulders to signal confirmation and attempting, cautiously, "It's hard for me to say. About being depraved, I mean. Our family always did OK. Just about whatever I wanted I got, which is my biggest problem I guess."

Ivy sat up. "That's *deprived*, you idiot. I said *depraved*. What am I doing here. What I said just went right by you, didn't it? God, sometimes I feel like going downtown to hustle someone I don't even know, and just have a straight fast fuck."

"Oh well, yes, of course." Robbie said, gamely. "Me too."

But Ivy looked at him and said, "No you wouldn't," and he felt ashamed that she was right.

One of her favourite bars, not least because they were lax about checking ID, was Rockhead's Paradise, under the Ville-Marie Expressway, down by the same set of tracks that ran past her family's apartment. During the days of the Montreal Maroons, black baseball players gathered there, up from the States with an evening to spare, and that's where the city's steamiest jazz used to go down; in the seventies, in the classy area upstairs, the bands were strictly stupid, disco-pated Motown with stupid, spangly choreography (observed *the* Robbie Bookbinder, Montreal's official music critic), but downstairs you could still catch three grizzled old guys grinding out grooves on a scuffed bass, a gnawed guitar, and a drum kit as honest as an alleyful of trashcans.

By the harsh white light, reflected in the mirror behind

the bar, Robbie was shocked to see what a wreck he made – perched on the edge of his chair, wild with suspicion every time Ivy so much as looked across the room, crazed when she went to the can for longer than three minutes. He wished he could relax like her – face puffy and flushed, voice grown hoarse, rolling ciggies endlessly and smoking like a locomotive, not giving a shit about anyone. And now he was monitoring her with bugeyes as she stood at a table of black dudes who were slapping their long thighs with long hands, every time she made a joke.

When eventually she sat back down again, heavily, she said, "God, *stop*, would you? Any time I'm off your leash, you get idiotically frantic."

Robbie put his hand to his chest, eyebrows up, mouthing, *me*?

"Yes, *you*. Like when I was talking to Gaston outside school this morning. Rushing over to give me lots of caring attention. I hate that."

"Oh, like *then*." (So, he was right when he saw what he thought he saw: Gaston puckering up his hairy lips at Ivy, and Ivy not instinctively tearing his tongue out for what he did to Robbie the week before.) "I just wanted to know you were safe," he ventured weakly.

"First, that's none of your beeswax, really. I mean what's wrong with *unsafe*? But, if you really must know, he was telling me he's been expelled – they caught him dealing – and now he wants to meet my brother to get in the gang. Nobody wants him, not even the Jean-Guys. He's incredibly pathetic. I was telling him to fuck right off as a matter of fact. But you, you were jealous, I could see it a mile away."

"Well," Robbie said, cautiously, "what's wrong with – doesn't jealous mean I like you?"

"It doesn't mean a thing. Just that you want me all to yourself."

"But you hardly give me any of yourself." Stating this plain truth gave Robbie's heart a little electric shock. In the

Bookbinder family, no one ever really fought – Mom said that families who fight all the time, and say it doesn't mean anything, are also the ones that hug and say I love you without meaning it either – but the consequence of constant kindness for Robbie, he realized now as the distance yawned between him and Ivy, was that he was terrified any rift, no matter how small, would be irreparable. He knew that challenging her was as bad as admitting they were no good for each other.

"I suppose I'll have to spell it out for you," Ivy said, sighing smoke in streams through her teeth. "Listen. Say we're at a party and I'm talking to someone, would you be jealous?"

"Uhh, no," Robbie said, rubbing an eyelid.

"And if I talked to this guy for a long time, would you try to stop me?"

He bought time in his beer, biting the glass. Finally he replied, "Which guy? No, course not."

"And if I said I wanted to stay late because we were having a good conversation, would you stick around like a watchdog?"

"Well, no . . . "

"And then if I told you the next day that we had talked till five in the morning, would you be jealous?"

"Uh, not if you hadn't done nothing, no."

"*Uh, not if you hadn't done nothing, no,*" Ivy mimicked, stubbing a butt out with the particular precision of a practised drunk, aiming at the ashtray from several inches up and bringing it down hard, like a pin representing the present position of her troops versus Robbie's on a map of ash. "Well, that makes no sense at all."

"Why not?"

"Because if we had been *fucking* all night, which is what you're worried about, this guy and I wouldn't have a thing to show for it in the morning. But if we had talked all that time, we would have a *real* relationship, and that should

149

give you much greater cause for jealousy. Look, Robbie, face it. You haven't the slightest clue what love is. You just want to own me."

"No, I don't," Robbie said. But he was unsure about that. He knew it wasn't – aum – to want to own – but wasn't it better than – fuck, his head was a misery-go-round. He looked at his beer, flat now. "K, OK," he mumbled. "You're right. Of course. Sorry."

"God," Ivy said, getting up again. "Roll yourself a cigarette while I get us a drink."

One thing Robbie had learned quickly enough about Ivy was that whenever she suggested going downtown for a drink, you didn't go for just a drink. You went for *all* the drinks. *Life will be convulsive*, remember? So, when eventually Ivy returned from the bar with burning cheeks and said, "Rockhead told me personally there's no more drinks," he had to dumbly follow her out to find some elsewhere.

He followed her to L'Enfer Strip, down in the disco zone between Bishop and Peel. He'd seen it from the outside often enough before, driving past with the family on the way to the Champlain bridge. He'd seen the entrance, on which were painted several crude nudes prodded at by devils in a pit of flames, and steamily wondered about its real contents all the way to the Townships.

"You *know* some people here?" he said, stamping snow off his boots. "Gee. Looks warm inside, at least."

It was so warm inside that most of the girls in the place weren't even wearing clothes. At least ten of them were standing on tabletops and boxes, nude as you please but for the strapped and stilettoed shoes they perched on. They were all up to their thighs in whooping men, and on the chrome-topped stage three were insinuating a ménage-à-trois to a throbbing disco rhythm. The whooping men were folding dollar bills lengthwise, and gingerly inserting them between the dancers' knees, and if a dancer was still wearing some thread of clothing, that's where the bill got tucked. The dancers harvested the bills with their long fingernails and slipped them between their fingers, building Spanish fans of money. With their hands splayed out like that, and the shadowy men all jerking about at their feet, they looked to Robbie like weird, nude puppeteers.

Scotch-taped to the walls were *Bosom Buddies* centrefolds. He averted his eyes from them, like old friends you don't want to admit having ever associated with. Beneath an illuminated plastic Molson clock there hung a Businessman's Lunch-Special menu. Above the stage a banner was strung that read in glitter-glue letters:

TITS FOR TOTS
X-MAS CELEBRITY STRIP-A-THON

and everywhere, instructions written on white cards in fat magic marker:

DO NOT TOUCH THE DANCERS
DO NOT ASK FOR THE DANCERS PHONE #
THE DANCER'S CANNOT LINGRE AT YR TABLE
TIPS ARE *NOT* INCL. IN THE PRICE OF ALCOOL
NO SPITING OR SWARING
THE MORE U PAY HER THE MORE SHEL'L SHOW U
YOU MUST DRINK TO SIT AT THE TABLE
THERE IS NO WALKING ROUND WITH DRINKS
NO COVER CHARGE
TIPING IS NOT A CITY IN CHINA

It was worse than school.

Now there was a ruckus at the lip of the stage, and suddenly three bouncers were roughly ejecting a man with several cameras around his neck. They dragged him shouting past Robbie and Ivy and threw him through the swinging doors. Robbie cringed at the thought of all that equipment scraping on the icy sidewalk. "I'm PRESS," the photographer was protesting. "You have no RIGHT."

151

"J't'ai *averti*," one bouncer hollered as the other kicked the fallen man's feet out from blocking the door, "Not de hathletes!" Then, extending a heavily tattooed hand and forearm, he kissed Ivy's fingers and courteously led her and Robbie to a table at the back of the room beneath the Molson clock. Robbie fished in his pocket for a tip, but the bouncer waved him off.

"And a-nowww, ladies an GENNELmen, mesdames ET messieurs," the emcee announced with the fluency of a racetrack commentator, but with the sort of sleazy innuendo that would not have been appropriate for horses, "veuillez bien réclamer pul-ease welcome all de way from Shawinigan Québec de lovely la CHARrrmante . . . Chastity CHURCH!"

Robbie felt weird about the gratuitous biographical detail the emcee felt everybody should know about Chastity Church – that she came from somewhere called Shawinigan – as if anybody cared! The expression, 'wearing nothing but your birthday suit,' entered his head and he considered that, while most performers are introduced by way of their childhood origin, it was pretty disturbing to even consider that these ones, spreading their thighs and yanking their pubic hair aside to demonstrate their inner genitalia for this whooping gang of men, had ever been born like regular little girls, anywhere.

Chastity Church, from Shawinigan, burst out of the dressing room over to the stage, bumping into tables. And *ouch!* it looked like she gave herself a real bruise banging against the fin of that jukebox. She stood over it, rubbing her thigh, made a selection, thumped it into life, and tottered up the stairs to the stage. She was dressed in a bishop's outfit, like a bizarre black chesspiece – chasuble, maniple, tunicle, the whole kit and kaboodle, all black, plus a satin biretta on her head mounted with little electric jewels, and a plastic light-up Virgin Mary. She held a black crosier in one hand, the coiled frond wound around with

152

Xmas tinsel, and a Bible in the other, with which she bonked the heads of the men in the first row.

The emcee began to auction off Chastity's clothes, item by item, as she slipped them off in a dance of the seven cassocks. The response from the crowd was half-hearted, Robbie would even have said *cowed*; her black alb went for only a dollar, the chasuble too, the frock for not much more. But when she got down to her Merry Widow the place went wild. One black stocking went for fifty dollars, the other for eighty, and when the winners stood up to twirl them above their heads like windsocks, flashbulbs went off. And there, Robbie saw, down by the stage, looking bemused but not at all involved, Olly Mills in a dark grey suit, arms folded, smiling coolly, sweeping his eyes around the room, like a man with shark's sonar. He stopped at Robbie – or was it only Ivy he recognized? – nodded, or maybe not, and continued sweeping, real smooth. Robbie wished he could be so smooth – to stand like that, crotch-high to a carnal vampire priestess unpeeling her stockings, and not bat an eyelid, cool as death!

"K, let me guess," Robbie shouted into Ivy's ear. "Olly's the boss here, right?"

"Not at all," Ivy shouted back, jabbing him with her elbow. "He owns the place."

Meanwhile, the elbow-length gloves went for a hundred dollars each, and when Chastity pulled off her black panties and ceremoniously crowned the top bidder with them, more cameras flashed. Finally, the corset. Whoops went up as the price escalated, and at last the emcee announced, ". . . GONE! Sold for two hundred fifty dollar to our fameux gardien de but de goalie number TIRTYTWO ladies an GENNELmen remember no photographs pas de photo S'IL VOUS PLAIT." And sure enough, there was another face that even Robbie, to whom sports were of unbelievably small interest, recognized. And when she awarded him her final stitch, he gave her nude body a bearhug that the bouncers didn't intercept. When he released her, she straightened out her headgear and walked right off the stage – she simply stepped out into the darkness and was gone. The room exploded with laughter. All the men in the room stood up to get a better look and thrust their beers into the air and whooped. Robbie couldn't see over their heads, but by the time they sat down, Olly was guiding Chastity by the arm back to the dressing room.

"C'mon, let's go say hi," Ivy said, and got up without waiting for him. Robbie followed her faithfully, and following her like that, *backstage*, in front of all these people, made it necessary for him to act extremely cool: he tossed his long hair behind his shoulders, wove around chairs smoothly like a wolf around trees, tucked his thumbs into the pockets of his hipsters, surveyed the room coolly, read the signs and assessed the Scotch-taped centrefolds with amplified boredom, and sniffed vigorously, wrinkling his nose, like he had just been out in an alley snorting heavy amounts of cocaine.

The dressing room was drab, smoky, cramped, and, he judged by the frost at the tiny window, would have been cold, too, if it weren't for all the hot bodies in there. There were reporters, hockey players, some heavy-looking guys with beards and greasy jean jackets, Olly with Ivy in tow, plus five girls sitting at the bulbed mirror, chatting in French as they applied sequins and makeup. And in the middle of the room, Chastity, enthusiastically displaying the bruises on her thighs for a photographer.

Robbie watched Olly from the corner of his eye, as the cool smooth guy massaged the shoulders of a stripper, whispering a cool joke in her ear and making her shriek rudely. When he winked back at Robbie in the mirror, Robbie took his big plunge.

"Hey, oh, Mr. Olly. Um, I was wondering – "

Olly smiled and held out his hand. Robbie was taken aback. Should he shake the hand in the conventional fashion? Or should he do it the cool way, hooking thumbs? He chose the formal option, out of deference, really, but Olly had stuck out his thumb, and Robbie ended up grasping it like a child will grasp his daddy's as they prepare to cross a busy street. Olly pulled away, swatting the air with something between amusement and irritation.

" – I was wondering. You ever hear of a guy called Gaston? Gaston Goupil, pimply dork. Goes to Blanchemains with Ivy and me?"

Olly smiled indulgently and shook his head. "No-o. . . . He steal your tuque in the playground, Robbie?"

"Well, not exactly. I'm only mentioning this by the way 'cause of how he hits on Ivy all the time, eh. I can take care of myself of course, but I can't always be with her, you know."

Olly put his arm around Robbie's shoulders. Robbie caught their reflection, and Olly was almost twice as big as him. Two of the strippers bumped heads together, giggling as they checked him out in the bright mirror. His gaze darted to the floor. There, at their feet under the makeup counter (five pairs of bare ankles, high heels and shoe-straps, one lost garter) he saw a brown paper bag lurking on its side, darkened at the bottom by some viscous liquid that had pooled stickily onto the linoleum.

"Tell you what," Olly murmured, winking at the girls. "You don't worry no more about Gaston, OK? Just go have fun with my sister. OK?"

"Yeah," said Robbie, pulling his lips down firmly in confirmation, pleased that he was party to an understanding. Whatever that understanding was. "Yeah, whatever you say. K, thanks. OK." They shook hands. He turned, bolstered, to Ivy, who frowned. "Chrissake," he said, pointing under the counter. "We know what this is." He opened it with the toe of his Beatle boot. Inside were several dead, blood-bloated mice. "Blecch. Just like Keef," he said grimly.

"God. I told you that haemorrhage thing's just a rumour," Ivy replied. "Right, Olly? Didn't the Bones just keep him on ice like Walt Disney until their career took a nosedive and they had to thaw him out?"

Olly smiled his cool avuncular smile as if to say, who'll ever really know, and isn't it cooler not knowing?

But Chastity got Robbie's real point. "Gross, isn't it? Some of us want to get a union together, you know." She said this with a steely look in Olly's direction. "But the girls get so scared it's hard to organize."

Emboldened, thrilled to be talking to a *stripper*, Robbie heard himself say, so maturely, so gallantly, "Scared of what? Why not get the hockey players to pick up the cause. Everyone out there thought you were great."

Chastity beamed at him. She told him all about the hypocrisy of family entertainers, and sportsmen and businessmen and politicians who go for the lunch specials but never 'fess to their wives, and the scum-bucket bikers who run the club really are scary, and Robbie was seized with pleasure because up until then he had been sure his innocence was peeking out like a soft pink baby's bottom for all the girls to see. Now he was like a reporter – intervening on their behalf, scratching his chin, super-concerned, just like Mom on TV, saying *somebody really should do something about all of this*, noting the rusty nails in the wall where their clothes hung, the frosted window too high up to look out of, the lack of a private toilet – only barely aware now of Olly's thinning smile, and the fact that Ivy was in the corner and having a demonic sulk.

By the time Robbie shook Chastity's hand, she had been standing around nude for so long that it began to look like a nude *outfit*, not real nudity at all, and when he took the hand it felt weird, like a glove, a glove of flesh.

"So!" she said. "You know the Millses, I guess. Boy, I can tell so MUCH about a person by the company they keep – I mean, I believe in reincarnation, but I still think it's the *quality* of your life that counts, eh, not the quantity! Just call me Rosie."

Out in the street two minutes later, Robbie slipped over the ice, calling after Ivy, "Whaddido, whaddido!"

She stopped and hissed, "I never want you going to that club again."

"But why?"

"If I have to explain it to you, then that's *double* reason why you shouldn't go." She walked away fast.

"Are you *jealous*?" Robbie shouted out, unable to conceal his joy, but she didn't answer. She stomped on, leaving him in her hot visible breath, disappearing several blocks later, near Ste-Catherine and Tower, through a cracked glass door marked Judy's Bar. At first he didn't follow her in, but leaned against the cinder-brick wall, picking at the weathered posters glued there, asking himself if he'd not be better to just go home. By the time he gave in, Ivy had already selected a table and was rolling another cigarette.

"Want one?" she said, all natural and nice, as if nothing had ever passed between them.

Robbie nodded, guessing she was pleased he had chased her so hard – that he had exhibited a sufficient amount of grovelling. He sat there panting like a whipped, resentful, but still faithful hound-dog, and hated himself for not just walking out on her.

"Look around you," she said confidentially, and he was grateful for the distraction. "Entire alcoholic families drink here."

He looked around. Elbows on their knees like marathon chess players, the families clustered around cathedrals of glasses on small, circular tables.

"Look at their incredible faces," Ivy whispered. "Like convicts transported to Australia, plotting. You're an idiot if you don't draw them one of these days."

157

A dented jukebox played Elvis records, so worn out that the scratches were louder than the music – shredded music, thought Robbie foggily – and couples, threesomes, foursomes, held each other up on the chipped-tile dance floor – blood-spattered like a butcher's shop – chewing butts like gum. Their cigarette breath burned his eyes. He could hardly see them for the haze. Ghosts going up in smoke.

Ivy said, "Look. *They Shoot Horses Don't They?*"

"They shoot what?" Robbie said, filled with weariness suddenly. "And how do you know they're alcoholics?"

Ivy blew her bangs up off her forehead. "I met some of them at AA, if you must know."

"You *know* these people?"

"Well, I took the mother." She raised her glass to her lips and drained it, watching Robbie over the rim with the alertness of a fox in the tall grass, as if, with her arm raised like that, she knew her soft neck and belly were rendered vulnerable to attack. She set the glass down and said, "Please stop thinking up questions about me. My life is boring. I have no stories to tell. Listen, I was reading Sartre. He's incredible. I wish I lived with him. He said that setting yourself at the centre of your own life story is like trying to catch time by the tail. He hated all the bourgeois getting drunk, and swooning over saxophone solos, like it was some soundtrack to a movie about them. He said, *Only idiots find consolation in the arts.*"

"Right," Robbie said. "Like people who go drippy when they listen to the HeeBeeGeeBees. Heh heh."

"No. That's not what I meant."

Robbie's head started to nod and the room was shifting queasily around him, long before Ivy showed signs of flagging. She smoked and smoked, and every now and then someone came up and asked her to dance. She always refused sweetly, and when they heard her lambent voice they went away shouting something like, "An angel! An angel of mercy in our midst!" Bursting with pride, Robbie looked around goofily, but Ivy glowered, crimson-cheeked, and rolled a fresh pinch of tobacco between her ochrous fingers.

At three-thirty in the morning, he crept into the house, holding his boots in his hands. Ivy behind him holding hers. Down into the dungeon they tiptoed on wooden toes to thaw out in each other's arms, drinking from Ivy's silver flask. In the buzzing silence, in the yawing, pitching room. He switched on a red light bulb. Ivy went upstairs, and brought a book down from the living room – a volume of sepia-tone photos by Brassai, of Paris in the thirties – the so-called *Secret Paris*: hookers with spitcurls standing in the chiaroscuro of cobblestoned streets; the damp atmosphere of dockside hump houses, a tart on a bidet and her client with a split in the back of his Macassared hair; the dozing, heavy-lidded clients of an opium den, hands limply cupping pipes of silver and mother of pearl; the lesbians of the Boulevard Edgar-Quinet; the naked showgirls of the Folies-Bergères; les bals-musette, rowdy waltzes, sailors on leave, and women with old-movie lipstick.

"I know I know," Robbie said. "You *wish* you lived there then. Beethoven, Caesar, Einstein, and the Pope all sitting around in cafés having incredible conversations."

He couldn't believe he said that – the words just slipped out like fish from a porpoise's mouth. Weird thing was, though, while Ivy stopped, a page half-turned in her fingers, and looked at him, there was no reproach in her eyes. She looked quizzical, disbelieving, almost apologetic, like the Wizard of Oz when they pull back the curtain. For Robbie it was an obscene moment, looking back at her so naked like that. He felt he had no right to see her from this reversed perspective. Quickly he added, "So show me more. It's incredible. Really."

The night swallowed them up in the basement of the old house. Finally, when his hair was in his face because his neck wouldn't hold his head up any longer, and he was sure his eyelids would thud shut and dunk him into a bucket of sickly sleep, Ivy said, "Do you have any crank in your *Cocaine* machine? Let's stay up all night and go to school together."

Choppily speeding through till morning then, Robbie's skin felt as dull and stiff as a mask of papier maché, his stomach an acid hollow, his fingers splayed like numb antennae. And Ivy showed him how she liked to burn herself with cigarettes. She held the glowing end close to her forearm and watched as moisture began to collect in a bubble under her skin. Robbie clenched his teeth and winced.

"*Chrissake!* Doesn't it hurt?"

Later that day, the sun's burning through the classroom window, and though it's December it's hot as summer in here. FUCK the outlaw biker's zonked out of his tree, but he can hug the road even on the tightest turns, leaning so sharp that the chains around the heel of his boot scrape the tarmac and shoot sparks behind him. He's got a crimson scarf tied around his neck, with batik designs on it. *Supit urang* and *kala* masks. The engine's monster vibrations thicken his blood, and the singular concentration required to keep the hog on the road hardens his eyeballs. He's warp-sped into a time-frame measured only in violent intentions. He shifts down to check out Soucy, a grunting porker with a neck like a stack of damp baloney: Soucy's hair is already shaved for the abattoir of life, his flesh reddened and sweating, a pen wedged in his trotter. When he notices Robbie, he curls his blood-pudding arm around his test paper, but Robbie's not attempting to cheat; no, to him that sausage is the sunburnt driving arm of some

160

long-suffering father at the wheel of his economy hatch-back Nip-job, with his squealing pigletty family in the back. FUCK shoots him a contemptuous stare before gunning his engine down the highway and leaving them to eat his dust.

All that day at his desk in class, his skull made of foam rubber and his eyes vibrating in their sockets, Robbie catches visible echoes of his night with Ivy, seeing the jumpy, fragmented scenes like photos in a flip book so well worn that the pages are soft at the edges. *Why do you do that? Doesn't it hurt?* His own voice loud in his ears. Drowning out the drone of the math class. And M. Nul is pointing a finger at him.

"Monsieur Bookbinder. Donnez nous un équation quelconque."

"Oh, uh. X + Y = Z?"

"Bien. Merci."

And Ivy's lips on his eyelids as he sprawls on the beanbag chair, the moisture evaporating like his own ascendant intoxicated soul. *Doesn't it hurt?*

"Et encore, Monsieur Bookbinder. X = ?"

"Uh. Y? Z?"

And the class chuckling now, looking at him with expressions ranging from contempt to awe. Robbie fires rapid looks back with a metal Gatlinger face. His body is stretched out so low at his desk that he may as well be lying on the floor. The wood of his chair feels soft as it slips under his shoulder blades. The pencil in his hand is fat as a baseball bat. He shivers, wonders how Ivy's holding out. Why is everyone staring? The class has ground to a halt. What's going on? There's a knuckle of chalk on his exercise book. Where did that come from? Oh, and now he feels at last the smarting pinpoint in the middle of his forehead. He reaches up to test for a lump or a wet spot. And the class erupts in guffaws. M. Nul is dusting off his fingers.

"Et une fois de plus, Monsieur Bookbinder."

"X + Y = Z."

Doesn't it hurt?

Ouaf ouaf ouaf. Dumbfuck pepsis honking like seals at the aquarium circus, clapping their fins for fish. And Ivy weeping helplessly in his lap and saying, *i don't feel a fucking thing.*

Robbie had heard that bikers were total scuzzbags, but he never really thought about the personal aspect until Ivy told him what they did to Gaston. Robbie lay late in bed and turned the image over and over in his head, like a pig on a spit: now that he was expelled from Blanchemains, the dork had been bugging the Dead Man's Hands to make him a prospect for the club. He'd been running errands for them, stealing little things like beer and ciga-rettes, lining up junior dope deals around the area of the school and generally being an overeager little asshole, and the gang had tolerated him until he showed up at the clubhouse in St-Henri one morning with a Dead Man's Hand tattoo on his arm. Big mistake. There are few things bikers hate more than an unauthorized person wearing their colours. So they pistol-whipped him and skinned the tattooed cards right off him with a red-hot switchblade, right then and there on the kitchen table.

Robbie was pretty pleased, in a way – after what the goon did to his tongue, skinning was maybe even even too good for him – but Robbie lay long wondering how much it was his fault. He hated Gaston's guts, and he was relieved that the guy would probably be too busy now licking his own wounds to come after him again, but still he couldn't help feeling sorry. Fuck, had he known Olly would take him that seriously, maybe he'd never have said anything. He thought of other atrocities Ivy had ascribed to her incredible brother: how one time he had sold a member of the rival New Hegelians club some crystal meth, which was

162

really Ajax solution, and then just sat around drinking beer with the Dead Man's Hands as the guy's skin bubbled up. Another time, one of the old ladies had been yammering too much to customers in the strip bar where she worked, about how heavy-duty the Dead Man's Hands were, and that had brought some heat on the club from the pigs. So Olly and the sergeant-at-arms had tied her to a chair and held her mouth open and poured boiling water into it. Chrissake! Robbie could hardly imagine. But he forced himself to, anyway.

While downstairs the family ate breakfast, he got to thinking of all the horrors in the world. All the ways of hurting a body he'd read about. Was it really necessary for him to list them? Yes! He couldn't help himself. In Paraguay they inserted glass rods into peasants' penises and then smashed them. The Nazis set prisoners in cement diapers and then force-fed them. Images of torture sliced his imagination into quivering slabs. And now, wriggling across the synapse between pain and pleasure, he found himself with an erection. Goading himself now. What else? He's performing a sadistic pyschic striptease, and loving it. Once he read on a Strolling Bones album jacket how the Spanish Inquisition paraded heretics around the cities, with their noses amputated and their genitals pulled off and their backs flayed open to expose their spines. To make them confess. But *really* confess. It was shocking to think that God should have made bodies so vulnerable. They have in-built thresholds of suffering, it's true, at which point the nerves mercifully switch off, but man has made a science of prolonging pain. Couldn't God have forseen that? With the blanket's cool satin border tucked under his nose, Robbie pictured himself being cowardly beyond belief in any number of gruesome predicaments, divulging war secrets before anyone could pull his toenails out, renouncing his religion and adopting any-one-you-please before they inserted the spike through his tongue, turning his family in rather than witness the loss of his fingers one by one. Well, for his family he'd endure most things, he supposed. It was unthinkable, one way or the other. All in all, it would be safer to be on the psychos' side; that way he could do the torturing rather than the thinking or the feeling or the fearing. Robbie the Reckless, medieval knight – biker of the fourteenth century – abandoned bastard child from a brutal time, weighted down with chain-mail and rusted armour, sweating off a hangover inside his helmet like boiled beef in a tin. He watched himself riding, drunk as a lord, fuelled with mead and the grim elation of violent living, his cock like the saddle's pommel in front of him. Time stripped raw by violence, violence the purpose and the reward, violence answering to no one. He lay in bed and listened to the thunder of approaching armies, the dull chink of iron, the sound of keys in bunches hanging from belts, the scrabble of hooves on rubble, him twisting in his saddle now to right his jittery horse. Then he turned on his pillow and sighed: Robbie Bookbinder of the twentieth century, safe in his bed at 218 Hillcrest Rd., Montreal, Canada, marooned in the seventies, the desert island decade, empty of convictions, void of intent, with next to no chance of torture rearing its ugly head at him to ever test his mettle.

Next morning, he found a note taped to his locker:

meet me after lunch –
i have something incredible

When he ascended he knocked, to be polite. At first there was no answer. Ear to the door he heard scuttling sounds. Things being put away. Then Ivy opened it, saw him, and rolled her eyes. To his enormous disappointment, she was not reclining nude on the wooden floor, nor straddling the banisters in nothing but a T-shirt, nor curled up in the alcove of the stained-glass window with her dufflecoat pulled around her goose-bumpled body.

"A shipment," she announced.

She had already opened a taped-up carton and pulled out more than a dozen boxes, each one a little larger than the size of a bar of soap. They were all wrapped in rough, turkey-red paper; on the top side, there were letters she said were Malayan, and what looked like a brand name motif – a dragon biting its own tail – and crude wax seals holding the folded paper at either end. She opened one, unfurling the protective tissue paper. When Robbie peered inside, all he could make out was solid wax. He bent forward to smell it.

"Wait," Ivy said, pushing him back by the shoulder. She shook the box and the block of wax slid out, landing on the table with a thump. She took a knife she used for carving off flakes of wax into the melting pot, and sliced the block in two. Robbie looked. Now there were two blocks of wax. Ivy tutted, and tried another one. Same result. She tried a third, from the bottom of the carton.

From a hollow in this block's centre, a small plastic pouch emerged, folded in four, and as it opened up on the table top like the petals of some unpleasant flower, Robbie realized what it contained, without having to pick it up.

"Oh, man," he said. "Is there, uh – in all – ?"

"One in four, maybe."

"But where – "

"In the mail. I also received some cloth today, and some metal stencils. Right here, c/o Lycée Blanchemains, Département Beaux Arts, via the school's broker. We did it again! That's two for two."

"We?"

" – "

"Oh, the Royal We."

"Want to try some? It's incredible. No one's stepped on it."

"Sure, but I – isn't it a little early in the day? I mean, I get kinda paranoid when there's people around."

"God," Ivy said. "You don't get paranoid with *smack*. The opposite. Oh. I see." She regarded him with her otter-brown eyes, still and cautious. "It's OK. Just watch me and join in if you want."

She held a very shallow tablespoonful above the kerosene burner. When the heroin had dissolved, she unlocked a drawer in her batik kitbox and drew out a syringe. She dipped the needle and pulled up the liquid. Then, when she slid the needle in the soft flesh between her thumb and index finger, Robbie had to look away. For her blood had momentarily blossomed in the barrel, like a crimson sea anemone in a warm lagoon, and he, the wimp, had gone faint.

The school bell shrilly rang and the shouts and stamping of students on the loose clattered through the building. Robbie took a step back and watched her go about her business: she gathered up her boxes, real slow. And meticulous. And put them one by one in her satchel. Locked her kitbox, put on her scarf. Tried tying it, twice. Slipped on her Afghan coat. Buttoned it with careful attention. Examined the frayed stitching and browning fur. Pulled the satchel onto her shoulder. Raised her head to regard Robbie with an expression of mild regret. Scrunched up her hair. And when the school was all quiet, wordlessly led the winding way down the stairs to the street.

"So-o," she said finally. "Want to come walking? I'm going to Olly's."

Robbie followed her eyes. Were her pupils constricted like that because of the glare of the snow – she looked to him like she was staring through the wrong end of a telescope – or was that the way he too appeared to straight people when he was stoned? His hands fidgeted in his pockets. He was grinding a semi-circle of dirty snow with the toe of one boot.

"Well, no. Thanks," he said. "I don't think you really need me around. So, mnn, I'll see you tomorrow. I guess." He held his hand up, palm to her. He shrugged. Made a thin smile. Said, "Bye," turned on his heel, and left her standing there. He walked away as fast as he could, feeling his own chilled skeleton shudder as he pounded the pavement home.

11

OCTOBER, AND FROM HIS APARTMENT ON BERDNIKOFF HE could see Mount Royal's flaming trees beginning to lose their leaves, which were descending now like crumpled embers to settle on the dampening, darkening ground. It was a bad idea, he reflected, to have plugged in all those amplifiers, turned them up to ten, and kicked the guitars screaming around the floor; the vibrations from the noise had been so great that the plaster on the ceiling below him cracked. And was it ever a good thing the old folks who lived there, the Grissoms, were in the habit of rising at dawn, because neither of them was in bed when the ceiling actually came down.

He lay on his own mattress on the floor. It was very crowded; all the stuffed animals of his childhood had been neatly arranged in a row beside him. Rosie was there too. He elbowed her.

"Hey. Don't you hafta go to work?"

She rolled over and exhaled sweet-and-sour breath that he imagined he could even relish, if only he loved this person. She leaned up to look out the window.

"No," she said. "Can't today."

"Why not?"

"Rain. It's raining."

He rubbed his hedgehog head. "You won't melt, you know."

He stumbled out of bed, came to a serpentine brook, busy with bullrushes and little riverbank creatures. When he bent down to look at them, he saw they had snarling faces with their skulls poking through the fur. The brook was clogged with stinging brown foam. He shrugged and stepped over it into the bathroom.

In the mirrored cupboard above the sink was his own personal tube of PH WOW! Green tube, menthol, 500ml – the man-sized format. He tried to read the instructions, but they were in French and it was all swear words: *calice tabernacle hosti maudit sacrifice calvaire.*

Ever weird, eh. Rosie was in fact asleep, curled up beside him, her warm bottom pressed against the small of his back. Through the open, curtainless window, he watched a ploughed field of muddy clouds scud over the neighbouring rooftops, dark and wet in the dawn. Under the sheets his toes met with Rosie's webbed ones. She stirred. He hugged his side of the mattress. He thought of all the chestnuts split open on the pavements, and breathed in the homey smell of soggy bonfires and leaves turning to compost, though the smell was tainted by the tang of gasoline and a stronger smell – something meaty and bad, heavy on the wind. And, he realized now, he had awoken with a nosebleed.

Rosie stretched and sat up. She reached across the bed, her breasts dangling, Robbie observed uneasily, like udders, and squeezed him from behind, reaching around to cup his penis in her hands.

"In the morning with guys," she murmured, "I can never tell – is it me or is it pee? Hey, Bob, I have an idea. You can draw me, like you used to Ivy. I can pose. Like this." She struck a bathing beauty pose, a leg and an arm stretched out like a water-skier in his wake.

Robbie looked at her webs. In one sense they streamlined her feet, like the fins on a classic Cadillac – and everyone should have them, really – but because they were alien they were also kind of repulsive, and Robbie felt their repulsiveness spread all the way up her skin to the limbs that were wrapped around him. He found himself bracing his body against her infirmity, and searching for an excuse to get up. She sensed his resistance, and pressing her cheek to the back of his neck, said, "You think I'm ugly."

"No, no, I don't," he said quickly, guiltily. "It's just, I have killer allergies this time of year – the annual Hay Fever Festival goes on until the first frost, fuck. So I need my mouth to breathe – mind if we don't kiss?"

"OK, Bob," she said, "so now let's work out if I'm *safe*. I release one egg each menstrual cycle, right, 'n my egg has only twelve to twenty-four hours to be fertilized. OK. So under favourable *cervical-mucus* conditions, your sperm can survive four or five days, tops, inside my uterus and fallopian tubes, *so* – I'm actually *fertile* about eight to ten days." Rosie counting it out on her fingers, squinting at the ceiling. "But lemme see, I finished my period only one, two . . . *six* days ago, so OK, *hi ho Silver!*"

Rosie had already introduced him to her bodily signs several weeks earlier – because, she said, the man's not sexually sharing unless he participates in the contraceptive process. K, thought Robbie at the time, but he didn't know this was her idea of *foreplay* – that she couldn't ever get aroused without reaffirming her personal femininity like a proud gardener in a greenhouse bursting with hot-house tomatoes.

He watched her gel and insert the diaphragm. Then he, he himself, shook the bottle and filled the applicator with stinging contraceptive foam and gently – *gently, Bob!* – injected it into her vagina. After that, she tore open the little square package and he extracted the cold wet lamb-skin. He held it in the air like a biological specimen for several minutes, while she coaxed him back up, and made a game Smiley face as she rolled the chilly squiggly thing down.

Eventually they were humping. Robbie pushed her head back in the pillow to bite her on the neck. Trusting this to be an expression of tenderness, she gasped and sent her legs up into the air with her toes fanned out. And Robbie, hating himself, thought, Where's Ivy. She's betraying me, and probably in a much smarter way than this; sitting up in bed in Sumatra, in a silk kimono with a dragon on the back. Sipping jasmine tea. Anyway, she's definitely not puffing or panting or slapping her belly against whoever or perspiring in the pits of her arms or making her delicate passage sore in frantic search of that elusive friend the orgasm. No, she's having a *convulsive conversation.* "Don't stop," Rosie said hotly in his ear. "Just a little more, sweet Bob." Robbie picturing Kiki Van Garterbelt in her most wanton *Bosom Buddies* centrefolds. Finally Rosie shuddered and grabbed, several times, going off like a string of firecrackers thrown into the street on Chinese New Year, and gasped, "Lions 1 – Christians 3. Mmmn."

After she'd gone, he surveyed the place, which he'd not exactly found time to clean up since he moved in a month ago: black broken record shrapnel lay everywhere, still; butts were strewn all over like spent cartridges; a pizza was on the turntable, the spindle neatly piercing a piece of pepperoni; a black bra hung from the handle of the *Cocaine* machine; and the black issue of an aerosol can's aluminum bladder was all over the walls and ceiling.

He started by picking up a few empty stubbies, but the odour of their dregs echoed the residue in his own gullet, and he lay down feeling nauseous, the mouths of six bottles stuck to his fingertips, three on each hand, like electric milkers clamped to the teats of two cows. The room swirled around. The noise-pollution machines sat stacked silently in the hall and in every room. Robbie looked at them and wondered if he'd not been rash. A stink of gasoline blew in from over the rear of the Parthenon Fil-U-Up, where an enormous tanker was nursing the pumps now, like a great smelly pregnant iron pig. He closed the window, got himself a fresh beer, a therapeutic brew, and told himself it was time to get serious, to do something of importance.

Hell's Yells. Brat and Louie Louie had not been impressed with the concept, so he'd just have to paint some inspirational images for them, in the same way stained-glass windows once told religious stories to illiterates. He'd design costumes, a stage set, record jackets, T-shirts. He'd get specific, write down lyrics, liner notes, souvenir program notes, a philosophy. And he knew that, just as urine was once used to make the golden glass glow, he'd have to pour the whole of himself into his work. *Convulsive, or not at all.*

No table, so he sat on the floor. He stirred a cup of tea with a pencil and chewed on the wood. Here he goes, he's free, he can think of anything he wants, anything in the world. This is a historic occasion, a big day, the first of the rest of his life. Life will be what he makes it. He'll prove himself now. He sat. Chewed the pencil. Got up for another beer. Sat down again.

K, seriously now . . .

The apartment was chilly; a faint smell of gas emanated from the kitchen. Periodically the radiators made a sound: *tank.* The window was a carapace of grime, the pale October light diffused through it dirtily. He sat, cozy in a luxurious Italian cardigan Mom had given him several Xmases ago. He picked at a cuticle, and noticed how the night's drinking had caused his fingers to swell up around his nails. He caught a whiff of Rosie's violent vagina on the tips. He drifted off, thinking about her cervical-mucus conditions . . .

Snapping back to attention now. Getting up and cracking open a fresh brew. Blank sheets lay on the carpet in front of him. His eraser stood up fresh and pink. He pulled a fresh pencil straight from the box. And sharpened it. No wastepaper basket either, so the shavings dropped onto the carpet. He ground them in with his knuckles. The radiator went *tank*. He pressed the lead to the paper.

Hell's Yells. To start: their outfits.

He chewed that ragged cuticle some more, and now blood crept under the fingernail. He went for a Band-Aid.

On the way to the bathroom, he noticed an article on an open page of *Blow Up* magazine, a thoughtful piece about French Canadians' passionate response to the Strolling Bones. Which he got to reading. Apparently, the sight of Keef with his arms outstretched, and Bile with his whip, and Spit Swagger at his electric organ (resembling an illuminated cathedral, in the writer's opinion) provided a significant benediction for pepsi fans who, in spite of the way they aggressively ignored their Catholic heritage, unconsciously desired it.

Robbie wondered what the writer would say about Hell's Yells. He plugged in one of his rented guitars and gave it a strangle. He made a lot of noise, but found himself quickly frustrated by the effort it took to make noise with any kind of significance. The effort left him feeling defeated, his fingertips smarting, his stomach craving lunch, and Mrs. Grissom thumping on her newly plastered ceiling with a broom.

Fish fingers for lunch, a knucklebone of ice in each one, warmed-up ketchup with grated parmesan on top. Plus another beer. Then he sat down again, pencil poised. He wasn't going to let himself get bogged down, just because his attempt that morning at imagining outfits had been a pathetic failure; he'd simply put outfits aside for the moment and move on to stage design. He cranked a new record up extra-loud, to concentrate.

The phone was ringing. He had barely heard it above the din.

It was Mrs. Grissom. She sounded quite hysterical. "Whatsamatter with you, dammit? You deaf or somethin?"

"No, dammit," Robbie replied calmly. "But if you are you old cow I can turn it up for you."

He'd really been too well brought up to speak so rudely, but he did it anyway; for a start, he'd heard her swear way worse, round the corner at Wu's grocery – she seemed to have that condition where people haul bags full of newspaper, and swear non-stop in the street – and he reasoned that this way, at least, he was speaking a language she understood. Then he hung up on her.

He couldn't seem to get started. Frankly, he had thought that working here, alone in his brand new apartment, would be way easier. For one thing, he had not expected the sounds of the radiators to bug him so much. He guessed their *tank*ing sound was made by the metal expanding and contracting as they heated and cooled. So he tried walloping them with a frying pan to settle the excited molecules. That worked. But not for long, and it painfully jarred the bones in his hand. He found that with a pair of pliers he could twist a valve at the base of the radiators, which let a rush of hot oily air out, and that made them go quiet for a little longer. Manipulating the pliers was a tricky operation, however; he pinched his fingers so badly he got black bloody marks in his flesh. Bummer. Then he had trouble twisting one valve closed again, and the rush of hot oily air became a jet of hot oily water, that spattered all over the carpet and the wall. Major bummer. He went back to the more cathartic solution: throwing the frying pan right across the room as soon as a rad made the slightest *tink*. The eighth time, or the ninth, he hurled it with all his might, and the pan glanced right off the rad, smashed through his front window, and landed with a clang on the street below. Seething, he patched the damage over with garbage bags and a great stretch of Scotch tape. And sat down again.

Smoke break. The piece of hash he had was as big as a golf ball. Soon the carpet before him was scattered with burnt matches, SUCCESS WITHOUT COLLEGE matchbooks, cigarette ash, flakes of tobacco, the fluff of torn-out filters, *Bambù* rolling papers, little copper screens, and smudgy pellets of hash. And the radiator going *tank*. He emptied out a *Ship* matchbox, broke off one end of its tray, and slid it back in so the box was open at one end; he poked a hole in the top of the box, inserted the joint, lit it, and sucked in the smoke from the open end of the box. Tell the truth, he's not overly keen about this method – when you put your lips to the box, you taste the sulphur from the match-strike panel – but it does make for a good strong toke and saves you in the end from burning your fingers on the roach. Go ahead, he thinks (the afternoon is wasting away, he's starting to feel dreadfully self-conscious, as if the ghosts of his own self-reproach are finding substance in the smoky air), try it sometime.

So anyhow: Hell's Yells' stage set.

Yes, a stage set . . .

. . . he's been picking his nose for a while now, rooting around in there like a robbing hobbit, and he wonders what to do with the mucilagenous specimens – the dragon Snot's treasure – which he's collected on the tips of both index fingers. He has his hands poised like a doctor awaiting rubber gloves. He wonders how long has he been up there, deep in the nose . . .

Gets up and goes to the bathroom for more toilet paper. Pulls at the roll a little harder than he intended (he's pretty woozy now, he admits) and yards of the stuff, the cheap kind that sheds white fibres, unfurl onto the floor. *Chrissake*, what does it take? If your ambition in life is to be a bum-wad manufacturer, how much work does it take to get it right? You make the stuff *soft*, K, you make it *strong* so it

175

doesn't shed, and you perforate it *properly* so the pieces come off without tearing down the middle and dragging the rest of the roll onto the floor. *K*? What in hell else have you got to occupy your day? Can you really say you're proud of your life? He catches his reflection in the mirror and glares at himself.

"Dopey," he says, aloud. "Numbskull."

And slaps his forehead. A wave of anxiety like a hot mist sweeps through his mind, condensing on the surface of his skin. He knows it. Almost three and he hasn't drawn a thing all day. His palms are damp. He's frightened and dizzy. And he's broke. The apartment is quiet. Except for the *tank*ing of the radiator. And the gas leaking from the stove smells like sweet burning vinyl. He gets a fresh beer, puts on a record and sits down again to really apply himself. Holds a *Bosom Buddies* magazine on his lap. He's going to draw a vicious caricature of Keef Richards. He'll illustrate the emptiness of the guy's life by piecing his face together in a *trompe l'oeil* of naked women. This will be Hell's Yells' first album cover.

Casually leafing. Hello, here's one of Robbie's favourite actresses, Kiki Van Garterbelt, having a nude pillow fight with some co-eds in the dorm of a Canadian university. She might serve OK as a model for his cartoon. Though he'd prefer something less lewd – here her knees are off opposite edges of the page . . .

There aren't any less lewd. That's what he concludes after fifteen minutes, or maybe more. Of stroking the bishop. *De bishop*, as Louie Louie would call it. The gronker's voice comes to him like that. *Shaking ands wit your wife's best friend. Aving a talk wit Mudder Fist and er five children, uff uff.*

Masturbate. The real word feels unclean: the long word, the long wrinkled word, with a personal odour to it. That you rub up and down. He stops, looks around, ashamed. He should be working. At Collège Blanchemains, M. Nul once told the class that some ancient Egyptian cults believed the moment of Creation was experienced in the ecstacy of divine masturbation. Robbie pictured the stars in the night sky then, and particularly the Milky Way, as this spray of sacred sperm. Then he caught Gaston Goupil's grin and one-fisted gesture, and grinned despite himself. And they had both got detentions.

These magazines creep up on him, infect him, cause him to stew in his own juices. The afternoon light has faded, the streetlamps are already switching on in chains, and from the electric billboard on Park Avenue, the crackling neon colors of Eccelucci's latest line of lingerie casts pastel shadows through the windows of the apartment. Brat, by the way, boasts that he never humps his fist, *'cause he can't reach*, but that if he could, he wouldn't feel guilty because he's Jewish and proud of it. *Jews are cool*, Robbie hears him hold forth belligerently at the Toe Blake Tavern, *I read the holy books. I been to shul. The rabbis of old said it was OK, as far as onanism, eh – they recommended that a man of whom his wife has a bun in the oven – and I quote, I believe, Eliezer – 'thresh inside and winnow outside.'* Louie Louie goes, *Et ça veut dire quoi, hosti?* Brat replies, *It means that the man may beat his meat, even in the presence of the baby.*

Switching on the light to pull himself together. These quicksand pictures. And the next thing Robbie knows, he's reading the letters. Though he's wise to them. He knows they're not real. You can tell because certain coincidences in the language always crop up, if you read closely. For instance, here are three supposedly different guys, all proud possessors of eleven-inch so-called joysticks, who each describe the object of their lust as a dripping honeypot. Now do you know one single person in real life who calls a vagina a honeypot, or a penis a joystick? So three in one magazine is just too much.

Another beer and he turns to a page of ads with men

sporting elephantine joysticks and endorsing Special Spurious Sex Pills. He's not taken in by these, either – he knows spurious means not genuine, because Brat once told him that when a mail-order customer tried to sue Lovely Things Inc. over the failure of their Spectacular Spurious IQ Increasers, the company's attorney successfully argued that the customer ought to have used a dictionary before ordering them – and Robbie feels sorry for all the ignorant men in North America who will be similarly disappointed after they receive the Special Spurious Sex Pills in an unmarked brown paper package, thinking that spurious means something between spurt and furious, and expecting to suddenly possess copious ejaculatory powers.

He turns a heavy glossy page. EASY LAYS, he reads, HOW TO SPOT THEM: Some are shy, some need a little warming up, others simply require cab fare. Interesting. And Robbie wonders, is there really such a thing as nympho housewives? And monopede mania – do some men really have a fetish for women's leg-stumps? More ads now, promising books and films available only in the U.S. The plot summaries revolve around partners with mammoth members and esurient appetites for swallowing, it seems, just about anything. Photos too: sex zombies, contortionists – Kiki Van in a special appearance! – with ink screens printed over their genitals. Robbie supposes this is to protect the reader from a sight he may not relish, and understandably so. Black bars conceal the men's joysticks; black dots disguise the women's honeypots. Problem is, the obfuscations have incited his imagination all the more, and now he's seized with a desire to own these books or films. Immediately. But there's nothing quite so explicit available anywhere in Montreal, so far as he knows, and it will take three weeks if he sends off in the mail for one. He'll have to draw something explicit for himself. . . .

Sitting with his pencil hovering above the fresh white

paper. His groin hot and tumid. And the phone rings again.

It's Barnabus on the line, sounding worried.

"Rob?"

"Yes. Hi, Barnabus. Bad timing."

"But I've got a stomach ache. I got sent home from school. 'Cause I can't go to the toilet."

"That's just constipation, Barn. Eat a banana."

"It's not that. I don't want to. It's . . . I saw something bad on TV. On Mom's show."

"What did you see?"

"About all the poolution in the world."

"*Poll*ution, you nit."

"No, it's *poo*lution, I know. I'm afraid to poolute the planet Earth."

"Oh boy, Barn, is *no* one taking care of you there?"

"Mom's away. Dad's asleep. And Miriam hates me. Will you come over and play?"

"Sorry, Barn. I'm way too busy. Go watch TV."

"But that's what everyone says," Barnabus whines in his ear. "Please?"

"Look, I really gotta go. Sorry. K?"

"K . . . Bye."

So, anyway: the trick here is to infuse each stroke of the pencil with a special sexy feeling. The fusing of his artistic skill with his figgy lust will produce something new: an image to make you go sticky, no matter what your sexual inclination. Just as Robbie feels it as he draws it, so'll you feel it as you follow the lines with your eyes. He plans a wild priapic scene, a hot fantasia with horny lickerish satyrs and fleshy nymphs bound with garlands of flowers. The satyrs will dance around, wielding their organs like giant soft cabers, great huggable totem poles with heaps of pubic hair as thick as dewy moss. With a flick of watery gouache here, and a dollop of creamy impasto there, he'll make the very paper writhe in pleasure. He'll swish and

179

dribble the paint so that even on an abstract level, or upside-down maybe, the picture will reveal itself to be one great climax, all marigold sperm and carnelian bollocks and wet wet carnation cunts. An arousing inflorescence. An aphrodisiac painting.

But when he finally puts his pencil to the paper he's too impatient to render the nymphs' feet. He's never ever been able to draw feet and fit all the toes in, fuck. Feet are tough for anyone to draw – look at a Picasso, even. Robbie should have got Rosie to pose for him after all. And now he hears her voice, close in his ear: *You think I'm ugly.*

K, so feet aren't the most important part of the picture. He'll go back to them later. But the hands are harder. He keeps erasing them, and he's wearing the surface of the paper away. Fuckshit, he's truly bummed out now. The knees of the satyrs look knobbly. The nymphs look lumpen and awkward. Plus, it's impossible to come up with twelve different expressions of lustfulness. *You* try three, even. His fingers are numb and damp, and the pencil squirms between them. He can concentrate only on their honeypots.

He makes a concerted effort to grasp onto his inspiration by detailing some roly-poly labia. Afterwards he'll fill out the bodies. He thinks of those Rubens he likes – how beautifully unashamed they are! And there's a Matisse he knows, nudes dancing in a circle – they're so simple! Why can't he do something lovely like that?

But what he ends up with is a quick, scurrilous sketch of disembodied sexual organs copulating, scratchy and smudged, lousy as toilet graffiti, the full coarseness of which he appreciates clearly only after he's ejaculated an albescent fountain onto the paper, like oyster-white oil paint squeezed from the tube.

A week or so later, several false starts later, Robbie decided that if he threw out his collection of *Bosom Buddies* magazines, he'd stand a better chance of concentrating. He'd clean up the place, too, get his mind together, do some exercises maybe, even limber up his voice. In the shower he was capable of howling his way, totally from memory, through all four sides of *Jesus Christ Superstar*, and that's what he did beneath the rusting faucet. He was a soap-spitting prune-toed one-man-band as he did the twelve-part harmonies of the Disciples, the thirty-nine lashes, the angels' lament for the dead Judas, the lot. And really *relating*. He stretched his arms out to see his ribs protrude. In the movie version, by the way, you could actually see JC's underwear through his loincloth during the crucifixion. Which was unrealistic. He thought about this. Fruit of the Loom, looked like. Ruined the illusion of those heavy Biblical times, which was typical since the director of the movie was *Canadian*, fuck.

Then the water turned freezing cold. Just like that. At first he figured there was insufficient pressure in the old building for hot water to reach the second floor, but, when he turned the tap just half a revolution further, it went scalding. Then, before he could twist it back, the water went freezing again. Call him paranoid, but that's when he knew for a fact that mad Mrs. Grissom was manipulating the taps of her bathtub downstairs just to get a rise out of him.

Turning the water off, he realized the phone was ringing. He ran to the bedroom, kneeled dripping on his mattress, and picked up the receiver, his tongue cocked to deliver abuse.

It was Officer Gaunt. The pig's voice was so pleasant that at first Robbie figured he must be satisfied with the investigations, and was calling to say thanks very much for everything. But then Gaunt barked at him to get his Royal Canadian rump in gear and present himself at Station 10 by nine-thirty a.m., sharp. Robbie protested that he had some serious work to do, but the line had already gone dead. He slammed the receiver down, put his face in the pillow, and yelled with all his might.

Sitting in the interrogation room on an empty stomach and only eight hours' sleep wasn't Robbie's idea of a good time. The bare white room buzzed in the light of a neon strip, and smelled like one enormous ashtray; in his ripped and safety-pinned KEEF SUCKS T-shirt he felt small as a crushed butt. Goose pimples came up on his arms – the temperature of the room had been set a few degrees below the threshold of comfort. He drummed on the table, buh-dumming a tune under his breath, picking lint from his belly button. Tried not to think about what was happening to him. Save it all and make a new T-shirt. But every thirty seconds, fear kicked his chest like a lizard in an eggshell.

Gaunt came in, wheezing, spilling coffee onto his hand. He cocked his head at Robbie and crossed his eyes and stuck his tongue out of one corner of his mouth: a man hanging by his neck. Robbie tried not to laugh. A crust of shaving cream still fringed Gaunt's beard, and the skin of his neck was raw around the Adam's apple.

"I'll tell you a secret, lad, if you want."

Robbie shrugged.

"No, really, you may find it hard to believe, but I used to be a lot like you are."

"Whut?"

"Well, confused, I'd say. Pushing mama's teat away, and bawling at the same time cause all you really want to do is suck."

"Speak for yourself, man."

Husker entered. He exchanged nods with Gaunt and sat at the table across from Robbie. Lit a cigarette. Closed his beefy eyelids and drew in smoke through his nostrils. Robbie fidgeted. Husker tilted his head back and held it there, like a man suffering from a murderous hangover. He was creased and balding and his flesh looked dense with booze and undigested meat. Behind his back, Gaunt pulled an unstrung face and fanned his hand rapidly. Robbie sent a grin back at the exact moment that Husker opened his eyes. Pulled himself together, did his Man With No Name for the detective.

"Oh, come off it," Husker said. "We're not going to eat you. Stop being such a pussy." Which made Robbie realize that he's not wearing a face like the visored helmet he'd imagined; that his tough iron grin is closer to a weepy wiggle. "OK, now. We're not saying you set this fire, so fucking relax. But we do think you know some things about it. Like the boy who died. Am I correct?"

"Uh, not exactly. . . " Robbie looking down at the floor. Inside his sneakers, his toes wiggled like maggots in a heel of bread.

"He was so badly burned it's hard to say, but we think he took a serious blow to the back of the neck – medulla oblongata, to be exact – which could've been enough to knock him out, kill him maybe. It probably didn't kill him, since he had soot in his lungs. Which means he was still breathing during the fire. It's also likely the amount of smack in his blood would've done the job just as well, had he lived long enough in the first place. The only thing in his stomach was a stick of gum and a pint of grain alcohol. This little idiot was headed for a fall."

Robbie propped his chin in his hand. He glanced over at Gaunt, expecting a clown face, but Gaunt was impassive.

"You look bored," Husker said.

Robbie, hand to chest, mouthing *me*?

And now Gaunt signalled his own boredom behind Husker's back by making like his eyelids were lined with lead and jerking them forcibly up again, and Robbie found himself on the verge of cracking up. What was with this guy? Was he doing this on purpose? To get him into shit?

"Or do you find it funny?"

"Funny haha," Robbie said, "or funny peculiar?" He felt like his lungs were full of laughing gas. His cheeks puffed out as he restrained himself.

"Look, you little FUCK. You think this is a *joke*?" He banged out a cigarette.

Robbie focused hard on Husker's fingers. The thick ridged knuckles. The split thumbnails. *Claws.* The mat of hair creeping out from the sleeve of his Human costume.

"OK, OK," Gaunt said. "Let's allow you're only hysterical. Scared, like. We can help you, if there's something you want to confide."

"Yeah," Robbie said. "I'll confide this much: I want to go home. You can't stop me. Am I under arrest here, or what?"

"No," Husker said, "but we *can* charge you with obstruction of justice. Your fucking smirking attitude totally baffles me. What do you think you are, a clever little nihilist?"

"No-o. . . . "

"No?"

"I mean, I don't know what that is."

Husker closed his eyes and summed up some energy. His face showed the peculiar concentration of a person working a fishbone out of a mouthful of trout. Robbie licked his lips.

"A dry mouth means you're hiding something," Gaunt said. "Did you know that?"

"I'm not hiding nothing, man," Robbie said. "Anything you wanna know, just inquire."

"OK," Husker said, opening his eyes. "What's that swastika on your arm? A tattoo? You a neo-Nazi?"

"Nah, got it in a cereal box. It's just a style."

"A *style*? Fuck me gently." Husker pounded his fist on the tabletop, and ash went flying from the end of his cigarette.

Robbie's ears went numb. The room filled with water. His mouth wobbled like a rubber life-raft on its surface. He wished he'd never saved Ivy to begin with. She didn't really deserve it anyway. He held his forehead in one hand, surreptitiously licking his thumb and rubbing off the ballpoint swastika. He gritted his teeth and looked away, scanning for something to distract him. He felt like a rattled window. He looked at the sky. The tumbling wet clouds. Some birds whipping away like black rags.

He confessed, "To bug people's ass."

"All right," Husker said. Now he was opening an envelope and pulling out some photographs. "I'm going to jog your memory. Brace yourself. This will make you sick, but I want you to see it to shake the fucking knee-jerk anti-authority compulsiveness out of you. Take a look."

A body. As black as the charred room it was in; you could hardly see a thing. Big deal, Robbie told himself, there's much better stuff in *Gutbath* – the special effects fanzine that features slasher flics like *Bloody Fucking Sadist Butcher Heroes of Rape County U.S.A.* – only in colour, and with better close-ups. For Husker's sake, though, he made a grave and thoughtful face, nodded the way he always did for Mom on sight-seeing holidays to Museums And Churches Of The World. Though in spite of his efforts he's shaking . . .

"Obviously," Husker said, scrutinizing him closely, "I can't ask you if you recognize this person."

"Nope," Robbie said, as regretfully as possible. "Oh, well. So, see ya, bye." He rose to walk out of the room, to recapture some of those lost z's. But his legs were unexpectedly rubberized and he fell over his chair.

It's a privilege of the truly inspired artist, Robbie told himself, to lose track of time. So, if another week later, or maybe two, he still didn't have his Hell's Yells concept drawn up completely – or if, in fact, he still hadn't exactly begun – that didn't mean he wasn't serious. Anyway, he had actually done one serious thing: arranged with the manager of the Roxy for the great and powerful Hell's Yells to practise in the cinema after midnight, when the movies were over.

That morning, Louie Louie had helped load the equipment from Robbie's apartment into his chicken factory truck, and stowed it behind the movie screen. Inside, they'd marvelled at the crumbling mock-Egyptian fixtures of the old burlesque follies, and examined the plaster-dusted dressing rooms up in the galleries. Louie Louie found the box of programs featuring Jacquie Diamantine and Regine Argent. "Uff uff. Uff. Look," he said. "Dey ad to ave de cock surgically remove from dis one's mout before dey take de picture."

Now it was the middle of the afternoon at the Toe Blake Tavern, and the boys were gathered to celebrate. Brat was buying.

"I'm on a generosity trip," he said. "Get this: last night I hold up a sealed envelope to my old man and I says, something's in here that's worth a ton of dough to any pharmaceutical company you care to name. Ever since the hippies stopped washing their hair, see, the toiletries industry has been in a slump, and I, Baimy Goldfarb, have the solution! If you don't want it now, says I, I'll sell it to the highest bidder, and you'll be sorry. How much do you want for it, he says. For you, Dad, one million smackers, I says. He thinks I'm joking, eh, but I hold out, and eventually we compromise on an executive position in his company if he likes what he sees."

"So – ?"

"So, he opens the envelope and reads one word: *Repeat*."

"Repeat."

"Yeah! Like, repeat *procedure*. I just doubled Lovely Bathroom Products' income." Brat snapped a claw. "Like that."

Six glasses of draught on an empty stomach and the air's looking very thin to Robbie – a haze of smoke is suspended in nothing, no oxygen at all, just hanging there, billowing aimlessly like sheets of miasma, gathering in pinwheel swirls, breathing in and out like Nicotine Nebula galaxies. Matter of fact, gravity's not taking care of anything in here – the light is jumpy, the front door keeps swaying open to let in a whipping frosted gust, and the TV's flipping *Hello World! Hello World! Hello World! Hello World!*

"Hello world!" Mom says sunnily, and it has to be a repeat; she's in the garden, attending to a rose-covered trellis. Robbie, meanwhile, is perched on the wooden chair, cuffs of his Italian sweater pulled over his knuckles and gripped there with thumbs, thighs crossed to keep warm, penis a hardened nub. He shivers deeply, the skin of his scalp crawling above his ears, his frigid bowling ball of a bladder announcing itself from amongst the organs. It's been cold in his apartment all November, ever since he threw that frying pan through the front window – plus, there's a three-inch gap under the kitchen door where now a ridge of snow piles up on the linoleum – but what's the excuse for *this* place? Chrissake, is heating not included in the price of beer, or what?

He tells Brat about Husker and Gaunt. He doesn't tell him the whole story – just how the pigs are hassling him, and how brilliantly he's stymied them in their efforts to nail him down.

"Fuck me," Brat says when he finished. "Are you ever an arsewipe."

"Whut?"

"Scuse, uff uff," Louie Louie announced. "Got to ang my rat over de porcelain."

"You're an innocent asshole not to tell anybody. You should know your rights. Like, SHAZAM!, get an attorney. The pigs are just taking advantage. Bet they've even promised you leniency in court if you tell them the truth."

"Yup."

"Well, you might be off the hook, at least, cause of what's in the Juvenile Delinquents Act. When'd you turn eighteen?"

"January 13th. One minute after midnight – Dad says I kept him up."

"And when was the fire?"

"Umm, January 12th."

"You're shitting me. Where're you hiding that horseshoe, guy? The Juvenile Delinquents Act, OK, is there to protect rubes like you who don't know their ass from a hole in the ground. To coin a phrase. There's a statute, OK, that says 'no confession or statement accepting responsibility for an act made by a person under eighteen is admissible if that person has been promised better treatment for confessing in the first place.' "

"Too much," Robbie said. "Talk about under the wire." He looked up and Mom was on the box with Mendoza. It's the Pets on Pollution part of the show. "Chrissake!" Robbie exclaimed. "He looks like an old doormat."

"Mendoza's only six," Mom said, and the camera closed in on his blotched muzzle, "but he's already got arthritis." She rubbed his face and kissed his nose, and now the camera panned down to his flank. Mendoza's fur had clearly been dropping out in clumps; his flesh was visible in raw, pink slabs.

"More or less what Gaunt's dog must've looked like on the inside," Brat said with a smirk, sucking his beer through a straw. "After I fed him that Drano."

"At first we didn't pay attention," Mom was saying, "but then he started licking his paws, and vomiting. See these cysts? And the mass on his abdomen? He's developed a thyroid problem and a tumour in his testicles. Now we're going to have to put him to sleep."

An interview clip followed in which a Kilborn doctor allowed, under pressure, that he'd noticed some insignificant behavioural abnormalities in his human patients since EPX moved to town.

"Must be hard to tell, out there in Kilborn," Brat said.

"Har har," Robbie replied, and got up to stand closer by the TV. Mom talked about how reluctant Kilborn's working townfolk were to make a fuss about little things like blackheads, bumps, boils, lesions, and pustules, even if they were showing up on their own children. Then she related reports of pets, in other places, drinking from orange streams and rolling in grass near other factories; in Midland, Michigan, where Dow operated, puppies were being born with water on the brain. This episode must have been made over Indian summer, Robbie calculated, but no one ever phoned to tell *him* about the mutt. He'd lost track of time. How long was it exactly since he'd spoken to the family?

"Fuck me," Brat said. "Living in your home must be a constant laff-riot."

"Yeah, well," Robbie said. "Ask me anything about boils and pustules, I know it off by heart."

"Naw," Brat said. "Don't bother me with details."

Louie Louie returned from the can. Robbie's turn now to cross the floor like a zombie and take a jet-stream leak, his eyes full of tears. On the way, lots of old guys, stringy as strips of beef jerky, watched him weave his way. Their bodies have been checked against the boards more than a few times, he observed, they'd taken their share of pucks in the teeth. The only chicks in the joint were on that TV, flashing their frantic jiggly bods to an audience that had come here specifically to escape them.

"*Colline de bines*," Louie Louie whistled when Robbie returned. "Dat fox in de Nissan commercial, she could

189

suck de chrome off a trailer itch." And now they're onto the litany of Louie Louie's regrets. "You know, guys, I'm almos tirty and I tell you dis so you don make de same misstake has me. I fart aroun for ten year wit my 'arley, living off classy girls – like Suzette, who run dat manicure salon, eh – and giving dem great doggies and getting waste. But now wit you I tink tings is appen real soon. I pay my debt and make my vieux père appy. E's get old and I wanna be someone before e die. I'll put is name on de halbum cover too, Beaulieu, in is honour. Make im proud, hosti." *The* Louis Beaulieu stopping now to close his buckshot eyes, and slug back a full glass of piss-thin draught.

Robbie swayed at a thirty-degree angle off his chair and made a face of slack-jawed, loose-lidded superciliousness, *hyulk hyulk*. He's not feeling a fucking thing, never will again. What's the point, the world's already gone to the dogs as it is, what does it need one more fucked-up perspective anyway?

Many more beers, and several bourbons later, off they went at last to become the world famous Hell's Yells. When the Roxy emptied out, the boys hauled their mountain of amps onto the stage in front of the screen, and the projectionist projected movies all over them without the sound. It was the best light show you could imagine – *2001: A Space Odyssey*; *Night of the Living Dead*; *The Rocky Horror Picture Show*; Robbie drunk as a skunk, staggering around, while Brat kicked his guitar screaming across the empty auditorium, and Louie Louie hammered his head with a mike. Robbie feels nothing but his stomach reaching hungrily up his raw bourbon-marinated throat. He's stripped off his shirt to become a fleshpad of moving tattoos. He expands his rib cage and stretches his arms out and opens his ears as big as ravenous mouths to guzzle this amazing noise down, till he's full to the brim. In this ocean of sloshing colour his body is numb, transparent, odourless to him, but he can watch the map of his neon guts flash and slither like the sign outside a pinball parlour – the bile route in electric blue one second, lip-gloss red the next, the sluices of booze and pills in cloudy white, his seething blood-stream a bolted gunmetal grey. When that snail-paced spaceship in *2001* goes by, he imagines himself plunging through a massive glass pane in the black and outer ether; plunging through it with his knees tucked into his chest, head first with the glass splinters slicing past his ears like shooting stars. He throws himself on the floor, again and again, heels pointing backwards like exhaust pipes behind him. He fires whole chambers of dum-dum bullets into his brain, and hollers in tongues like a born-again lunatic. The pigs and their little enquiries, fuck 'em. Bang. Old people, authorities, good health, *fuck* it all. Bang. The future the past my lungs my heart my nerves, *fuck 'em. Bang.* And Ivy, Ivy Mills, *FUCK HER. BANG.* He blasts and reels and thrashes and lunges about. His knees and the palms of his hands scrape and bruise and bleed, but he just can't feel; in those blinks of jagged time, with the bourbon and the black beauties and the heat of his rage as his nuclear fuel, there's no time for reason or respectability or conscience or disappointed adults. He's doing it mind-lessly, meaninglessly, convulsively, like a biker on acid, like an embattled knight, blind and deaf and sweating bullets inside his helmet. Like Keef, he's abandoning himself, at long last, to his own thing.

12

IN SPITE OF THE FACT THAT HE WAS HAVING THE WORST time of his life with her, it always struck him, when he stole a glance, how simply beautiful Ivy was, with that leaping polecat nose of hers and that tussock of bracken-brown hair. His chest swelled up with a shout of joy. He had to clamp his jaw shut. Suppressed, the shout dissolved like intoxicating bubbles throughout his flesh, causing his limbs to tingle, and leaving him weak with anticipation.

Baimy Goldfarb's Holiday Season party, and Robbie knew how everyone would envy him for owning such a beauty. But Ivy chose an armchair that sat only one, and he was forced to kneel at her feet like an obedient puppy.

"Let's play the game," she said, "where we invent characters and meet again for the first time."

So, Robbie thought sadly, it wasn't good enough any more for them to be just Robbie and Ivy. He shrugged, and watched as she retreated still further from him.

"Hi there, guy." Silky Ivy, like she's done this before. "You know anyone here?"

"No way, I don't know nobody, hosti," Robbie said, putting heavy inflections on the words, pepsi-style: *Hi don know no-boddee*. He'd do his best to play. He'd be Gaston. Just to check.

"Gotta light, man?" Ivy held out a joint. "Boring fucken party or what?"

Chrissake, he thought, who's she being? She's so excited she's just about got goose bumps.

"Ayy, tabernacle, it might develop." *Tabarnac, hit might developp.* He watched her beadily, and there was no doubt: she was aroused. Her lips were swollen like the lobes of a Red Delicious apple, a dimple in the middle where moments ago the stem had attached it to the branch of the tree. Her eyelids drifted drowsily down, like leaves in a humid orchard. She put the joint in her mouth and drew it out to wet the rolling paper. Then she did the same to Robbie's index finger. He could smell her saliva, rich, like mulched earth.

Trying now to make conversation, but nothing comes, and she just sits there looking like death warmed-over. Occasionally, she blows her bangs off her forehead. He's searching, really riffling through his mind for something, anything to say. It's an incredible sensation, being utterly blank like this. And being stoned makes him hyperaware of being utterly blank. Well, maybe this is what it's really like to be Gaston, arf arf. He finishes his beer, fuel for thought, maybe. But it's like the Earth has stopped spinning, and every subject that ever existed has flown off the face of the planet.

He goes to the fridge for fresh beers, where Brat says in his ear, "She's not overly cute, but – *coochie coochie coo.*"

And Robbie snaps back, "Don't razz me, man. That's not what our thing's about. I don't give two shits if she's cute."

Brat takes Robbie upstairs to meet his grandmother. She's sitting alone in her room, knitting. There's so much wool in her lap, and she's so round and compact and fleecy, Robbie has the impression that she's knitting herself. She looks up, and listens to Brat with applied concentration, nodding after every word and looking at Robbie

193

like he were the Eighth Wonder of the World. Robbie smiles a lot. His face hurts doing it.

"She's deaf as a coot," Brat says.

"Are you behaving yourselves?" the old lady says.

"NICE AS PIE, GRANDMOTHER," Brat shouts.

Downstairs, the party has taken off. Several couples are making out on the couch, several ashtrays have coughed up their contents on the carpet, and someone has knocked over the Chanukah bush. Robbie goes to the stereo, rudely lifts some fucking disco piece of shit off the turntable, and puts on the Bones instead. From across the room, Ivy makes a grave face and thumbs up, and begins to bob her head determinedly. He sits down again and strokes her shin. With fresh hope, he goes, "I would like join de club of your brudder."

Ivy looks at him for several beats, her head still bobbing. She looks really stupid, Robbie thinks, much too intense. Then she says, "God. You're a complete and total idiot, you know that? Ever since we fucked, up against the playground wall, I've wanted to kill myself. *L'enfer c'est les autres*, do you understand *dat*?"

"Sure," Robbie says, shaken, unsure if she's talking to him or to Gaston. Is that what they did, *fuck against the playground wall*? Or is she just testing him? He should have thought of that, and now he's in too deep. His nervous system feels like it's short-circuiting, burning his flesh from the inside. "Right. Dat bad, huh? I shoulda tought of dat."

"No, you shouldn't, Robbie. You think too much, that's your problem. Don't dream it. Be it. That's existentialism. That's what I'm talking about."

"Yeah." He's lost his grip on his character completely now. "I know what you mean. It's like sometimes I feel like smashing things. I want to throw things around the room, but I'm, I. . . . "

While he searches for the right words, Ivy lifts her beer

194

bottle over her head and whips it clear across the room at a glass-front cabinet filled with chinaware. The crash brings even Brat's grandmother, fretting, to the top of the stairs. The whole party stands around the shattered glass and froth on the carpet, silently, and then turns to Ivy and Robbie. Ivy's tugging at her hair, making fleabitten ears, and grinning like the Cheshire Cat.

"Time to disappear," she says, sweeps up her overcoat and flies out of the house.

Robbie lingers. He's worried that people will think they're breaking up. Grandma Goldfarb is hysterical. She shrieks and beats at him with her cane and drives him out the front door.

Outside it's quiet, way below zero. Under the late-night crushed-ice sky, Ivy's on her back in the snow with her winter clothes scattered all around. A broken column of breath rises from her mouth. She's laughing so hard she's barely making a sound. When she notices Robbie standing there, she claps her red, mittenless hands and scoops snow up at him and manages, "And I bet you were terribly worried what everyone in there thought, too!"

Robbie forces a laugh and sits on top of her and beats her up playfully. She resists ferociously, shoves his nose with the butt of her palm.

"Oww! Hey," he cries. "We're being *convulsive* now – right?"

"Not at all. Or at least, I'm glad I don't have to spell it out for you. Now, will you please get off of me."

Charcoal on his fingers, he spent most afternoons the week preceding Xmas holidays sketching Ivy in the attic. He had heaps of studies of her now, in all her moods – Ivy looking distant, Ivy being moody, Ivy brooding, Ivy being morose, Ivy guarding a secret, Ivy with an abstract thought, Ivy saturated with liquor and longing, Ivy doing her batik, absolutely nude.

He asked her if she was addicted to smack. She said, "God, no. You know me."

"Ha! That's what everybody . . . "

Ivy's response to that was to look up from her batik, and gaze through the window with a flinch of irritation. Then, just as he expected her to dunk the canting into the molten wax and bend over the cloth again, she sighed and said, "God. What makes people dangerous addicts is not having stuff around to chip. I have all I want. Only problem I get is, well, constipation. Real bad, you have no idea. The other day I had to pull the log out with my fingers."

As for joining her, meanwhile – forget it. He was paranoid of needles to begin with, but he also considered himself a real smart head, a most discerning individual, to never even smoke the hard stuff or skinpop it or anything stupid like that. K, to explain: some stones are cool, 'cause the drugs will do the thinking for you in times of stress, of which there are many during the teens; you don't always feel too clever – in fact sometimes you feel dumb as a dog – but at least when you're stoned, the blues zip by like lightning. Time is your friend, for once. Anyway, here are some of the drugs he figured a person can handle in moderation: Maryjane, obviously, kif too, honey oil, all that. Bennies of any variety (blackbirds, cartwheels, cranks, dexies, greenies, jelly babies, lidpoppers, pink amps, green amps, crystal meth, you name it). What else – snappers, gunk, stinkweed. All the kitchen conveniences: catnip, mellow yellow, wild lettuce, kola nuts, nutmeg, parsley, fennel, dill. And the stuff in the cabinet; paregoric and Valium and Demerol. What else? Yellow jackets, Christmas trees, goofers, Mexican reds, red devils, rainbows, Seconal. Canary Island broom, sweet flag, calea, California poppies, camphor, betel nuts. Jeez, what else:

wedgies – you know, flats of various kinds like sunshine, pearly gates, blue cheer, windowpane, strawberry fields, purple microdot. Then all the alphabet: MDA, STP, PCP, DMT, MBD, DOM. Ummm. Mesc, ludes, mandrakes, quacks, laughing gas, peyote, passionflower, percs, magic mushrooms. Most of that, if you're sensible, like Robbie, and don't overdo it and don't mix too many of them together at once or with booze or nothing, is cool. Go ahead, he'd say, try 'em all. You're only young once.

But Robbie did have a bottom line of KEEP OUT OF REACH OF CHILDREN items: death's head, because, well, the name speaks for itself. Ahh . . . what else? It was a very short list. Hard to think. Belladonna, that's pretty dumb, unless you want to look like the Bride of Frankenstein with a wicked hangover. Black Henbane. Spanish fly, but that doesn't do nothing, anyways. Cocaine's too expensive, so he'll cross that bridge when he gets to it. Opium, well, you almost never see it. Except when you know Ivy. And if you do and you do it, your stomach feels like the bottom of a bird cage saturated in fermented parrot droppings. And top of the list, the *numero uno* no-no, is junk. Who can really handle it, except Keef Richards, and he regularly flushes his blood out at a Swiss clinic and never had to hang out on the Main at Ste-Catherine at midnight to score some horse that you just know is going to be cut with baby laxative. Why bother? Everybody knows it'll drag you down. Just look at Ivy, fuck.

"We-ell," she said in an amused drawl, her nose to the cloth, when he expressed his concern, "it shouldn't come as such a surprise to you. How else could a person find the concentration to do all this detail? Heh, heh."

Robbie discovered that, when she was stoned like this, she was kinder to him, and more wistful. "Java," she'd say. "Can't you just picture it?" Robbie would look up and see her smiling to herself, meticulously trailing beads of wax on the coloured cloth. A long silence. The wintry wind buffeting the windows. The concentrated silence of class-rooms below, punctuated occasionally by the shout of an irate teacher. The spinning and spitting of tires on the snow-choked streets. Robbie contentedly sketching. Then she'd murmur along some more.

"Olly said one day he'll let me go. It'd be warm and humid. We'd just wear these cotton sarongs or something. And hike to the ocean when we felt like it. Mellow, breezy, you know? Maybe we'd eat spicy goat stew, with bamboo hearts, and tea. And the purple mountains all around. God. Can't you just picture it? You would have your head shaved with just a plait at the back. Me, too. I could also be a boy, just about. I'd wear a Bones T-shirt. . . . "

Now, when he said kinder, Robbie didn't really mean *kind* at all, since kindness requires some conscious effort, and he had come to the conclusion that Ivy was barely conscious at all, at least not of him. This was confirmed the morning he presented his Xmas gift to her: the last week of school, the cold slush had soaked through the shankless soles of his boots, and he was under a cloud; if there was one thing he hated more than studying, it was sports. He was nowhere near good enough a skater to make the school hockey team, so he was forced to play with the misfits, the leftovers and the losers. Worst of all were the chill showers, plus the smells of sweat and steam and mouldy towels and rotting wood, which he had hated and feared since he was six: boys with bellies and thighs as red and thick as boiled hams, blotchy bums. Shoving and shouting. Robbie self-conscious about being circumcized, shivering in a corner. He'd hide his underwear behind a radiator, so no one would steal it in the changing room. Then, when he pulled it out, it'd be matted with dust and spiderwebs.

Ivy hated gymnastics class equally, so they *fucksed* together, and sat in Pendeli's.

"The whole school thing's a joke," Robbie said, "I've decided doing well isn't so much to do with studying as using your head."

"That's a perilous rationalization from someone like you," Ivy said.

"Right, sure. Ahh, look, I'd like to give you a present."

"Over my dead body. What for?"

"Christmas of course! And because I, I . . . "

"No. Don't even *think* of saying it."

Here's what he gave her: a new pair of mittens with the fingertips snipped so she could read at bus stops, and an anthology of Albert Camel's poetry.

"I had to sell some of my records," he told her proudly.

Ivy held the book at arm's length, turned it over doubtfully. "Who's Albert Camel?"

"One of your favorite *writers*," Robbie answered with a trace of irritation in his voice, for he was starting to suspect that she hadn't bought him a thing in return. "You've said so a hundred times. He wrote a book about a plague, you said."

Ivy gave him a condescending look. "That's Albert *Camus*. Thanks, anyway. Oh, hey. Look, I can see it in your face. That's exactly the sort of pain I try to avoid at Christmas by not buying presents for anyone. You can never please people. And if you do like what you've been given, you can't be sure what the person's motive was in giving it to you. I don't have to prove my affection for you by giving you a gift. I could give you a gift and not mean it."

Robbie shrugged unhappily. "You mean, if I didn't give you a gift, you would have been happier?"

"No, but I think *you* would have. Anyway, don't worry. It's not worth me explaining."

"I'd like you to explain, so I can understand."

"If I have to explain it, then you wouldn't understand it."

"K, then," Robbie said, and made a scrunched-up, resentful mouth. "Sorry." But he wasn't. His spirits had sunk to an all-time low. Why was it, he wondered, that when you're with the person you love, you can so rarely manage even the simplest things? On his own, he had inspired conversations with her all the time, but those flights of giddy fancy always eluded him in real life; the rehearsed hilarity, the solemnity, and the moments of special intimate fusing never took place. And here he was again, severed from all natural experience, void of wit and energy. He barely recognized himself. She'd probably leave him now, and who could blame her? He pulled back his ears, felt the skin stretching over his face, widening his eyes like fleshy satellite dishes to pick up clues. Some distant signal of love. And only now he saw how the pupils in her eyes were constricted. And how her skin was pallid and damp. That was all he needed to know. And only now, he knew how much he hated her.

Xmas Day, and Robbie was elbow-to-elbow with her bizarro family, having a hard time dealing with what a privileged middle-class kid he was. He was casting his eyes around and going, *These are poor people.*

He hated himself for thinking it, on this day of all days, but the words came up involuntarily: *What a pathetic meal. Is this all?*

The thing is, he'd never eaten in a poor family's home before. Well, once before, when he was about eleven: a friend of a friend, at a pickup hockey game on Staynor Street, had taken him home for a Mae West and a Dr. Pepper and a TV dinner, and while they were watching *Dark Shadows* on a snowy UHS channel, the friend's baby sister had hauled a foot-long tapeworm out of her throat, like a translucent linguine, right there on the carpet.

Anyway, now Robbie was the guest of a solemnly Christian family, whose few joys were being summed up in a prayer and a supermarket meal. He was wondering how he was going to finish this glutinous mess – a slice of a deboned turkey sitting in a pond of just-add-water potato mash, some sugary gravy, and a bank of diced mixed vegetables that are paler than they appear in the colour supplements.

Is this all?

He knows the whole do will set the parents back enough to ensure their January Blues last at least two months, and he can see that Ivy's elder sister, Julie, for one, is filled with simple joy and forgetting herself in all this luxury, but he can't stop the hot, vomitty voice in the back of his head, *Is this it? If this is the best they can come up with . . .*

He wants to slap his own face. He doesn't want to think these thoughts. He's not like this.

This place stinks. They're ugly, too.

Chrissake, stop.

The dining room was two rooms really, cut in half by a fanfold wall on a floor-rail; since this was the big Xmas meal, and ten people were eating, they'd opened up the wall, laid out tables end-to-end, and now right behind him was the parents' bed.

Olly was there with Karen and the two kiddies. "Hi," Robbie said, pumping Karen's hand, "Remember me? I'm Mr. Big Balls." She looked more surprised than shocked, but Robbie was satisfied that he'd scored as the NEW! IMPROVED! him he was planning to be for Ivy from now on – an armoured, insensitive Robbie, giving nothing away for free. Meanwhile he gathered that Mr. and Mrs. Mills thought Olly was in real estate. Olly had brought gifts. For Ivy, *The Trembling of a Leaf* by Somerset Maugham, and something even for Robbie – the Bones' *Cambodian Relief* charity album, autographed by Keef himself. Robbie thanked him, but avoided his eyes (so much for the NEW! ARMOURED! Robbie); since Olly had apparently done so much for him the last time they had spoken (and Robbie had said so little, been so unspecific), he was afraid just exchanging glances might have some deadly consequence. And Ivy had given Olly a present in return – a batik scarf, with intricate *kala* mask designs and TV sets and hockey sticks. Robbie watched as he proudly wrapped it around his neck.

Ivy's younger brother, John, had a family method Robbie could relate to – he holed up with a coil heater in the alley garage, tinkering with a chemistry lab which he financed by holding down five paper routes – another way of keeping clear of home, and who could blame him – plus, apparently, Olly paid him for the occasional assignment. Out in the garage, John showed Robbie his latest explosives experiment, utilizing just everyday chemical products.

Julie was troubling Robbie, meanwhile; she appeared just a few degrees too full up with delight at this Xmas banquet. Her teeth were creamy, she rolled her eyes a lot, and, horror of horrors, she seemed to be flirting with him.

Mr. Mills sat at the head of the table, carving the turkey with frightening enthusiasm. Mrs. Mills was flushed with merry energy, intoxicating herself with her own chitchat. "So this *Cuckoo* movie, how fun it was!" she called out from the kitchen in her bleating voice, a voice that rode hysteria bareback, always threatening to break, "It remind me of birds, how cruel to putting them in cages, like those hostage in Amsterdam, *hein*? Are you kids see the big Stroll and Bone show next week?"

Robbie's mouth was stopped up with a lump of hardened potato powder. He tried to swallow. His cutlery felt heavy in his hands. He thought of how dwarf stars are so dense, that a teaspoon of their magma weighs a million tons. Mrs. Mills bent down to pull a dish from the oven.

Mr. Mills found his opening. "You are idiots," he said,

his smug smile wet with wine, "lining up all night just for a rock show."

"AYOI!" Mrs. Mills screamed. She dropped the dish full of pudding, buttered glass scattering around the floor, and vigorously shook her fingers in the air.

"Hey, hey, let me do it, Ma!" Olly said, leaping out of his chair. "Sit down, OK. Maybe you've had a little – "

"I am NOT DRUNK," Mrs. Mills shouted gutturally, her face as red as her fingers, "so SHUT UP." Then she turned pleasantly to Robbie, awaiting his answer, and placed a spoonful of glass-spiked pudding on his plate.

"Well, um," Robbie said. Now the potato was lodged in his throat, and squeezing down like a croquet ball in an ostrich's neck. He avoided Julie's lopsided, attentive, admiring face. "I think it's interesting to see the city come alive – delivery trucks, workers coming into the greasy spoon for their coffees and dogs and westerns. . . . "

"We had once a dog," Mrs. Mills started, "a chi – "

"That's my point," Mr. Mills said quickly. "If you found the same time and energy – kids today are all over the place, like an old woman's piss. What have you got to be angry with? When I was your age I worked at that greasy spoon. Every morning I had to haul buckets of chicken, giblets, legs, livers, breasts, into that same kitchen – "

"Oh, *cher*," Mrs. Mills butted in. "Not buckets, you telled me – pails."

"What, *cher*?"

"Not buckets – *pails* of chicken. That's what you telled me."

"Buckets, pails, what's the – "

"Oh there's a big difference. They're not the same."

"OK, *pails*, if it means so much to you."

Robbie dug a trench in his muddy turkey. Ivy nudged him with her knee below the table.

"Well, it does. I think a person must speak properly well."

"Yes, of course, ma bonne femme, but I – "

"If you don't have command of the good English, how can you earn respect? You said that to me much times."

And Robbie thinking, This is not a well family. How could a person as imaginative and beautiful as Ivy have sprung from the loins of these Nazi humanoids from outer space. I must *rescue* her from all this.

"You should call them pails," Mrs. Mills warbled.

While the family bowed their heads to say closing Grace, Robbie looked around: a set of Coronation plates up on the wall, a stumpy Eskimo sculpture on the coffee table, a set of Russian doll-eggs, set along the mantlepiece in diminishing size, and unbelievably (but *someone* must be buying these things, so you have to believe it) a portrait of a weeping clown on black velvet. There were dozens of Hallmark cards with doe-eyed angels, pussycats playing with Xmas baubles, and gauzy portraits of the baby Jesus. Plus a plastic light-up Santa Claus face and a scrawny aluminum tree on top of the TV set. It was all enough to make you very sad. And, Robbie thought to himself, What have they received that they've got to be so truly thankful for?

As soon as the prayer was over, John climbed out of his chair. He left the room without a word; off to the lab.

"I'm so anger with him," Mrs. Mills said to Olly.

"Aw, relax, Ma," Olly said, good-naturedly, little Cissy bouncing on his lap. "Give the kid a break. Give him time."

"Time. I'm run out of time. I've waited long enough for the respect. I want it now."

"The whole family's here, Ma. What more do you want? Merry Christmas, OK?"

But Mrs. Mills wasn't listening. She was tickling Julie in the ribs. "Aiy ma pauvre minoune, would you like one of my chocolates now? Oui? Well, come and give Maman a kiss, first." Julie squirmed, and cackled with delight. Mrs. Mills tickled her harder and Julie, her eyes rolling wildly, her teeth in a froth, tried to squirm free. Now it was clear she was hurting. She sent her head back and bonked her mother on the nose. Mrs. Mills tossed Julie to the ground, and now the tender moment was spoiled. Mr. Mills sat and watched. Ivy sat, looking at her lap, scrunching her hair. She hadn't spoken in an hour. She was drinking wine, nose in her book, she was in Java. Karen was changing a stinky diaper on the bed.

"French-Canadians are incredible," Mr. Mills announced pleasantly. "Did you know that 75 per cent of them have not read a book since high school, much less a French book? Statistics show they watch seven hours of TV a day – American sitcoms. They refuse to give up their big American cars, they holiday in Miami and Maine, and they talk about French heritage – HA! – the way they're going, they'll be calling the energy crisis theirs, and end up trying to make *Florida* independent."

Silence around the table at that one. Ivy sipped her wine. Even Mrs. Mills was quiet.

"What *d'you* think? This language commission they're proposing, the French language cops, it's an inquisition, isn't it? Don't tell me none of those FLQ thugs and murderers got jobs with the party."

No one said a word, though Robbie was wondering if he really said, *Whajew think*, or if he was only slurring his words because he was drunk. Ivy scrunched her hair, gripped her wineglass tighter. Mr. Mills moved his glass to his lips, but poured too soon and wine spilled down his chin. He took a different tack. "What's your family doing today? Working?"

Robbie jumped. "Who, mine? Oh, no, not today. We have Xmas, sort of, Bookbindermas really. We have Easter, too, and Passover, the whole shabang. It's just my parents feel you shouldn't have one single religion stuffed down your throat before you're old enough to decide."

Ivy's leg under the table.

"The problem with you kids, is," Mr. Mills said, little pig

tails appearing in his cheeks, twisting his chunky wine glass (the kind of goblet you get FREE! after purchasing ten litres of gasoline) between his thumb and forefinger, and examining it like some precious jewel, "you're not aware of how short life is. You just screw around, devil may care, when you have no idea. You think that money grows on trees – "

" – but," Mrs. Mills jumped in, "you won't shake a limb to get it! That's not your joke, isn't it, cher?"

"Yes, *cher*, that's my joke," Mr. Mills said, wearily. And his stitched-on smile completely unravelled.

"Let's dance!" Mrs. Mills exclaimed, and yanked Robbie up by the arm. She was strong, and her breath was as warm as the bottom of her stomach. The room whirled around, she was whooping. Robbie caught a glimpse of Ivy as he turned. She had snapped the stem of her wineglass in two. Her fingers were bloody, and she was licking them calmly.

A dull POOM from the back of the apartment. Everyone jumped. Olly leaped from his chair again, hopping over other chairs to get to the door.

By the time the whole family had stamped down the back stairs and gathered at the door of the garage, Olly had already picked John off the floor and was holding him in his arms.

"I knew I put in too much potassium permanganate," John said, with a stupid smile. The family looked stupidly back. The skin was burnt right off John's stupid face. The Stupid family, Robbie thought. The Stupid family have a very Merry Christmas.

He felt pretty grown-up, sitting in this taxi with his luggage on his lap. It was the first time he had ever paid for one himself. He was watching the meter with an eagle eye now, too amazed at how quickly it clicked by to enjoy the moment fully, but riding high and proud as if the cab were a royal carriage, and seeing the world renewed in the light of love. Two days after Xmas they were taking a secret holiday trip. To Montreal. It was Robbie's idea. He was asserting himself in this relationship, now. He had sold a hundred more of his beloved records, and Ivy had borrowed money from Olly, lying to her parents that she was staying in the burbs with him. They checked into the grandest hotel they could afford – the Hotel Bonaventure, a poured-concrete mammoth of a building situated above the Bonaventure shopping mall.

They stood on street corners, making a show of being lost; holding their street maps upside-down and squinting at them and thanking people for their help in wild accents. They bought postcards with Mounties on them, fumbled with foreign currency Robbie had stolen from the parents' dresser. They were loaded with brandy and laughing helplessly. Robbie posed for a picture outside Ben's smoked-meat restaurant. He stood with his hands on his hips and breathed in deeply, savouring the illusion cold air has of always smelling clean, even in downtown traffic. They went to the planetarium, and the Musée des Beaux Arts, visiting sights in town they had taken for granted all their lives. They bought swimsuits for the hotel pool. Robbie was full of joy that their relationship was so rejuvenated, and at one point, when Ivy was looking the other way, he looked at the sky and winked heavenward, real chummy, like, thumbs up, man.

How humiliating to be treated like a child, at his age. Moments after they had sat down in this snooty hotel restaurant, with its suffocating drapery and undead waiters, the maitre d' smoothly inquired if Robbie was paying cash or credit. Cash, Robbie answered pleasantly, and only after the vampire asked if he'd like to pay in advance did he feel a creeping sense of indignation. He had nicely combed his hair, parting it down the middle. Now he sat with it drawn close to his cheeks, which made the long face he pulled look even longer.

"When Hell's Yells are a big success," he promised Ivy, "I'm gonna stitch together a jacket of hundred-dollar bills and wear it specially for dumps like these."

It was no fun here at all. You couldn't shout or burp or eat sitting on the floor in front of a TV if you wanted. And old people were everywhere, murmuring. Even the air seemed like old air. All this formality. His shoulders felt as stiff as a coat hanger. People *pay* for this?

Ivy wasn't enjoying herself either. She rolled one cigarette after another, making vertical creases between her eyebrows as if this was a punishment Robbie was imposing on her like a parent, as a prelude to a spank. She was doing her best to make him feel responsible for everything that was ugly and pretentious about the place; each time she made sneering faces at the luxury-liner decor, or shot her eyes over at some snatch of artificial conversation, it was as if she were saying he had done this to her on purpose.

It was coming over Robbie, like the first twinge of nausea, that this so-called relationship was still as delicate, as uncertain, as a hungover stomach. Maybe Ivy had been right all along; they just weren't made for each other. He skimmed over the menu. He could make out about half of it, but just to prove to the seethingly solicitous waiter that he didn't need help with the rest, he ordered the most expensive item: *riz de veau*.

"Fifteen bucks for rice," he grumbled to Ivy, after the waiter had strode away. And he knew now he was competing with her to be pissed off the most, as if finding fault here was a special mark of sophistication. "What's the point of being rich if everything you buy costs more? Life is really fucked."

Ivy absently brushed breadcrumbs into rows on the tablecloth. She said, " – "

All right, so *riz de veau* turned out to be sheep's brains, which took him by surprise, but even Robbie could tell that the gazpacho was cold and the crème caramel was barely set. The espresso coffee was shitty too, served in an insultingly tiny cup with mud at the bottom, and the bill arrived much faster than any of the courses had; the *Night of the Living Dead* waiter plopped the vinyl folder on the table and gave him a look of royal disdain, as he lingered. *Braiins*, Robbie thought, and said, "I s'pose you think we're just gonna take off, like run out on you."

"Yes, *monsieur*," the waiter said, bowing politely with a smile like the crease in a starched napkin.

The hotel's rooftop swimming pool was the best place in the world to air your head out after a nightmare like that, and even better because Robbie and Ivy were the only ones there. They swam out through a tunnel and emerged beneath the night sky in an emerald pool sliced with underwater scimitars of light. The surface steamed thickly, as if it were boiling and evaporating into space, and the sides of the pool were piled high with snow. Craning their necks, Robbie and Ivy could see the tops of Montreal's skyscrapers illuminated, and the aerial beam atop Place Ville-Marie stirring up drifts in the refrigerated heavens. To the south, FARINE RED ROSES FLOUR blinked on and off in red neon, and that was the factory you drove past on your way to Kilborn and the Eastern Townships.

"Later, I'll read from my diary," Ivy said to him, nose to his nose. She was panting as she paddled, blinking water from her eyelashes, her otter eyes all icy and dark.

Robbie now with the curious sensation of swimming with an erection, like a rudder below him. Rolling over, and his swimming trunks looked like a shark's fin slicing the surface. He lay still in the mist and watched the stars twinkle above him. By narrowing his eyes to eclipse his peripheral vision, he could feel as if he were floating alone in ripply space, unravelling time, erasing memory, expanding in all directions at once, convulsing ecstatically.

"I wonder what that sheep's last thoughts were," he said, still feeling queasy.

They swam back to the changing area and, shivering, hugged. He grasped Ivy's wet rubber body and was seized with panic; this was all too beautiful, he feared, surely it couldn't last. He held her tenderly, taking care not to squeeze her breasts too hard, or crush her thigh, lest her precious flesh be accelerated on its road to softening and decay. Desperately, he thought that if he held her gently like this, for as long as possible, maybe time would cease for them both. But then Ivy wriggled free.

He changed and waited for her where they had hugged. After ten minutes he went back to the pool and asked the attendant if he had seen anyone. The attendant shrugged. Robbie went down the hall to the women's locker room. No answer. He pushed the door open cautiously and peeked in. No one there. There was Ivy's gym bag, there were her clothes and shoes, but there were no other signs, not even wet foot marks on the floor.

He felt sick. Had she been kidnapped? Had she gone off with someone else? *Downtown, for a straight fast fuck.* She was capable of it, but in her *swimsuit*? Was it a game, then? Where could she be hiding? He went down to the hotel room, but she wasn't there. He sat on the bed, and despondently watched TV. And Mom was on, of course. A rerun: about the way dry cleaners routinely pump masses of chloroethylenes into the atmosphere; the piece started off breezily – Paris runways, flashbulbs popping, Eurobeat music, women shopping and wearing the new styles – just to suck you in, but ended sneakily with a shot of a toxic cloud. Rain fell, women got drenched, their clothes went to the cleaners, and then Mom laid on the fact that these and other emissions contribute to the contaminated atmospheric sink, and may soon add up to cleaning bills no one can afford to pay.

A knock on the door. Robbie looked through the peephole and there, in the convex distortion of the lens, was Ivy in her swimsuit. He opened the door. She was dry, and in a fury.

"You want to know what happened, I suppose. Well, I pushed the wrong door up there. I locked myself in the stairwell. I banged, but you never came. So I went down the stairs, fifteen flights, opened another door at the bottom, and I was right in *the middle of the Bonaventure mall*."

"You were right in the middle of the Bonaventure mall?" Robbie repeated incredulously. "Crack me up!"

"God. It's not a bit funny, you know. It's still late-night shopping down there. People are bringing back all the stupid Christmas gifts they've had dumped on them by their relatives. The place is packed."

"Were you embarrassed?" Robbie said with a snorting laugh. "Even *you* must've been."

"You know me. I walked through the crowd with my head up. Maybe people thought I was a promotional gimmick for a travel agency, I didn't care. Anyway, that's not the point. The point is I was walking along and I bumped into the father."

"*Fucksake!*"

"He was returning presents. His arms were full of them, he almost didn't see me. Now he's in the lobby settling our bill. I *told* you no good comes of giving Christmas presents. *God*."

Even if there had been time to flee, where would they have gone? So they packed their bags. Robbie fixed his glare at a reproachful heavenwards angle, his hot skull like a Trojan helmet with iron eyes. In the hall now, Ivy moved like a ghost – in the way he was accustomed to seeing her, only now he understood why – hugging walls, sliding from one place to the next as if she were afraid of being swatted. And just as she said, her father was there in the lobby as the elevator opened. He was winding his thumbs and looking like The Stuffed Toy from Hell. No doubt he was in a rage after discovering the amount of brandy they had ordered up on room service. Now he was marching towards them and, some ten feet away, raised his hand to strike. Robbie ducked instinctively, but it was Ivy Mr. Mills swatted.

"Let's go," he said. "Fun's over."

"Later for *that*, man," Robbie said, taking his most challenging stance: hands clasped casually behind his neck like this is a walk in the park, his dry gulch eyes flaring, and an arid smirk on his lips. "I say let's rap."

"I say this better be good," Mr. Mills replied. "You've got five minutes."

Back in the suffocating restaurant then, and a funky cocktail lounge act had hit the stage. The pantywaist musicians with their poodle haircuts were going at a repertoire of chart-toppers with the keener enthusiasm of boy scouts doing camp activities. Robbie was alert to the minutest change in the atmosphere, sensitive to the molecular vibrations in this dead place, to Ivy's rapid breathing. He stood by the table, legs apart, one knee resonating madly, his hands where a holster might be, his neck cocked back. Mr. Mills sat down, elbows on the table like an opponent in an arm-wrestling match, and stabbed the tablecloth with a heavy index finger. Robbie obediently sat. Ivy sat too, and rolled a cigarette.

"What's this?" Mr. Mills demanded. "Has he started you smoking, too? Dear Lord, what have you done to my daughter?"

"K, wait," Robbie said, supersmooth. "Cool your jets. What exactly is eating you?"

"What is *eating* me? What is *eating* me?" Mr. Mills was apoplectic. A waiter arrived. Mr. Mills ordered water, all around.

"Will that be mineral water, sir? Perrier? With lemon? With lime?"

"TAP water," Mr. Mills snapped, and Robbie was amazed at how briskly the waiter turned on his heel and took off. He sought Ivy's leg beneath the table, and rubbed their shins together. But Mr. Mills must have had his leg stretched out too, and that must have been the one Robbie was rubbing, because it abruptly withdrew.

"STOP that!" Mr. Mills barked. He stood up and grabbed Ivy's chair from behind, yanking it several feet back from the table with Ivy still on it. Ivy didn't register one iota of surprise. She held on to the side of the chair for balance, that's all. Then she crossed her legs, scrunched her hair, and reached to the table for her tobacco pouch.

"What exactly is up your ass, man?" Robbie said, and he could hear his voice wobbling. "I mean, sorry. I'll say that more politely – you seem about to have a heart attack. Why is that?"

"Because I love my daughter. You kids don't think up here," pointing at his own head, "you think down there," pointing at Ivy's crotch. "My wife always told me about your kind. Taking advantage of French-Canadian girls."

Robbie knew exactly what Mr. Mills meant by *your kind*, because you never feel more Jewish than when you're accused of being it. No one has to say the words – you just know. And since when did this guy ever listen to his wife? What a cheap shot, how obvious – Mr. Mills had to be only going for *Jew* because, for want of a nigger or a chink, Jew was the nearest available target. Like really, Robbie thought, what real reason was there to dislike a Jew more than anyone else? He suddenly found himself taking a stand against all prejudice everywhere in the world, because it is so cheap, and so promiscuous. However much Robbie would have liked to change that word *Jew* into something grander-sounding, like *Mesopotamian* or *Atlantean* or *Carthaginian* – something with a prouder architecture, with more than just one syllable, that you couldn't just spit out – however embarrassed he was to catch himself unawares in the mirror and see that old melancholic, hunted look in his own eyes (wondering if, in Nazi Germany, he would have been pegged for a Jew as he boarded a train to escape the country), it still didn't jibe with him to be pigeon-holed. So he said, "Hey, man, watch what you say, I'm Robbie Bookbinder."

"I know who you are," Mr. Mills said. "You're just an angry young man. And I know you've been corrupting my fifteen-year-old daughter."

Fifteen? Jeez. She always said she was *seventeen*. The waiter brought a tray, with three glasses, setting them down with laborious precision, one by one.

"I told myself it was OK if she missed a curfew or two," Mr. Mills said, at last. "I told myself, what's a few beers. I told myself, they'll break up soon enough without my help. My daughter isn't stupid, I reassured myself. But I will not take any more now I know she's on the pill."

"The pill?"

"Don't bullshit me, you little sneak," Mr. Mills said. "You've got two more minutes to say your piece, then we're gone."

Robbie looked at Ivy. She didn't look up. She was concentrating – perversely, Robbie thought – on striking a match. "Ahh, how do you know she's on the pill?" he ventured.

"I don't have to tell you."

"I wanna know, K."

"All right. I was borrowing her clock-radio. The cord was tangled under her bed."

"You call me a sneak," Robbie exclaimed, and slapped his own forehead. "Look, man, we haven't exactly made love yet, but to be honest we were planning it. And it wasn't going to be in some sleazy dive or nothing. That's why we came here. It was going to be, like, a celebration, really beautiful, with chocolates and – "

"I don't want to HEAR about it," Mr. Mills shouted, pounding the table. The water and ice jumped from the glasses, and ashes were dashed from Ivy's ashtray. People turned their heads.

"Hey, man, hey!" Robbie said. "Is that how you bring up your kids, by punching 'em out?"

"You'll have kids one day, you'll see."

"No way, José."

"You ought to be horsewhipped yourself. I'm going to your father to explain my methods in person."

"Good luck. Corporate punishment is against family policy, I'm afraid." You can't really take him seriously, Robbie thought, lancing him with a look. His chest ached. Whew! he thought, I've hated people before, but those hates were farts in the wind compared to this. "Haven't you heard," he said, "these are the *seventies*."

"That's *enough*," Mr. Mills shouted. "Ivy, sweetheart, we're going. And you – if you so much as dream of her again. . . ."

He hauled Ivy out of her seat by one arm and dragged her out of the restaurant. Ivy didn't resist; she expressed her indifference by fussing with her tobacco pouch. Lots of people were looking over now. He ignored them, pretending to enjoy the band. He drummed his fingers on the tabletop, tapped his foot, took a sip of water. And in the din inside his skull, he replayed the event, word for angry word, and wondered if there was anything he had said that you could really blame him for. And Mr. Mills would surely repent once he cooled down; the fat fuck would soon see that, unlike Robbie, he had let his dignity slip. It would all work out fine in the end.

13

MRS. GRISSOM HAD HIS NUMBER AND SHE LIKED TO USE IT. She had no consideration – at six in the morning or eleven-thirty at night, she had her bony finger primed to dial. And sometimes she phoned before Robbie'd even had a chance to put the record on. What, he wondered, was she standing on her dining-room table with her ear to the ceiling, monitoring his every approach to the turntable? He tossed in bed over the fact that the more useless people become in society, the more you're supposed to respect them.

The phone rang. Now it was Rosie on the line.

"Hi!" she shouted in his ear above the din of the strip club. "I'm just calling to let you know how happy I am. REAL happy. I'm on my break, I have a little time, so – how about you tell me why you don't love me, and I'll tell you why you're wrong!"

Robbie had figured a phone of his own would allow him to gab with friends without getting razzed by family for once in his life, but he never expected it to be a liability. Unravelling the dusty mummy bandages of sleep after his slumber of centuries is difficult; his arms are bound by the sheets, he can hardly roll over, there are heavy pennies on his eyes.

"Whatsamatter Bob, can't you show me you miss me? I still have to *work*. I was getting frisky'n I was thinking I'm going back to *astrological* birth control – it'll be less messy for you. Dr. Eugen Jonas says women have a SECOND fertility period called the *cosmic* period'n that occurs each time the sun and moon are in the same ANGULAR relation to each other as they were when the woman was born'n that's every twenty-nine and a half days, like the lunar cycle. . . . "

Robbie's trying hard to rise from his sarcophagus, but his body is thick with muzzy embalming fluids. "I'm a Capricorn," he manages. "Capricorns don't believe in astrology."

"Really? I didn't know that about Capricorns – oh, wait, wait. You shouldn't make fun like that, Bob. I'm starting to believe you're not the romantic I once saw you as. You're too much in love with cold hard facts."

"Yeah, well," Robbie retorted, "it's better than you, clinging to the sixties like a burr on the pants of time."

"Oh, thanks a lot. Hey, Bob, are you *with* somebody?"

"Rosie, quit getting jealous on me. You're always – I can't get a handle – "

CLIK.

And it dawns on him for the first time that she thinks they're going out. Then he sinks back under, reassuring himself that, when next he sees her, she'll be too sensitive to bring the matter up again.

Three weeks before Xmas now, and he'd not paid a single month's rent. The first month he hadn't come up with a payment, Queenie Graves, the super, was unexpectedly sympathetic; she told him she remembered how difficult it was for her moving out the first time, being a single mother and all, and how she could only imagine the hard road a young *artist* must have to follow. At the other end of the dingy, narrow, cabbage-damp hallway, Robbie had caught sight of Mr. Graves, who drove trucks, Queenie said. He had upper arms the size of Holiday Season hams, standing sideways and looking over his shoulder, like a pitcher sizing up a batter from the mound. He wore a sleeveless, cheesecloth undershirt and elephant-ass pants and looked, from Robbie's perspective, capable of knocking the teeth out of any tenant who didn't pay the rent. Robbie suspected he might already have knocked a couple of Queenie's teeth out; she wasn't all that old – no more than thirty, he reckoned – but she already wore dentures, which she liked to click around with her tongue while she considered things.

Thankfully, the time the Grissoms' ceiling caved in Mr. Graves had been on the road, and Queenie had remained easy even then, saying how old the building was and how inevitable little accidents were. That's how Robbie had the courage to report, cheque-less, at the end of November, assuring her, "For sure I'm a professional artist. Only last week I designed an exclusive pass card to that disco on Bishop – used to be a church – Gino's Paradise – ever been?" Robbie rubbing his eyelid like mad. "But when I asked about my money they said if I bugged them again they'd break my legs. What could I do?"

One grimy rugrat clung to Queenie's leg, another – older, warier – watched from a distance. Queenie stood, planted in a quilted dressing-gown that must once have been a lively canary yellow, but was closer now to grapefruit rind in a garbage bag. She leaned against her doorway smiling easily, fixing him with bright blue eyes, casting all over his face for more information. Then she rolled them up to the ceiling like a flirtatious schoolgirl, producing dimples in her ruddy cheeks.

"Well, I'll tell you," she said, and smoothed her dressing-gown over her hips. "I don't wanta go too hard on you, eh.

218

No lectures, okay, I don't think you should be forced t'stand here for too long and see me dressed not altogether at my best, you bein' an artist and appreciatin' beauty and that. F'you kin keep the front walk clear of snow and ice for the older folks in the building, you kin pay late this month and, who knows, we maybe kin come up with an arrangement. We'll see."

Robbie gratefully agreed, and reached out to shake her hand. When she smiled her heavy wide lips slipped up her teeth like the husk pulled back from a cob of corn.

"De ting dat crack me up de most, hosti," Louie Louie told him, "is when de cock chase de hen. E chase and chase till e wear er hout. E got appy feet, e pull her on like a rubber boot. I get such a ardon to watch dat I can't close my heyelid."

Robbie craned his neck back to look at the lofty ceiling of the slat-and-litter house. Hanging from the rafters were neon strips, whose jittery light cranked up the nervous atmosphere of several thousand chicks awaiting debeaking.

"This your job, too?" Robbie said, pulling his T-shirt over his nose. "Shovelling out the doo doo?"

Louie Louie told him chickens have such cast-iron stomachs they can eat their own waste, and human waste, too. The thrifty farmer who owned this place had housed the chicks near the workers' can, and channelled a sluice over to enrich the mash that flowed past them on conveyor belts. Robbie had come with near-serious intentions, but he knew immediately that this was one more job that made not paying the rent look attractive.

He sat while Louie Louie de-beaked. It wasn't just a joe job, Louie Louie pointed out proudly, it required precision and experience. If you didn't do it right, either you risked cutting off the chick's tiny tongue, or the beak grew right back again, and de-beaking a chick that's older than ten days is way more difficult. Robbie watched as Louie Louie positioned himself in front of the machine. *The* Louis Beaulieu held a chick with his thumb at the back of its head, and his forefinger under its throat. He squeezed its throat lightly, causing the chick's tongue to pull back, and inserted the beak in a hole on the face of the machine. The beak hit a trigger, a hot blade dropped down and sliced it clean off.

"It look cruel," Louie Louie said, "mais faut le faire, t'sais, in crowded cage like dese, cause chicken are cannibal and are gonna peck each another raw, udderwise. Mos funny ting is," he chortled as he picked up a squirming chick, "you're not suppose to de-beak when dey're hunder stress. Hunder stress, uff. Uff uff."

"Chrissake. How many do you do in a day, man?"

"Two tousand an hour, maybe."

"Two *thousand*? Fuck. That's your *job*?"

"Halso, I clip de toes of de female. Just like Suzette, wit de salon, who I gave de great doggies. Uff uff. And I de-wing too, and I dub, which is cut off de comb of de pullet."

"Chrissake. What's left of 'em when you're done?"

"Kentucky Fry Rat, mon chum. Uff. Uff uff."

Louie Louie treated Robbie to lunch in his cubbyhole – Pepsi, tourtière mini-pak, tarte à sucre, Mae West. From his locker, he handed back a book Robbie had lent him, an erotic classic Ivy had once lent Robbie: *The Autobiography of a Flea*, by Anonymous.

"C'est-tu ben platte, cette affaire là," he said. "Where de dirty part? Explique, hosti, ça pas d'sense."

"Let's see," Robbie said. *"Thus she pumped from Clement a fourth discharge, and reeking in the excessive outpouring of a seminal fluid, as well as fatigued with the unusal duration of the pastime, she disappeared to contemplate at leisure the monstrous proportions and unusual capability of her gigantic confessor."*

"Taberslaque! Qu'est-ce que ça veut dire?"

"Fucked if I know. But it used to turn Ivy on, I'll tell you that much for free."

"Now *dis*," Louie Louie said, pointing to a *Bosom Buddies* calendar on the wall by his desk. "Dis hi unnerstan. *Ayy*, Robbie mon vieux, when you jerk off han de baby batter go in your navel, you hever dip your celery in dat?"

Several midnights a week, Robbie skidded over downtown blocks of matte black ice to the Roxy, the streets flecked with hunched up figures, the massed steel-wool clouds foaming overhead. His ears as red-and-white as candy canes. His forehead a burning slab in the knife-edged wind, tears streaming from his eyes.

Hell's Yells' practices were already drawing a crowd. Kids congregated at the foot of the fire escape; after the Roxy staff switched off the marquee lights, Louie Louie lowered the metal stairs and let them climb up. They occupied the first three rows, and watched the boys work out the kinks in their act.

If you could call it that. For an act requires some planned co-ordination between performers, plus some articulated sense of purpose. Robbie hadn't wanted to rehearse at all – he believed that spontaneity, uncertainty, and violent instability were the keys to their success. It irritated him that Brat and Louie Louie were so stuck on conventional concepts of music, like playing together. More than anything, he told them, Hell's Yells demanded stamina. Hell's Yells was a protest against blind tradition and pointless subtlety and pretentious technique. There should be no lyrics to learn, no songs as such, nothing you could call a rhythm – only a furnace blast of heat and energy, gunning from point A to point B, a music to end all musics, a meltdown of music-less particles, a riot of negative ions, *anti*-music.

He roared and leapt and raged and mooned the crowd, but when all they did was sit listlessly, watching, and not taking part, he had to figure he wasn't giving enough. He attacked the front row and sat on the lap of a fan and pulled her shirt up to bare her breasts, and when her boyfriend just laughed and didn't try to stop him, he knew he really wasn't giving enough. He whipped an empty bottle at their heads, and when a barrage of litter didn't come hurtling back out of the darkness, he shouted *"No fucken IDOLS*," and shot himself in the head with an aerosol spray can. "Don't believe a word I say!" Black paint streaming from his ear, he yanked them out of their seats and wrote, one letter per cushion,

N O   I D O L S !

and when all they did was cheer him on, he knew there was still a lot of work to be done.

One advantage of having the Roxy for a practise space was that the band could fuel itself with junk food; Brat broke open the office door with a credit card, and there Robbie found the key to the candy counter. Night after night they gorged themselves on chocolate bars and cold popcorn and flat pop, crashing at dawn to sleep off the rawest stomachs. Problem was, Robbie soon developed a bad case of diarrhea, and found he'd have to supplement his diet in some way. His parents had given him a heap of tinned supplies when he first set out, but that had been exhausted in no time, and he was amazed at how quickly food can become a person's paramount concern; world domination by Hell's Yells was going to take a little while longer, he could face up to that, but he needed food now. At home he made stewy tea and re-used his teabags. He boiled spaghetti and ate it without butter or oil. And he mooched like mad: Monday night, Louie Louie's for a feast of processed meat and cheese-food product, layered between damp slabs of white bread; Tuesday night, Rosie came over and did her best to impress him with a dessicated slice of veal, topped with withered onion shreds and gluey corn niblets drowned in maple syrup; Wednesday night, he went with her to L'Enfer Strip and got free beers; Thursday the same; Friday night he got shit-faced again and did a whole lot of her diet pills and repeated a joke he had heard from a bloody-minded Dublin punk group that was climbing the charts at the time: What's an Irish seven-course meal? A potato and a six-pack of Guinness, arf arf; Saturday night he was back at the club; and on Sunday night, Brat's mother fed him his only nourishment for the week: vegetarian chili, unchafed wheat bread on the side, pineapple juice, and bran cakes with boysenberry cream, which sent him farting happily home.

Hunger makes a person keen. His senses became sharpened, his judgement quicker, his vision polished; no mirror above the aisle of Wu's grocery store was convex enough to reflect him, none of Mr. Wu's sons were fast enough to catch him. That was also because he was fuelled with benzedrine. Crackling like a spark plug, eyes in the back of his head. He was bristling, with eyes like rear-view mirrors on a Vespa, and a good mod one, as anyone knows, has more mirrors on it than arms on a head-shop Shiva. He wore his mod parka – it had so many handy giant pockets it was like a green canvas kitchenette. Meat here, in flat frozen slabs; thin packets there, of Jell-O, soup-in-a-mug, chocolate, diet pills.

Brat showed him some Dine 'n' Dash scams, one of which went like this: they order two *souvlakis* all-dressed, K, two *doner kebabs* with spicy sauce, two *gyros*, and four Molson. Under the seat, in a footprint of iced sludge, Brat surreptitiously drops a wallet – a real cheap plastic one, courtesy of Lovely Things Inc. – with Mounties on it. It's stuffed with old bus transfers and a couple of dollars

223

conspicuously sticking out. After they scarf their meal, Robbie makes a big deal about having found this wallet on the floor. He asks some good folks at the adjacent booth if it's theirs. At first they look fearfully at him – he's all hammer-and-nails – but he's very very nice and says, "Well, I'm going to return this at the cash, eh, but there's only a couple of dollars in it, which they might think is – I mean, who carries just a couple of dollars, in a nice wallet like this, and take a look at me, it's not as if I'm always trusted! So, when I tell the cashier about it, would you just wave to say I'm telling the truth? Oh, thank you. You're very kind." Then Robbie and Brat go to the cash and point to the nice folks and say to the cashier, "We found this wallet. And see those people there, they're paying for us, OK?" Go ahead. Try it sometime.

"FULL SCAM AHEAD!" Brat said, as they snowplowed up the street. "Oh, and by the way, I've got something for you." From his jacket, he pulled a rolled-up T-shirt, black with white lettering on it. He unfurled it. Robbie stamped and blew breath into the bowl of his hands and, sucking the tang of onions from the walls of his cheeks, read,

TO THE PIGS:
AM I UNDER ARREST?
NO? THEN POLITELY LEAVE ME THE FUCK ALONE
YES? OK, I'LL IDENTIFY MYSELF FULLY
BUT I DEMAND MY RIGHT TO CONTACT A LAWYER
IMMEDIATELY

"Cool, eh? I got it done specially for you at my Dad's factory. He says he likes it so much he'll put out a line of Lovely T-Shirts with messages about social injustice on them. I had another idea, too, a novelty, eh – tin cans that'll supposedly contain *authentic* FRESH AIR from the Canadian Rockies. Pay off is, he's gonna make me director of the division next year. Anyway, you better wear it, man. I can't always bail you out when you get in trouble."

That night Robbie went to L'Enfer Strip again, mainly to bum burgers and brews, but also because he always sort of hoped Ivy would show. Or at least it was only a matter of time before Olly turned up, and when he did, Robbie would screw up his courage and ask him.

At the adjacent table, three black guys in pinstripe suits the colour of chocolate milk were taking in a gloomy dancer on their table top. "Yeah, BABY! Show us some TRIM! Give us some fair-haired PUSSY PIE!" The dancer, Florida-tanned, was listlessly thrusting her white bottom at the guys' faces. They resembled dogs sniffing. Robbie watched her face and, with a lurch in his stomach, saw her lips were horribly swollen, as if she had been drinking boiling water.

He visited the cramped dressing room, where Rosie allowed him to sit against the wall at the back. She was pulling on a black-lace clerical collar she'd made to match her brassiere. Robbie sat, feeling supercool with his spiky hair, shredded black bondage pants, Lovely T-shirt with the sleeves torn off, and studded dog collar like Mendoza used to wear.

"Hi'm not so sure e should be ere," said gloomy Dolores. She was stark naked but for a cigarette in her mouth and stilettoes on her feet. She wore her mascara like rings under a raccoon's eyes, which made her look woebegone; she also had a way of facing the floor when she sucked on her cigarette, and looking up at the same time, half submissively and half suspiciously.

"S'OK Dolores," Rosie said. "He's quiet and gentle."

"*Ouais*, dat's de kind dat worry me de mos'," Dolores said. "De ones who can't look you in de face." Making a glum and sarcastic *moue* at Robbie, who looked down. He dug his fingers into his plate of *poutine* and slouched, doing all he could to feign nonchalance, as Dolores cupped her startlingly white breasts in her hands to glue a gold star on each nipple.

After she'd left the room, Rosie said, "I saw you stare, Bob, but don't go getting a crush on her. She's not your type. She's not *happy*, she's doomed to be one of those victims of society, some people just are. Like Little Miss *You-Know-Who*. I'll tell you how bitter Dolores is – she got herpes on her lip from a guy, right, one of the Dead Man's Hands, so what she does now is, if anyone in the club is being an animal, she kisses the lips of the beer bottles before she serves them. Gross, eh, but in a way I don't blame her; I mean, we're talking rapism and gynocide. We're fighting in the trenches, anything goes. It's like, OK you guys, your two thousand years are UP!"

Robbie reached forward to give her shoulder a friendly squeeze, but when she purred and held his hand fast for an extended back rub, he was suddenly put off. Why did she have to behave so needily? It was irritating. *Always* the tense shoulders – for what reason, he wondered angrily, considering the easy life she led? This had become a duty, not a pleasure. His arms itched unpleasantly. He withdrew. Picked up a book from the counter, opened it, and frowned. *Wimmyn In Herstory*, two thirds of it underlined in pencil.

"What's all this, Rosie?"

"So I can go back to the interesting bits, of course."

"But – " He leafed through. Page after page, entire passages, paragraphs, pages, meticulously underlined.

"Oh, forget it," she said, "you wouldn't understand."

She fussed with her lacy push-up bra, her nipples erect, he slyly noticed, served up now like a couple of juicy plums. She caught his gaze in the mirror. "Cos it's *cold* in here, in case you haven't noticed. Silicone's bad enough in winter-time, but OUCH do my boobs ever HURT when I'm about to have my period."

"Boobs," Robbie said, by way of apology. Trying out

consideration like an ill-fitting pair of pants. "Ugly word. Makes them sound like – I dunno – mistakes."

"Sometimes I think they *are*," she replied mournfully, and got up to go take her clothes off all over again.

"Ladies and GENNELmen, once again please welcome vieullez réclamer de loverly la CHARmante . . . "

Rosie had added a kink to her striptease: in between articles of clothing, now she read passages from the Bible into a microphone – *Classics of Misogyny*, as she introduced them: "*I permit no woman to teach or to have authority over men*," she intoned gravely, pulling down a stocking from under her frock. "*She is to keep silent. For Adam was formed first, then Eve; and Adam was not deceived, but the woman was deceived and became a transgressor.* I Timothy 2 : 10–14."

In Robbie's humble opinion, this was a bit much. Well, it was boring. Who in their right mind comes to a strip club for Bible class? Rosie tossed a frilly garter belt to the front of the stage and read, "*As the Church is subject to Christ, so let wives be subject in everything to their husbands.* Ephesians 5 : 23–24."

A man in a grey raincoat stood up, blocking Robbie's view. He seemed to be whispering to Rosie, for she was leaning towards him over the lip of the stage. What was he doing, slipping money into her panties? Maybe not. For now Rosie had her distressed face on, apparently looking around for help. Then the man in the raincoat grabbed her shoulders, and nearly pulled her off the stage, lappets flapping. The music was loud, but you could hear her shriek. Several bouncers rushed over, grabbed the man, roughly and efficiently, and ushered him out of the club.

Slouched in the rear of the club under the placard of rules, with his belly full of greaseburgers, poutine, and seven-odd beers, Robbie takes it all in. *Interesting.* No one pesters him to buy overpriced beers here – he's been on nodding terms with the bouncers since Rosie cleared him. From this perspective, he can eyeball a dozen girls at one time, not unlike the women in those old paintings featuring harems or hell or catastrophes befalling all of mankind. He pictures them bound and helpless, some being ravished by Romans, others devoured by monsters. He thinks, my harem. Yeah. Weren't there famous French painters who did tender portraits of the whores in Paris? One day he'll bring a sketch pad in here, too. He could easily be famous too, if he just got around to it.

After Chastity Church is done, Robbie, Cruel Lord of the Concubines, drunkenly reclines to watch an overweight stripper do her aerobic number: dimples in her buttocks, boobs just one more fold of flesh above her belly as she bends to disentangle her panties from a heel. She's performing ludicrously unerotic contortions; touches her toes with her arse presented to the tiny crowd like a pummelled face, clumsily does the splits and lands with a bump, lies on her back like a stranded beetle and grabs her ankles, all with the enthusiasm of a beast at the circus. And Robbie despises her for it. . . .

Sometime later, Rosie's at his side. He looks at her blurrily. Her underwear's stuffed with paper money, like a costume at a Caribbean carnival. Her temples and upper lip are glistening, her eyes gently searching his.

"Robbie, are you all right? You look OUT of it. Boy, did you catch that *weirdo*? Know what he gave me? A pamphlet, look – JESUS LOVES EVERYBODY. He said I was a fornicator and a blasphemer. Well, at least SOMEone's taking me seriously! Oh, and guess *what*, we're taking care of Dolores tonight. Did I tell you she recently had a baby but she gave it away? Last week her old man threatened to *eat* it or something. I would of taken it off her, eh, but the adoption people said I wasn't any more suitable a mother than she was. What're they looking for anyway, the Virgin Mary?"

On Ste-Catherine the three of them walk with their heads down against the wind, the butt of Dolores' cigarette flaring brilliantly in the gusts. Rosie wraps one half of her fur coat around Robbie's shoulders and tries to button the front around the both of them. Robbie shrugs her off roughly, and goes to pee against a wall. After he's shivered and turned around he sees he's attracted quite a crowd. What, have people never seen spiky purple hair, or what? Feeling reckless and mean, and knowing he looks like he's stuck his cock in an electric socket, he jabs the middle finger of one hand at them and makes the other hand into a livid codpiece.

"*Chriss*," Dolores says, grimacing against the wind. "Soon as I make henough money – pas compliqué, chu partie à la Floride." And singing that old Charlebois number, "*Sur Québec Air, Transworld, Northern, Eastern, Western – pi Pan American.*"

Two blocks on, something moves in an alley. Just as Robbie notices him, he steps forward with a groan, his raincoat flapping like a raven's wings.

"*Blasphemer! Fornicator!*"

Rosie jumps, grabs Robbie's arm again, and grips it tight.

"Oh ayy, bis mon cul," Dolores spits.

"Yeah," Rosie says. "Get outta my life, you weirdo."

"*Prostitute!*" the man hisses.

"Weirdo!" Rosie says. "Captain of the Raincoat Brigade!"

"Jesus loves everybody!" Robbie calls out merrily (he's bobbing and weaving around, above it all somehow, witnessing the whole scene as if through a glass-bottomed boat), and pulls the girls down the street on his arms.

"Devil's gateway! Demons suck your body! How easily you destroyed man, the image of God!"

They scoot away, turn a corner, until the rasping's out of earshot. "Weirdo," Rosie says, and shivers vigorously.

By the time they arrived home, Robbie hopping from car roof to roof (enjoying the percussive pop they made when

229

he jumped off), it was past three, but Mrs. Grissom had her face pressed to the glass of her front room, forehead and cheeks illuminated in the lamplight. She rapped on the glass and shook her fist and shouted. They heard locks unbolting as they approached. She wrenched the door open, and winked darkly.

"You're quite a hit with the ladies," she said. "Ain't you."

Rosie and Dolores shrieked with laughter, but Robbie wasn't so amused – he was noticing the garbage bags he'd taken out earlier that day had been slashed. It couldn't have been an animal, because other people's bags were untouched, while junk-mail envelopes with his address clearly marked on them had slipped into the muddy snow; and to his dismay, the colourful, lurid, incriminating pages of several *Bosom Buddies* magazines. While Rosie and Dolores climbed the stairs, he gathered the messy bunch of tits and bums in soggy wrinkled wads, and rammed them into a trashcan.

Rosie poured a bath, and whipped up heaps of bubbles with an egg-beater. Dolores sat on the bathtub rim, smoking and looking spiritless. She had taken her shirt off and was clutching it to her breasts. One thing about strippers, Robbie observed smiling, they're modest when it comes to their civvies.

"You're in a good mood," Rosie said. "Well, don't cream your jeans – this bath ain't big enough for the *three* of us."

"I know, I know," Robbie said. His stomach a sunken tub of disappointment. He went to put on an Environments record: a lapping lagoon with chirruping insects and a distant mackaw. He lit some incense to cover up the smell of burning vinyl that emanated from the kitchen, carried several candles into the bathroom, and sat on the lowered toilet seat. Drifts of bubbles glimmered on Dolores' shoulders and breasts where Rosie had playfully scooped them up, but she was looking gloomy again, and when she drew strenuously on her doused and soapy cigarette, vertical lines appeared on her upper lip as if she had been developing muscles there from years of applied smoking.

Robbie's thinking, Cool, this is like a *magazine*. Dolores' erect brown nipples. Rosie's heavier boobs. She's bursting too big a bubble of gum, and now there's a skin of it on her lips. They passed around a hash-oil spliff and Rosie murmured how womb-like water feels when you're stoned.

Then Dolores farted. Rosie shrieked and, for the first time, Dolores smiled, too; her laughs came out, reluctantly, in a series of little short explosions. Those muscular lips of hers made an upside-down smile, and laughter spurted out. Robbie made a skeletal roof with his fingers and, resting his chin there, sat in stern judgement on his flush-handled throne.

"Hey!" Rosie said. "Don't you here's the church and here's the steeple at *me*." She howled again and Dolores sputtered, the two of them thrashed about like stupid smiley dolphins and banged their heads on the bathtub rim. Rosie choked on her gum and swallowed it, and that made them laugh some more. "Oh what, do you think Marilyn Monroe shitted *ice cream*? Girls are only human, Robbie, get a grip."

Rosie and Dolores weren't exactly moving in, Rosie promised him. They were still offically shacking up at her apartment in Nôtre-Dame-de-Grace, with Dolores' old man, Bill the Beast, but since the Dead Man's Hands had started running their own highly profitable methamphetamine-still, up in Nitro, Bill and his friends had taken to mixing the stuff in its liquid form with their beer, and smoking killerweed – parsley sprinkled with PCP – and they were getting rabid and unpredictable. They were partying hard and, Rosie said, starting to show up at L'Enfer Strip a lot more than usual. Rosie had convinced her to hide out at Robbie's until the guy burned himself out, or got killed playing chicken on his bike, or something pleasant like that. Robbie wasn't so sure what he felt about harbouring a biker's runaway mama, but so it goes, that's what friends are for. The only bad thing about having girls around is you have to remember to lower the toilet seat after you're done – the first night he forgot and at four in the morning, short-sighted Rosie fell in.

The next night, or the night after, in spite of Robbie's spray-painted memo re: NO IDOLS!, a Hell's Yells fan surprised him with a blowjob behind the cinema screen. In his electrostatic haze of speed and booze he wasn't ever quite sure how it started, but suddenly, during a break in the sonic onslaught, he was up against an old Egyptian god and she was on her knees looking at him as if to ask permission. All he could manage was eyes as round as buttons, a smile with teeth as tight as a zipper. Problem with this particular BJ was, it wasn't enough like those letters in *Bosom Buddies*, for she never said anything really filthy to him. She didn't murmur or moan, or sit back from time to time to admire his joystick. His mighty schlong. If anything, it hurt. Then he sort of guided her head to help her. He looked up at the screen, and thought of that movie Ivy once brought him to, *She Stoops to Conquer*. The pictures came to him, like a film projector was between his ears shining images on his eyeballs; the celluloid strip snaked through his head, twenty-six frames a second. He thrust a little more eagerly, and he was welling up, and she looked up at him with her long face to see if he was close, and he was, and then a shocking thing happened: his semen came spurting out through her nostrils. Chrissake. He had only ever seen that in a *Fritz the Cat* comic, and assumed it was something that could only happen in a comic. She stumbled off to blow her nose. And after he'd pulled himself together, he walked out onto the stage to accept the crowd's applause with open arms.

If there was one thing he hated more than raking leaves, it was shovelling snow. Out in front of the apartment building, perched up on a ridge of ice, he raised the shovel above his shoulders and brought it down with a clang. The corners of the blade curled up like paper. His hands stung with the impact. He thought of the first pioneers, bravely battling off Indians and the flu and building log cabins with their bare hands, and how they must have got one fuck of shock the winter of fourteen hundred whatever. To find it lasted five months of the year. They must have lain in their beds through the dark mornings, under heaps of beaver pelts, watching their breath condense in columns above them, and had some serious second thoughts about the whole enterprise. Why didn't they listen to their better instincts and take off home? If they endured it for the sake of future generations, well, they ain't getting a monument from Robbie, he'll tell you that much for free.

Grumble grumble like that, and when other tenants stepped by, especially Mr. and Mrs. Grissom, he felt bitterly degraded.

By December it had looked like it might be a mild winter. Or it might not. It was indecisive, which meant that the snow Robbie had so meticulously shaved away in the mornings, melted and trickled across the walk in the afternoons, and became a skating rink by night. Daily he chopped in a fury, sometimes taking an axe to it and hewing up chips of concrete and ice that flew in all directions.

Two weeks before Christmas he'd still not paid any rent. Queenie Graves looked out of her window and invited him in for a cup of rosehip tea laced with rum. He gratefully wrapped his fingers around the cup and sat on her couch. Queenie turned the volume down on The Newlywed Game and sat beside him with her knees pressed primly together, her cup balanced uncertainly there. Her freckled cheeks were glowing like stewed apples, and Robbie guessed that she was already halfway through the pot. She watched him while he sipped, her eyes roving all over his face. He looked back at her, taking details in – the fine web of blood vessels at the edge of her nostrils, the freshly ironed creases in her jeans and George Jones T-shirt, the snail's trail of silvery-blue mascara around her eyes – and the bobbing motions their four eyes were making, reminded him of moths in mid-air.

"The girls're in school," she said at last. "The littlest won't be back till after noon." Robbie nodded, put his nose in his cup. He looked at her bare feet. Tiny spots of dried blood speckled the skin between her ankles and knees. She smelled of clean, static-free laundry. "I know what-chou're thinkin," she said. "I put her in as soon's I could, see. I'm not one of them people who claim they kin provide all the education of a child in the home. I'm only thirty-one, I don't know everything, I'm the first to admit it. Anyways, I shouldn't be selfish, spoilin her all the time, pickin up after her for hours on end, when she could be out learnin to take care of herself in the company of other children. By the way, I been meanin t'ask, ever since the Grissoms started complainin about you – I'd of come to your door, eh, but I don't feel I'm in a position to invite myself over – are you *punk*, by any chance?"

FOLLOWING THE DEBACLE WITH MR. MILLS AT THE HOTEL
Bonaventure, Robbie spent the last days before New Year's
Eve moping about the house, waiting for Ivy to call. He
snuck a lot of booze from Dad's liquor cabinet, and sought
solace in music, like Sartre's sentimental idiots. He caught
himself feeling grown up for having had such a heart-
break – being pleased he could feel such volumes of
emotion, that he was so *convulsively* alive – and he hated
himself for that. When at last Miriam called him to the
phone, he had exhausted himself flailing at his pillow and
weeping, the soaking self-indulgence made all the more
delicious by the silence he imposed on himself to conceal
his woe from the family. He rushed to pick up the receiver.
"How you *doing*?"
"Oh," Ivy replied, her voice furtive. "You know me."
"But how are you *feeling*?"
"Not a fucking thing. So stop asking. I've been drinking
like a fish. Pure revenge, really – I'm giving the parents a
taste of their own medicine. This way, at least I don't have
to *feel*, which you seem to think is so important. Anyway,
listen to this: *The crimes you have commit are worse than
Hitler's you have disgrace the family I wish you have been born
ugly or retarded. If you cannot redeem yourself I will wish for your*

235

death. A note from the mother, can you believe it? And she's been telling all her sisters about my crimes, too. Half of Outremont now knows about Robbie's girl. You know *Robbie*, Robbie Bookbinder, son of the famous television host, Abigail Bookbinder! I tried to leave but she caught me packing and hit me with one of my books. She doesn't blame you, not as much as the father does, at least – she blames books. She picked up that Canadian poet you gave me, Albert Camel, but it was such a slim volume, I barely felt a thing – but the humiliation still hurt."

Robbie was surprised that Ivy had strung so many energetic sentences together in one breath. She seemed to be enjoying the danger of the secret phone call, and the thrill of a denied romance, much more than she had ever enjoyed the so-called romance itself.

"Your mother's a psychotic windbag," he said.

"Oh, you're a big help. Look, she's not a rational person. Here's what she told me after she hit me – she said, *I never want that you make love under my roof, I never want that you make love under Robbie's roof. If you want to make love, go in a motel.* Can you believe it? I told her that's what we were doing, and she hit me again. Even if I run away, what am I going to do, work at one of Olly's clubs? I just have to accept, the mother is not a rational human being. Anyway, I'm calling quickly to say I've got passes to the Bones concert – it's their First Final Tour of Triumphant Return! Want to meet me? It may be the last chance you have to see me before the father locks me up with the Ursulines."

New Year's Eve, and the Alexis Nihon Plaza was bristling. Outdoors a freezing dark had fallen, and the sidewalks were glazed with ice. Cars jammed around the Forum, exhaust illuminated in the headlights and hugging the street, as if the cold had made the air itself heavier. Crowds massed around the main doors, under the elevators shaped like crossed hockey sticks. Ticketless fans hung around stamping their feet, trying to outwait the scalpers who were blowing into their hands and pacing. Robbie was feeling pretty dumb; one of the heels on his cheap shankless Beatle boots had got so soggy and rotted with salt that he lost it when he leapt off the bus at Atwater. Finding himself stepping unevenly, he turned around and saw the three-inch heel standing there on the bottom step, all alone with nobody on it, as the doors closed and the bus pulled away.

The other thing to bum him out was – just as he was approaching the West entrance of the ice rink, since now he had to walk so lopsidedly, like a man on a peg-leg – the quart-size bottle of apple cider he was concealing under his parka slipped out and smashed on the sidewalk. The liquid fizzed and froze almost instantly in a thin white crust. *Major* bummer.

"Hi! I got a ride," Ivy said, boldly handing him a roach, right there in the street. "Olly's a personal friend of Keef's, did I tell you? They did time together in jail!" Robbie took a toke and held her round the waist proudly. Hey, maybe they'd get in the papers! For Ivy had dyed her chopped hair electric green and stuck gold stars on her cheeks and put on one of her father's business suits with a pair of studded motorcycle gloves, mirrored sunglasses, and a flaming eight-foot fluorescent pink boa, whose feathers fluttered off to land and extinguish in the muddy slush behind her as they walked.

The Forum's outer halls were filled to the brim. Dad joked that rock 'n roll crowds resemble a compost heap, but Robbie enjoyed being stinky and ragged. It was an improvement, at least, over smells of Vitalis and Barbasol, which was the way he imagined those famous old hockey players in the photos on the Forum walls; he looked up at them and their coaches, all crewcuts and shiny chins, and he knew he couldn't have hacked belonging to that generation. He just closed his eyes as the stone came on and allowed the warm and fetid crush to carry him along down the narrow corridor. . . .

As the pressure squeezes tighter, he's lifted off his feet. He can just see past the curtains, into the bright arena. Fans are hurling Frisbees and toilet rolls, and unfurling ink-blotted bedsheet banners, while they wait for the show to begin. A recorded Bones number is pumping out from the ampstacks (the rhythm track rumoured to be the hyper-amplified heartbeat of a girl climaxing in Keef's bed) and the atmosphere's already hazy in the rafters. Suddenly the lights go down and a grid of spotlights switch on like skeletal pillars in a massive miasmic cathedral. And the crowd explodes. Still stuck in the corridor, people shove harder, pushing up on each other's shoulders to see; it's as if this giant music has a fist, and is pounding on the ground to send people flying up off their feet. Ivy squeals from somewhere – under Robbie's armpit – and pink feathers fly up. The music's so loud it makes the air as thick as wax, plugging Robbie's ears, unbalancing him. The guitars scream like molten plastic like blue fruit like all the sadness of his life like something enormous and soft and majestic. He wrenches his arms free and throws them up like he's on a roller coaster.

The ushers open a door to divert the urgent flow of fans. Bodies are sucked to the right like clumps on a current, and as he goes this way, he realizes it's the same route hockey players take to get to their dressing rooms. Fans are being herded to an entrance at the far end of this corridor to emerge, he guesses, at the east side of the stage. So this is it. His big chance, possibly his one and only. One of these doors must lead to Keef's dressing room. All he has to do is pick the right one, and wait.

He's alone and in darkness. The crowd's on the other side of the door, and in this oily smelling dark a *plip plip plip*. He fumbles about. Feels sticky fur on pipes, the ribs

238

on an aluminum cable, the bristle of an upside-down broom. There are also rags in piles, a rock hard paint-brush, a greasy tuque. When at last he finds a switch and flicks it on to see where he is, a crown of prickling heat descends over his head and the muscles of his temples grip him like a metal helmet. He looks at the great white Zamboni, only three feet from him, its cab some six above, and his mind goes utterly blank.

The door to the corridor has no handle on this side. He bangs with his fists and shouts, but no one will ever hear him out there. He bangs again anyway, and again, then rests his forehead on the asbestos wall and looks at his shoes. His fancy duds look suddenly goatish and irrele-vant: the dumb blue Beatle boots, the flared jeans with the ridiculous slogans stitched onto them – QUESTION AU-THORITY and KEEF LIVES – the big stupid studded belt slung low about his hips. He stares and stares and listens to the room hum indifferently around him. And as he hears *Keef Richards AND THE STROLLING BONES!* take the stage in the arena, his eyes fill with tears and his mouth starts to go all wiggly.

How old is he now? Eighteen in two weeks. What's he doing with his life? SFA. One hour earlier there was noth-ing more important in his life than seeing this concert. Now it seems like a stupid waste of time. He knows it seemed important only because, by comparison with the apathy and uselessness of his life, it's a major event. How ridiculous. He's read innumerable interviews with Keef, and one thing he's noticed is that the guy can rarely remember anything he's said or done; he's had so many vital experiences in his life – from the Bones' riot-ridden central American tour, during which he threw a toilet out a hotel window and beaned a Third World dictator on the terrace below, to the time he was taken to a Monte Carlo hospital after swallowing 50cc's of semen (the wad of Alba-nia's entire Tour de France bicycle team) – but because he lives such an abandoned life, doing nothing that isn't pure creative instinct, he can't remember any of it. Robbie, on the other hand, is hobbled in the present by the memory of all his insignificant achievements, his every puny puerile problem and utterly uninteresting failure. He gnashes his teeth and calls himself a fuckingly fucked-up fuckup, and a dumbfuck hole in the head, a bona fide shit for brains, and more, besides. Through the door he hears the screech of a guitar solo, so loud it rides feedback's spine. Then he begins to yell. To the rhythm of the Bones' music that pounds on the walls and ceiling of this little box of a room, he roars blue bloody baby talk with his neck pitched back and his eyes scrunched shut. He can feel his throat heat up like a motor burning oil in first, painfully, but he's determined to punish himself.

Half an hour later, Ivy and a security guard opened the door. Robbie was sitting up in the Zamboni's seat.

"God. You're unreal," Ivy said. "You look like you've lost your mummy at the funfair."

"Arf arf, so funny I forgot to laugh," Robbie said hoarsely.

"So get down, it's the intermission now. I'm with Olly, and you know who I just met, just one door down from here? Go on, guess. Keef Richards! The whole band, too! He was so attentive, he even invited me for a drink before they go back on. That's now if we hurry, so let's hurry."

The hockey players who regularly use the dressing room would not have recognized the place, but from fan mags Robbie knew every detail of the Bones' backstage rider by heart, and had long dreamt of seeing firsthand what he now beheld.

The neon lighting had been pulled out and replaced with black candles, tall as spears, on eight silver octopus candelabra, which were flanked by the dozen Dead Man's Hands contracted to provide security; the skate-scraped

240

concrete floor was covered with plush Persian cushions and carpets, and in the corner, Robbie recognized Keef's famous grandfather clock, whose hands had been bent around like Dali's moustache by Dali himself. Guests sat on the floor smoking and drinking, and on the mahogany four-poster bed (the posters like May-pole penises), a girl in hot pants was giving two men in satin Bones tour jackets a blowjob; there were blood-red lava lamps arranged along the shelves where the Canadiens would normally store their gear, four state-of-the-art pinball machines, and in the showers, enough jeroboams of champagne on ice to keep the Bones' entire entourage crazed (for if the supply ran out, the band wasn't legally bound to play the concert).

The group had developed an appetite for Northern African food during their Morocco days. Now an indecent heap of it was loaded, à la Bones, on an oak table that ran the length of the room: Spit Swagger was carving into a platter of *b'stila* – cuts of cornish hen, lemony scrambled eggs, and crushed almonds, layered between pastry flakes, dusted with sugar and cinnamon, and spread out on a thick, undulating coverlet of white lacy lingerie; Bile was pulling a boiled rabbit by the ears from a sauce of spiced tomato and honey, grinning at it, nose-to-nose; and Jerusalem Slim was using his spoon to cut up two molded aspic breasts, rising up like denuded islands out of a libidinal salad of eggplant *zaalouk*; guests were feasting, too, with honeysticky fingers, on *briwat al hobb*, "love letter" pastries; and at each end of the table, a marmalade gelatin mermaid bathed in a brass basin of orange-flower water.

Dishing out the feast were several little girls (as close to eighteen as possible, the contract stipulated, but not a day younger), wearing ribboned frocks of rose satin hiked high to show off their stiff muslin petticoats, filigreed garters, and just an inch of tantalizing thigh. Their hair was artfully disarranged by the famous Michel Froufrou who travelled with the band, their faces daubed with thick

241

white pancake and smudged black lipstick, their eyes hidden behind black webbed domino masks.

And boy, standing there in his lobby concession Bones Tour T-shirt, did Robbie ever feel dumb.

Ivy was already off talking to a spindly man with a peacock green hairdo. He wore Saigon mirrors and a ruffled shirt, a death's head coke spoon around his neck, and shells bristled from the shoulders of his jacket like a stegosaurus. He was dreadfully pockmarked, a real crater-face, and he looked very sly.

Chrissake.

Keef Richards.

Robbie insinuated himself at Ivy's side. He said to her, super-nonchalant, "Oh, hi. I am look you for all the place, uh. It's so crowded here there's no room for your little panties."

People say pretty stupid things when they're nervous, eh? And Ivy did nothing to help him out. And Keef's drawn, grey face just flinched with amusement.

Up close, he was amazingly tall, much taller than he looked in his pictures. Besides his mother, Robbie had never met a celebrity in the flesh. In 3-D. Only inches from Robbie, his body appeared to possess a denser mass than most people's bodies. It was as if air had been unnaturally displaced to accommodate this man's bulk, after he had leapt from the two-dimensional world of album covers and TV screens. He was incredible. And to Robbie, it was like time had been displaced as well, for he was staring and unable to stop.

"I'm Robbie Bookbinder," he managed. "I'm in Hell's Yells."

When Keef smiled, the skin of his whole face crept and gathered reluctantly into furrows to achieve the expression, which eroded with equal indifference. He said, "Mmm?" and that was all. His voice had a flatness, smooth as raked ash.

Robbie heard himself blather on. "Well, you know, my group. Didn't Ivy tell you?" He could see his own image reflected convexly in Keef's mirrored glasses – tiny chin, pointed head, *Punch* nose, a constellation of pinpoint candleflames – in stereovision like a satanic ViewMaster. And Keef still said zilch. His lips crawled around, like he was about to make words, but stopped dead. All he did was twist his nose, the infamous silver-lined nose, the bone in which had been eroded right through from snorting too much cocaine.

"Um," Robbie said, last ditch now. "I always wanted to ask you – in the song "Hush-A-Bye-Baby," when you sing, *the cradle will rock,* right, are you really talking about, well, underage girls?" Good question, he thought, Keef was surely impressed now. But Keef just drew on his cigarette, drawing hard, as if he needed the very smoke to breathe, and said,

"Read into it what you like, man." Then he turned to Ivy and said, "So baby, mmm. . . . "

A voice called out, "TWO MINUTES!"

Keef kissed Ivy's forehead and slipped off, without so much as a nod for Robbie.

Back in the arena, sitting there on his cold seat, Robbie relived his Big Encounter, word for word, stupidity for stupidity. And sitting beside the world's biggest Bones' fan, in a crowd of twenty thousand fans, turned out to be the loneliest experience he had ever had; for Ivy was just about drooling. Robbie watched her more than the show: standing on her seat she mouthed along to every song and struck her fist at the air to emphasize the lyrics she believed in the most; she swayed like an Arabian belly dancer; she shrieked with her eyes squeezed shut and her hands clamped to her ears; she smoked joint after joint, passing them generously around, as much to strangers as to Robbie; and never once, not even once, looked at him to share the moment. When everyone else was standing on their seats for the spectacular finale, he was sitting in a sulk. Around him the twenty thousand metal-headed rivet rats ate it up, indiscriminately, as far as he was concerned, as indiscriminately as garburetors. All he could see was the backs of their legs. Ivy's legs were snapping and stamping away beside him and he hated them. He hated the very fabric of the pants that were on them, and those sexy snakeskin boots she wore, the boots themselves, were hateful to him, too. They reeked of frivolity and faithlessness.

At the very final peak of the performance, the house lights went up. People screamed and jumped on each other's shoulders. Ivy kicked Robbie in the hip. He looked up at her. She jerked her head as if to say, *Stand up, you baby*. So he did. The stage looked naked and vulnerable without the magic of lasers and strobes and dry ice, and the Bones looked unexpectedly small; the same size, really, as any of the members of the audience. Keef had thrown himself head-first into the crowd, and now it was tossing him about on its bed of upstretched hands. And swallowed him up. What was happening? Everyone on tiptoes to see. Then he was on the stage again, with a fan cradled in his arms. He was hugging her, dancing with her slow, rocking her, and then very deliberately, as the house lights went out again and a single white spot focused on him, magnifying the movement for all to see, he slid his hand under her skirt. He looked at the crowd and grinned that crawling grin of his, and the lights went out completely. The music screeched to a halt, and all of a sudden it was over. The crowd erupted. They lit lighters and yowled. Ivy wrapped her arms around Robbie, holding herself up by his neck. She was hot and fragrantly damp and breathing hard. But Robbie stood with his arms hanging limply by his sides.

When he gets home, his family's preparing to ring in the New Year. He kicks off his boots down the basement stairs, slush flying, and spits after them. He's in a foul temper, he knows it, because he was stupid to have taken all five points of that star blotter he was saving for the so-called celebration with Ivy. Not that he's hallucinating overtime or anything – this stuff has turned out to be little more than a hefty dose of methamphetamine. The days of serious LSD, he concludes, are over; none of his friends tell stories any more of plucking gas-flame flowers, no one sees faces in the walls, no one surfs on lawns turning into great green tidal waves, no one ever feels like a banana and wants to peel himself. No, seventies acid is a rip-off, pure and simple. All you get is trails at best, and now the air in this house is buzzing like the inside of a TV set. He goes scowling into the living room, socks wet on the warm carpet. The room looks flat; one dimension has been sucked right out of it. And here's his paper-cutout family. They come with a variety of outfits for all occasions and their underwear is printed permanently on their bodies for modesty's sake. They come FREE! with every box of Sugar Krunchies. And they're all facing him.

"Where's Ivy, darling?" Mom asks. "Why didn't you invite her home for champagne?"

"Well, she had to be with her family, so."

"Mom's a greedy guts for joy juice," Miriam says. "She runs on it."

At midnight, he phones Ivy's house. He has to dial ten times before he gets through. He sits down by the phone, his champagne bubbling joylessly. Mrs. Mills says, *"Allo?"* He thrusts the phone at Miriam.

"Hi," she says. "Can I speak to Ivy." Miriam listens, then covers the receiver with her palm. "Some cow says she's out," she says to Robbie.

But that's impossible. They parted an hour and a half ago. He flushes hot. His heart yawns up blood. And the thought of the long speeding sleepless night ahead, with only his wriggling nerves for company . . .

Back in the living room Mom says, "Are you all right? Did you get through?"

"Yes, no," Robbie hears himself say. "S'OK." Pulling as nice a smile as possible. He's not going to start to explain.

"No, really, Robbie. You seem upset."

"I told you I'm perfectly fine," Robbie snaps.

"Are you – have you been taking pot?" Dad now. "It's all right – you don't have to – aum."

And Robbie thinking, if you didn't ask so many fucken probing questions, I wouldn't have to lie so much. "I am fine," he enunciates as precisely as can be. "I am fine. Thank you." Doing his utmost to appear super-normal now, performing complex mental and physical exercises to discipline his hyper impulses at the same time as he jolts awake the dormant ones. Don't stand funny, he's telling himself, keep your eyes open, you are not messed up, you are in perfect control, just look alert, don't act crazy, smile, but not too much, don't mumble, don't laugh too hard, keep your hands in your pockets so you don't fidget but not for too long, don't overly concentrate on little things like the binding of that book or the lipstick on the butt of that cigarette, please them with whatever but don't get too eager, don't get weird, weird? what's weird, relatively speaking, fuck, I'm losing track.

To the family, who are watching him with no small measure of concern, he is not handling it well: swivelling on the ball of one hip, dragging shapes through the carpet with a toe, making that heavy-metal devil salute with both hands, tossing the hair on his head like a female film star, inspecting the ceiling when there's clearly nothing there, and chattering like a baboon.

"I may as well get real with you," he's saying. "I've done one or two drugs in my time. I admit it. But I'm not the kind of son who's gonna get busted, you know, 'cause I'm smart. I mean, whaddo I mean? I mean, I smoked my first joint, K, in like Grade 6, which I believe is too young for most people.

They can't handle it, eh. They don't know their limit. I never do nothin I can't handle. You don't hafta worry, K, 'cause like I don't see drugs as making me have a good time. Uh-uhn, no way, I wouldn't want you to think that I relied on them. I see it as having a good time while I'm doing the drug. Catch the diff? Which is what most of my friends think, too. Why are you all looking at me funny?"

"No, no, Robbie, go ahead. . . ."

"Uh, well. Sometimes it's really hard to talk to you, 'cause, like, there's certain types of way I'm s'posed to speak."

"What do you mean, Robbie?" Mom looks like she's about to cry, which he cannot understand. Why's everyone so quiet? "First of all, it's like you always call me Robbie. I mean, I know that's my name, but you always say, *What is it, Robbie?* and *Are you all right, Robbie?* and *Now look here, Robbie.* Do you dig what I'm trying – ?"

"Aumm – "

"K, what I really wanna say is, there's certain types of way I'm s'posed to speak, like, if you ask me if I'm OK, whaddo you want me to say, exactly. I can't just say *yes* or I get the third degree. It's like, I gotta say it just right all the time. It's like there was a special secret way, like:

RIGHT   WRONG

"Now do you dig what I'm – "

After the family goes to bed, he creeps down to the dungeon to listen to music on the headphones, and try to survive the night. His heart's churning like an egg-beater, his flesh feels saturated with sadness and uncertainty. His bones are aching, the muscles stretched taut along them. Where's Ivy? He pictures all the dark and frozen streets of the city, all the doorways and steps, all the clubs and homes and her empty bed. He gnashes his teeth and the tears stream hotly down.

Music provides some solace. In stereo, especially, zinging through the core of the pulp of his brain, scrambling under his scalp and over the top of his skull, seething through all the porous bones in his face. He closes his eyes and pictures his synapses flashing. He grimaces a lot to express what he feels. When a guitar solo goes WAH, he makes his eyebrows shoot up; when it goes NEEAUW, he curls his lips; when it goes DIDDLYDIDDLY he flicks his tongue like a snake. And when he opens his eyes, there is Mom in her dressing-gown and slippers, watching him with worry all over her face.

She tucks him in bed and kisses him goodnight again, but he still can't sleep. He goes to the bathroom. The towels on the rack are a blazing radioactive red. The water from the tap is thick as plastic. The noise in his ears is like the boiler room of the USS *Enterprise*. What's the point. He just wants to die.

He was finally extinguished by five, and slept till noon. When he awoke he was zombied out. His limbs were as soft as cooked vegetables. He was sore, as if water-filled blisters were on his feelings. He couldn't wait to call Ivy. When he did, she picked the phone up herself.

"Hello," she said flatly.

"Hi," he said, affecting the game jollity of a clown warming up a crowd that wants its money's worth. "What's up?"

"You woke me up, that's what," Ivy said. "Family's out. I was just taking a nap."

His spirits sank instantly. Why a nap? Had she been out *all* night? Did he sense resentment in her voice? "Gee, I'm sorry," he said. "I was just feeling real *up*, you know, real positive, and also wanted to apologize for being a baby last night. Sometimes, well as you said, I get a bit jealous. I'm getting a handle on it, though. I've thought a lot about your theory." In fact Robbie didn't feel that his behaviour merited an apology at all, or that her theory was worth shit – she was the one who should be sorry. She was selfish and obtuse. He was pathetic to have relapsed into this state of helplessness with her – he knew it – and worse to be wheedling a response this way, but it would be worth it to him if she would only exhibit some kindness in return.

She said, "That's nice."

"Ahh, you're not irritated, are you?"

"No, why should I be? . . . but look, you obviously called in such a fever, it's as if you expected me not to call you."

"No, no – I was just – so, uh." Real casual now. "What did you get around to doing last night? It fun?"

Ivy didn't answer at first. Robbie heard the strike of a match and the flare of sulphur. Then she said, "Yeah, great fun, as a matter of fact. I'm pretty tired, so."

"So you wanna get some winks. I can call you later if – "

"No, I think we better get this out in the open right away."

"Ahh . . . what do you mean?" His voice cracking like puberty all over again.

"I didn't go home after we said goodnight. I went to a party with Olly."

"Yes," Robbie said. "I know. I mean I called. I was sorry you weren't there. I wanted to send you a kiss on the phone. Happy New Year, by the way." These words, limp and forlorn, not at all as crisp or flounced as they're supposed to be.

"That's nice. So I stayed pretty late. Wait till you hear. I partied with Keef."

"Oh wow did you that's far out." Robbie's whirling head.

"He showed me this little watering can he has that used to belong to Anastasia Romanov. He keeps myrrh in it to sprinkle the smelly carpets of his hotel rooms."

"Oh, boy," Robbie said, emptily.

"And, well. I don't know how to put this to you any more kindly, but I . . . I spent the night with him."

"Oh, wow." Robbie said, smiling like a goof – a ventriloquist's dummy staring blindly into the lights. His wooden words now. "Did you have a great talk and everything?"

"No-o, not really. God, what am I saying. Not at all. You know me. He's completely vacuous. It was nothing. We just had sex and did Olly's cocaine. In Keef's hotel room. We watched a lot of TV. Nothing for you to worry about. Understand? OK?"

"Yeah," Robbie said blandly, trembly. "OK. Look, maybe you wanna get back to sleep. See soon, K?"

"If you want."

"If I want?"

"Well, I'd like to," Ivy said tenderly. The cunt. "So – it's up to you. Keef says you're a nice guy. He didn't mean to be rude, it's just that since the Bones are the loudest band in the world he's virtually deaf. You were mumbling, he had a hard time reading your lips."

There weren't too many options. The bitter disappointment lay solid, unsublimated, undigested, in the pit of his stomach. It would never go away. Living the rest of his life with the knowledge of her infidelity was unthinkable. The pain, the shame. He pictured her nudely nakedly naked in Keef's bed, in his hotel room with the TV on. He pictured her very vagina, unfurling. He forced himself to think of it, the way you punish a dog by sticking its nose in its own shit and then swatting it.

He didn't really hate her; it wasn't her fault he couldn't manage the simplest things in life. So now he'd just spare her and everyone else the boredom of being with him. Look at him, skulking through the house, catatonic, with a long stupid face. *Gather Ye Rosebuds* – in the dull winter light, the glass was the colour of dried petals. On the terrace below his bedroom window the newly fallen snow gusted about. And this house all full of the smell of some thick, savoury New Year's dish Mom's making. He paced his room. Sat on the bed. Beat off, numbly, and wiped up after himself.

Love will be convulsive or not at all, isn't that what Ivy said? What's the worth of it, arrested halfway? But she still thought he was a little wimp, a bumbler. Now he'd have to do something to show her he was capable of going all the way. It was so clear to him now: they say adolescence is the best time of your life, but if that's true, what shit-ass misery was in store for him in *adult* life? Forget it. He wasn't going to stick around for *that* bogus set-up. Better to burn out, he resolved, than fade away. They call suicide a cowardly escape, but what do They know? When They blab on about responsibility, maturity, consideration for others, getting real, what do They know about the suicider's state of mind? Robbie felt a gush of relief when he realized what he had decided for himself; the release of all the binding, sensible emotion was like moisture evaporating off his body. Now, for once in his life, he was going to do something for himself and nobody else.

"Just going to see a friend," he announced at the kitchen door, and his voice resonated dead in his ears.

At the pharmacy he asked for the biggest bottle of pills they had.

"Pills?" the pharmacist repeated.

"Yeah. For my Dad, eh. Too much partying, ha, ha."

"You want aspirin. Over there on the open counter."

"Yeah, but I was thinking more like codeine phosphate with, like, butalbital. D'you have that?"

The pharmacist dipped his head and looked over his bifocals. "You need a doctor's prescription for that, my boy."

"Right," Robbie said, "I knew that." He was shifting now, from foot to foot. What else was there? Demerol, Percodan, Darvon. If he said too much, would the guy get suspicious, or would he then believe Dad really had sent him? He ran through the list in his mind, all the ones he knew with acetaminophen or codeine – Phenaphen, Tylenol, Proval, Alorain, PAC, Bufferin, Empirin – did they need prescriptions, or what? He was confused now, he just couldn't think. His resolve was wavering. Fuck, at this point, he'd take anything.

He felt pretty stupid out in the street again, with a bottle of 222s in his hands, but what choice did he have? He bought a beer at a dépanneur and sat high on a snow-covered bench in Westmount Park to wash a handful down. Five, ten, another handful, fifteen. It was hard getting them down his throat – they were dry and sticking and made his mouth sting, and the beer made him burp and bring them back up.

After twenty, he was starting to scare himself. Was he serious about this? What was the point? He hadn't left a note or a will, he realized. Well, Ivy would know the score. And would she ever be sorry. But how about Miriam and Barnabus, would they understand? Would they take it personally? Maybe they'd take it more personally than Ivy would. Another handful now, twenty-five, and another gulp of brew.

The park is buzzing now, the snow seeming to jump off the ground like a huge white trampoline, and his stomach's raw. He pours more pills into his mouth, directly from the bottle this time, but there isn't enough beer left to wash them down. The bitterness is unbearable. His tongue throbs. He spits out in the snow. Now he's starting to weep. He's afraid of what he's done, and yet he's ashamed to have stopped halfway; he's ashamed by his behaviour thus far, but he just can't face the future any more bravely.

He looks around him, at the naked trees, the indifferent traffic across the park, the Kiosk locked up and icicled over. The clap of a hockey puck on the boards of a municipal rink. He tries another mouthful, scooping up snow, now, and chewing it, too. It's useless. Spits again, and shivers violently.

Taking an aimless walk downtown, his ears begin to whistle and his legs turn to rubber. It's not at all like the amused and jellied stroll you get with shrooms; now he just feels queasy and weak. He might throw up, although that would be a relief. Stops at McDonald's and buys three Big Macs with large fries – something to make him really vomit. But it doesn't work. Down in the toilet he tries to gag himself with a finger, but he can't manage it that way, either. Back in the street, he bumps into pedestrians bracing themselves against the winter wind.

And suddenly someone perfumy is clutching him and shouting in his face.

"Hey wow! *Bob* – Bob, isn't that your name? We met at the club, right? I can't believe my *eyes*, you're just the person! I was just thinking, Why do men always have the hots for really BITCHY distant women? I mean, mystery is never all it's cracked up to be. What is it? Oh dear . . . hey, you look *awful*. Should I take you to a hospital?"

At the Montreal Central, the nurses were utterly indifferent to his plight, and the doctor treated him with rough disdain. He felt puny. In a small voice, embarrassed not to have a more serious complaint, he said, "I took too many pills."

"Pills? What kind? How many?"

See? No sympathy at all. And then, he's forced to wait for over an hour in the waiting room, Rosie chin-wagging the whole time about her Xmas Tits for Tots Strip-a-Thon in a very loud voice: "I get forlorn just *thinking* about it, Bob. We got a photo in the *paper*, all the proud girls in their *G-strings*, did you see it? Us propping up a giant blowup of the check, for $14,000, imagine, four-teen thousand dollars, and Scrooge Central here won't take it because they say it's dirty money! The *nerve!*"

All those pills are actually giving him a crushing headache now; his ears are screaming like there's a TV off the air with the volume up, right inside his head. He tries to keep pace with Rosie, saying anything, just to stay conscious.

"Maybe you should spend the money to start a union. Like you talked about once." It hurts to move his jaw – it feels bolted on too tight. "You were right, it is gross where you work, makes me mad . . . what? Why are you looking at me funny?"

"Cos it sounds like – like you *care*. I think. I mean no one ever gives a shit about *us*."

"Um, I . . . sure, why not?"

"I *like* you, I've decided. You're *together*. Not half as out of it as you look. I don't mean to be rude. It's just great that in a way we're both such *losers*. You know, I tried to stick my head in the oven once – just last week! – but I couldn't go through with it cos I got claustrophobic."

Finally he's admitted, undressed, and laid in bed. A nurse stabs a needle in each of his wrists and tapes them there. He watches, vaguely pleased that it looks so dramatic – one tube for plasma, another for some kind of serum. It's weird – his veins are swelling up like inner tubes.

An hour later, he's growing concerned, however; no one's spoken a single word to him, and now the serum bottle has quietly emptied out. The liquid's a third down the tube. He's afraid that air will get in his veins. Maybe he'll die, which now he most assuredly does not want to do. But he doesn't want to make a fuss, he's probably being silly, so he lies still and hopes for the best.

Rosie pulls back the curtain and peeks in. Just in time. She sees the tube and shrieks. That brings two nurses in. One tsks and quickly switches the bottle of serum for a fresh one, while the other whisks Rosie out and returns to prepare some instruments in a kidney-shaped aluminum dish. A doctor arrives. The first nurse hands him a length of rubber tubing she's coated with Vaseline. He holds it up, and the nurse with the tray fixes a funnel to the end. Robbie watches and wonders. Then the doctor shoves the free end of the tube up his nose. *Chrissake!* He didn't expect this. The tube slithers up around his sinuses and then descends, like it's alive, down the back of his throat. He gags, his throat closing on the tube.

"Just relax," the doctor says, impatiently. He's got more important, more *deserving* patients, elsewhere.

Robbie looks at him through a veil of tears, tries to allow the tube passage.

"Breathe through your mouth, that's it. Easy."

When the end of it has passed the involuntary swallowing muscles in Robbie's throat, the first nurse produces a big plastic bottle of what looks like grey poster paint, and the second nurse places the dish beneath his chin. The doctor holds the funnel up high, and the nurse pours the paint in. "Just liquid charcoal. Go with it. Don't resist now."

Robbie nods stupidly as he feels the cold, thick stuff ooze through his nostril and esophagus and into his stomach. This is what drowning must be like; the stomach filling up like a cool balloon. He wants to upchuck. Is he supposed to? No one said. Go with it, what does that mean? He doesn't want to throw up in front of these people – it seems like an indecent thing to do – but he soon finds he

255

has no choice. With the tube still snaking inside him, he brings up a tidal wave of grey bile that washes all over the bedsheets and the nurses' uniforms, everywhere, in fact, except in the dish. The second nurse gingerly places it lower on his chest.

Now his stomach's filling up again. It's such an unfamiliar sick feeling; you normally associate nausea with hot acids and a lumpy puddle, but now his belly feels chilled, and the vomit that leaps forth is smooth as paste and doesn't burn – not like in *The Exorcist*, he thinks, humour being the only way he's going to handle this little nightmare – but the second wave looks more familiar: *oh hello*, there are the Big Macs and the fries, there's the frothy beer, and there, like buoys bobbing in the swill of a harbour, are the pills. Well, thank God, he thinks, at least that's all over. But he's wrong. They fill his stomach and make him vomit, spectacularly, twice more before they pull out the tube and leave him soaking in his own vile juices, panting for breath, stinking, and feeling like those cows he's read about in the early days of seafaring, who got so sick they disembowelled themselves bringing up all seven of their stomachs right there on the deck. . . .

He was discharged around eleven that night. Rosie had waited the whole time, so they walked along the Boulevard together, arms linked, past the dark Westmount mansions. His stomach gurgled clammily. The night was mild; unnaturally so. A ceiling of fog lay under the sky, bright as day as it reflected the lights of the steaming city. He thought of all the observatories in the world, whose once crystal view of the universe was now obscured, as urban grids expanded round the globe. And way beyond, piercing the mist, the docks and the bridges and the Expo '67 site sparkled across the St. Lawrence River, the solid-state city glowing in between, holding out the promise of a better year, a life worth enduring – maybe.

After a considerate half-hour of walking in silence, Rosie said, "So, why'd you do such a crazy thing, Bob? Not over that strange little stray cat, I hope."

Embarrassed, Robbie nodded.

"Wow. Well, if it makes you feel any better, I've seen her at the club a few times, eh, 'n there's heavy guys hanging out there who *I* wouldn't cross, but she's all over them like a dirty shirt. Is she ever a *minx*! Leaves 'em with blue balls half the time, 'n she can get away with it, too, cos of who her brother is. She told you she almost went to juvenile court last summer on *assault* charges, right?"

"Uh no-o, not exactly. . . ."

"I heard about it cos the kid she almost tore out the eyes of is always bugging the Dead Man's Hands to be a con-script, or what do they call 'em, a *prospect*, and he sort of hangs around the club. Or at least he used to, haven't seen him in a couple of weeks now. He's quite the slime himself but still, like normal human beings, even he has parents 'n *they* were going to press charges, eh, until Olly paid them a polite visit."

"Yeah, well, Ivy and Gaston deserve each other is all I can say."

They stopped at the Lookout to take the city in, the wind blowing through the bare trees of the bird sanctuary behind them. The blood-red lights of late-night traffic streamed away intermittently along the Ville-Marie Expressway, distant enough to be silent, not to wake the rich residents here. Closer, a car's tire crunched as it rolled over a ball of gritty ice, and popped it, skittering, into a gutter. Two dogs did the midnight yelp. Robbie grit his teeth tight together, breathed resolutely through his nose. Rosie rested her head on his shoulder and her hair went up his nostrils like spikes of fragrant grass. He pecked her forehead with his lips. She looked up at him, lifted her chin, and they kissed. And while they kissed, tentatively, tenderly, he listened to the heavy tide of sorrow roll up, roll up, roll up repeatedly, like a record stuck in its final groove, from his heart to his bruising head.

15

WHEN ROBBIE DESCRIBED THE GRISSOMS TO ROSIE, SHE had a simple solution: "Make *peace!* Let them get to know what a sweet guy you are, Bob. Share your vision of the WORLD with them. I'm sure even they were *young* once too!"

One more beer, then, and a joint for good luck, and they left Dolores to play records and be gloomy on her own. Downstairs, Mrs. Grissom answered the door, her husband behind her. They looked surprised at first, but Rosie was so effervescent they closed the door only to slip off the security chain, and welcomed them in. Both Mr. and Mrs. had white beards, and mottled onionskin stretched over their skulls. Mrs. Grissom had white powder caked on her face that stopped at her chin; the neck that hung in folds below was naked. She had pencilled an almost continuous straight line across her forehead where her eyebrows had been, or a little higher, maybe, and Robbie was struck with the impression that wherever she looked, whomever she addressed, she was waiting, querulously, for answers to questions she'd been asking all her life.

"Nice walkway, these days," she said, and Robbie stiffened, radar tuned to the sarcasm frequency.

Old people – he'd known a couple: Grandma Bethel and

259

her sister, Dinah. Robbie's considered opinion was that, being from the old country as they were (though he couldn't tell you *which* old country) . . . well, forget it, you don't need to hear what his considered opinion was, you can guess. On sweltering afternoons, anyway, Grandma Bethel liked to wear pillowy bloomers with Canadian geese migrating across them, and Great Aunt Dinah had a taste for jewel-encrusted horn-rimmed spectacles. To slobber over Barnabus, they both had to painfully bend their bowed legs with the thick nylons rolled down about the ankles. Barnabus making a wiggly mouth and bursting into tears, and Miriam and Robbie just killing themselves at that.

"Look, Bob!" Rosie exclaimed, while Mrs. Grissom went to fetch them a glass of sherry, and Mr. Grissom lowered himself into a tatty overstuffed chair. "Look at *this*." On the mantelpiece were numerous photographs in ornate silver frames. Eons old, from before the war: Mr. Grissom looking sharp, with Brylcreemed hair and a smart mustachio, plunging through the air, with his heels tucked under and pointed behind him like a couple of exhaust pipes. Robbie whistled with admiration. And here was Mrs. Grissom, posing proudly in a sequinned muu-muu, with a headdress of rhinestones and ostrich feathers, and standing *topless* in one, with one bare thigh thrust forward (not at all the leg she has now, Robbie notes uncomfortably, with the varicose veins like mould in Stilton). Her eyelashes were clotted black, her face was creaseless and shiny with luminescent lipstick.

"The inscription says, *Empire Burlesque Follies of Montreal*," Rosie said.

"Yeah, I know," Robbie said. He'd made the connection quickly, impressed, suddenly sorry he'd hated them all this time for just being old. "Jacquie Diamantine, and Marcello 'Red' Manzoli, of the Flying Manzoli Brothers. They were famous in their time, eh."

"You *know* these people?" Rosie said.

"You got it, young fella," Mr. Grissom said, getting up again with difficulty. "Direct from the Lido Cabaret." Robbie observed that his long lanky body moved as stiffly as an old deck chair now, taut-hinged, hauled out from the shed when the winter's done.

"This was your *job?*" Robbie said, meaning to compliment the old man, but thanks to his indelibly mean little gunslinger eyes, and his habitually sharpened tone of voice – plus, now, his punked-up haircut that looked like a wig of nails – the remark came out as a taunt, and right on cue an almighty noise started like a chainsaw through the ceiling. The Grissom's chandelier rattled, and knick-nacks walked across the shelves.

"I'd like to see you try it," Mrs. Grissom shouted. "I'd say you have trouble just jumping out of bed – only reason the ass of your jeans is worn out is, you sit on it all day." The old lady started it, remember that. "You are a noisy little bugger, ain't you?"

"Free country," Robbie retorted.

Rosie tugged at Robbie's sleeve. "Why don't you ask Dolores to turn it down, Bob? That would be the *nice* thing to do."

"Don't get a wedgie over it," Robbie said. "I guess it's just not your kind of music. Free country."

"C'mon, Bob, let's go. You're wasted."

Mr. Grissom's face was shaking. His eyeballs swivelled in their sockets. "I can't hear myself think," he said.

"That's cause you're hard of hearing," Robbie sneered.

"Go to hell, you filthy young creep," Mrs. Grissom said.

Robbie struggled to undo the half-dozen locks on the front door, flew out leaving it open.

Rosie called out, "Bob, wait!" but he was going going gone.

He stomped away, kicking fences, Robbie the marauding knight, swinging his fists at bare bushes, heading for the Roxy. The first heavy snow of the year was drifting down out of the darkness, teeming in the light of the streetlamps. It was accumulating on staircases all down the street, all over this free country; it was collecting on windowsills, and the windscreens of parked cars; it was gathering in the bark of trees and on the handles of trashcans and in the folds of scraps of litter huddled against the curb; and, as it melted on Robbie's hot head it made his ferocious spiky hair go all limp.

Next morning, still charged, he's tilting homewards with a bleeding throat and a whole new fan on his lap, riding with her in the back of Louie Louie's Oldsmobile Cutlass, with the back hiked up high over mag wheels, furry dice hanging from the rearview, 8-track, and fuzzy plastic bobbing-head doggie in the back. The car filling up with dope smoke just like in a Cheech and Chong skit. Robbie and Brat laugh about the stupid broads who take them seriously enough to get in the sack with them just like that. It's hilarious: three Joes, K, just three fucken nimrods throw together a band, hack their way through some so-called songs, and in two weeks, look what happens.

"I got a Lovely souvenir streetmap of Montreal," Brat says. "I put it on my bedroom wall and stuck little flags on it. Green ones is where I got laid, red ones is where the chick comes from."

"Uff. Uff uff," goes Louie Louie, punching the roof of the car.

"You throw a party, right," Robbie guffaws, "and invite all the chicks you balled," exhaling, and passing the joint to the fan. "They show, and they're checking each other out the way chicks do, and you say, Well, I guess you're all wondering why I invited you here tonight."

Ironical thing is, he's actually going off sex. The boys drop him off, and soon he's back in his bed with the fan,

262

(relieved that Rosie and Dolores appear to have crashed chez Bill the Beast for the night), his tongue beneath the hood of her love button, one finger up her honeypot, another in her asshole, when he realizes he's bummed out. Weird, eh? He just feels like an animal, humping in the age-old tradition – millions of years of it, what a bore. Sex, he decides, is definitely an old-fashioned concept. Anyway, it's hard to concentrate on sex when he's so completely wasted – the air is buzzing flies in his eyes and ears – and she's taking so long he thinks his tongue will fall out at the roots. He can't remember the last time he's enjoyed doing this, if ever. He periscopes up over her belly. The muscles of her abdomen are heaving happily, and now she lets out a vaginal fart. He crawls up and bites her neck, as hard as he can. Now she's really alive, digging into his back and nipping back. He bites her again, on the lips, hard, and draws blood. He looks down to where his penis is beached like a soft eel on her shorebelly. A wave of nausea washes over him as his stomach brings up a solution of fizz and that oily stuff they have the nerve to call popcorn *butter*. He and the fan look at each other, nose to nose. She makes a quizzical expression. This is a drag, he thinks, and pushes his face into the pillow. She sits up and wipes the blood with the back of her hand. He feels bad, but turfs her out, anyway – nicely enough, telling her that it serves her right if she refused to listen to his dire warnings about star power. She leaves with her clothes in her arms. He holds his head above his pillow and waits for the front door to slam. Then he hauls out his secret pile of magazines from beneath the mattress, pores over them, licks Kiki Van's glossy pussy, and rolls over into a boiling sleep. . . .

All of this time, he didn't miss the family one bit. Had he heard from them? Of course not. Dad would have spouted some bromide about a son returning only when he's ready; and Mom would insist that, unlike other mothers, she would never bother him on the phone or embarrass him by turning up at his door unannounced. (In truth, she couldn't phone if she wanted to, because Robbie's phone was dead; earlier that week, a woman with a voice like rusted iron filings had grated in his ear that he had twenty-four hours to pay his bill, which was two months overdue already, or he'd be disconnected. Robbie saved her the trouble and yanked the cord from the wall.)

It was a good thing Mom had started sending him care packages, though. Robbie hungrily ripped the first one open as soon as it arrived. He found sesame seeds, turtle soup stock, *loukhoums* imported from the Middle East, iron pills, seaweed. And a miracle hangover cure in her racing handwriting:

> Before going to bed, darling, take 1 or 2 g vit. C + drink 1 cup of herb tea w/honey.
> On waking, drink juice of a lemon with molasses + 1 or 2 vit. C. Go for a run or walk a mile or 2. Shower cold. Try not to eat – liver is busiest removing toxins in the midnight hours.
> Lunch: if you're only feeling well-ish, grated apples and alfalfa should do the trick. OJ, o-oil, lemon j., 1 or 2g vit C.
> Dinner: cammomile tea, steamed veg. Gd way to eliminate poisons, indigestion, muscle aches, fatigue, SLUGGISHNESS.
>
> love ever,
>
> Mommy.

A brisk December afternoon and, *Happy Chanukah!*, Brat was on another generosity trip. He picked Robbie up in a cab, and they headed for L'Enfer Strip. Brat was nervous as a buzzsaw. Angel dust'll do that to you, Robbie the discriminating substance-abuser observed warily. Wag your fingers in front of a neon strip and that's the way the world must look from Brat's perspective now.

"Hey, Rob, now that the pepsis rule Quebec, right, there's language laws that says the Lovely Fruit Company's gotta remove all the stickers that read *banana* on their bananas. My Dad protests that that'll make it too expensive to import them, so the fucken PQ goes, Eh bien, de Québéçois will do witout *bananes*. Is that like, WHOA, or what?"

The cab was still a block away, gridlocked at the lights, but the driver switched off his meter and said pleasantly, "Bon, les gars, trois piastres – ça va."

"Nice!" Robbie said.

But Brat spat, "Wassat? Speak to me in *Hinglish*, man."

"Hey, hey," Robbie said. "Read. Says three dollars."

"Yeah, well, I'm SICK of this. I'm gonna punch him out! Either he tells me in English, or I ain't forking over a fucken nickel." Brat opened the cab door, stepped into the street without closing it again. Traffic swerved around, honking.

"Hey, buddy," he shouted through the driver's window and kicking the door. "Come again. Tell me how MUCH?"

The cabbie signalled with his fingers, *trois piastres*, not at all nicely now. He opened his door. Brat wasted no time. He headbutted the driver. The driver held his nose, plopping out heavily onto the street, one foot jammed under his seat. Brat kneeled on his chest.

"ENGLISH ENGLISH, you pepsi FUCKER," he shouted. "Tell me how much I OWE!"

A knot of pedestrians had gathered to watch. One couple cheered.

"Hey, cool out, man," Robbie said, dragging him back by his neck. Now there was the old familiar siren screaming. They took off, cackling like bats out of hell.

When they got to L'Enfer Strip, Rosie gave them a look that would sour milk. No free beers were forthcoming, no hot dogs, nothing. Brat was still acting like a dickhead. He even looked like an erect penis, sitting three-quarters in his chair to ogle girls dancing at other people's tables, his neck thrust as far as it would go. "Ever thought what a vagina is, Robbie?" he said. "A wet, smelly, sucking hole with flaps. And that's what makes men crazy with love. Weird, eh? All it is is we all wanna marry our mothers. I know cause I read Freud, eh."

Robbie watched as Brat talked to everyone, calling strangers *buddy*, addressing the strippers by the names pinned to their brassieres; he was still on his generosity trip, buying beers all around and grinning, thumb-things up, as they stripped.

"The ugly ones appreciate it when you're nice," he confided. "Whoa! When a broad has great jugs and she can dance, knowaddimean, Rob, you arsewipe? I really *know* dancing when I see it."

Robbie found himself feeling suddenly prudish and censorious. He could just picture Brat at the ballet, knowing dance when he saw it.

"Hey, guy," Brat said. "You're weirded out these days. Still hung up on that chick Ivy, I guess. Fuck me, you've got lousy taste in women. This Rosie chick, like *whoa*, toys in the attic, or what? You hear her on the radio the other day?"

"No, what?"

"Phone-in show about divorce, right, and she comes on, says her real name and everything." Brat leaning over, confidential now. "She goes, 'My Daddy's got a new girl-friend, and I'm worried now he won't want me any more.' Can you *believe* it? What is she, twenty-three, right, she

266

hangs round with dorks like you half her age, and she wants to marry her father, fuck. I'd steer clear if I was you, dude. Slap the salami instead, pull the pud, it's disease-free. I took French Lit, it's like Sartre said, eh, 'the pleasure given coincides with the enjoyment received.' "

Brat turned to the next table and picked up a conversation with a man in a polyester jacket with extra-wide lapels and a kipper tie. A stripper was engaged in contortions on the top of his table: she had propped her heels on the back of his chair with her legs suspended over his shoulders, and gripped the edges of the table behind her to hold herself up, spreading her thighs in front of his face while he ate his lunch.

"Hey, buddy," Brat said, "is this seat taken?" The man gave him the look of someone interrupted at his reading for the fourteenth time. "Hey," Brat said. "I *know* you from somewhere, don't I?"

"That right?" the man replied. He pushed his greasy plate under the stripper's suspension-bridged body – and nibbled a toothpick. He fixed Brat with eyes as slitted and grey as sharks' gills. "Where from?"

"Jeez, lemme see, now," Brat said.

"You know Olly?"

"Olly, lemme see. Yeah. Course, we go way back."

"Yeah?" the guy said. "I ain't seen him in a dog's age. I hear he's out. How's he doen?"

"Well y'know . . . " Brat said. "I don't know him that good really."

The man stared at him, shunting his toothpick around. He stood up and walked away, leaving the stripper to clear away the plate and cutlery.

"Et maintenant, MESdames et MESsieurs, vieullez réclamer la charrrrmante CHAStity!"

Rosie climbed the stage and pointedly ignored the boys as she started up her bump and grind. Robbie wasn't sure if he should watch or not. By way of compromise, he stuck his nose in his beer and snuck glances. She was dancing without much conviction, cautiously back from the lip of the stage. She hadn't even troubled to wear an outfit, and chewed her gum like a cow at her cud. Robbie followed her childish, myopic face and thought meanly, She barely knows she's alive. It was the most obscene thing he could think of, but he thought it, anyway, and added, What is she doing with her life?

Leaving the club an hour later, they shielded their eyes from the afternoon sun, and Brat told Robbie he was quitting Hell's Yells. To be a male model, he said. He showed him the set of photographs he'd had done at an agency: Brat sporting a foulard and looking like his horse is coming in; Brat in a hound's-tooth jacket gazing earnestly at a distant horizon; Brat in spiffy tennis shorts squinting into the sun and looking determined.

Robbie, who had now glued and knotted actual nails in his hair and put a zircon stud in his nose, said, "Don't you think they're gonna need other poses? Like, with arms?"

"Equal opportunity, man. I plan to sue the first bastard who rejects me."

"But I thought you're gonna work for your dad?"

"I want it all, man! I get featured in the national talent catalogue. The head office is in Toronto, which is where I'm bound, anyhow – 'cause of all this PQ shit coming down, my old man's moving Lovely Things to where money counts, in the language that counts. First of the new year."

"I don't get. I was meaning to ask. *What* PQ shit, exactly?"

"The election, numbnuts. Montreal's the pits now. It's going to the dogs as far as foreign investment, eh – the Yanks are backing off like we've switched to Communism. Maybe there's gonna be a revolution, like *hup against de wall, Hinglish.*"

"Oh, right, right. The election. But what about Hell's Yells, guy?"

"Well, I could of went the other way like you, but I'm opting for success. I want my bananas."

That evening, Rosie was in a rage because, after Robbie and Brat had left, the weirdo in the raincoat had come around again and called her a fornicator. Plus, the editor of the *Montreal Star*'s Lifestyle section turned down her idea for a photo-story on the Second Annual Tits For Tots Yuletide Stripperama.

"*Inappropriate subject for the Christmas season.* Tell that to those poor little *kids*," she said. "*Shit*. Maybe I'll set up a home for battered women, I don't know, a REFUGE from the *Church*."

They were elbowing through the last-minute shopping rush, Rosie homing in on every free sample, every demonstration, every give-away item the department store had to offer. She squirted *eau de toilette* on her wrist, answered a questionnaire and received an indestructible pen that was guaranteed to write underwater and in outer space, and scored a microwaved meat pie for Robbie. He chomped at it greedily. People stared.

"Hi! I'm Robbie Bookbinder," he said, "and that's my Mom." For there she was, on forty-five TV sets at once: a Holiday Season Special! presented from resorts around the world with a complete guide to sunscreens, six ways to recognize mercury poisoning when you catch fish, and how to tell if battery acid's been dumped in a stream – *before* your children swim in it!

What a dinful season – piped-in music, Salvation Army bells, Ogilvy's in-store bagpiper blaring away. And now, with these commercials, they're arranging carols like rock songs. The soundtrack to his youth, quit fucking with them. Who are the cynical old scumbags responsible for this? Own up. A security guard asked him to leave or stop yelling.

"Bug OFF!" he shouted. He was ejected by two security guards.

Rosie clung to him as they vaulted over a lake of curb-side slush. "Blows me away how *heavy* life's getting," she said, and she was talking a mile a minute. "Like, I don't think you should even come to the club any more. Did you notice in the club how all the announcements are French ONLY? I thought it was all that PQ jazz, and it *is*, but in a *twisted* sort of way – there's been a buyout or a gang war more probably, cos the Jean-Guys from the Châteauguay chapter are all over the place, and they're like RABID separatists. Dolores tells me things are heating up real bad on the biker scene generally in Quebec, eh – they say the Satan's Choice have been absorbed by the *Outlaws*, and the *Popeyes* are facing off against the *Angels*, 'n they're like animals salivating BLOOD from their *glands!* Even smaller gangs like the Dead Man's Hands used to have a strip of the road, right, but these days everyone's being dragged into the fight. Guys like Bill the Beast are just itching to DESTROY. I'm real scared for Dolores, I do hope you don't mind us shacking up with you for good now, I mean that boiling water incident was one thing – she ASKED for it, sort of – but yesterday Bill tried to pin her hand to the BED with a KNIFE! For no good *reason!*"

A second care package, which Robbie opened guiltily. He knew Mom's birthday was shortly before Xmas, but for some reason this year he couldn't remember the date exactly. She wasn't the type of mother to remind anybody how many shopping days remained before her birthday, and he hadn't had a chance to ask. He intended to call Miriam and check with her, but since he didn't have a phone, he kept forgetting. He knew all Mom wanted was

270

flowers. That's all she ever wanted in wintertime. He could have simply stolen some and sent them any old day, she wasn't a stickler for dates. But he couldn't seem to get around to it.

He delved in. Bag of wheat germ, seaweed strips, box of liqueur-filled chocolates. He ate the chocolates while he read the note:

> Remember, darling Robbie, yr body seeks always to get rid of waste. Junk food is exhausting because it's toxic. Aver. human has 5oz undigested meat in intestines. People like Daddy who live on coffee: blood vessel dilation, irregular h-beat, high blood p., kidney probs, ulcers, restlessness, stomach trouble, blood sugar levels, and pancreas secretes insulin. Don't! Preserve good PH balance, don't make digestive juices counteract one another. Laughter, happiness, etc. is alkalizing. Anger – acidifying. Try the occ. all-juice gesundheitstag – good health day.
> Must go,
>   love always,
>   M.

"An all-juice day," Robbie repeated aloud. "Now there's one fuck of a good idea."

The bones in a woman should be implied, thought Robbie the Famous Artist, but never pronounced. You wouldn't say Queenie Graves was fat, but at least she wasn't like most of the girls he knew; Rosie was as jumpy as a pinball machine about to TILT, Dolores was thin as a wire, Ivy was another rack of nerves, and, in a flash, he realized he was tired of all the skinny rib-caged junkies, anorexics, stray cats, waifs, fans, and unpredictable runaways who invaded his space.

"Hey," Queenie said, peering in. She had brought him another package, arrived Special Delivery while everyone was out. "How many books d'ya have? Ever counted 'em? Art books, right. You paintin today? Maybe I could come in and watch one day? I betcha see the world in a whole different way than other people."

December the twentieth, and Mr. Graves was due home on Xmas Eve. Queenie had appeared at Robbie's door three times already, clicking her dentures and apologetically demanding the rent. Soon, Robbie promised her, soon. He tried to shut the door on her face. He was afraid she'd see what a mess he'd made of the place.

The living room was a demolition zone. Those taped-up garbage bags did a feeble job of keeping the winter out. The radiators dribbled black oily water down the walls. Plaster, pencil sharpenings, flakes of white paint, pizza gunge, beer mould, and puke mould were all mashed into the carpet which, far from the Mediterranean blue that had first greeted Robbie like a holiday resort, now resembled waters that would only support the most undesirable life-forms. He'd torn up the Formica countertops in his kitchen, which were the colour of baby's shit, intending to replace them with something more punk but had delayed the project until he finished the paint job on the walls; he had begun to paint the walls in red, white, and blue stripes, but his brush picked up dirt and hair and bugs from the floor and ended up smearing the matted muck all over. His iron pots had grown hides of rust, and his cutlery was just as foul on one end as on the other. The oven was a place so evil that even Rosie would hesitate sticking her head in it, even if she had been cured of her claustrophobia. Nor could he use his toaster; on an impulse one morning, he had brushed in a plump cockroach he had caught crawling across the top, and fried it – now, when he switched it on for toast, a sickening, meaty smell arose from the slots.

After Queenie left, he didn't even look into his latest care package; what was the point, health-junk probably. He took off downtown in search of meat for his intestines, leaving by the back porch. The front path could take care of itself. His junk mail too, which he left stuffed to bursting in his box. That's how he'd avoid Queenie from now on – pretend he wasn't there at all. Garbage he'd leave indoors, and lights he'd never use. He'd tiptoe around a lot. As for playing records, well, wouldn't the Grissoms be relieved. And Merry Xmas to them.

The fire escape was rippled with baby icicles, as round and regular as a dog's lips, and it was perilous. When he slid down the steps, the frozen metal shrieked against its bolts and braces, and the gums of ice peeled off. He clung tight, his ass on a cushion of snow, his fingers sticking to the rail, waiting breathlessly to see if Queenie had seen him from her kitchen window. Across the back alley, up over the back of the Parthenon Self-Serve, Eccelucci's sumptuous dollface watched him like the Mona fucken Lisa. He slipped off down the alley.

One thing about not letting on that you're home: you can't turn on the taps. And Robbie was getting mighty stinky. He noticed this for himself the next day, waiting for Dad in the lobby of the CIBC building where he allegedly worked. Robbie was visiting just to say Hi, see what Xmas plans the family had this year, and to see if the old man was free for lunch, maybe. The security guard phoned upstairs, nodded, looked Robbie up and down, nodded again, hung up, and asked him to wait – Monsieur Bookbinder was in a meeting, he said.

Robbie sat on a chair and paged through a newspaper.

The ink was still too fresh to hold it close to him, so he stared into thin air instead of reading it, rubbing his inflamed nostrils, chewing on his tongue, and slipped a hand inside his shirt to feel if his underarms were wet. He smelled his glistening fingers delicately. The security guard frowned.

Men with suits were striding briskly in and out, their rubbers on their shoes squeaking foolishly across the marble floor. At first Robbie felt superior, just slouching there in his X-ray specs and dog collar and chain, but after three quarters of an hour Dad, apparently, was still tied up. He stood up, stuck the guard his middle finger, and strode out into the late-afternoon traffic.

The world was dark, the drizzled snow sparkling ruby-red in the brake lights of cars. He lifted a six-pack from a dépanneur and drank it sitting on a stoop overlooking the exclusive girls' school on Côte-des-Neiges where Miriam went. He watched the girls cluster and squeal and smoke cigarettes at the bus stop. A couple of them flirted with him. When their bus drew up, he went to piss behind a snowbank. He filched an aerosol can from a hardware store – having seen photos of the graffiti that covered New York City like a cartoon fungus, he figured he could get people wondering all over Montreal, maybe in the papers too, with sober concern, What is this phenomenon, this, ah, *Hell's Yells?*

First, he ducked into an alley and leaned behind a garbage haul. He broke a glass ampule of amyl nitrate beneath his nose and inhaled the rotten apple odour with his eyes closed. When he opened them, his body was humming. The slushy snow was a laugh. His loneliness was the bestest way to be, the world fell away from him like a flimsy toy theatre.

Graffiti artists require strong fingers; in less than five minutes, his thumb is aching and sticky. The paint won't build up satisfactorily on the drizzle-streaked walls, and he gets nabbed by a pig. The pig's in a holiday-bonus mood and only asks him to hand over the can, but Robbie's in a frenzy, buzzed and dripping.

"Get away!" he blurts, "I'm improving on the cityscape, man. Who built these buildings? Who let 'em? Thirty floors of ugliness. Horror stories, I call 'em, skycrappers. Seriously, these concrete bunkers. What does it say on it? Sir George Williams University. Chrissake, Hitler died in something that looked like this. It's depressing. Looks like World War Three. Physical graffiti, is what it is. It affects people and they don't even know it."

"It's private property, sir," the pig says, patiently. "Now give me the paint can and go home before I book your ass."

By the time he snuck back through his kitchen window, every little thing was driving him crazy. He had to pee badly from all that beer, and he was in an irritated snit about the whole world. He had a headache from the poppers, like someone was kicking at the back of his eyeballs. And cold, he decided, is not funny. His forehead was screaming – it was so cold outside that blood had come up on the skin of his temples. He kicked off his sneakers because he couldn't manipulate the laces, leaving slush all over the kitchen floor. Cold made his stomach cramp too, and he was sick of being poor, and he sincerely wondered why he should be in this state of virtual eviction.

The falling dark, and a shower was just what he needed to soothe him. He put his fists up on the wall and stood there with his head under the faucet, glorying in the rush of water. Scalding, just this side of pain, thundering against his eardrums, coursing over his shoulders and streaming down his back – the waterdrops with their tadpole tails licking his ears and trickling ticklingly inside, the way they used to when Mom washed his hair, with his neck resting over the cool lip of the bathtub. He shuddered, felt like he was slipping his skin off. Like an onion in a bubbling hot soup. He was dissolving, he felt as if he could breathe in water. He was an amorphous wriggling sensitive creature, swimming through the water mains beneath the mucky sidewalks of the city, to emerge up the drain of Ivy's bathroom to spawn. There she'd be, scented with lavender oil, rubbery wet, her pubic hair tapered to a dripping ducktail as she showered, and wouldn't she be surprised.

. Which was when the stream went freezing cold. Out of nowhere, just like that.

IT WAS HARD FOR HIM TO SAY WHICH WAS THE GREATER failure: his life to date, or his bid to end it. He'd slept most of the weekend down in the dungeon, but by Sunday morning Ivy's silence was unendurable. He sat by the telephone with a palpitating heart and nerves that itched like rusting steel. When she hears what he's done, he thought to himself (and hating himself as he dialled), how concerned she'll be – contrite, even; she'll see how cruel she was. His suicide attempt will be a bonding experience for them both. She'll see how spontaneous he really is. It'll be a lesson to her, too; she'll see how there are limits to that convulsive business.

But all she said was, "God. You really do make all kinds of demands on me. *God!* OK, OK. Let's meet at Chang's. At 9:00, OK?"

He hung up with an awful sense of disintegrating resolve. He had miscalculated somewhere. All he had for certain, now, was a killing headache and cheesecloth for brains. With slow, sickening cognizance he saw that he might have damaged his brain. His stomach felt exhausted, and his head was sizzling with the residue of all that codeine. It was weird; all those happy drugs he had come through safely in his life, and now, an overdose of fucken aspirin has him toxically wasted. Obliviated. Of course, he might be suffering from the longer-term consequence of the acid, the hash, the beer, the brandy, the speed, the champagne, *and* the aspirin he's done non-stop since the Bones' show, but what did it matter now? He almost wished he'd gone through with killing himself properly. Now at least he could tell Ivy what *thinking* felt like: like pulling the soggiest blackened leaves from a week-old bag of spinach.

You could call human beings juicy radiators sometimes, he thought that night as, balanced precariously on a squeaky ledge of snow by the bus stop, he hugged Ivy hard; she was ribby, tepid, a wrought-iron rad. He hugged her, with passion, but was surprised to find himself remembering how much bigger, how much softer an embrace Rosie had given him – more mature, more comforting – and just thinking about her now, with her perfume and her plummy warm lips and the fresh shape of her tongue, the tongue of someone new, gave this bony hug the lie of a weirdly formal occasion.

Ivy pointed with a mittened hand to the restaurant at the corner of Girouard Park. Inside Chang's Mountain Jewel Palace, strings of gold and silver announced Glad Tidings, but no one was eating there. The staff were clustered around a booth in the back, playing a vigorous game of mah-jongg. Robbie and Ivy sat down, and were soon warming their hands around an aluminum teapot.

"It's not even Chinese tea," Robbie said. "Look. A Tetley tea bag."

"I wish I was in Jamaica," Ivy said. "I can picture it now. A ridge of hot white sand, you go over the top and then there's the sea, blue as a jewel. Ganja in cone spliffs. And a bassy sound system from out of the mountains of Maroon County."

278

"Yeah, well, you're not."

Ivy looked at him. "Don't make it worse," she said tersely. "You started this. I suppose you want to talk about yourself, now. That's the problem with this relationship – we don't have one, we only talk about it."

An explosion of laughter at the mah-jongg game. Robbie looked over, searching for something, anything, to look at. Ivy took his hands across the table and squeezed.

"Hey," she said.

Robbie flinched. His body was pulsing erratically, idling on an arrhythmic heart, fuelled with hatred and shame.

"Your family," he pronounced, "it's jinxed, you know. It's sad to see. And I just hate your father."

She whipped her hands back, narrowed her eyes. She was hissing, her nostrils flared.

"*You* hate my father? You're so insensitive sometimes I ought to stick a fork in you. It'd let some air out. God, what have you got to be mad at? How do you think *I* feel?"

"Why don't you move out then?"

"It's not that. I just need to have my own space."

"That's what I *said*."

Robbie shunting his shoes under the table and picking at a cuticle and thinking I'm right I'm right I'm right. She never listens, she drags me down, she doesn't understand me. She's incapable of expressing herself. I just want to go home. I love my family. And I want to phone Rosie.

Ivy sighed, drew a deep breath, said, "Actually, I'm psyching myself up for it, but I need a job, obviously. I'm thinking I could be a nude model at the art school at the Musée des Beaux Arts."

Robbie's blood going thin at that one. "A nude model? That's nice. Maybe you'll meet somebody."

"Maybe I'll meet somebody? God. Listen to you. You're already jealous and I haven't met him yet."

Robbie's throat is tight; it's like a boa constrictor crushing his heart. He's thinking, vertiginously, We could break

279

up tonight and I don't care a bit. Merry Xmas, Happy fucken New Year. He wants to spurt the venom all over Ivy's face. He thinks, she drove me to madness, she made me damage myself. She's heartless. There are nicer people in the world. She's only being nice now because she regrets what she did. Well, I never liked her in the first place. I had a crush, that's all. The chase was fun, but now it's over. Ivy was staring at him, but he wasn't going to be fazed – he stared back, unflinching. A waiter came around.

"Flee compremantaly," he said, smiling broadly, and placed a pair of eggrolls and plastic envelopes of plum sauce between them. "Onna house, you kids."

"Hey man, cool," Robbie said.

"Yes, Melly Chlistmas," Ivy said, giggling.

Robbie frowned and shushed her. "Hey, that's not funny, that's rude."

"What's the point of funny if you can't be rude?" she snapped. "God, I wish I were a child again. In another family of course. Remember when you're a kid and you believe it when they sing about products on TV, that all the problems of your life can be solved? Well, the other day I was standing over the sink, and I picked up a bar of soap they used to have an ad for – where the girl says that corny line, *Mommy how come your skin's so soft?* – and for a moment, for a split second, I felt I was six again. I went all hot and faint. I knocked one of those ridiculous little mascara brushes down the drain. God. Imagine having your life epitomized by a TV commercial."

"Acid flashback, man."

"No, 'cause I never did acid."

"I was *jo*king. That was a joke."

"Then it wasn't a good one, was it?"

They glared at one another. Robbie's ears were humming. His throat a sluice of sadness now. What has he done? Why is he repulsed by Ivy the first time she expresses some real need? He doesn't know. *I'm* OK, he's thinking, *she's* fucked up. He wants to say he's sorry, but he can't bring himself to do it. The sentence is all in there, crouching in his mouth like a spring, the words all coiled together. No, he won't. *She* never would. She'd say, If you can't read my mood, what's the point of explaining it to you.

"You don't really listen to me, you know," she said. "You don't care what I say or what I'm going through. You and I are completely and utterly different, and you know that as well as I. Have you any idea how selfish what you did was? How was I supposed to feel if you really went and *killed* yourself? How could I have lived with that? God, you must hate me."

Robbie's heart must be a fleshy yo-yo, spinning up and down his throat on a catgut string, because now he's scrambling with an apology. "I didn't know what I – I thought I was doing it for you. I'm sorry. Maybe if we try explaining ourselves more."

"NO!" Ivy slamming the table. Robbie darting his eyes over to the mah-jongg players. "You haven't listened to a thing I've said. If I have to explain now – "

"Then I wouldn't understand. I know I know. K, forget I ever mentioned it."

In the dead of winter in Montreal, when the streets are dark and the wind is still, the distance between the Earth and the sky appears to diminish; the night seems truly to have fallen, thin and inhospitable, and the planet they've paved beneath your feet is more palpably a planet, spinning alone in the refrigerated galaxy.

He walked her home, kicking meteors of spiny ice out of his way. Neither of them said a thing; they just tucked their heads into their coats. When they reached her porch, she broke the silence. She grabbed him by his shoulders. Her face was wild. They were nose to nose. She shook him and spat out, "What are you *doing*? Don't you understand *anything?*"

"No," Robbie said, coolly. "I guess I don't. I never understand you cause you never tell me a damn thing."

"What do you want to know? Why do you need everything spelled out?"

"But you never spell anything out, fuck. Pardon the language."

"*Fuck* the language," Ivy hissed. "You want permission from me to swear, now? You never take a chance. You never just *grab*. You've been well brought up, haven't you? Well, you *bore* me. You're a coward, always leaving it up to me. Know what I did last week? I picked up a taxi driver. Don't even ask, it was disgusting. Yeah, yeah, I can always feel you admiring me – like a prize pig – but that's not enough for me, for God's sake. You think I *like* myself? I'm a real vixen, a sex-bomb baby. A double-bagger, more like. I bet you think I parade in front of my mirror every night. Ever thought maybe I don't *want* to be sexy? I see your eyes follow every girl in the street. I know you'd love to flip through every *Bosom Buddies* magazine in every dépanneur we pass. I have to know you want to sleep with *me*. It's like my brother – I love him, but when he talks about girls, like on the reserve in Caughnawaga, 'they've got either TB or VD, one or the other, so you only fuck the ones that cough.' Ha fucking ha. You don't know what it's like. To be gang-raped. By bikers. You don't know *any*thing. For all it's worth, for all it makes a person feel *something*, you should try being fucked, for once. Hung up on a hook. Also, by the way, you should feel what it's like to shove a dry tampon up your cunt, just hoping for blood. It was all a false alarm, by the way, you never even asked. You just don't know what it's like. *You* ought to be signed up for Home Ec, just once. *You* should try being Daddy's girl, peeling his fat fingers off your thighs. Why don't *you* surprise *me*, for once. Make me feel wanted. Here." She grabbed Robbie's hand and jammed it between her legs and said in his ear, "Why don't

282

you ever get tough with me. C'mon, squeeze me. I can't feel a thing."

"It's cold out here, that's why," Robbie said, helplessly.

"Don't be a child. Let's go upstairs and fuck."

"*Upstairs?*"

"Yeah, c'mon. What d'you want, permission? What have we got to lose?"

Robbie shaking his head and making his eyes wide with incredulity as they tiptoed up the stairs, climbing up on the rubber ridge of each step to exert as little pressure as possible on the complaining wood. They pulled off their boots and placed the hard heels with infinite care on the mat. Sliding on solid-cold stockinged feet down the linoleum hallway. All the rooms dark, still smelling of reheated turkey dinner.

In the living room, the tablecloth had been folded up and laid on a chair, the tables had been put away, the fanfold wall was drawn to. Mr. Mills was snoring on the other side. Ivy guided Robbie to the couch, hands on his hips, pushing from behind; Robbie widening his windpipe and nasal passage so as not to let air out audibly. Ivy slipped away and returned after several agonizing minutes, nude, and white as a ghost, with something in her hand. She gestured at him to take his clothes off.

His parka was as loud as a chip bag in a theatre; each and every tooth of the zipper on his jeans made a sound like thick cloth tearing. Ivy laid one hand on the radiator by the couch and then took Robbie's frozen niblet of a penis in it. As he thawed out in her grip, he couldn't help but shoot glances at the parents' bedroom wall, drawing his lower lip down off his tensed teeth to make a face like a person in the front seat of a roller coaster.

Putting his hands on her shoulders now, trying to relax. Ivy jumped, for his hands were cold, and she nipped him in the bud. He twiddled his naked toes to get some feeling into them, and it occurred to him that it should not be taking so long, since his heart was pumping overtime. And now his penis was in bloom, although he wouldn't describe Ivy's technique as consummate. She looked up at him with a very serious expression, yanking him up and down, and what's in the other hand? Chrissake, a condom. He'd never used one of those before, except to fill with water and throw at buses. The main reason was: he was still a virgin. Oh, he'd fucked around, you know, been with all kinds of girls and done some sticky things, but he's never actually, um . . .

Ivy pulled it on. For a moment that made him think of Keef, and how she was really a polluted canal. What will this be like? Will it be like taking a shower in a raincoat, as Louie Louie described it? Or making mudpies with rubber gloves, like Baimy said? He no longer cared if the parents woke up. He was going to shout with joy. He would slide back their bedroom wall and tell them all about it. Or would he, for now he heard a sound. Was it his imagination, or were Ivy's parents being disgusting with each other in their bed? Ivy didn't seem to have noticed, but Robbie was sure that was a man softly grunting. And that, without a doubt, was Mrs. Mills talking again. Does she *ever* stop? This was ridiculous, this was no fun. Now Robbie was perspiring. He jerked a thumb in the dark, trying to communicate his fear to Ivy, but she was squeezing him, like a shopper testing fruit for its ripeness. And now, Robbie had wilted inside his condom; it clung only half on now, and dangled down like a pom-pommed sleeping cap. Ivy gave him a ferocious look, and he sent back a miserable shrug. And somewhere outside, from several streets over, the brittle bells in the tower of St. Henri chimed, once, . . . just once.

The first excruciating week of this fresh new year has come and gone, and tomorrow it's back to school.

As if the caf wasn't dreary enough to start with, with its industrial toilet-orange paint; every day, Robbie also has to sit through lunch hour, stoned out of his brain in his TOO COOL FOR SCHOOL T-shirt, watching the pepsis play Ping-Pong with animal concentration on their faces, and wondering why Ivy hasn't shown the whole first week of school. Pharte meanwhile has started piano over the holidays, it seems, for he is picking out some Favourite Melodies for the Beginner, stabbing at the keys with two fingers like he's crushing bugs: *The Godfather* theme; "Chopsticks"; "Moonlight Sonata." Robbie is feeling homicidal; only his drugs prevent him from getting up and wasting the nerd. From inside his head, the world sounds like a party balloon does when you put it to your ear and bonk it.

In class, Robbie orchestrated a pretty funny joke: he had all the kids put on their winter gear and sit nonchalantly at their desks with their pens in their mittens and their glasses on the outside of their balaclavas, and he opened all the windows to let the worst storm of the winter in. By the time M. Nul entered, there was a heap of snow on the teacher's desk, papers were blowing all over, and everyone's breath was visible. Thing was, M. Nul didn't find it funny, for some unknown reason, and Robbie was out on his ear (three scumbags stooled on him at once).

He didn't exactly vandalize, but he did take out his frustration on things: Tuesday, he kicked his locker so hard the door refused to close afterwards; Wednesday, he watched a stray ember from a joint he was smoking tumble into the crease of one of the foam lounge chairs, and more or less deliberately allowed it to smoulder there; Thursday, he mistakenly broke a window with a grit-packed snowball, plus he spilled some 7-Up onto the blackboard eraser – just to see what would happen – and sort of accidentally turned it to rock; Friday, he misjudged his own strength and broke the fire alarm glass with his elbow, which emptied the school out onto the sidewalk. The director, M.

Boutaric, called him to his office a second time, even though Robbie was the picture of innocence, and gave him a month's worth of detentions topped off with the threat of expulsion if he didn't reform. Which didn't mean a whole lot to him anyhow. His mind was a heavy-duty organ grinder, full of spiked tunes, winding round and round and round. *All teachers must die.*

Gaston, of course, had already been expelled, but he still haunted the area – there were at least three other schools in Outremont besides Blanchemains, and he sold *ash* and *hacid* to kids when the Dead Man's Hands weren't in sight. He looked like a real Cro-Magnon now, his face erupting with boils and scabby acne, his hair matted like horns; a grinning, smelly trafficker in souls. Worst of all, his elevated, if still inferior, status as a Devil's Disciple had invested him with a cranked-up arrogance, and Robbie had to be as nice as could be. Except one time when he risked, "Gee, Gaston, do you keep your mouth open like that to catch your dinner? It's January, dude, didn'tcha know – blackfly season's not till May." That's when Gaston pulled a knife and pressed it to Robbie's stomach and breathed in his face,

"Ayy, parle français, maudit bloke," and punched him in the breadbasket. Robbie didn't fight back. Curiously, he felt sorry for Gaston – vaguely sorry – for if Ivy had in fact put him through the wringer as Rosie described, then in the most unexpected of ways, he and Robbie were buddies of a sort. And so, when a lousy seedy twiggy joint Robbie bought from him snapped like a firecracker under his nose, he didn't even ask for a refund.

Monday morning, by which time his memories of Ivy had already shrivelled in his guts like a bitter gallstone, and all the blacker because it was his birthday the next day, he found a note in his locker:

i'm back. meet me after lunch?

He spent the rest of the morning in a state of loose-bowelled consternation. He asked permission to pee, and toked up in the can. Now the desks in the classroom are bobbing about like a flotilla of life rafts. And here's what the teacher sounds like in his ears: *moombamoombaooom.*

After lunch, he grabbed his chance to sneak up to the attic, but M. Boutaric caught him in the corridor before he even reached the stairs. For the next two hours, in the chilly gymnasium, he listlessly followed the class, doing rubber-boned push-ups and indifferent, calamitous high-jumps, escaping finally between classes while M. Nul's attention was engaged in admiring the showering boys.

He charged down the corridors of the school, scrambled up the old staircase, knocked hard on the attic door with his fist, once, and barged right in. Ivy was there all right, with a bunch of little red boxes opened up on the table by the kerosene burner. But she wasn't alone and she wasn't exactly waiting for him: she was snarling and hissing like a polecat as he burst in, pummelling Gaston's chest and trying to scratch his face; Gaston had his baggy-ass jeans halfway down to his knees, and his Devil's Disciple colours emblazoned on his back. He was grappling with Ivy's hips and dry-humping her, ignoring her ferocious scratches, and making a repugnant sound, something like a laugh.

Robbie shouted, "Hey!"

Gaston turned around, his grin dissolving. Ivy shoved him with a shriek. He fell backwards, tripped up by his dangling belt so heavy with keys, and banged the back of his head on the workbench, where Ivy had been doing her batik. He flopped stupidly on the floor and lay still.

"God," she said. "Fuck!" She was breathing rapidly, one overall strap off her shoulder. She blew the bangs off her forehead and looked at Robbie with a wild expression. Her cheeks were flushed, and her fists were clenched like she was holding a pair of grenades. Robbie was frozen to the spot. It had all happened in the space of two seconds. A dreadful thought flashed through his head: in two seconds, our lives are utterly changed. He went over to Gaston.

"Chrissake," he said. "What'll we do?" He crouched down. Gaston was breathing. Robbie looked up at Ivy. "What happened? What *happened*?"

"What do you *think*? He wanted my ass. He wanted my boxes. My *stuff*! God, he's been waiting for me all this *time*." She trembled violently. She was scraping her body with flattened palms, as if to scoop off muck. Now she was looking at Robbie as if he were a werewolf, too. Her mouth wobbled open, gasping for air, chewing feelings to make digestible words. "He snuck up here during lunch hour. I was expecting you, so I opened the door. He was decent at first, and I thought I could get rid of him if we talked. He said he wanted a hit. The goof. I thought that would take care of him for sure, especially if I gave him too much, but he did it himself, then he got horny on me. How *disgusting*!"

"Chrissake, Ivy," Robbie said again as she began stuffing boxes into her satchel. He shook his head. "This whole scene and everybody in it. Sometimes I feel like burning the entire fucken place down."

She turned around. They watched each other. Robbie stood up. He wished he hadn't said that. They were on either side of Gaston's body, like coyotes circling. Ivy looked crazed. Those wary eyes of hers, the fox in the grass.

"Don't dream it," she said flatly. "Be it."

She knocked over the kerosene burner with the back of her hand. Just like that. Never taking her eyes off Robbie's. The flame slithered across the tabletop like a blue snake spilled from a basket.

"What're you *doing*?" Robbie shouted. "Don't be crazy!"

"What's wrong with crazy," Ivy said. She stepped over Gaston, grabbed Robbie's hand and hauled him out of the room. She locked the door from the outside, took Robbie's hand again and pulled him into the little room across the landing. She kicked the door closed behind her, and slipped both straps off her shoulders. Then she was on him, biting his lip, pulling his ears, knocking their foreheads together. She was halfway between tears and giggling. She kicked Robbie in the shins and said, "Come *on!*"

Robbie dumbly obeyed, fumbling with his jeans, crouching to pull them down, fending off her kisses, trying to do everything at once. Ivy was shaking her head vigorously with her eyes closed, like someone needing desperately to pee. She dragged her dungarees down to her ankles and pulled him close to her. They plopped onto the coarse wood floor, clothes around them like straitjackets. Ivy parted her legs under Robbie, and speedily guided his wagging penis inside her. He was amazed how easily she swallowed him up. He pushed his nose to her breasts like bobbing for apples. With his groin he bounced up and down the way he thought he should, feeling ridiculous, but Ivy threw her hands on the floor above her head and whimpered. It was boiling hot in the room, and their bodies were slickening fast. Robbie kissed and kissed, expressing in kisses all the desperate, pure, unadulterated feelings he had ever had for her. He felt an orgasm rising in him, tried to suppress it. Ivy gripped his buttocks and pulled him in and out of her. He closed his eyes and held her slippery hips and felt the great swell suspend him, like a surfer coasting out on his board for the mondo waves. He was plunging, plunging, his heels in the air behind him, defying gravity and all good sense, and as he ejaculated he moaned and heard Ivy whimper again in his ear, caressing both sides of his face at once, squeezing him to her chest. What, he thought, did she have an orgasm too, or is she just pleased that I did? He felt like he was being petted for having done something good. He opened his eyes to sneak a look, but in the early darkness of winter dusk, it was hard to see her face.

"Happy birthday," she said grimly. He looked up into her nostrils. Now she was sniffing the air. He sniffed too, and there was smoke. He pulled out of her. It was baking in this room. His skin seized up and crackled with fright. He stood up, switched on the light. Tendrils of smoke were creeping around the door.

Stumbling back into their clothes. Ivy was the first out. Dark on the landing. Robbie fumbled for another light switch. Now they could see the haze of smoke, collecting above them in an angry restless ceiling; it was claustrophobic here, the attic was a hot lung hissing, and Robbie and Ivy were stuck to the floor, like in a nightmare. They could still see the stairs. He pushed her towards them, but she resisted. She pulled the art-room key from her pocket and inserted it in the lock. She put her hand on the brass doorknob to push the door open, but withdrew her hand with a scream.

"So OK, fuck," Robbie said, "let's go, for Chrissake!"

"No!" Ivy snapped. "Give me your parka. I want my stuff!"

Robbie stripped it off again. Ivy wrapped it around the doorknob, twisted and pushed. Robbie helped her. The door opened almost two inches, but stopped. Something heavy was on the other side. They pushed again. It gave, a foot or two. The room was full of smoke. Fragments of carbon floated about like in zero gravity. As Ivy squeezed in there was a terrific whooshing sound. Robbie could feel air sucked into the room from behind him, and a great tentacled arm of fire scrabbled across the ceiling, reaching for them from the far side. The flames illuminated the room. They looked surreal and dry, thickened with smoke, boxed up in this room with the sloping eaves, like a set in an infernal theatre, the whoosh like the audience's collective reaction as the safety curtain is lifted. And now he could also hear a fire alarm ringing distantly.

That great flashover had singed his eyebrows and the top of his head, but it took him a moment to realize it; his body seethed with heat and fright, and when he reached up to wipe the sweat from his face he discovered his forehead was smooth and raw. Ivy, meanwhile, had swooned in the heat, and now lay prostrate, clutching her satchel under her. The smoke had almost filled the room, from the ceiling down, leaving five feet or so of penetrable, breathable air. He was nauseous. He kneeled down and crawled over to her, dragged her back out by her wrists. They were slimy as eels, slipping from his grasp. He grabbed her sleeves instead, and by the time they were out on the landing, he had pulled her Afghan coat over her head. He pulled the door shut to contain the flames. He started hauling her down the stairs, like a sack of potatoes, but the back of her head bumped on every stair, so he strapped the satchel around his neck, and lifted her up in his arms. Down the attic stairs now, into the darkened building and already sensing the cooler temperature of the lower corridors; past the director's office, past the eerily empty classrooms and halfway down to the main entrance. There he met the first fireman, a giant in massive flapped armour, looming up out of the shadows, who grabbed Ivy and slung her over his shoulder. A second fireman did the same to Robbie. He squirmed as the blood rushed to his head. He felt stupid and childish. The world was upside-down and bouncing like a rubber ball. Out in the street the whole school was teeming. There were fire engines and squad cars with blue lights flashing, crowds of neighbour-hood rubberneckers, and policemen making cordons. Robbie wanted all of them to know he was in control of this thing, he didn't want to be seen coming out like this, like a child deserving of a spank. The fireman set him down at the back of an ambulance and wrapped a heavy

291

blanket around him, and someone else slapped an oxygen mask on his face.

"I'm OK, *fuck*," he yelled, but no one understood him through the mask. The pure oxygen made his head swim. The air was swelling in front of him and popping, displaying for his enjoyment the elastic surface tension of enormous soap bubbles. He was shivering violently. He could feel his nerves and muscles slamming and shunting around, like tracks in a haywire train terminal. He looked up to watch the aerial blaze, the gables and wrought-iron trellises of the old school silhouetted against the stony sky like an antique fire grate. A colossal rope of bright smoke twisted heavenwards, fraying on high and weaving into the wind and clouds. Firemen were on ladders with their hoses; streams of water collected in titanic icicles on the building's windowsills, filling up the gutters and freezing over the parking lot and sidewalks.

He was grateful for the oxygen now, struck by how delicate his stomach and lungs must be, how paper-thin, how outraged. And now two policemen were guiding Ivy past him. She was trying to wrench her arms free, hissing and spitting. He caught only a glimpse as they put her in the ambulance; her hair was singed and shrivelled, and her face was wet and flecked with ash. She struck out with her elbows until she was allowed to stand on her own. Then she walked, without assistance, without a look to the left or the right, into the ambulance.

Someone in a uniform bent down in front of Robbie, hands on knees, and said, "Qu'est-ce qu'y s'est passé, p'tit gars?"

"Don't ask me, man," he replied. The tumult on the streets made an insulating wall of sound around him. He slapped his shoulder instinctively to ensure the satchel strap was there beneath the blanket. And then a lie came to him, a simple lie told in a moment of utter enervation, for which he could hardly take responsibility:

"I was in the can, eh, when I heard screaming upstairs. So I went up to save her. Good thing, too. She was all alone and almost passed out. No one hurt? Too much, man. Quel miracle."

17

HE OPENED THAT THIRD PACKAGE FROM MOM AFTER ALL. Kelp, bag of dried figs, bag of Jerusalem artichokes, some other useless junk labelled *dulse*. Chrissake. He read the letter. It was more hurried than ever, terse even, and no "Dear anything" at the top:

> Don't improperly combine foods. Digestive j's overworked. Food may be forced undigested into intestines. Animals don't need Rolaids: in fact carnivores go for predigested veg. in victims' stomachs first . . .

He stopped. What was the point, this made him want to rowlf. There was another page, but forget it, she had obviously got her poo in a knot about that birthday business. He tossed it aside. What was the big deal. The country will be full of flowers in the spring, don't you worry.

Dolores's leather-brown leg was nestled up between his thighs, and his warm erection was riding it like the pommel on a saddle. Rosie was shaking him. And there was someone banging on the door. He got up, resentfully. It was early – about one in the afternoon. Rosie leaned up on an elbow, squinted around, and rekindled a roach from the night before that lay beside a hardened blob of bubblegum on the bedside table.

Two earnest-looking ladies stood to attention at the door, offering copies of *The Watchtower* and any amount of spiritual enlightenment for absolutely free, or a small contribution, if he wished.

"Yeah, sure, step right inside," Robbie said. "My friends are keen to learn, too."

He led them to the bedroom. It smelled heavily, muskily, of sleep and hash and Rosie's patchouli body oil. A veil-thin canopy of smoke hung above the mattress. Rosie and Dolores were nuzzling in the sheets, Dolores curled up like a seahorse, Rosie hugging her from behind with her Medusa hair, all sharp-headed adders, a black nest between the pillows.

The Watchtower women fled.

Robbie returned to bed, and Rosie was asleep again. He stood by and watched them. He scratched his head, crusty-dry, as congealed and spiky as yesterday's muddy cleats, and thought with satisfaction, They say when people cuddle in bed they're like spoons, but we're a drawerful of knives and forks. Then he fetched a pad and several sticks of charcoal, and sat cross-legged by the bed. The charcoal was loud against the paper. He sketched lightly, gently, so as not to wake them.

He woke alone, with a full bladder and a dribbling, inflamed nose. His arms were burning, he had been scratching them in his sleep. He held them out above him, and there was a rash in blotches from his elbow to his fingers. What time was it, the middle of the night. He went to the toilet. Squinting in the light as he peed, what's in the sink? Sea sponges. Rosie uses these because she refuses to get toxic shock from tampons. In the living room, he could hear her voice speaking low.

Stealthily tiptoeing down the hall. He stood naked in the dark – holding his bag, his belly like a fireplace full of smouldering coals, as it struggled to digest the spicy souvlaki he punished himself with yesterday – to eavesdrop.

"He won't even *touch* me sometimes," Rosie was saying. "I only ask for backrubs sometimes because my doctor says I have a pinched nerve, but Bob treats me like a leper."

"Ow long you been going togedder?" Dolores said.

"Since last summer. St. Jean-Baptiste. We've seen each other almost every single day, but I don't feel I've even scratched the surface, 'n I know he screws around. I don't care about *that* too much, I guess, it's just when he makes like I'm *invisible*. He's worse than my Daddy, I think. The more freedom I give him the more he thinks I'm penning him in. We haven't kissed in *months*. I'm doomed to compete with the ghost of sweet little Ivykins. Boy, did she ever do a number on him," Rosie whispered, and maybe now she's drying her eyes, Robbie can't tell from around the corner.

"Ow come you're wit im?"

"He's got a gentle soul. I just know it. And he loves me. I *know* it. He hasn't told me in so many words, I mean *spontaneously*, but he does whenever I make him repeat it after me, so that must mean something."

Sneaking back into bed now, Robbie moving in slow motion, the darkness thick oatmeal in his ears, his belly on fire, his tendons snapping like twigs underfoot. Back in the bedroom, he quietly quietly tears into little pieces the tender drawings he had made of Rosie sleeping. And stuffs them in the wastepaper basket.

The wind buffeted the apartment windows. The garbage bags swelled up like sails in a storm. Even though he had waited until Rosie and Dolores had left for the evening, and he knew he was alone, he jumped at the smallest sound, guiltily looking over his shoulder. He felt his ears in stereo, one chicken-sized heart pumping inside each of them. He picked out the little fat key on his key chain and inserted it into his *Cocaine* machine. The door's rubber lining was sticky from years of grime and syrup, but gave with a yank. The thick, acrid smell of hash and shrooms wafted out. Sealed inside the machine, Ivy's satchel and the red boxes with the tail-biting dragons on them had accumulated little dust. There were a dozen boxes in all. If each contained an ounce of pure smack, he guessed, each would be worth around twenty thousand bones, twice or three times as much if he stepped on them with Mannitol or baby laxative or crank or dextrose or something. He'd make this deal anonymously, of course – he'd have to find a buyer he didn't know, a friend of a friend of a friend. For if the Dead Man's Hands knew the stuff had *not* been lost in the fire, that *he* had it, he'd be cold meat by morning. He'd never seriously considered selling them before – he'd been too scared, frankly, and he'd hoped Ivy would show one day – but he was desperate, now. Broke, jobless, friendless, hopeless, and three months rent to pay. What choice did he have any more?

The eve of Xmas Eve. Arthur's Hideaway was a fleabag hotel with a bar and a matchbox stage on the ground floor, just a hork away from Boulevard St-Laurent. When Robbie got there, some band was busy spitting its guts through the PA. He leaned against the rear wall of the club, looking around him anxiously for whoever might show. Three punks were dancing up front, friends of the group, probably. Then someone lobbed some beer at the stage, bottle and all, and that really livened things up – in a flash, people were spitting Guinness-Book-of-Records-distances, and the guitarist nearly got beaned with a beer-stein, and Robbie thought, draught dodging, that's what bad musicians do when the crowd is roused to anger, arf arf.

The music was so loud he felt his sternum resonate and his bowels weaken, and he could imagine the throbbing gristle of his body. And, once the violence started, the music had definitely improved. Now there was Brat, and Louie Louie a head and a half taller than the rest, wading chin deep in a field of black razor-grass, redolent of hairspray. Rosie and Dolores had saved a table in the corner. Dolores looked gloomy, but Rosie was stunning in a Victorian lace bodice, clamped tight, her bosom squeezing out as white and plump as yeasty dough.

"Hey, Rob!" Brat shouted in his ear. " 'Member I said you had lousy taste in women? I stick to that, but two at once, YOW!"

"Yipper," Robbie replied sullenly. "Dog eat dog world, ain't it?" But he wasn't really listening. He needed this dope deal especially badly because he had only one more shopping day to buy presents for the family. It hadn't exactly slipped his mind before this, but it sort of had. It's hard to concentrate on stuff when you're skint.

He went for a quick private pee before the set ended. The can was fairly quiet, empty except for a guy standing a foot back from the urinal, due to his bear-sized beergut. He was a mountain of leather and oil-soiled denim, chaps and studded wristbands, and enough tattoos on his arms and chest for three regular-issue circus freaks. Stitched across his back, a hand of poker: aces and eights, riddled with bullets. Hearing Robbie enter he turned around, all greasy beard and dark glasses. In his hand he held his hog and it was tattooed too – a bright, viridian peecock – F.D.W. That was enough for Robbie's bashful bladder. He dipped into a cubicle, closed the door with his elbow, kicked the toilet seat up with his sneaker and unzipped. Thought of Niagara Falls. Instantly there was a pounding on the flimsy wall.

"Hey, FUCKhead, what am I, a *faggot*?"

Robbie jumped. Zipped up fast. Too fast, pinched his penis. Saw himself reflected twenty times in the chrome plumbing, each little Robbie as wimped-out as the one before. He looked down and saw the toes of a pair of battered motorcycle boots, BILL in studs on one, BEAST on the other.

"Hey, FUCKhead, I said, are you callen me a fucken FAGGOT?"

"Whaddoyoumean, I didn't say nothen, guy."

The guy thumped on the wall again. "Any guy hides his whang's gotta be scared of sumpen. What're you, scared I'm a FAGGOT?"

"I don't know what you're *talking* about, man. Leave me alone, eh."

"There's room out here for three tuh take a whizz, ya PUSSY. I ain't gonna molest you. You're goin roun callen me a faggot, ya TURDBURGLAR."

Now the psycho kicked the wall, hard. A bracket rattled loose in the concrete wall. Robbie pulled a bunch of keys from his pocket and arranged them between his fingers like a gladiator's spiked glove. His heart was flapping madly as a bird in a banged cage. His arteries felt too small to accommodate this massive flow of blood. He could feel his teeth pulsing, his temples come alive. This animal was clearly wild with crank and killerweed, and didn't care if he woke up in the morning with a broken nose, but Robbie did, man, he really did.

In his panic, he hadn't heard the concert thump to an end upstairs, but now the can door was thrown open and a clot of people burst in. Bill's boots stepped back, mingled with others. Robbie yanked wildly at the door of his cubicle, but it wouldn't open. Then he unlocked it, shouting, "Chrissake!" and plunged into the crowd.

When he returned to the table, Brat and Louie Louie had taken off somewhere, but Rosie was still there, in a sulk. He wiped his forehead, miming relief, zooming with adrenaline, and jerked his thumb in the direction of the can. He laid a hand on her thigh and let it linger for an ingratiating moment, but Rosie stopped him with a face that could kill cockroaches. She chewed her gum at him, and then she said, "A party for all the girls you've slept with."

"What what what?" Robbie said. He knew exactly what. He looked her right in the eyes, real earnest.

But Rosie spat, "Once there was this sensitive guy I thought I knew, but now all I see is a juvenile jerk-off."

Then she and Dolores stood up and stormed out, leaving him with a skull like a bowlful of seething brothy guilt. And now, as he looked around, he saw there were maybe half a dozen Dead Man's Hands lurking in the crowd. What, is there a *convention*? Robbie thought that under normal circumstances he might have asked them about Olly, and maybe found something out about Ivy, but now he didn't dare. In the meantime if he could just connect with his man, get a deal done, any deal at all, and go home.

Now look. Pigs. Great. He froze. What is going *on* tonight, may he ask. He was a sitting duck, all alone at this table. He got up to mingle. The headlining band walked on stage, a hail of spittle went up, a shriek of feedback, the biker mamas flashed their tits at the band, and the front row pogoed away like the springs in a motel mattress. He leaned behind a pillar, sucking on the dregs of Rosie's beer. There was Brat, putting the make on some doe-eyed vealcake in a freshly laundered Sex Pistols T-shirt. Robbie dragged him out of the club by the fins and shoved him against the wall by the entrance.

"Hey, guy," Brat said. "Don't crease the suit."

"Whydjou say whatchou said to Rosie, fuckface?" Robbie said. "You've no business, man."

"It was a *joke*. Whadda you care what she thinks? I was teasing her, that's all."

Robbie had to think for a second. How much did he care? A lot. A whole lot. And he found himself taking pleasure in Brat's shit-eating grin; he had his hand on his chest, preparing to push.

"*There* you are, you FAGGOT."

A 427 Camaro drew up in the parking lot and three more Dead Man's Hands climbed out (it's degrading, but neither the Dead Man's Hands, nor the Popeyes, nor the Hell's Angels, nor the Outlaws drive hot steaming hogs in winter, in Quebec – the salt'll get to them long before the cops ever will). They strode over, exhaling in the lamplight, it looked to Robbie, with the quiet menace of the Nazgûl.

The crunch of gravel underfoot. Robbie panicking immediately. Not waiting for them to open their mouths, even. With his heart in his mouth, he just said, "I know what you're gonna say. Well, there's nothing I can do. It's like this – there was a fire. What a waste, eh. There wasn't much, anyhow. Small potatoes for guys in your league. K? Like, I been trying to get in touch with you for ages about this. How's Olly?"

The bikers looked at one another with smiles in their beards, and then Bill swung a leather fist at his ear. Robbie saw it coming this time. For some reason the guy had chosen to punch him in slow motion. But Robbie's metabolism turned out to be working even slower. Maybe that's an explanation for ghosts, he thought: maybe they've got an incredibly speedy metabolism and their molecules vibrate so quickly, they become invisible to us. Another clout, square on his nose. At first he felt nothing, then disgustingly queasy. His legs turned to rubber, standing was like trying to tread water. He grabbed for support.

301

There was Brat, watching with the rest of the crowd. Bill the Beast grabbed Robbie by the throat, and squeezed his Adam's apple. Robbie tried to swing back, but he was held at arm's length. He couldn't draw a breath through his windpipe. The world was dancing like it does when the camera jiggles in a warzone newscast. The lurching ground. The trails and pops of light. Thinking, This is no fun, and sort of giving up. Now he's being dragged into the car. Three guys in the front, two with identical jean and leather uniforms, aces and eights on the back. Hey, here's a familiar face: John Mills, Ivy's mad-scientist brother. He's smiling, but he's not being friendly; his face is covered in burn scar tissue, he's holding up a syringe filled with clear liquid, and he's not troubling to tap it clear of air bubbles, neither. A head turns, and it's Olly, Ivy's batik scarf around his neck. At last! Now Robbie can say hi, he can explain. But he gurgles up blood instead. He hears the crunch of leather and vinyl inside the car. John squirts some juice into the air. It lands on Robbie's leg, eats right through the denim and ouch, Chrissake what *is* that, *battery* acid? Olly speaks.

"Touch Dolores again and you're history. Get it?"

Robbie nodded, swallowed blood. Sweet, metallic. Got it.

"Good. Shake hands with Bill, now." Through the open window, Bill the Beast thrusts a spiked leather fist. Robbie extends his hand feebly. Should he shake Bill's in the conventional fashion? Or the cool way, hooking thumbs? Bill squeezes his hard, harder, harder, *Chrissake*, his hand is numb, but he hears a snap. Like a splintering baseball bat like a polystyrene egg carton like a dropped egg. Here's what else he hears: *Ivy sez hi.* Now he hurts all right, like barbed wire's being dragged through his veins, up to his elbow, and out through the not-so-funny bone. His nerves rise raw to the surface of his flesh. He whimpers, rolls his eyes up, blacks out.

There were voices. He was sobbing. He covered his face from shame, and dunked his head between his knees. He was a nerd, he couldn't fight. This was what the end of the world was like. Robbie became aware of sitting on steps, watching his blood blot the snow. A throng of punks stood around his head, all tattered knees and dangling buckles. There were pigs, and a cruiser flashing crisp blue light. Brat was saying to Louie Louie, "I tried to help, eh, but it all went by so *fast*."

Robbie raised his head.

"Hey," Brat said, doing a wobbly boxer's dance. "Don't look at me. I could of taken him out with a headbut, but I figured, why have two of us get slaughtered instead of only one. And what about my suit, no just joshing, fuck. Hey, don't look at me like that. I didn't do nothen."

Officer Gaunt crouched down beside Robbie, rubbing his hands together. Robbie opened his mouth to speak, but the cold air sent a stab of pain up the exposed nerve of his front tooth, an icy skewer jabbed right into his nose. He couldn't feel his hand at all.

Gaunt winced and said, "Don't you know those biker boys are out of their skulls. I'm amazed they behaved with such restraint. Often as not, they'd kill you for sneezing in their oxygen."

"Bikers' motto," Robbie replied. "One for all and all on one. Ouch, fuck."

Gaunt helped Robbie to the cruiser. Louie Louie got in, too. Husker was at the wheel. They headed for the Montreal General, speeding along De Maisonneuve. Robbie's head lolled on the back seat. High above, the searchlight atop Place Ville-Marie stirred the clouds, just like in the opening skyline sequence on the hockey game. His head spun following it. "Guess what," Gaunt said. "We know who that kid was, eh – the one who perished."

"Aw, for Chrissake," Robbie moaned.

"No, listen. Did you know a tattoo survives a fire? It's not

303

as colourful as before the body turns to toast, but you can still make it out. Gaston Goupil wore biker colours, so we just checked him against a list of missing members."

"You're just trying to snow me. When did you find out?"

"Ohh, close to a year ago, I'd say."

"Yeah? Well, I happen to know he got his colours skinned."

"Did he indeed?" Husker called out. "Dead Man's Hands colours maybe, but when he died he was with the Disciples. We'd been watching him as a matter of fact, and the others – Ivy's big brother included – for quite some time. We figured you're such a stupid little dickhead we were bound to stumble onto something with your help. What does it take? Do you know now to keep your fucking nose clean?"

"It's drug wars these boys are fighting," Gaunt said. "Or have you already heard? We jumped the gun this summer with Olly, so to speak – we got cocky, too much publicity in advance of the case – and they caught us on a technicality. But, in the long run, all these psychos are on self-destruct. We're going to just stand by and watch from the sidelines from here on in."

"Me, all *I* was trying to do was take a whizz," Robbie said.

From the hospital, Louie Louie and Robbie stopped for one more beer at the Toe Blake. It was the last thing Robbie wanted – his nose was a bloody, tender fruit whose pulsing roots probed painfully about in his head, and his hand throbbed maddeningly inside the fresh cast – but Louie Louie insisted.

"To tell you de truth, it's for mon vieux père. I'm quit de chickens, too. I ave save lots of cash. In de New Year, I start a store in Chicoutimi."

There were sixteen glasses of draught on the little round table between them. Robbie had asked for a straw.

"Great," he said. "Kick a dog when it's down."

"Ayy," Louie Louie said, slapping his arm. "Ça serait beau, peux-tu l'imaginer? A record store. I could give you great discount."

"Louie, you gotta shoot higher than that, man. Hell's Yells are gonna get more than a fucken discount."

"Non non, ç'a pas d'sense. I'm so ugly I coulden get lay in a women's prison wit a andful of pardon. I'm tirty, right. I fart aroun for ten year wit my 'arley, living off Suzette, you know – "

"Yeah yeah," Robbie said. "Giving her great doggies."

"C'est ça. An now I gotta get serious. In is honour I call de store, Les Disques Beaulieu. E gonna be proud, mon hosti. Hanyow, check dis." Louie Louie handed him a piece of important-looking stationery. In French it read, '*According to Article 58 of Bill 101, regarding the language of commerce and business: all signs, posters, and commercial advertising on the premises shall be solely in the official language.*'

"So?" Robbie said.

"So dey took my *Bosom Buddies* calendar down from my hoffice. Some broad squeal on me cause it's Hinglish an bring in de Commission de Surveillance. Shit la marde, Robbie, when hi tink of de Québéçois fight for hindependence, quand *Je Me Souviens*, t'sais, dis is not for what hi do it. So now, hi do for me. You wan four more beer?"

The next morning, it sure felt weird waking up in Queenie's bed. For one thing, it was a lot softer than Robbie was accustomed to – his back and bum were sunk into a hollow that had been made by big Mr. Graves, and for another, there was a little girl at the foot of it wanting her daddy. And Chrissake! Wasn't he due back today? Robbie's arm was trapped under Queenie's head, and he thought of that sick joke guys make, about being with a broad so ugly that chewing your arm off is preferable to waking her. The little girl was rocking the bed by Queenie's ankle and making the most outraged face at him, and Queenie was roused. She only glanced at him. Her eyes were bloodshot, stained overnight by the red wine they had shared. She pulled on her dressing-gown and hustled the kid out of the room.

Robbie's nose was so plugged with crusty blood he felt he could snap the whole thing off his face, like plaster. He stood up, saw the room black out in a checkerboard pattern, lost his balance, sat down again on the bed. When his vision cleared, he crouched over, gingerly, to the vestibule mirror and took a look. Two glorious shiners stared back, dirty yellow, divided by a blackened bridge. The swelling was massive, in spite of the ice compress that now lay in a bowl of water by his pillow. He pulled on his clothes with his left hand, snuck a $20 bill from the night table, tiptoed down the cabbagey corridor, and slipped out as quietly as he could.

By the time he reached the Voyageur station, he had missed the first bus of the day; he went to look for a dépanneur, but when he returned the driver wouldn't let him on with his beers. He sat in the grimy terminal and drank five in the space of an hour; by the time the third bus arrived, he was stupid and drooling. He staggered to the back, sat next to the latrine. The other passengers, their laps loaded with gifts in jolly wrapping, twisted in their seats to stare at him.

Speeding down the Eastern Townships autoroute now. The snow by the highway fluffed up with earth. The fields lying fallow, and the frost in the furrows. The china-blue dish of sky above. Robbie with the last of the beers between his knees, blasted with all the thoughts of Xmas in Kilborn Bay. How the family will find him changed; how

306

mature, how well balanced, how sharp with knowledge of the real world. Yes, he's looking forward to home.

Well. How could it be worse than what he's leaving behind? It's as if Montreal had been sprung overnight like some intricate booby-trap. He was stunned by how quickly life could seize up on a person. He saw that Ivy was right when she said people are fools to set themselves at the centre of their own life story; stories have a hero and a purpose and a moral, but in reality, life is a series of ever-worsening enstranglements.

Scenes from last night, flipping by: weirdly enough, none of the bikers had even mentioned the subject of dope, or told him to empty his pockets. *Ivy sez hi*, that's all. Returning home, he had found Dolores and Rosie gone, and his place trashed to pieces; five cards, aces and eights, had been left on the hallway carpet. His couch was slashed, the contents of the beanbags were scattered like a polystyrene snowstorm. The Dead Man's Hands had ripped open his books, spilled his records from their sleeves, and torn the guts from his stereo speakers. They had pulled the carpet up and left it in waves. The question Robbie asked himself was, had they trashed the place just to drive home their point about Dolores? Or, if they were looking for drugs, had the dummies not thought to look for drugs in a place as obvious as a *Cocaine* machine? Maybe they weren't looking. Maybe they didn't know he had the stuff at all. After what happened in the school fire, only Ivy could have told them – told Olly – how it had come into his possession in the first place. Maybe for once in her life she had kept a secret *for* him, not *from* him.

Anyway, Queenie had waited up. He thought she was holding a present for him, but it was only another care package from Mom, this one marked URGENT. He had rolled his eyes, kicked it in a corner.

Queenie was quiet and shy. And had the softest body.

Well, she had had children, that's why. She was like tumbling in baby powder. And that morning, as they lay there, she had smelled to him of the heavy process of living; a sweet-and-sour, inside-out odour, laced with dead perfume. And her dog-tooth dentures in a glass by the bed.

Two old women across the aisle from him are dragging on cigarettes and gabbing. He gives them the Evil Eye. They look so dessicated they can't just have aged in the regular course of time; the cigarettes they're sucking on must have dried them out like strips of cod. Their grey hair seems singed to ash, lifting high above their foreheads like smoke on the wind. They're cooing over a *National Examiner*:

NEW EVIDENCE OF REINCARNATION
– BABY BORN WITH PEG LEG AND JOLLY ROGER TATTOO –

All the old, smoked women on this bus have short hair. As if, Robbie thinks, they've been shorn to announce the shame of growing old. Clothing stiffens around them like a petrified shell. He looks the other way, presses his boiling forehead to the cool glass, and passes out for the duration of the trip . . .

At Kilborn Centre, the driver had to carry him off, and dump him on the steps of the station. He had no luggage, just Mom's unopened package under one arm. Nobody was there to meet him. He hitched the twenty kilometres or so to Kilborn Bay in a farmer's pickup. The farmer was jovial, but spoke in joual so thick Robbie could barely communicate at all. The day was already falling dark. He looked across the purple snow to a column of silhouetted pines, the bristling guardians of the lake, massed in silence and waiting as he approached.

He decided he would help in the kitchen this year, if you can believe that. Yes, he could really get into preparing the turkey stuffing with Miriam and Barnabus. He liked the feel of the hot and slimy water full of chestnuts, each one's shell marked X with a knife, and the way your fingers wizen and unpeel too, wherever you've been gnawing at your cuticles. He could already smell the pine in the living room, the port and marbled Stilton, the aroma of the turkey with pepper and garlic and raisins, of glazed ham with burnt sugar and cloves and bourbon peaches, of roast duck with quince, hot stollen, panettone, and mincemeat tartlets with nutmeg, allspice, cinnamon, bourbon, and rum, crowned with sprigs of pine and holly. The farmer was talking, between swigs from a bottle of Molson he kept snug between his legs, but Robbie was in the ruby dining room that's upside-down in a glass of wine, the trembling liquid light in that truffle paté's aspic jelly, the featherlight texture of those gingersnaps, that dark fruitcake so thick with candied lemon and currants it looked like it'd been cut from an oil painting. And, Jesus Fuck his hand hurts. He remembered how Dad likes to stick bottles of champagne in the snow outside the living-room window and how, when he opened it, the sound of ragtime jazz danced out across the twilit lake, echoing to and fro across the bay, losing its way in the listening, glistening woods, and finally giving up the ghost in the navy blue snow. He thought of Mom, tucking him in tightly and kissing him on his eyelids, her dinner-party jewellery rattling reassuringly above his nose. And, thinking of it, as the moisture of her kiss evaporated in the dark, he felt the way he imagined his soul might feel, if he had one, ascending.

18

HE SLEPT LATE, IN THE BEDROOM OVERLOOKING THE BAY that once he shared with Barnabus. Lying in this tiny bed, snug as a sardine in its tin, his body was firmly packed in the blankets and sheets and his feet stuck out at the end. He felt too big for this room with the Snoopy poster and the model aircrafts and, by the bed, the patch of fresh wallpaper where once a hide of pick-a-nose had been; and the thought that this single bed was intended only for *sleeping*, and that his sleeping and waking had been so chaste, made the morning heat of his body seem rude.

From the window, he surveyed the glistening confection of pine trees and snow. Under a navy sky, Kilborn Bay cracked and groaned. Somewhere out there lay Mendoza's iced bones. Robbie thought of his empty grey apartment in town, that chilly hollow whose rent was still unpaid, smelling of gas, graffiti on its cold walls, and his throat felt soaked with sadness to be in the hug of home again. He wondered how Rosie was doing, down in the empty city core, gathering with the girls and the bouncers for some special matinée performances in that horrible club. And for their Xmas meal: a special Santa's Helper Take-out Chicken Sleigh. Louie Louie meanwhile in Ste. Agathe, snoring the morning away after midnight Mass with his vieux père. And Baimy, watching Yuletide TV with his feet up, indifferent to it all, scheming, pissed, caustic.

Robbie would be nineteen in two weeks, but he still got an Xmas stocking. He ransacked it greedily with his good hand: a Lovely "punker" safety pin, with a notch permitting you to wear it without piercing your cheek, shoe fresheners, *Saturday Night Fever* gum, Walter T. Foster's *How To Draw The Nude*, gourmet turtle soup.

He also opened that care package he'd carried all the way from Montreal: food, mostly rich stuff, like sweatmeats and shortbread, and a note:

> Dearest Robbie darling,
> tried to reach you, but phone o-o-o. Sent 3 pkgs begging quick response already. Did U not receive? Time running short. Coming to Bermuda Xmas or not?
> Worried sick,
> M.

Major bummer. Arriving last night, the house on the hill had been dark. He'd been forced to tear through the mosquito screen – Mendoza's emergency entrance during lightning storms – dragging snow and mud over the carpet. "Hello-o," he had called out, "is anybody ho-ome?" There was an artificial Xmas tree, beside it a menorah with all nine lamps burning, and a heap of gifts, all marked with his name.

In the living room now, with a stomach full of champagne and chocolate, wild with avarice, still hot with fever. He opened his gifts: sweaters, socks, a bottle-cutter kit, a *Stars on '45* extended mix, a poster-sized all-dressed cheeseburger blueprint, and a book of David Hamilton photographs, which he immediately took upstairs.

Whoopee. Five minutes later he was down again, feeling

pretty sore that no one had given him any *money*. He roamed the room for anything else that might have been left, then raided the kitchen to make eggnog, grating orange rind and nutmeg into a jug, bitterly disappointed that Xmas was already over, with a full fallow year to wait before he'd be reaping again. The phone rang. It was Miriam on the line.

"Guess where *we* are, you big tool!"

"Arf arf. No need to rub it in."

"We're in a land where Dad says at least you can speak the language of your choice. Here, I'll give him over."

"*Hi!*" Dad shouted down the line. "Robbie! How've you been? We missed you. We thought perhaps you'd been arrested for speaking English in the street."

"No . . . ? I mean, not yet, I've escaped – "

"Just *joking*, son."

A silence followed, and now Mom's voice. "We were so worried about you, darling! How *are* you? Actually, we were very worried. We never heard from you, and things have been so unpleasant. Did you read about that barber?"

"No . . . "

"In St. Henri. The one who's calling the language laws *Nazi* laws. The thing's got out of all proportion, don't you think? Over a little sign."

"Oh, *yeah*," Robbie said. "I bet I know the one. Says, PLAIN HAIRCUTS – NO NONSENSE, right?"

"Oh, I'm so glad you're keeping up with the news. Did you see it in the *Gazette*? What's the latest?"

"See – what?"

"Well, his window was smashed when he wouldn't take the sign down! And then somebody painted a swastika on his door . . . "

"That'd serve him right," Robbie said, his bandaged fist stabbing his cinnamon stick in the air. "I mean, that would've been Ivy's dad. The anti-Semite hypocrite."

315

"*Ivy's* father? Darling! How *is* Ivy?"

"How would I know? I'm *sick* of her," Robbie snapped. "Uh, we decided to take a rest from each other."

"Poor darling, she really broke your heart. I can hear it."

"Well, I've been handling it pretty well, I think. Both her parents are such straight arrows, y'know, so marriage with me was out of the question. And it was such a long time ago, fuck."

"I'm so sorry. Anyway, have a merry Christmas, darling. We do miss you so very much. Will we see you when we get back?"

"If I see you," Robbie replied, vacantly. The fumes of whisky and rum were overpowering. Chewing on some grains of nutmeg now, he remembers how he tried snorting some of this one sneaky afternoon last summer, but all he got was a sneezing fit, and a wicked headache.

He went to bed early, watching the moon over the trees. He made a high-pitched sound as he wept, similar to Mendoza when he used to need to go out. He asked himself how he could possibly have taken Dad's joke seriously. And not known about Mr. Mills. How could he be so out of touch? First he had missed the election, the biggest thing to happen to the province in over a hundred years, and now this. He was seized with self-loathing. Was he *so* stupid? Was his life so completely unconnected with any teensy-weensy part of the real world? Was he even alive? Sure, he had been working hard on Hell's Yells, but that seemed like a pathetically puny and irrelevant concept now. The rest of the time he had just jerked off. When he could have been part of something. It was all Rosie's fault. Her understanding of politics was even vaguer than his. He heard in his hot head the closest they'd ever had to a discussion about current affairs: "I hate my thighs more than nuclear war," she'd announced, standing nude in front of her dressing-room mirror.

"It's weird," he'd said, trying to steer the conversation in a meaningful direction, "the way the word *regime* is used for military governments and also for diets."

"Makes perfect sense to me," she'd said. See. She was dumb. He needed to spend time with people who were better informed. It was time for a serious change.

When he returned to town a few nights later, Rosie had not only forgiven him for what she called their little tiff, but she'd moved all her belongings in, as well. She gave him little choice in the matter, as she'd already paid up his rent. Plus she'd cleaned up the entire apartment, filled the fridge with fresh vegetables, and done the laundry, so that was that. She had done a fair job, pinned all his sketches and paintings to the walls, turned his slashed mattress over, drawn the curtains, lit a dozen candles, thickened the air with frankincense, propped his disembowelled stereo on the chest of drawers, and put an Environments record of the Pacific ocean on endless repeat.

"I've been looking into *books* while you were gone," she announced. "Since you won't trust in the STARS, what about the *sympto-thermic* method? It's more work than the ovulation method, and there's more responsibility on the man, but it's *mathematical*. First you take my vagina's temperature . . . "

He gratefully crashed. He'd been wrong about her, maybe. He'd try harder with her after all. In stages, just holding hands at first, which is the way it should have been from the start. Plus, it occurred to him that having her here would also put off Queenie Graves; it was awkward that they had slept together, he thought, as the surf rolled up onto the sand; she didn't seem at all desirable now, just dowdy and fat. Now the rhythm of the waves, chewing on a distant shore, lulled and disoriented him; he awoke believing there was a magnificent storm outside. He pulled the blanket over his head and tried to wriggle back into the warm womb of sleep, only slowly realizing the rumble was made by infinite waves doing bellyflops on some inaccessible stretch of sun-bleached vinyl sand.

"Drop kick me, Jesus, through the goalposts of life!"

A Tuesday afternoon in January, and he was watching television from his bed. Rosie had bought him a second-hand TV from the Sally Ann for his nineteenth birthday. They were in the Information Age now, blasting from channel to channel, getting the global picture. Weird thing was, even with eight amazing channels of shit to choose from, Mom's show wasn't on in its regular time slot, or any time slot, it seemed. He couldn't find her at all.

"That's right, sinners! Put your hands on the screen, go on. You, yes you! Place your palm against mine and pray hard with me. Out, devils, OUT!"

Rosie huffed indignantly at that, but Robbie obeyed with his good hand.

"If the faithful out in *Stupid*-land think the *static* on the screen is divine interference," she said, "then the world is in even worse shape than I *imagined*."

"One day, Hell's Yells are gonna be the house band on their own twenty-four-hour talk show," Robbie said.

"Yeah!" Rosie said. "*The Atheist All-Star Revue*! With celebrities and comics and just plain ornery people – and hopefully even my favorite *weirdo* – coming on to testify about how GREAT their life has been since they shrugged *off* religion!"

"*Hyulk hyulk*. And instead of this K-Mart Garden of Eden, with plastic shrubbery, it'll be a realistic street scene.

There'll be a toll-free number you can call for advice on how to live life in the Here and Now, how to channel your time and energy into Reality."

"YES! And instead of blackmailing old ladies with fear of HELLFIRE, anyone who mails in their devotional paraphernalia for the on-air BONFIRE, will actually be sent money in *return!*"

The two of them were getting along like houses on fire, suddenly, and it felt queer. Life was short – he asked himself, was he investing precious time in the right relationship? On the one hand, how could he have been so stupid not to appreciate her charms and her smarts; on the other, was he being stupider now to think she was charming or smart at all. He really couldn't tell. He didn't know. He no longer knew himself – who was he to judge?

Two Tuesdays after that, or maybe three, a snowstorm was whipping up outside, fringing Eccelucci's sumptuous lingerie with a lace of frost. Robbie sat up in bed and set his jaw, asking himself what Hell's Yells could ever realistically accomplish. The rent on the equipment was up in a month. He drew the blanket up to his chin; now Rosie's hip was bared and she moaned in her sleep. He had to force himself to care, to gently tuck her in; he was disgusted with her now, for one very good reason: without even knowing it, she had left a square of bum-wad in her asshole the night before; this morning her bottom barked, and he saw that it had fallen out amongst the sheets, shaped like a shitty shuttlecock, while she was still sleeping. He drank half a warm beer, felt his eyelids thicken, as the alcohol seeped in and the throbbing in his hand receded. He stared out the window to watch the snow fill the sky. A shred of laundry blew off the clothesline over the back alley like a frostbitten gull, and the window threatened to pop inwards. He watched the chill grey

319

flurries in the alley and thought of Kilborn Bay and how the mist there used to sit like a sweet pillow on the water and linger on the cool sand until as late as breakfast. And, as he heard the first stomps upstairs of children preparing to go to school, it occurred to him that memories like these were a privilege; most of the kids on this street had probably never been out of town, even for a weekend, to see such a thing as a shore with the mist evaporating off it . . .

He got up and went to the living room. Idly, he opened the *Cocaine* machine and stared at the dull red boxes with the dragons biting their tails. Still there, still tempting. He thought of something the Dead Man's Hands had done to someone who tried to cut in on their drug monopoly (Rosie had told him this for a fact): fed his balls to Bill the Beast's doberman pinscher. But was that really true? How do these stories get started? He just stood there and stared. Maybe it was better to flush it all down the toilet. *What*, twenty thousand bones worth? Was he crazy? But what else could he do? He could give it back, he supposed, but after the incident at Arthur's Hideaway, those animals would slaughter him for having deceived them so long. He was paralyzed, flushed through with anxiety. The boxes sat there; evil things, hibernating.

"Where are you, Bob?" Rosie called out from the bedroom. She did that, all the time. If he so much as went to pee. He flinched with irritation. Though he also had to admit to a secret twinge of pleasure – of knowing he was wanted so. But that secret twinge irritated him, too – it might oblige him to love her back. And he didn't like anyone telling him how to feel. He locked the door of the *Cocaine* machine and slumped back to bed.

Rosie worked mostly nights, and spent the days in bed beside him sleeping, waking, demanding neck rubs back rubs foot rubs calf rubs scalp rubs, and reading. She read just about anything; in his view, she had a myopic imagination; not discerning but stumbling over whatever random interests lay in her path – Aspasia of Miletus, Colette, *The Female Eunuch*, poetry of Sappho, Madame Blavatsky, *Our Bodies Our Selves*. The books piled up by the bed, and he resented her for being able to read so fast. Could she really be absorbing anything? It wouldn't have been so bad if she didn't insist on underlining as she read, but as he lay trying to watch The Price Is Right in peace, she sat there underlining with her pencil, underlining, underlining, underlining, underlining. And it wouldn't have been so bad if she were more selective, but she was maniacal. He seethed as he sat there, listening to the pencil stroke the pages.

"Rosie," he finally said. "Have you thought of only underlining the things that *don't* interest you? You'd save on pencils."

He hated himself for saying that. He had promised himself he'd make efforts to be nice, but it was tougher than he'd anticipated: *nice* felt unpleasantly supersensitive, like a layer of his skin had been peeled off, while *not nice* felt good and warm, heavy blood moving sluggish beneath his thickened hide. It occurred to him that he was *addicted* to being not nice, because it was true – he could actually feel his glands responding contentedly, relievedly, to his nastiness.

He awoke one night with stabbing cramps in his belly, got up for water. Rosie was at the kitchen table all alone, doing something industrious with dozens of little scraps of paper.

"Robbie!" she said, startled. "You SCARED me, creeping up like that." She was trying to gather up the scraps. She knocked her coffee cup over, and swamped a few.

"Careful," Robbie said. "What is all this?"

"Nothing of consequence to you, I wouldn't imagine. I

mean, before there was a person in this house who was interested in me truly, but I don't see him around too much these days."

"C'mon, Rosie, lemme look. Watercolours, oh," he said, suppressing his bemusement. "I didn't know you could draw."

"I can't," Rosie said defiantly. Though she was blushing, chewing her gum furiously. "That's not the point."

He inspected them more closely. They were tiny, but numerous – more work than he'd done in years – amulet-sized, filled with delicate, feather-brushed, kaleidoscopic designs. You had to hold them to your nose to make them out. There were dripping Gardens of Eden, it looked like, with alizarin skies and blue weeping willows and wispy white sprites frolicking on the duck-egg blue grass. There were green streams with lilac trees, in one a pink canoe, in another two minuscule nymphs fluttering on lemon wings.

"You *can*, you know," he said, impressed. He looked some more. What's this. Heart-shaped butterflies, and childish handwriting: *with love from Rose to Bob*. Chrissake, a Valentine. Is it already February? He set it down quickly. He remembered the way Ivy had proven the uselessness of giving gifts. Well, that's why he hadn't thought of making anything for Rosie.

"Wow," he said, guiltily. "This is like Matisse. You should have an exhibition. And they're so tiny you could show in a bus shelter. Serve Aqua Velva to the rummies."

"I don't *want* an exhibition," Rosie retorted. "They're not for anyone but ME. I don't *want* people's judgements. I don't *care* if they're like Mateus, or anything else for that matter. As far as I can see, they're like *me*. Which is all I'm looking for."

She was becoming quite difficult to get along with. Robbie shrugged. He'd been working on some secret art of his own, as a matter of fact, a complicated idea for some erotic art, which he hadn't quite finished. It was secret because if Rosie found it she'd be sure to misunderstand: a Barbie doll, bound and gagged, the legs twisted about like that pornographic doll of Hans Bellmer's, an image of all women everywhere who've been submitted to the abuses of men, exactly like Rosie raved about; he had put a match to her, cut her breasts off with an Exacto knife, glued on fresh body parts snipped from the pages of *Bosom Buddies*, and painted a mad airline stewardess' face on it with acrylics. It was a fine piece of work, but in the process he had become a little too feverish, and ended up masturbating on it. For one brief, hopeful moment, he'd imagined this would add to the integrity and horror of the art object, but it wasn't long before he changed his mind, and dumped the sticky obscenity in a cupboard.

What day was it? What night? He felt he hadn't slept at all; he had twisted and rolled, and his dreams were shallow, like blisters on his conscience. Rosie was underlining, underlining, and the dreams had come in aggravating, repetitive episodes, stamped again and again, as if on some brutal assembly line: "Bob," Rosie says, over and over. "Bob. How many times have I told you to be considerate of others and scrub the bathtub when you're done?" She beckons him into the bathroom and demonstrates with an outstretched palm. There, clinging to the inside wall of the tub, is an embryo the colour of fish guts. Backstage, Dolores had talked to him filthily, and he'd ejaculated a thick fountain. The semen coagulated like eggwhite in boiling water, globbing and searching for a surface to cleave to . . .

He felt like the Swamp Thing, reaching out from his marsh of sleepy molasses to drag the phone off its cradle. But it was the doorbell. And now knocks, on the front door. He got out of bed, tiptoed down the hall. It was pigs. He tried to sneak back into his bedroom, but one of them saw him through the window and rapped on the glass.

As it turned out, they had no connection with Husker or Gaunt; they said they'd been asked by the Montreal Central Hospital to look him up – his phone was out of order, they said. One asked him, reading from a slip of paper,

"Are you acquainted with a Mizz, er, Church? Chastity Church?"

The smell of antiseptic, and the waiting room was filled with murmuring, moaning people. At least two of them were nursing sore or splintered bones from slipping on the ice outside. Robbie paced. He knew about this place.

Time went by. No one fetched him. He was still in the dark. What had she done, killed herself because of him? No, that was a selfish thing to think. But maybe she had. It flattered him to think it. Finally, a nurse opened a double door and beckoned. She led him down a corridor, and then another. Nothing was said. He was told to wait some more. In time, two nurses wheeled an aluminum crib down the hall. He stood up. There was Rosie, with a tube up her nose. Her cheeks and forehead were a blotched yellow, her eyes swollen and black, her neck bandaged up.

"What'd you do, Rosie?" Robbie said. "What a dumb thing, when you know you got friends. You look like you put too much makeup on. Arf arf."

They held hands, and Rosie smiled a little smile.

"No, you stupid boy, I was raped, I think. Look at us war vets now."

"You *think* you were raped?"

"I don't remember it all. Oh, Bob, it hurts so *much*, if only you knew."

Robbie looked around him self-consciously, though no one was paying any attention to him at all: the busy corridor, patients in wheelchairs, doctors with a purpose, chattering nurses. He thought he saw one of the nurses who'd filled him up a year earlier. He resented them, hated the insouciant atmosphere that cheapened his personal drama.

"They said I can be out this aft, if I want," Rosie said, tugging at his arm. "If I have a place to go. Take me home, won't you Bob?"

Having Rosie convalesce in bed with you was like being stuck with the sequel to *The Exorcist* in your very own home. For two days and a night, wearing one of Robbie's T-shirts, she hugged a pillow to her stomach and slept fitfully, rising up to suck liquids past her split lips, and allowing Robbie to mop her forehead with a cool face-cloth. He fixed her boysenberry tea and sandwiches too, that were easy to swallow, like tomato with cream cheese and fresh cucumber. She looked especially horrible at night in the light of the candle. Her eyes were reddish-brown and swollen and stared with a zombie's stare, as if the real Rosie was locked up inside this body, crying to get out. Robbie had to look away. He sat beside her on the bed and watched a lot of TV.

At last, several days later, she sat up and unravelled the bandages from her neck to reveal a necklace of bloody stripes. Some were cuts through the skin, where her larynx had provided a hard base, and all of them had stained her flesh with lateral bruises. Gingerly she felt under her neck, and then closed her eyes and swallowed painfully, as if a thought as threatening as a wave of nausea were coming up.

"I was walking home, eh, so it must have been three or three-thirty, 'n I had to catch the last bus which leaves you by the overpass not far from Rockhead's, right. At the best of times it's gloomy, but last night or when was it, three nights ago, it was windy and made you skip along the sidewalk. I thought I sensed somebody move behind me, although when I looked of course it was all blurry shadows. Most of the time I'm used to that, but I couldn't hear anything, it was so windy. Then a cop car comes cruising along real slow 'n I ran up 'n said something nice like, Hi, I think I'm being followed, but the cops just looked at me and didn't stop, so I kept up with them, which was like hard on high heels eh, and I'm thinking Oh they think I'm a *hooker*, which makes me real mad because why should a hooker not get protection from the law if she needs it. I'm banging on the roof and saying, well begging, really, *Please I'm scared couldn't I catch a ride?* and I was crying, too, and getting even madder just on *principle*, but you know what they did, Bob, I swear on my mother's grave, you know what, they smiled, they *smiled* at me and took off and left me . . . " Rosie sucking in a sudden breath now, holding back a sob. " . . . all . . . on . . . " and making an *ugly* wiggly mouth as Robbie watches, all filled up with his own discomfort ". . . my, my owwwn."

Crying now in her lap with heaving shoulders, and Robbie's mighty uncomfortable, clasping his hands and pressing his teeth together. Crying is a drag. Ivy never cried. Rosie looks too foolish in his KEEF SUCKS T-shirt and nothing else, the flushed flesh of her bottom and thighs creasing his sheets like a brass bedwarmer.

"Go on," he said.

"Thank you, Bob, it's good to see someone who understands, which is not what I found with the doctors or the cops after – you know, asking suspicious questions like What were you doing out so late 'n Why are you dressed like that 'n Where do you work 'n Why were you in that part of town 'n Did you know this man 'n Have you ever been in a situation like this before, can you believe it, as if it were my fault what happened. It's *sickening*."

"Well, uh, did you know the guy? I mean, hopefully you'll describe him when you're feeling calm and rational."

"I *am* being rational, for Jesus' sake," Rosie wailed. "I *am*. I am telling you exactly what happened, except that I couldn't see *at the time*. All I knew was he was mauling me and I was crying and trying to pull a nail file from my purse to gouge his eyes out, but he grabbed the purse and was strangling me with the strap. It was so *dark*, and I choked on my gum, and my legs were so *cold* on the sidewalk . . . " She paused to mop her eyes. "But, Bob, I know exactly who it was – that creepy weirdo. The regular, you know. The pud-puller, the captain of the raincoat brigade, remember? He was whispering, hot, wet disgusting words in my ear all while he was pulling on his thing, like *blasphemer, harlot, mistress of Satan*, stuff like that. Gross me out. He said, like, *vile abjurer of Faith*. Then he goes how he shudders at the sight of me, and rips my panties aside. Oh God, oh God, I can hear him in my ears, *eeulch*, he goes like, *fornicator. Meat, mucus, and blood*. Then he stuck his fingers up my nose and said *what's here what's here, filth* and then in my mouth and said *what's here, filth. And inside your belly. Filth. Beauty beauty. Skin deep*. He kept repeating that, and said my skin is a sack of mucus. Oh, *Jesus* how disgusting. He said I'll hatch evil things, *me* of all people. . . . And I think I've just decided. . . . " She straightened her shoulders, looked at the ceiling and snorted. "I don't want to think about any of this again. It never happened that's all. S'OK. I'm fine now. . . . Except, Bob, what if, what if his ugly semen has made me . . . *pregnannnt*."

She abandoned herself to sobbing again, and although it obviously hurt her throat to sob she did it anyway, drawing back abrupt and ragged breaths, sucking anguish up from the depths of her being, without any regard for what a mess she looked. Robbie watched her. He was sitting precisely three feet from her, but he didn't move a muscle. He had caught himself thinking, *She's laying it on a little thick*, and slapped himself mentally, with an imaginary hand. Then thought, The kindest thing I can do for her is be honest. He'd already decided he didn't want to lead her on, as far as going out together was concerned, so he didn't touch her. Sounds heartless, but it was honest. Well, listen to the way she talked, like someone running down a hill, unable to stop. She didn't really merit his compassion, because she was dumb. He hung his bandaged hand limply on her shoulder. She didn't really feel things as deeply as he did. She doesn't keep a diary, he was thinking, like Ivy does, and she never talks about her dreams, just moans in her sleep; she doesn't mark time. She'll die one day and leave no record of herself. Returning as a ghost, she'll find no traces. Ivy would say that even the most self-conscious among us, the most intelligent, do little more than scrawl graffiti under the overpasses of life's highways, but that that is better than nothing. Most people just eat and shit and feel, and all their lives' works are washed away in time. Even being nice to a person is only an act that washes away. But the achievements of the intellect endure for the betterment of the world. Like Hell's Yells!

He knows he always hated it when Ivy went silent on him, so why would he want to inflict the same treatment on Rosie, now? He doesn't know. It's partly because he doesn't like thinking about the vulnerability of Rosie's honeypot, or the damage to it – that soft pink flower, its petals just about torn off. It's too disgusting to think about. Also, he's thinking, Rosie asked for it. In a way. Maybe. . . . Doing that act. . . . And since she likes to make love so roughly in the first place, biting and all, is being raped *such* a big deal? So he just sits there instead, exalting in the power of this silence of his, while she cries. He resisted at first, it didn't seem decent, but then he embraced it. And he senses he's fucked for life, that of all the lessons he could have learned from Ivy, this is the poisoned one, the one that'll get under his skin. But it feels too good, this silence – it's narcotic. He's addicted to not being nice. He should know better, but he doesn't. Because he doesn't know himself at all.

19

THE APARTMENT SMELLED OF CINNAMON, SWEAT, AND overripe fruit. A week later, Rosie was still afraid to go outside, and wouldn't go to work. She asked Robbie to go to the club, and explain on her behalf. He was glad to do that, if only to get outdoors. Once he was out, though, he got to worrying. There were secrets in his apartment. He had become a keeper of secrets like bees in a hive. There was that heap of magazines right under the bed, in which Rosie lay like a kicked cat. And in the hallway cupboard the dreadfully abused Barbie doll. What if Rosie found those things?

Pornography, he'd discovered, was like a bottle demon; it promised high times, but took a major toll on delivery. And putting it back in the bottle became harder as it grew bigger. This devil, Porn, cursed all he visited and spawned in them infectiously. And now Robbie was hungry in a new way: with this infected appetite, like Prometheus' liver, desire regenerated inside of him. He enjoyed those pictures, just as he knew they were bad for him. The gloss on the pages was a skin on his emotions. The more he enjoyed them, the less he liked the flesh and blood they professed to be about.

The game shows he watched from bed were a fantastic

circus of organized greed, but Robbie wasn't into the washing machines or fabulous kitchen accessories; instead, morning after morning, he lay with an ache of yearning for the hostesses with their impossible smiles and tempty hooters. He'd lie there and wait for them to bend over and open an oven door, or caress the fringe of a carpet, in the hope that he'd catch a flash of bosom or thigh. He wondered, did that make him a pervert-in-training? Surely he wasn't the only person in the world who did it? But one night, he and Rosie were watching *The Nutcracker Suite* (Rosie *listened* to it), and instead of appreciating the dancing, he found himself waiting only for glimpses of the ballerina's panties beneath her nightie. At times like those, he bitterly wished he could put the demon back in the bottle. But he didn't know how.

What he told Rosie was that he was going for some beers with Louie Louie, and did she mind if he spent a bit of the money she was saving for supplies. Rosie looked distressed.

"I don't care about the money," she said with a swollen mouth, "but I'm afraid to be alone in the house for too long. I see shadows. Please don't leave me in this place at night."

"Yeah, yeah, no problem."

What he really intended to do was a take a bus to the nearest border town in the United States and buy some porn in person. Coming back across the border, he'd hide the magazines in a suitcase stuffed with drawings and paintings, and record jackets into which he'd have slipped the magazines. Go ahead, try it sometime.

From all he had read about the rising tide of immoral magazines and movies in the States, he imagined the country as a pornographic playpark. You could get *anything* there. In a community newspaper from Vermont that he had found at the cottage on Xmas day, he saw a double bill playing till the end of February that looked promising: *She Stoops To Conquer*, and *School For Scandal*, starring some stud called Richard Brinsley Sheridan, if he remembered correctly. (It was amazing how Robbie could remember names and facts if he really put his mind to it.)

It was a four-hour bus ride from Montreal to Granby, Waterloo, Magog, Sherbrooke, on to North Troy, Newport, West Charleston, and then Derby Line, where the Constitution Playhouse had been since the turn of the century. As the bus pulled out of the terminal, Robbie couldn't believe what he was doing. Was it so important to go so far? He was jittery, his blood fizzing with tiny air bubbles that propelled him on this desperate journey. His head was filled with forbidden delights: honeypots and joysticks galore. He pictured the location of the Consitution Playhouse: a special street, lined with throbbing sex stores and massage parlours. Since Derby Line, Vermont, was only a little bigger than the community in Kilborn, he didn't imagine there would be a strip the size of a major fun fair, but he had his hopes up. All the American cities had them; wasn't every mayor embroiled these days in trying to shut them down? Boston's Combat Zone, New York's 42nd Street, L.A.'s Hollywood and Vine. And one of the reasons he was going now was he feared the mayors might succeed before he ever got there.

On his way home again to Rosie, it was dark inside the bus. In the headlights, a galaxy of snowy stars zoomed in and out of the infinite. What a total goof he felt. He put his nose to the glass and replayed his day while he watched the cat's-eyes light up and the highway's centre line peel up off the tarmac like a strip of luminous tape. . . .

He had stood nervously in line at U.S. Customs; all the passengers on the bus had been required to step off for inspection. When his turn came, he had been asked for his passport or a birth certificate. That was a shock – he had been across the border with his family so often just to eat at that little country restaurant in the mountains of Vermont, and the officer had never asked them for a passport. The customs officer was young, brush-cut, and wiry, and smacked of men's soap. He had only one arm. He looked Robbie up and down, and curled his lip in displeasure.

"What is the purpose of your trip, *sir*?"

"The purpose? The purpose is sightseeing and – uh – friends."

"And what do you have in that bag, please?"

"Oh, nothing much. Some art. If you can call it that, arf arf."

"Open it for me, *please*."

Robbie unzipped the suitcase. He wasn't worried. The inspection that would make him anxious was on his return, when the suitcase would be several magazines heavier. The one-armed officer had trouble flipping through the sketches and rolled-up canvases and album covers and scraps of paper, so Robbie helped him, doing a real eager salesman trip on the guy. "This was going to be my first professional gig, for a nightclub, eh, and these are my album cover designs, like them? And this one I don't dig so much, but these – "

"Is your trip for business, *sir*, or pleasure?"

"Why, for pleasure, like I said. Friends, like."

"Bull*shit*. Whut are the names of your friends?"

Robbie scrambling now. That swear word has had quite an unpleasant impact on him. "Uh, well, there's Rosie and Baim – *Abraham* – and Louie."

"Bull*shit*. Looey is a *French* name. Whut is your business, sir? Do you have a work permit? If not, I shall have to refuse you entry, *sir*."

It was pointless to insist. Robbie stuffed his artwork back, gnashing his teeth, and carried the heavy portfolio back out into the terminal area. He found a dépanneur on this, the Canadian side, bought a six pack of Molson, and sat in the foul-smelling, piss- and dust-filled waiting room till dusk.

After a while, he felt some relief that it was all over, that he hadn't gone to Pornville after all, and sated his repulsive seething desire. Mainly, he felt the old goatishness grow all over him. He slapped himself. *Stupid.* A traveller glanced at him from the bench by the door, quickly returned to studying the hem of her skirt.

On the bus back, he pees a torrent into the toilet. He's drunk again and full to bursting. *Drunk as a, as a . . . trout,* he thinks to himself, for his vision's a fuzzy fish-eye lens inside this tiny room. The bus is lurching wildly on the snow-covered country roads, and his pee is looping all over the place like a skipping rope that's been let go on one end. The window, frosted over like ground glass, lights up periodically as cars overtake the bus. He turns on the hot water, which comes out scalding, and mists up the chilled mirror above the sink. He rubs it and looks at himself. He's hard to see. He can barely recognize himself. The image looks like the ghost in him. Moisture collects and dribbles down. He feels sick. He has sunk to this.

He was thinking about Rosie, curled up in his apartment and licking her wounds as, three hours later, he rounded the corner by Wu's Grocery and the Parthenon Fil-U-Up. It was snowing heavily now, and bitterly cold. He stopped still.

A small crowd had gathered outside his apartment. The dim streetlamps and Eccelucci's billboard made the falling snow fizz with electric light. Robbie's stomach clenched, tight as a fist. He hesitated, considered ducking down the back alley, but there was Rosie at the top of his stairs, and she had spotted him. She waved him over frantically.

The crowd was made up of tenants and neighbours. Queenie Graves was there, and her husband. Mrs. Grissom was standing in her nightgown and overcoat, moaning. Big Mr. Graves and another man were laying a dark body on a blanket. Mr. Graves slipped on the ice as he bent down to lift the body up, and landed hard on his knee.

"Hi," Robbie said, stupidly. "What's up?"

Everyone turned to look at him. Their faces were shrouded and shrunk beneath their hoods and hats. They lifted old Mr. Grissom and carried him into his apartment, and Mrs. Grissom followed after him. She shot an evil face at Robbie. He shrugged. What did she want him to say? All right, it was his fault, maybe he hadn't done his shovelling job as well as all that – anyway, he'd thought he was off the hook after Rosie paid the rent. There was no use in getting on his back about it now. Sorry. K, satisfied?

He climbed his stairs. He was wondering how he was going to explain his suitcase to Rosie. In the end he didn't have to; she was so distressed that, when everyone had dispersed, he was able to distract her by cracking a feeble joke.

"By popular request," he said in a TV announcer's obituary voice, "Mr. Grissom, AKA Marcello 'Red' Manzoli, has flown through the air with the greatest of ease. For the very last time, it is feared."

When Mr. Graves told him he better clear out that very week, Robbie was not surprised, but he was aggrieved; when he asked Mr. Graves for a good reason, the guy just made a fist, and called that one.

His relationship with Rosie was strained to the limit of their endurance, as well. Robbie was sick of the way she analyzed his every move, his every word. He didn't have to be told he was afraid of confronting his own failure; he didn't need to hear he was building patterns of procrastination; it was none of her business that he rationalized his ignorance by hurling abuse at the status quo; he never asked anyone to tell him he pursued impossible dreams, or, that like most men with a problem, he put Ivy up in an ivory tower of unattainable desire.

"You didn't use to have any of these clever-dick ideas," Robbie said. "Don't get so high on your horse. You're just getting them now from books. You should stick to women's magazines. I can't get a handle on you any more. You're the one in need of shrink-rapping."

"Ha ha. You can't discredit my ideas 'cause I get them from books, you condescending male-chauvinist jerk," Rosie retorted, chewing her gum militantly, with marching jaws, chewing *at* him.

"Hey, I only say that 'cause I care for you."

"So care for me a little less."

"So I suppose you didn't like the Valentine I gave you yesterday."

"Oh *that*. A shoebox coffin with LOVE scrawled in blood on the inside? That's when I *first* saw the light of day."

"Hey, I did it my way, OK. Whaddo you want? Least I'm *here*, aren't I? Least I'm *around*. Isn't that a show of, um, of love?"

"Oh, Bob, why couldn't you just give me *chocolates*? I can't get a handle on you, either. Before, there was someone who was compassionate and brave. Now I see a person all wrapped up in himself and projecting his insecurities on others. On me."

"K, OK. Since you put it that way. *Here's* something funny," Robbie snapped, "You always talk about seeing 'this person who' and 'that person who', like I'm someone who's not standing right in front of you, which I am. Well, if you don't want to see stuff, s'OK with me, but don't deliberately put me out of focus, too. That's how you sound when you talk about me – like I'm out of focus."

He said that weakly, because he knew he was only resentful of being nailed down. He especially resented her when her analysis was dead on. He wouldn't permit her such conceit. He didn't like to seem so transparent. He fancied that he had a personality as bewildering as a house of mirrors. He flattered himself that he reserved judgement on other people until he had given them a fair chance.

"You're just jealous of everything I do," Rosie sniffed. "You're so jealous you even hate it when I'm involved with a book. Typical male – to you women are footstools or pedestals. You wish I'd pose for you all the time like, like . . . " She pointed out the window. "Like that horrible *billboard*. You liked me better when I was at the club because I was caged there. You're no better than the bikers who took over the place. Poor Dolores, she'll never get out, now. But I have. I'm different. I'm fed up with being forlorn. Oh, and by the way, I've got a brand-new method of contraception – staying away from men like you."

"I'm not jealous," Robbie said. "I just don't GIVE a fuck."

To add insult to injury, he learned that during his frequent absences, Mrs. Grissom had helped Rosie convalesce and they were now fast friends; the old lady had recommended that Rosie adopt Robbie's apartment, and Queenie said that was fine if it meant Robbie never showed his face again. "One good turn deserves another," Rosie told him. "That whole hospital experience was a trauma for Mr. and Mrs. Grissom. The nurses and staff are getting real uppity these days. Mrs. Grissom was given a form in French which she couldn't understand 'n she couldn't communicate Mr. Grissom's allergy to penicillin. It was a real bad scene – they almost finished the job you started. Anyhow, now that Mr. Grissom is pretty much incapacitated, I don't mind running errands for them. We're a mutual appreciation society. I'm the apple of their eye."

He goes walking on the mountain, to retrace the route he and Ivy took after blowing off class that magnificent first day of their so-called relationship. He climbs up to Lac Aux Castors, his belly bubbling with two pints of warm apple cider he lifted from Wu's grocery, and the snow fills his sneakers. The great iron cross on the Eastern bluffs looms dark against the whale-grey afternoon. At night, it must look comforting to some people, illuminated and seen for miles, but up close by day it's cold and utilitarian. From its base he can see the paint peeling off its steel stilts, and more than a quarter of the lightbulbs have been smashed. Arching his neck, he also sees something fluttering in the wind, hooked high up on one of the surviving bulbs; a bit of cloth perhaps, a weatherworn shopping bag. No, it's a pair of panties. Robbie looks around him, almost as if he were the guilty one. But there's no one around. A tidal wave of frost blows up over the crest.

He always liked to believe the legend that once upon a time Mount Royal was an active volcano. Now, skaters cut shining curves in the ice where the plateau stretches across the lake to the north. Southwards the slope jumps away steeply to where Montreal lies, belching up thick stacks of gas to scud and dissolve in the heaving air. The storm clouds suck up all the colours of the land and the sky, which become indistinguishable from one another; the glass of the skycrappers reflected grey, the snow loses its glint, the solid-state city rusts, fizzes, and crackles out. Lac Aux Castors is an abcess on the hip of this old man mountain, the chilly pollution rippling below the ice and accumulating on the shore in a pale scab of frozen sand.

He stands there and stands there. When the snow begins to fall, the skaters throw their gear in the trunks of their cars and drive away. Robbie just stands there, hearing the mountaintop bristle with speech; the naked trees seem to be mocking him, criticizing him, throwing their arms up in exasperation. The wind howls abuse, echoing all the voices of his experience and stirring them about in his ears. The wind pushes at his back with a huge, forceful hand, actually shoving him forward. It's as if Nature's fed up with him; she's been raped and beaten and ignored, and now she's had enough. For some reason, she's going to take it out on him first. The mountain seems to want to buck him off, for Robbie finds himself tripping and falling the way you do in a frustrating dream, and always landing on his bad hand. He's hot and flushed as he tries to make his way home. Home? He has no home. He's made a terrible mistake and he knows it. Can he ever make it up to Rosie now? He loses his bearings and finds himself overlooking the great Mount Royal graveyard. His teeth are clacking uncontrollably. He has a nasty tumble down the east slope, back towards Fletcher's Field, and bashes his head on a rock. He slinks downtown on weak legs and numb feet, bent over with a morose epiphany: life giving his arse a damn good kicking.

He wandered blankly for an hour, kicking trash cans across sidewalks, throwing gritballs through apartment windows and running off, stopping occasionally to take a whiff from a bottle of airplane glue, and found himself passing by the school on Côte-des-Neiges just as a flock of girls was being released. He walked briskly on this time, looking down at slush. He heard his name called. He looked up. It was Miriam, clutching her satchel to her chest as she galumphed towards him the way thirteen-year-old girls do: shoulders chugging, ankles flying up in opposite

339

directions, head thrust forward, and ponytails whipping about like snapped reins. She was out of breath by the time she had crossed the street.

"Hi! Hi! Let me take you for tea, big brother."

In the Toman café, Miriam paid, and Robbie hoovered up two slices of Black Forest cake, three Florentines, and a bowl of cappuccino.

"Yes, folks," she announced to the old ladies at the adjacent table. "My brother, the Amazing Human Garburetor." Robbie smiled shyly, licked chocolate from his fingers.

They sat silently for several minutes. Then he lied about gigs for the group, and a windfall lottery win, and a growing friendship with Rosie.

"She's a nutcase on the outside," he assured her, "but dead serious on the inside. She loves me. We love each other. So – do *you* have a boyfriend? 'Cause if you do I'll kill him."

"S'matter of fact, I do," Miriam said, blushing. "Funny 'cause I wanted to ask you if I, if he, like, if he wants to go further than I want to, you know, well, should I let him?"

"What're you *talking* about?" Robbie said. "Of *course* not."

Miriam looked down, sucked noisily on her straw. Robbie picked up his fork and scraped a thin film of chocolate from the enamelled rim of his plate. When he put it in his mouth, all he got was a tongue-zap from the fork's burnt prongs.

"But then maybe he won't like me," Miriam said, chewing on the straw.

"*Miriam*," Robbie said, getting very excited suddenly and raising his voice. One old lady looked over. He leaned across the table, nose to nose with his sister. "You gotta always remember this, OK? If he's not thinking of what *you* want, first, you don't need the stupid creep near you. Get it?"

"OK, OK, I got it," Miriam said, sitting back. Now the straw was just a scribble of plastic between her teeth.

"Good. Sorry if I scared you, but I've been *experienced*."

"Nothing scares me."

"Well, it should. And don't lay that sort of talk on me, it doesn't mean a thing."

"OK, OK. Oh, guess what. Mom's show got dumped. Lousy ratings. Then she got arrested again, just for a day. She went on a march to try to close down the EPX factory, there were dozens of people, the most ever. She chained herself to the fence this time and threw the key in the snow. First they had to clip the fence then they arrested her. It was so great. By the way, Mom and Dad say you'll never come home until you've well and truly left it. What does that mean, exactly, and have you left yet?"

20

THE ROXY WASN'T SUCH A BAD PLACE TO LIVE, EXCEPT that it was dark and cold and Robbie couldn't tell anyone he was there. He laid out blankets in one of the old dressing rooms, hid Ivy's satchel under a cardboard box, and called the place home. After midnight, he fed like a rodent on the goodies at the candy counter. He learned to thread the projectors, too, and sat alone in the cinema, front row centre, watching *Woodstock* as often as he pleased, stuffing himself to the gills with oily popcorn.

During one unnatural thaw, the snow outdoors had melted away to reveal bedraggled red tinsel on muddy shitty lawns, but now it had frozen over again and the sidewalks were blistered with the skin of icy puddles. He went out to sit on walls and benches. On a crusade of joyless destruction, he tilted at mailboxes, spilling envelopes into the slush. How he hated the city suddenly, this environmentless place. He watched the pigeons – skyrats – and observed why their shit is so corrosive: they eat stuff even he'd turn down – there was nothing of value here for him, nothing he could save or call his own. Nature had been kicked out, exiled to the mountaintop, where she brooded acidly. He was wondering how he could ever have been so in love with the city – this giant garbage compactor, this concrete compressor of soured desires. A truck roared by, hitting a pothole, and its rear section slammed down onto its chassis, brakes screaming. Robbie held his ears and thought of Kilborn and how pleasant it would be to bask on the terrace overlooking the lake.

He scanned the windows of high-rise apartment buildings, took some small solace from all the erotic possibilities there, like a thousand drawers of ladies' underwear. He thought of Rosie; the way she both embraced and laughed at sex. Why hadn't he appreciated her warmth, and her wit, when he had the chance? This regret he felt was entirely unlike the regret he once felt for losing Ivy. No suicide this time around, thank you very much; this time he would learn the lesson properly, he promised himself, he'd find strength in himself, he'd make things right. He'd improve himself. He'd win her back with tenderness and imagination. If he only knew how or where to begin.

He perused the head shops, stealing stupid little things, and prowled the warm Métro like Gollum, watching for people to drop precious items onto their seats from their pocketses. No one ever did, not after they noticed him sitting beside them.

He glowered all around. Life is what you make it, was one of Dad's Top Forty bromides, but Robbie had sussed *that* out for what it was worth: life *can't* be what you make it, 'cause no one lets you. All these senior citizens past their usefulness, with their blue-rinse hair and rhinestoned glasses, tutting at Robbie as if *he* looked foolish; all these other prissy people, swallowing Muzak and process cheese-food and shit TV; all these drones bowing down to the gods of mundanity; all these cowards and nestbuilders, making like their lives were achievements of note. Mr. Mills had said that Robbie was just an angry young man. Oh, is that all? Robbie hoped that at thirty he'd be an angry *middle-aged* man. People said he wasn't nice, but weren't there a thousand reasons to be *not* nice? Does he have to list them? It drove him crazy to think of the myriad petty proprieties, the routine humiliations life had ON SPECIAL! this and every other week. He felt unprepared to be civil at all, ever again; he'd step on people's heels and not say sorry, he'd burp up their noses, become violent at the slightest provocation, anything to challenge this crushing routine. By being a nasty little prick, right in society's face, he'd be doing his thing, he'd be his own foul artwork incarnate, demonstrating how trite people were to be so preoccupied with little rules, with niceness, with the seven deadly-boring sins those evangelists cling so dearly to. Envy, he'd howl, so what! Jealousy, greed, and anger, how petty! How dull! Sloth, avarice, gluttony, what puny stuff! How unexceptional, how plain, how mean. Robbie's got way worse, if you want them, he doesn't give a fuck – there are way more urgent matters in life than good manners.

"I am Robbie BOOKbinder!" he shouted. People hid their noses in their bluespapers. "I am UNLIKE you!"

He hung out with some street kids for an afternoon, doing scams and watching them get skanked. He got friendly with a foxy fourteen-year-old in a Spandex mini-skirt and barrettes. She was pretty wild; passing by a Brinks truck outside Birks, she minced up to the armed driver and with her scabby wrists outstretched, cried out, "Hey, handcuff me!" They were chased away. Later, down by the old Windsor Station, one of the kids had a chicken seizure on the pavement with the rig still wagging from his arm. Robbie took off when he heard the sirens.

He snorted at weathered posters glued up around the city for bar bands he knew were doomed to fail. He stood in the heated doorways of pinball parlours, just as he'd seen winos do; for an hour he stood beside one, watching how the guy passed time, like gas, smoothing down the pleats on his tuxedo dickey.

He stood outside department stores and bummed quarters. Thing was, where once he had relished appearing

344

down and dirty to passers-by, now he was ashamed because he had no choice. It was embarrassing to find
himself at the level of all those derelicts whose panhan-
dling he'd disdained all those years, but what could he do?
Like a rubby and his bottle of bitters, he and his life were
now distilled down to several small, all-consuming, animal
concerns.

In Dominion Square, the black snow- and skyrat-spat-
tered statue of Sir Wilfrid Laurier bore the inscription,

The governing motive of my life
has been to harmonize the different
elements which compose our country

but someone had gone at it with a key or a knife so that
now it read *which compose our cunt.* The flower pot at its
base was filled with trash in frozen filthy water – cigarette
butts, grit, bus transfers, ciggy-pack silver foil, Kentucky
Fried Rat bones like Arctic mastodon remains – a record
of twentieth century civilization. And here was old Joe
Smolij. Robbie brushed a pillow of snow off the chal-
lenger's seat. The chess pieces were spangled with frost.

"Moof, moof," Joe told Robbie. "Time is money. Money
is freedom. Freedom's for the birds. This I tell Spassky
when I beat him." He offered him some Canadian sherry.
Robbie accepted.

"You beat Spassky? So how come you're here, Joe? You
could be rich."

Joe looked at him. Such crazy people downtown. "I got
health plan in Quebec, boy without a brain. Boy without
money. You want to talk or moof?"

Robbie found some money, later that afternoon, in a
wallet on the sidewalk. He splurged on a BIG BIG HAPPY
PIZZA, wolfed it down and got a wicked case of indigestion.
Then he visited Classics, thinking of buying an art book.
He bent over the heavy volumes, melted snow dripping off
his head, and felt his toes thaw, as his imagination bloomed.

New names, new pictures, new ideas for him here – De Chirico, Ernst, Miró – which he was committing to memory, to tell Rosie all about, to help redesign their future, as in-store security once more ushered him out.

He would have bought something decent if he'd been given the chance. Passing by a newsstand now, his attention was drawn by Andy Warhol's *Interview*, the Xmas issue, with Keef Richards on the cover. He went to Gino's Paradise and read it ostentatiously there. As he drank bourbon and beer, he read about the beautiful people and imagined that he could be one of them, only even more beautiful, and in his own fashion. These vain, conceited people with their gossipy lunches and mindless hedonistic pursuits; Robbie's interview would be more interesting by a mile, his reputation for fun and smarts unmatched, his Avedon portrait truly a register of style and the enviable life.

Moving on for cheaper booze when almost all his money was spent, he discovered that Judy's Bar, where Ivy and he once drank and rolled cigarettes, was burnt to a crisp. He sat in the charred doorway, like the entry to an abandoned coal mine, the dancing miners all gone up in smoke. He bunched newspapers about him the way he had seen the rummies do. He had no intention of actually reading them, but boredom got the better of him in time, and he foraged for the latest on Mr. Mills' barbershop, perhaps, or the Dead Man's Hands, anything.

Chrissake! Here was someone he knew, in *Allô Police*: Louie Louie, *the* Louis Beaulieu. Who'd been busted.

On Brat's advice, Robbie knew, Louie Louie had begun to import reggae records from Jamaica for his new store, only some of them weren't exactly reggae records; they were ganja, pressed in the shape of reggae records. According to *Allô Police*, the hapless pepsi had not bargained for the fact that Jamaican records aren't shrink-wrapped, and so a dog in customs had smelled out the very first shipment. *The* Louis Beaulieu was now doing five years in St-Vincent-de-Paul.

Rolling his eyes, Robbie saw a jet leave a short slice in the sky, a luminous paper-cut in the pale flesh of the heavens, and he wished he could be on that jet. When he looked down again he was surprised to see an old woman coming fast at him, all in black with a shawl and a cane. They almost bumped: Grandma Bethel! He hadn't seen her since that fiasco of a Seder; she looked so small and hunched now, like a beetle, picking her way across the ice. The city is no place for old people, he thought. He stopped, waited for her to recognize him. He found himself smiling. Hey, maybe they'd have some tea and cookies at her house – he could tell her all about himself. She did look up, finally, but the gaze she gave him was uncertain. Her eyes looked huge through her glasses, darting like startled fish in a bowl, and she hurried right past him, leaving him to wonder if she had deliberately shunned him, or if his appearance was so spectral, his smell so alcoholic, that *anyone* would be scared, and shy away.

Back in the Roxy, he tried to sleep off his hunger, folded up like a skull and crossbones. In his dream, he walks the streets alone. For this crisp day he's surprised to find people have made a decision: they've had it with city life. Ice-blue sky above the silent skycrappers and there's no traffic down here at all. He can breathe the air, it almost smells of the sea. A cool breeze, and a chip bag blows by like a laughing silver kite. It lands on a rich, green verge where the snow has melted away. He bends down to pick it up: the last one on earth, the final piece of rubbish, and what a sense of satisfaction to have finished the job . . . then when he was awoken by a heavy-duty jet roaring overhead, he had a ridiculous reaction: he whimpered for them not to drop the Bomb, to let this not be the end. He had so much left to do with his life.

He tried to sleep, but hunger followed him under the

blanket and kicked him in the stomach. He sat at the window, listening to the bleat and gurgle of the skyrats, his forehead slick with perspiration, his eyes closed, absorbing heat from the winter sun, the blood volcanoes erupting. He watched the specula slide over the jellied surface beneath his eyelids, jumping like zooplankton, like a cartoon cash register, like one of those Mirós he saw in Classics, whenever he moved his eyeballs.

How long was it since he had eaten properly? In the Roxy can there was always the row of toilet bowls, unoccupied, their open mouths howling for more than he could give. He felt like a character in a high seas drama, cut adrift by mutineers, and becoming as preoccupied as children with their own stool; marking detailed updates on the size and state of it in the ship's log. *Woe. Six mere pebbles today, akin to gull droppings. No sign of land. Now will someone please wipe my bummy?* The fever clung to him, sending shivers all over his skin, pulling the muscles over his rack of bones, and frequently sending him back again in a dash, only to make a paltry offering. Sitting on the freezing seat, he realized that what little he had dislodged was at least sending up warmth. So he sat a while longer. Sitting in the pitch-black toilet, trying to evacuate some spicy tacos. Delirious, perching up one half of his pelvis to give the muscles of his miserable ilium a better grip, he found himself thinking, Maybe this is what it's like to have it up the ass. Kind of ecstatic. Painful euphoria. The walls of the rectum alive and hot. The outer body blooming with goose-pimples. His nose running. Other concerns just fall away; all the world is well during this little struggle, all the world is well. His life will change soon. Concentrating like this, he can make a change.

Hunger makes you tired, he found, if only because you exhaust yourself thinking about it all the time. He wearied himself thinking about his body, worrying about his deadened senses, his dribbling sinuses, the lining of his bleeding stomach – ulcers planted there by cheap, spicy junk food and liquor breakfasts – and the cramps and hemorrhoids and the wasted nerves and loosened teeth he'd developed from all that bad speed. Go ahead, try it sometime. What he didn't know, but could feel, was a duodenal ulcer that had inflamed his lower stomach, in particular his pancreas, giving him pancreatitis, and his liver, giving him hepatitis; the increased bile pigments in his blood had given him jaundice, which explained his yellow eyes, and the internal bleeding led to a case of pernicious anaemia, and frightening bouts of bloody vomiting and excretion. He didn't just have *heart*burn, as he thought; it was his whole bloody gut.

He watched a fly struggle to defeat the invisible wall of the windowpane. It had begun to bang and baffle itself the day before, and this morning it was still there, slower, bruised, still crawling stupidly across the glass. Robbie went out to get a job.

He will change, and here's his plan: to offer his creative services to the new management at the L'Enfer Strip; he had all sorts of ideas for renovating it, and for a reasonable price, too. He heard Rosie's delighted voice in his ears: *it sounds like you care. No one ever gives a shit about us. I like you.* Even if she wasn't working there any more, he might do something, at least to give Dolores' life a lift.

He presented himself to the doorman, some new guy with a wide kipper tie, and eyes as grey as shark's gills, and asked to speak to the manager about work. The doorman made a face as dull and heavy as lead in a sock, and told him to wait. Robbie paced the lobby, taking in the nude posters, not for the tits and ass, but considering ways to lend the joint some class. The doorman returned with an

349

application form. Robbie was disappointed. He said he wanted to speak to the manager personally, but the doorman held out a pen.

"Hey, guy, look," he said. "I'm a friend of Rosie's – I'm Robbie Bookbinder. Also I know Olly. You know, this was his joint once."

"Is that the fucken say so. You know Olly?"

"Yeah, sure," Robbie said, encouraged. "We go way back, fuck."

"Olly's fucken history, buddy," the doorman said, shunting a toothpick around his mouth.

"Fuck. Yeah?" Robbie said.

"Fucken, eh."

"Fuck. Where'd he go? I haven't seen him in a fucken dog's age."

"He's *dead*, fuck."

Robbie quickly took the pen and the form. He read –

RENSEIGNEMENTS PERSONNELS
PERSONAL INFORMATION

NOM/NAME . . . .

MENSURATIONS/MEASUREMENTS . . . .

DEFAUTS PHYSIQUES/PHYSICAL IMPAIRMENTS . . . .

VOS PREMIERES QUALITES/YOUR BEST QUALITIES . . . . .

VOTRE AGENT/YOUR AGENT . . . .

COURS DE DANCE/DANCING SCHOOL . . . .

NOM D'ARTISTE/STAGE NAME . . . .

– and carefully folded it down to a tiny square. Then slunk outdoors again with burning ears.

He went into a department store to scrounge free samples, but was given the bum's rush by the in-store security. He shuffled on along the sidewalk, thinking black and tangled thoughts, ruminations on how to destroy the world, enraged by the noise of the city now that he wasn't making it himself, and ended up accepting a coffee at the Christian Mission Drop-In Centre, after an eager young fellow with a brush-cut and polyester slacks called out to him,

"Hey! Yes you! You look in need of some SALVATION!"

No one knew Robbie lived at the Roxy, but Scurvy knew that's where he'd been storing the equipment, and now it was the end of March and the six-month term was up. Bummer, because Robbie'd been hatching a plot to take the world by storm with a solo show, one in which he'd plug in a cacophonous kitchenful of appliances, TV sets, hairdryers, and other symbols of terminal consumerism and middle-classness, over-amplify it all mightily, kick it around, and let the feedback roar as he sang. If you could call it *singing*. It would be a stunning performance, the wild amplification of all his desires and frustrations. This was his new thing. Art on paper and canvas was dead; it had all been done, it affected no one any more. To be noticed today you had to perform your art noisily, force it on people, be a sharp stick in society's eye. Like Mom; she'd made anger an art and performed it on TV. He'd howl in his own angry style; he'd wiggle his prick through his fly and grimace from ear to ear, splitting his face open to show how much he cared, too. That was the problem with the deadhead seventies – people didn't care enough about anything, they'd stopped demonstrating anger. . . .

So it was a *major* bummer to wake up one morning to clattering sounds, peek down from his gallery, and see men lifting the equipment away from its storage space behind the cinema screen. He crouched on the scaffolding stairs and watched in agony as they carted his last hope away.

He still had Ivy's boxes, and now in the Roxy he guarded them the way a dragon will jealously sit on its treasure; fearful of its theft, with no use for it at all. He sat on it, jumping at every creak the building made, sleeping with a steak knife at his chest. Out on the street he was watchful of slow cars, and he made paranoid detours whenever he returned to the Roxy, sneaking up the fire escape only after dark.

Breakfast of eggs, with the white all runny, at the Mission, and Robbie found that he was the most despised of men, because even the rummies here looked down on him; they, at least, were on welfare, while he had never worked and did not qualify. He was a scummy punk with dirty fingernails and a mod parka scrawled with incomprehensible slogans, scrounging a free meal and smelling fiendish, when he should be out somewhere contributing to society – that's what was written on their hoary faces. But Robbie knew he was better than them; he had been brought up in a lovely family, he had been to the theatre, his favourite artist was Rubens, he was blessed with possibility. There they all were: Joe and his chessboard, the bus-worshipper, the lunatic with the mat of hair, and all the other grubby bums, murmuring together and nodding smugly in his direction. He glared back and fired a finger pistol at his head, opening his mouth to let his eggs drool out like pus.

Bingo! All it cost was a couple of bucks, and then you took your chances. He had earned six bucks giving blood at the Red Cross, and bought an evening's supply of cards. Looking around him now in the church basement: ladies mainly, scrawny old ones with plastic net shopping bags, obese ones in cotton dresses, toothless ones masticating their gums; couch potatoes, welfare abusers, hunchbacks, alcoholics, the disappointed of the earth, the abused and the neglected, the halitosis-stricken, the slimy piss-poor, all those fallen through the nets of government statistics.

"Under the G, forty-three . . . B eight . . . N thirty-one . . . "

He found it hard to keep up. He was scanning his cards like a madman, six of them taped to the table the way he had observed the ladies doing it, placing his plastic tokens down as fast as possible, asking *what* number? *what* number? and getting shushed.

"I twenty . . . B two . . . B thirt-teen . . . "

The Knights of Columbus officer read the numbers from the stage in a monotone that Robbie found unendurable after a couple of hours. He was stunned by the listlessness of the game. He remembered how once on a childhood cruise to Europe with the family, in the brass-railed lounge of the *Empress of Canada*, he had giggled at the caller's delivery: Under the B – men from the ministry – number 11 . . . under the N – pregnant ladies – number 33 . . . under the B – the day of God's rest – number 7. . . . The Knights of Columbus version was as bland as corn chips and an afternoon soap. In fact, watching TV was a lively exercise compared to this; there was a surge of electricity in the air as boards filled up, but when someone won, no applause – just the collective sigh of envy, and the massive swish of tokens being swept up. The woman across from him had her own deluxe wire-meshed tokens, which she swept up by means of a magnetic plastic wand, and tapped into her own personal plastic pouch.

"Been playing long?" Robbie asked, but he was told to shush again. *Planet of the Zombies*, he thought. They could beam us all up and put us in forced labour camps on Mars to irrigate the canals and no one would bat an eyelid. Just so long as we got our Bingo.

"N thirty-eight . . . G fifty . . . "

Robbie mechanically laying his tokens down now, banishing all thoughts so he could concentrate on the task.

"G forty-seven . . . I twenty . . . "

Hearing the buzz of excitement all around and the women across from him saying, accusingly, "You're close."

"Yeah. So I am."

"G sixty . . . "

"Chrissake, BINGO!"

Hey, all he'd won was twenty-five bones, and it's not as if he whipped it directly from out of their purses, but when he stood up and walked down the aisle to collect his winnings, the room had stopped and stared at him like he was Oliver Twist asking for more. Feeling faint for lack of blood, he had shrugged at the whole ballooning room and fired a blunderbuss into his nailed head. He flew out into the evening like a bat, and blew close to the whole wad on beer at a dépanneur, plus shrooms from a dealer he met in the street.

He was making his way back to the Roxy, wondering if he should swallow the entire stash in one session, when a car pulled up slowly beside him, and it was Husker and Gaunt.

"Not a bit cold, eh?" Gaunt said.

"Colder than a witch's tit," Husker said. "Climb in,

boy. Just to get warm, nothing else." Robbie got in, gratefully.

"Oh hey, want to see some dirty pictures?"

"Nah," Robbie said. He blew into his red hands. He felt as if the liquid in his ear canals had frozen and sound was skating hard on it, now. "Not into that stuff, thanx."

"Just look," Gaunt said, and passed an envelope over the seat. "Might be someone you know."

Kiki Van? No such luck. When Husker said dirty, he was speaking literally: swollen bodies dragged up from the bed of the St. Lawrence, vomiting mud. Four or five of them, each half-wrapped in sleeping bags, chains, and cinder blocks. Robbie flipped through them over and over. One of their bellies had bloated up so enormously it was clear the coroner wouldn't be able to close the coffin lid. The face had just about loosened off the skull; it was eyeless and toothless, like a rubber King Kong mask. Robbie hadn't recognized him the first flip through, but then he saw the studs on the boots: BILL on one, BEAST on the other. He looked another time, and another. The air buzzing with flies. The grotesque figures flopped on the shore, in river-gorged poses like dancers in some foul ballet. One had a batik scarf around his neck – you could just make out the peacocks and *kala* masks. He was wearing a KEEF LIVES T-shirt too, and his mouth was open and his tongue was sucked back, plugging his throat.

"Chrissake," Robbie said. "I *knew* these people. Olly. And Ivy's other brother, John. He wasn't pretty to begin with. How come you're showing me these disgusting things? Makes me wanna puke."

Neither Husker nor Gaunt turned around. Husker was sipping coffee. Gaunt was peeling a triangle from the plastic lid of his cup. The back of Husker's neck looked like a stack of damp baloney, Gaunt's was red and dry-blistered as a carnatzel.

"You know," Husker said, at last, "the other day, we received a funny shipment down at the station. Forwarded it was, by the old school's broker, to us. On account of who it was intended for."

"Hey, man, don't *start* on me."

"No, no, we was just wondering. You wouldn't know anything at all about that, now would you?"

"Course not. What shipment?"

"Good, good. Just wondering, you know. We'll take care of it ourselves from here on in, OK? The whole affair's over anyway, so far as the Dead Man's Hands are concerned. Unless you're planning to pick up the franchise."

"Pull the other one," Robbie said vehemently. "I've had it with those psychos."

"Good," Gaunt said. "Wise decision. So give me the pictures back and fuck off, all right. See if you can't go out and make some nice friends, for once."

Robbie fucked off. He circled the block and hung out in Girouard Park for five minutes to make sure he hadn't been followed, then hauled the fire escape down and slipped into the cinema. *Woodstock* was playing to a packed house. He would have loved to stay and watch it – in reverse, from his perspective – but he had a more urgent agenda. He foraged for Ivy's satchel, slung it over his shoulder, and bussed down to Nun's Island, where the damaged St. Lawrence froths up yellowish on the shore like clotting fibrinogen. He filled the satchel with rocks, buckled the leather straps tight, and hurled the package out with all his might. He was giving the stuff back, a little late perhaps, but with the best of intentions. It wasn't his thing. It splashed, floated for a moment on a heavy eddy, coursed swiftly down river, and then sank, gobbled down by the dark water.

By the time he returned, the cinema had emptied out. He dangled his heels over the lip of the stage, the great screen above him, chewed his shrooms, and systematically wasted himself. He thought of the Indians who roamed the land long before we fucked it around, and of how young prospects would fast alone in the woods, eating roots and magic mushrooms and hallucinate, waiting for the spirit wisdom to visit. Plus Rosie had said once how Christ and his disciples were enlightened by *A. muscaria* mushrooms. And Viking beserkers were emboldened by it. And it's what made Santa's reindeer fly. . . .

He starts by yelling at the empty seats of the cinema. Hoping his anger will at least flush out the uselessness in him, he yells till he gargles with blood. Nothing happens. He finds he's the same Robbie at the end of it, just hoarser.

Tries again, pounding the floor now. Knocks his head with his fists, spits phlegm back in the faces of all the people responsible for ruining him. Sees his parents' faces at the end of the lineup, shocked, close to tears and wet with his spittle, unable to comprehend this venom of his, this grotesque breach of reason. Then, with terrible regret, he sucks the spittle back.

The Roxy small as a fishtank now. Robbie curls up like a luminous mollusc, curling tighter to suck his own cock, tighter till he snaps his own spine. Sees himself spatter the cinema screen with his own gore and slash the giant canvas with his teeth and nails. He lies in the dark and listens to his breathing. Beginning to feel himself unravel . . .

. . . the images are projected on the screen above him: under a sky of whipped black clouds, the banks of the St. Lawrence, and bodies being dragged out of the freezing mud. The image is like old newsreel. Buzzing flies. Camera closes in, who is it in this soaked KEEF LIVES T-shirt, whose face has thickened and fallen off the skull? His *own*, of course. The stupid flippant FUCK. *Night of the Living Dead. Braiins.* He's watching himself, sickened, vertiginous, as time's wheel slips off its pin and rumbles round deafeningly like a great granite coin in accelerating, ever-diminishing spirals. Down the sink, into the sewers of the city. Here's Joe Smolij, naked but for his sprawling, brambled beard, his hands flopping in his wrinkled lap like old moths in a jar, the way they always did while he waited for you to move. Robbie goes nose to nose with him and looks into his face. Joe's eyes are white, like a baked trout's. There's a tattoo on his left wrist, little numbers in blue ink: QP5-KP6xR= CHECK. Robbie looks around, and everyone's here: Kiki Van Garterbelt grinning like a gargoyle stewardess. Ivy naked bone-white and skinny disgusting, with two rows of teats like a bitch stoat, offering her white slippery wrists for him to grasp. He grabs, then deliberately releases his grip looking around instead for Rosie. Where's Rosie where's Rosie he howls he never meant to hurt her he's so sad he's done such wrong he's choking on his own swollen Adam's apple. No. It's cool, he's in control of this thing, he can't feel at all, his heels are exhaust pipes, shooting sparks behind him. He's a knight on a smoking field, playing dead and struggling to unhitch his own iron coffin as villagers pick their way through the corpses, harvesting for jewellery with knives. The great granite wheel grinds, he's up in the filthy clouds, up and over with a heave in his stomach, plunging with terminal aban-

don the way he always wanted to, rising again as a
jealous devil just like Ivy always said he was; in a
medieval play, licking the powdered cheeks of petti-
coated whores, he holds his horn-shaped cock in his
skeletal fingers, pricks it with his own fingernails and
has them catch the blood on their lips like molten
rubies. Over again, heave ho. He's barely aware of it
but he's vomiting now. Back through time. He's a
Viking, drunk on mead and enjoying a good rape,
propped up on his palms, slipping in his own puke.
Now he's a sorceror's apprentice battling brooms, an
Australopithecus crouching in a cave and sharpening
sticks for the hunt, something more primitive than
that, something grunting, barely on two feet, with
claw-things for arms, and meatbreath, and bloodpoo.
His fur peels back to display his nerves and muscles
like the Visible Man kit, his body is jelly, heaving and
veined on the exterior, opening and throbbing like
bloody porridge. His mind peeling away before his
eyes, layers of a multicoloured crystal onion. His very
DNA unravelling. Light-splinters slice out of the darkness. Great writhing vaults open up to him supported
on walls of ribbed black rubber or is it flesh swelling
and bursting open with *kala* masks and *supit urang*.
Bill the Beast and mud-fat Olly. All the wriggling
souls of the creatures he's ever eaten are gathered
round him for the vengeful feast. Passing through his
own digestive system, his spine arching overhead like
the ceiling of a sinister cathedral. On and on, down
the drain, till the din of voices recedes. He passes
through a constricted canal, whimpering aloud now,
struggling to breathe. Plopped out onto a warm, sandy
plain, a primordial beast. Eohippus? A dog. Woof. He
barks, like that. On his hands and knees, on the
Roxy's stage. Woof. Snarling too, should anyone be
hiding among the seats. The air is brittle, snapping,

tiny sparks, synaptic explosions in front of his eyes. He curls up right there, panting, naked. With no desire but to sleep, dreamlessly, and to wake refreshed as someone new.

. . . he sees a shadow-dappled park, up on the screen. He walks into it, ducks golden clouds of aphids. It's a Mediterranean scene, a De Chirico, suffused with sandy light: ochre piazza, olive groves and fields of chalk, a duck-egg blue sky. A small town at high noon, the melancholy and mystery of her streets, dusty and quiet, shadows falling like the very stuff of silence, the clock tower arrested in time, a steam train pulling noiselessly away. He squints at the sky. Gulls are suspended over the coast, over the roof of his own little house. He's sitting there now, with a simple but adequate meal of apples and cheese and wine. On a rough-hewn table he's laid out a canvas, and on it he's painting a simple still life. He has nothing to prove; it doesn't matter if this has been done before by anyone else. He's doing it only for his own pleasure. And Rosie is there, painting too, contentedly . . .

21

OVER KILBORN BAY, WOBBLY ARROWS OF GEESE WERE already bowing back, this way north. As he watched from his tiny bed, clouds passed rapidly overhead, their shadows gurgling up the trunks of the maples and along their branches like blood through arteries.

"Wow," Barnabus said. "Where'd you get that tattoo?"

Tattoo? He'd forgotten all about it. He looked down and there it was on the cusp of his right deltoid; a large, articulated spider in black and blueberry ink.

"Oh, yeah," he stammered. "It's fake, like, what you get in boxes of Sugar Krunchies and stuff. Fun, huh?"

"How come there's a scab, then," Barnabus said, gripping Robbie's arm and peering closely. "Looks real to me. I saw a show on TV." Indeed, the skin was still raw and raised where the blood had come up. And Robbie's appalling realization was that, in the context of home, a tattoo suddenly seemed like the most meaningless, inexplicable thing on earth. He felt sick to think that it was embedded in his flesh for good.

That was the first time anyone had discussed Robbie's appearance since he'd joined them for Spring Break a week earlier, though he looked like a wild animal in captivity: dog collar, torn net T-shirt, spiked glove, skull earring, rabid haircut, missing tooth, black-and-yellow bruises under both eyes. It should have been a relief to him all this time, but instead he was on tenterhooks, waiting like a sprung trap for the first snide remark or joke from anyone. He'd been skulking around the cottage, looking out of windows. It was weird being home, feeling like a kid again, all paranoid of the parents; just doing normal things like flushing a toilet or making a sandwich, but expecting a harsh reprimand. Passing Dad on the stairs, he'd pull a little contrite smile, for no good reason, as if he were on his way up to steal something, or who knows what. The whole cottage seemed to resonate with a lifetime's history of scolding.

His rueful revelation: out on the street he feels scary, looks scary – a nasty piece of society's work, a nail pulled bent from the burnt plank of experience – but here he's just one of the family again, a babykins, going through a harmless phase. He's almost a joke, an out-of-season Hallowe'en treat, Junior-gone-wild, that's all, and he feels deflated for not being able to impress on them that he's certifiably dangerous.

By the window, the drainpipes were clogged with thawed leaves. Down below, the terrace was cracked where the ice had worked at the stones like a crowbar. The lawn had sunk where moles had busied themselves, and the rose-trellis was bent after the weight of snowfalls. He heard the scratching of a rake over stone; Mom out there already, cracking the whip at Nature. He rose and went out to help.

The spring earth, marbled with loam, flecked with root and fern, was still hard and unyielding. Robbie hacked, Mom pressed bulbs in the holes he made. He pictured the two of them from an aerial POV as unremarkable scratches in a great grey landscape, investing so much hope in these stupid little things. Mom stood up to stretch her neck and grip the small of her back. Robbie looked out. The lake was luminous in this light, and jumping. One curious thing about lakes with too much acid in them, they develop an electric clarity; you can see right to the bottom, and in the summer they're exquisitely blue. That's because all the environment has gone out of them.

The clouds were a helter-skelter fox hunt now, hounds scrambling out over the lake with their tails streaking behind them, mud flying from their paws. Robbie, in tuque, big boots, and ski jacket, said he looked like the village idiot; Mom, in her fingerless gloves and frayed straw hat, laughed and said she felt like a mad bag lady.

"Life in the post-nukular world," he joked. "At least we'd be self-sufficient."

According to the *Farmer's Almanac* he'd consulted, there's invariably a day halfway through March that's warm and sunny. It's a dirty trick, however, because at least three more snowfalls are in store, and there's a good month before the hills switch on green and the lilac and apple blossoms light up. Right on cue, the following Monday was so toasty Robbie had his shirt off. All around the land was alive with the thaw, the house's eaves dripping snow water into barrels, the smelt brook rushing over exposed rocks. The ice had already melted off the lake, although Owl's Head's peak was still white, and Robbie pictured babes skiing in bikinis. He crouched down by the brook and scooped up two handfuls of chilly melting mud, rich as chocolate. He held it to his nose, pressed it to his lips.

He was really getting into this nature business.

He was basking on the terrace, half-snoozing beneath the weight of *The Thirty-Nine Steps*, "a novel of mind-numbing suspense." Miriam was stretched out on a deck chair beside him. *Sonny Daze and Sandi Beaches*. She was wearing makeup, he noted out of the corner of his eye, almost as much as him. He sniffed the air, frowned, snorted phlegm. A smell of burnt toast or rubber. Some farmer must have a wet bonfire going.

"Hey, Miriam," he said, absently scratching a rash on his chest. The roof of his mouth itched unpleasantly. "Did you know, if a wet leaf leaves a blue stain on a window-pane, that means it's been soaked in acid rain. That's Nature's litmus test. See those patches of brown pine needles? That's because they've been sitting under acid snow all winter."

"No guff," Miriam said.

"Death to the sugar bush, Mom says. Drag, or what?"

Miriam shrugged. "Whatever turns your crank, man," she said, without even turning her head. "Hey, Rob, I got high with Pinch at a party the other night. We made out, it was ama-a-azing. Roman hands, Russian fingers, and more arms than Israel."

"*Miriam*, Chrissake."

Robbie's enjoyed some scenes in his time, but teenage girls getting banged senseless by grizzly acidheads is not one of his fond memories. He opened his mouth to give Miriam hell, but bit his tongue.

"Whatcha doing, Rob?" Miriam said. "Catching flies?" And did the air ever smell bad. He could actually taste it.

That night, not long after Robbie had hit the sack, Barnabus began to cough in his sleep. The cough had been irritating Robbie all day, every day, since his arrival in Kilborn. Now he lay awake. There was a knock; Mom's soft knock, and then her head in the door. Robbie leaned up. She put a finger to her lips, and went over to Barnabus' bed. She sat him up gently, holding him in the crook of one arm. Robbie saw for the first time how frail he had become. His body was drawing rapid, shallow breaths. In the moonlight his ribs seemed bare, white, and dry, like naked bones. He watched Mom apply some tube gadget to his mouth, and squeeze. Puff. Barnabus coughed in his sleep, sucked gratefully on the tube. Mom dabbed his lips with the collar of his pyjamas, and allowed him to sink back into the sheets.

Robbie followed her downstairs, on tiptoe. They sat in the covered porch overlooking the lake. Alone with her like this, he felt unspeakably physical, overcome with the naked feeling he associated with concealing guilt. Why guilt? He watched her. She was beautiful, but tired and tense, the very bones of her head somehow strained, as if all the pressure of her life was squeezing the skull smaller. He wondered how different from other old ladies she'd look in twenty years. He remembered the first time he had inspected the lines on her forehead. Eight years old, and his navel had opened up and given off a sicksweet baby smell. You could see right in. He stood up and showed it to her at the dining-room table. Her forehead was at his eye-level as she stared back down the umbilical tube of her first and favourite son. Now he understood: he was aware of having been born by her. Weird, why would he feel guilty about that? For the pain he put her through back then? Or *since*? He had always raged about wasting his life away, his precious adolescence, but now he wondered how many years had he robbed from *her*. He broke the silence.

"Barnabus OK, Mom? What's he got?"

"Well, probably just asthma. I'm giving him Ventalin until he learns to wake himself up. He had such a rough time around the lake last summer, after Mendoza was put to sleep. Then he had indescribable food poisoning from a fish he caught around the Hogsback. Then one morning, after another night on the dock in his sleeping bag, well – he coughed up blood."

"Chrissake!"

"It's simple, in my mind – he breathes in acid mist for several hours every morning and then his little bronchioles

are eaten right through. But really, I don't know any more.
I may be alone in this. I'm told I get hysterical. I can't get
a straight answer from anyone."

Weird thing about that Monday in March was, it turned out
to be the first day of spring, after all. The temperature
stayed high, the blackflies rioted, and Mom and Robbie
had no idea whether to plant and risk frostbite to the root
of the vegetables, or wait for the snowstorm and risk
missing this freak spring altogether. It was the talk of the
countryside; you couldn't pass a farmer on the road without stopping to discuss it. And that burnt-meat smell was
definitely not some bonfire; Robbie checked around, and
everyone was curling up their nostrils. It was as bad as
being in the city; you wanted to stay indoors with the
windows closed.

Dad took the kids back to school in town, but Mom and
Robbie stayed out, for Mom had a plan. Robbie was mightily impressed by her energy; in one afternoon she pulled
together half a dozen locals – all with maple trees on their
property – and set a date for a community sugaring-off
party to be held on the field, right outside the gates of EPX
Chemicals Corporation. She had to argue fiercely, for most
of the farmers had long abandoned maple-sugaring; their
trees were producing only small amounts of sap these days,
and it wasn't only the maples that were blighted – the
beech and birch, too, and higher up on the Hogsback, the
spruce and the fir. Several said they weren't inclined to
take on such pointless work, and one was particularly
bitter; he had built a sawmill on his land, and several times
his saw teeth had been sheared right off by old forgotten
sugaring nails buried in the butt logs of maples. And his
son had lost an eye to a piece of flying metal.

In spite of all that, Mom arranged for a temporary

sugarhouse to be built, and managed to borrow a disused evaporator so maple sap could be boiled at the party. She and Robbie drove out to barns collecting old cedar buckets and newer tin ones, patching them up if they needed it, and redistributing them to the farmers who were going along. They found spouts that hadn't rusted, and several augers for drilling into the bark; they polished up the sugaring arch and painted its metal frame a fresh fire-engine red, and even hauled out a rotted sled and scrubbed the mud and cobwebs down. They borrowed twenty trestle tables and long benches, and hammered together a low stage.

All the while, Mom explained to Robbie the art of mapling. Robbie never knew how abundant sap could be; when she first snapped off a twig, so much dripped out he feared the tree might haemorrhage; what maples were healthy were just about bursting, and to Robbie the land suddenly flowed with honey. He helped her stuff dozens of invitations, which went out not only to friends and neighbours, but to the mayor and sundry politicians, the Kilborn police station, environmental groups, and all the media friends she had made during her years on TV.

A week to go, and Dad was on the couch drinking scotch, watching the hockey; whenever he did make it to the country on weekends, he was so knocked out he was good for nothing. Robbie considerately asked if he was preoccupied with his latest contract, something – was it? – related to exercise.

"No, Robbie," Dad said. "*Excise*. Customs and Excise, you lunkhead." He punched him in the shoulder, right on the sore muscle with the fresh tattoo.

He must really be drunk, Robbie thought, to touch me for no good reason. The Canadiens scored on a power play, Dad shouted, but Robbie wasn't really watching. His brain was buzzing angrily: every year, Dad comes back from his fishing trip on the Moise and says, Well, the salmon aren't spawning this year, like it's just a freak of nature, at best something that merits aum, a study. Robbie wished he would think *microscopically* for once; if the old man had ever dropped acid – the psychedelic kind – *then* he'd appreciate life's tiny secrets. But instead of struggling with words and fighting him, Robbie pretended to enjoy the game – *Cournoyer scores!* He punched the air. He had something better up his sleeve.

Although the local police had given her no more than a warning after her arrest that winter, Mom had obviously acquired some notoriety since her show was taken off the air. The weekend of the cabane-à-sucre, Robbie and Miriam and Barnabus went down with her to the site, and though it was not yet noon, a horde of camera crews had already set up camp, and the EPX Chemicals Corporation had deployed security guards along the fence. The fields were busy with farmers' families stringing up striped tents and pastel bunting and tables to display their maple-sugar products. Two trestle tables were laden with pots of steaming beans and deer stew, and the air above a row of barbeques was wobbling. Robbie sat on the edge of the stage, closed his eyelids to feel the glorious sunshine warm them over his eyeballs, leaned back with his palms on the hot planks, and took the sounds in: the flapping of canvas in the wind, the ping of sap as it dripped into the metal buckets hanging on the trunks of trees, children giggling as they stuck their tongues out under the dripping spigots, a radio scraping out *Tam ti de lam* on a fiddle. He breathed in deeply, and for the first time in weeks he couldn't smell the sour rotting odour on the wind; only the pungent fragrance of boiling maple sugar. He opened his eyes and went to help.

Because the snow had melted so early on the lower ground this year, he had to hitch a ride with an old farmer in a pickup to the top of the Hogsback. It was the same old guy who had driven him that battered Xmas Eve; he still had the bottle of beer wedged between his thighs.

"Awayy," Robbie said, and shook his huge knotted hand. Ça va bien? Good to see you, guy."

Together they shovelled snow into the back of the pickup, and from the crest of the hill Robbie surveyed the fabulous 3-D topographic map of the Townships. What a high; natural, too. They drove back down and transferred the snow to a trough set up in the shade of a canopy by the lakeshore. Soon people would dunk sticks in fresh-boiled maple syrup, roll them in the snow, chew the hardened stuff like taffy, and lose all their fillings in it. Robbie stood back, put his fists on his hips, and admired the unsullied whiteness before anyone started dunking.

The field rapidly filled with people milling, people catching the rays, people linking arms in fours and dancing on the grass, and people dipping their toes in the lake and lining up for the hogfest of maple-sweetened stew, waffles and maple-baked beans, maple-glazed squash, eggs and sausages and ham drowned in pure maple syrup, maple apple crisp, maple tarts and maple-fried bacon rinds that curled up like ears – *les oreilles de Christ*, as Robbie's old farmer buddy called them.

While people ate, several men set up a pretty big sound system on the stage. When they were done, Mom introduced herself to the crowd. The mob of reporters jostled for a view, and if you were sitting on the grass to eat you could hardly see her at all. Robbie sat and listened as she did her number: sulphate deposit acid mist aluminum phosphate indigestible to trees EPX air pollutants, and so on. It was passionate, and Robbie was proud. Barnabus got up and said the immortal word POOLUTION. Then, one by one, the farmers took the stage and, hesitating, described how their woods were depleted, how their livestock were falling sick – how their cuts weren't healing good – how the air smelled like an abattoir, how brown foam was washing up on their shores. The crowd applauded and waved banners and booed EPX and made disgusted faces for the cameras, and in the heat and excitement, the sweet afternoon air bent and stretched.

Children in threes were carrying the heavy buckets of sap and sloshing it about and making the grass sticky, and what looked like a pack of Mendoza's bastard pups licked the ground after them. A lone French-Canadian fiddler mounted the stage and scraped off tunes as fast as any heavy-metal guitarist Robbie had ever heard, stamping his foot on the bowing planks. People whooped and spun one another around, and already one local had had too much syrup and beer and was upchucking onto the ground. Plus there was an accident in the little sugarhouse; too many people had crammed in to watch the raw sap being poured into the evaporating pans, someone had jostled the hot arch, and the whole thing had tipped over. Maybe that had been Mom's and Robbie's fault, for in their haste they hadn't set the contraption on a proper concrete floor; since the ground had only recently thawed it was still soft and uncertain, so the arch tilted over, sap spilling onto several pairs of pants and spattering the lens of one television camera, and the air quickly filled with the smell of scorched syrup. Robbie shrugged, went to the car, and with Barnabus's help, unloaded his equipment.

On a table by the microphone he laid out his things. It looked like a domestic or industrial trade show. Mom climbed the stage and introduced the afternoon's final feature: ladies and gentlemen mesdames et messieurs the one and only *Hell's Yells!*

He plugged an Environments cassette into his tape machine and approached the microphone with deliberate slowness. As he approached, the sounds of nature were amplified louder and louder until the fields around EPX were alive with the chirruping of huge mutated insects and birds as big as cattle. Nature run riot. Some people looked at one another sceptically, some were amused. Most of the cameramen and reporters just stuffed their faces on all that free food. Robbie concentrated mightily on all the things that had ever made him angry. He knotted his cheeks up and fired at his temples and glared at the crowd through slitted eyes. For a start, he was saying with his magnificent glare, most industrialists should be hanged, drawn, and quartered. Several people in the field seemed to understand, for they had stopped smirking. He made an animal growl; if he were prime minister he'd stir up such shit he'd end up assassinated, but the things he'd do are what should be done by any decent leader in a dirty land. He picked up an aerosol can from the table and sprayed it into the mike. A jet-stream roar went out through the PA, and people covered their ears. He'd made himself clear. The camera crews were wiping their hands on their pants and picking up their equipment. He pictured himself as PM, his snarly face on a dollar bill, a halo of nails around his head. Kill an industrialist. That's all there was for it. Hunt an executive down and fucking drag his spine out. Throw him down a chimney. Feed him to a smelter. Fess up, who's responsible here?

That was enough to get him going, and the crowd had pressed around the stage to get a better look, too. Cameramen were pushing children out of the way to get the perfect vantage point. He pulled the cord on a chainsaw and left it buzzing where it was. Gunned a lawnmower, too. And a hedgetrimmer. He thought of Ivy. To her, other people were always having a better time on other planets. He used to believe that was true, but now he had run out of energy to keep hating himself so much. You can threaten suicide for only so long, life is what you make it. He switched on an air-conditioner and a Mixmaster. Dinful! Plus an electric mosquito-zapper, and when insects were drawn to it they combusted in a snap and a flash that amplified unpleasantly and bounced off the walls of the EPX Chemicals Corporation. He suddenly understood how Mom, who loved nature so mightily, could find little pleasure in it, because she knew how fucked it was; when she raged at people's indifference she raged not only for nature's survival, but also the survival of caring. You had to care, you *had* to be angry, or you didn't deserve nature at all, you could just rot in hell. 'Cause Mother Nature herself is mad as hell, he thought, you better believe it. Do people really believe that Nature in her pure state is some kind of Garden of Eden? People speak with regret about the way we've raped her. They talk of dead lakes, but mainly in terms of us and ours. *Our* health. But in reality, she's not some sweet defenceless thing, some easy lay. The notion of Nature as something pure, Robbie thought, is science fiction. That's what all those National Geo shows are on TV: SF. Nature cares no more than the average Bingo player about being in good shape. Nature can be a fat woman too, a smoker, a couch potato, someone who farts in public; she'll eat white bread and Cheez Whiz, and be happy as a pig in shit. 'Cause it's perfectly natural. Nature, Robbie discovered for himself, will exist in any state – acidified, radiated, inseminated with rusting stuff and plastic junk, cold all the time, quite indifferent to our needs – and still be Nature. Now he's trying to project the idea telepathically to the crowd: use your *braiins*. When you dump on her too much, she'll get vicious, volcanic, and primordial all over again. She'll welcome the release, the chance to punch holes in some walls; she'll burp it all back at you without thinking, break wind in your face, slap you around with a hurricane, let too much sunshine in. She'll be an angry god, demand the sort of respect pagans once gave her. So Robbie's offering sacrifices: plastic wrapping, aerosol cans – the kitchen counter as the altar of modern times. He's starting his own career of caring angrily, and not just aiming at his own temple. This is his new thing.

372

Cranking up a portable air-raid siren now, he screamed hard. Some children clung to their mothers' legs. At the back of the crowd, he saw the family hatchback draw up, and it was Dad at the wheel, taking a conservative look, Miriam smirking in the passenger seat. Robbie wasn't fazed, he was too far gone, now; his nose was running, his naked chest was slick with sweat and red with that nasty rash, he was bellowing, mostly meaningless raw-throated blue bloody baby talk, but with a nasty, tuneless refrain that came to him out of the sky:

"STINGing in the rain, just stinging in the RAIN . . . "

The crowd applauded madly, but he was barely aware of them. Some were singing with him, some just shouting. There was a bristling garden of upraised hands, the fiddler made his fiddle cry along, and now people began lobbing their hardened maple-syrup apples at the EPX security guards. Robbie thought of Rosie, and how her violent caring had always embarrassed him. Caring that strangled her, made her angry and petulant – had driven him away – but now he saw that without it, you're nothing. A couple of farmers started up their pickups and gunned their engines. Many folks were hollering now, really venting their spleen. The guards looked nervous, one pulled out his pistol, and the cameras were pointing in every direction, gobbling it all up. And if Robbie wasn't mistaken, there was Dad, pounding his car horn.

22

A STEWARDESS NUDGED HIM, AND HE AWOKE TO A HOT OK meal, smelling of soggy sneakers. He looked at the limp selection, presented with such gusto in individual plastic envelopes, and was struck by a burlesque echo of the adolescent's sinking heart on being presented with life's agenda: What you see is what you get, boyo, and lots of luck to you.

He was flying to Ottawa, joining Mom for a rally, to help kick off a commission studying, among other things, the behaviour of the EPX Chemicals Corporation on Kilborn Bay. An environmental group had invited him. Well, they'd invited Mom, and when she got there she'd called to suggest he come along. The EPX party had gotten a ton of coverage on TV, and he'd bought a heap of bluespapers to see how he featured. Poolution was clearly in vogue, a hot topic, and everyone had found an angle: THE 'DINFUL' SPRING, said the *Star* – and it felt great to be quoted like that; there was a crowd shot in *Allô Police*, and he could just see the spikes of his hair poking up over the shoulder of a cop, with a list of the important people who'd been arrested for trespassing, and although he wasn't mentioned by name, he was definitely one of them; even the *National Investigator* had an article about him – about the

374

Loch Ness Monster's cousin, really, being attracted by the noise to the surface of Kilborn Lake – with him saying, "It was farm out!"

A couple of papers were critical of the mess left behind all over the field after the event, even though it was mostly the media who had done it in the first place, but Robbie thought that was cool; it was a lot like the garbage you see at the end of *Woodstock*, and it made him feel he had been a part of something, at last.

The plane touched down. Having worked so hard for the past two weeks, and partied with the locals all night, then drunk as much in-flight liquor as the stewardess would give him, he was numb and giddy and savouring the euphoria of inebriate travelling. All those stories he had read of Keef's twenty-four-hour binges, that tailspin life-style he had envied so, this is what it was like; once you're over the hump of the first night, anything is possible. As he strode through the doors three teenage girls were squealing. One of them wore a wedding dress and a chainmail coat, another a tie-dye T-shirt and a green Mohawk, the third an industrial jumpsuit with glowing liquid phosphorescent bangles on her wrists and ankles. He smiled and waved, really getting into this. But the girls passed right by him, clutching one another and suppressing groans as if they badly needed to pee.

Across the hall now, he saw an entourage, a ragged, spangled rock group hauling luggage and loudly looking for the bar. They were wrapped up in scarves, dark glasses, dusters, and heavy campaign coats. One of them yawned, slipping out a great green tongue from his grey face: the weariness of a man in the saddle way too long. These dusty, aging ghosts of groove, Robbie thought. These skeletal freaks. This cool clique. Vampires eternally wandering the earth, shuffling through airports, thriving on spectral neon light, using people up, cursed by the reputation of their youth. Their clothes had that faded lustre of

the 70s pop-aristocracy – Moroccan, Victorian, psychedelic. What a crippling, lingering hangover, Robbie
thought. Figures from the Invisible Decade. The Great
Hangover. These wealthy misfits with their utter disregard
for anything. Across the way, Spit Swagger and Bile were
putting their booted feet on the glass table-tops of the
airport lounge, throwing lit cigarettes at one another,
roaring over dried-out in-jokes, showing tombstone teeth,
carrying casual to an extreme, and Jerusalem Slim was
flirting with the waitress by pulling on her apron strings.
This strangely knotted family tree of drug dealers, assis-
tants, hip travelling maids, hangers-on with trans-Euro-
pean acents, amanuenses, biographers, reporters, and an
exclusive, groovy old fraternity of chums that Keef must
need at least as badly as they need him.

Then Robbie noticed a woman with them – a girl, really
– in black lace and velvet, sorting out her belongings on
the floor. She was transferring a jumble of books and
tassled, mirrored clothes into a flat cardboard box the
airline had provided for her. She was just dumping the
books – beautiful ones with satin moiré endsheets, and
fringed suede pagemarkers – in with everything else. She'd
dragged a black broad-brimmed hat over her face. When
she stood up again their eyes met at last, and Robbie's
heart clambered up his throat.

She looked startled, too. She stood up, blew her bangs
off her eyes. Robbie hesitated, pulled a tight smile, took a
step in her direction, his heart pumped up with air. Bile
looked around in mid-grin, Spit Swagger, too. Keef gripped
the girl's arm in skeletal knuckles, but she wrenched
herself free and stumbled forward over her baggage. Robbie stopped dead. He thought, – .

Then turned on his heel, just like that. Abandoning
himself. To his better instincts. And passed through the
automatic doors into the fresh air and sunshine.